The Highly Improbable Adventures
Of
WALLACE and FANG

EPISODE ONE

The Highly Improbable Adventures

Of

WALLACE and FANG

EPISODE ONE

God is Good
and
Life Seems Better when Lying in Mud

Incidents recorded as accurate as humanly possible
by

Hank Perry

XULON PRESS

Xulon Press
555 Winderley Pl, Suite 225
Maitland, FL 32751
407.339.4217
www.xulonpress.com

Paperback ISBN-13: 978-1-66289-752-8
eBook ISBN-13: 978-1-66289-753-5

THE ROCK WON'T MOVE TRILOGY
A Story of Love
A Story of Forgiveness
The Power of A Cross

Acknowledgements

I am truly indebted to Ellen Weston. It would not be an over-statement to say that this book was greatly improved by her involvement. For you see, Ellen is my editor. Without her patience (with me) and her skill at untangling literary errancy (my work), much of the story would have been lost to misunderstanding or worse... incomprehension. Trust me, dear reader, any nonsensical narration that remains in this book is due to my insistence that it remain. Thank you, Ellen.

To my eldest son, Alex, for taking the time to read my manuscript and write the foreword. One can only imagine the pressure he faced knowing, if he were to say the wrong thing, he could lose his inheritance. Of course, the only things of any significant value are my coin collection (from when I was a kid), my Washington Redskin Super Bowl souvenir collection (the Jack Kent Cooke/Joe Gibbs years), and the vast collection of classic Walt Disney movies on Blu-ray (conspicuously missing from this collection is the garbage Disney puts out these days). Naturally, he will have to fight over these priceless treasures with his younger brother.

To my Lord and Savior, Jesus Christ. You are the same yesterday, and today, and forever (Hebrews 13:8). May all my words glorify your name.

Table of Contents

Acknowledgements vii

Foreword xi

Letter from the Author. xv

Chapter 1   Prophets and Profiteers. 1

Chapter 2   Bright Eyes and Fang. 24

Chapter 3   The Passion. 45

Chapter 4   Enchanted Forest. 69

Chapter 5   That Wiccan Boy Can Sing 88

Chapter 6   Cabin In the Woods 107

Chapter 7   In God's Hand 127

Chapter 8   Palm Sunday – Part I 149

Chapter 9   Palm Sunday – Part II 171

Chapter 10 Say You Love Me 191

Chapter 11 It's Hard to Explain 210

Chapter 12 Music to My Ears 230

Chapter 13 Good Friday 250

Chapter 14 Dueling Cantatas. 269

Chapter 15 You're Just Who I Needed. 289

Notes 311

Foreword

It was around ten years ago that my dad started writing his first book. I was probably about twenty at the time (man, time flies) and will be turning thirty in a couple days as of writing this foreword. It is a little bit wild to me that Dad has already been an author for that long. Like most of us, before being an author, Dad was a reader. He instilled an appreciation for the written word in my brother and I at a young age, partially through reading books to us. When Jake and I were kids, we would all lay in bed, and he would read. One of the most common entries to this activity was the *Hank the Cowdog* series of books, written in the 80's by John R. Erickson.

We grew up with dogs and Dad always had a love for "man's best friend." I think one of his favorite things about reading us these books (other than getting to spend time with his wonderful sons, of course!) was that they were written from the perspective of a dog. After all these years, I can't tell you how personal and exciting it is to read something with his own interpretation of this concept.

If I had to sum Dad up in just a few words, it would be that he is caring, giving, humble and loves the Lord with every ounce of his being. You would be hard pressed to find a more committed, dedicated man. My Uncle Randy wrote the foreword in Dad's first book, *The Rock Won't Move*, in which you start to get some semblance of how great a man my dad is. He has been such an amazing father. I need to stop here because enumerating all the things that Dad has done for me and others would end up filling as many pages as are in this book.

To those of you who have read Dad's other books, you will be excited to meet lots of new characters (human and otherwise). A fascinating aspect about this fourth offering is getting to see the individual characters and their relationships with each other change and grow. If you haven't read any of the first three books in his original trilogy, I implore you to do so.

One of the most exciting parts of these books to me is that you get to witness the creative journey of his writing style. If someone was to ask my dad how much he knew about classical concert performances prior to writing this book, he would probably start with a laugh and say "...not much." It is evident how much fun he has had researching concepts that were previously alien to him and then building it into his characters and settings. This creative exploration has been a constant throughout his books, be it Japanese samurai or the Roman Empire, and it is absolutely one of my favorite parts of reading them. You will also get to see so many of his own ideas come to life. From his squirrel naming conventions to the inner musings of dogs, there is no shortage of fun, charming abstractions.

There are also a lot of Dad's personal interests and passions sprinkled in: American Civil War history, dancing, surfing, and most of all, his love for the Lord. You are bound to see some of his frequent contemplations as you progress through his books.

I hope you enjoy reading Wallace and Fang as much as I did. You can't imagine how special it is to read something that your good ole' Dad wrote and you REALLY can't imagine how special it is to have the honor of writing the foreword to his latest edition. Sit back, relax and get ready for an exciting adventure.

Alex (Perry)

Letter from the Author

"Man, I love God!"

Oops... too vague.

"Man, I love Jesus!"

I suppose in today's topsy-turvy world, that statement might need a bit of clarification as well.

Alright then, let's try this.

"Man, I love Jesus and the Christian's Bible that professes him to be God!"

Ooo, that's better.

Or is it?

Alas, in this topsy-turvy world I just spoke of, being considered a "Christian" no longer requires a person to accept the Bible as the primary, or even a necessary, resource for who is, and who is not, God. Granted, the concept of aligning yourself with Jesus Christ - without also aligning yourself with the main account of his life and earthly ministry as your fundamental reference - is nothing new. Some go so far as to add their own set of creative "Prophetic" books to their doctored Bibles (just invite a Mormon or a Jehovah's Witness into your home). As bad as that is, however, you can't get much more disgusting than those "Christian" TV ministries who have built lavish empires preying on the elderly, the sick and those with acute physically disabilities (check out K. Copeland, J. Duplantis, C. Dollar, et al). The claims they make about having conversations – *not praying to, but having conversations* - with Almighty God on a routine basis, boarders on schizophrenia. In other words, they pretend to be something they are not... Apostles and Prophets.

> [Note: this is not unlike those who are caught up in their extreme form of "wokeness" and identify as something they are not]

Now, to be clear, I am not - *suddenly* - concerned about these fake religions and ministries of the past. Just as I am not - *suddenly* - concerned about the many other religions of the world that do not claim to be Christian. Religions such as Judaism, Muslim, Buddhist, Hindus, Scientology, Jedi Knight immediately come to mind. Heck, even atheists don't - *suddenly* - concern me. None of them - *suddenly* - concern me.

What does concern me - *suddenly* - is the assault on fundamental Christian principles coming from within the body of mainstream Protestant and Catholic churches themselves... causing huge divisions. The classic "house divided against itself" syndrome (Mk 3:25, Mt 12:25).

[Caveat: I am about to play the Christian victim card here]

With that being said, I have a big problem being lumped in with the ever-expanding umbrella of "Progressive"

Christianity. You know - the really cool group of Christians (and who doesn't want to be considered really cool?). This new assault on who Christ is has essentially abandoned the absolute and objective truth of Scripture - in whole or in part. In its place, the purveyors of this "Progressive" ideology have slipped in a nebulous and subjective truth. Sound familiar? It should because they all seem to take their cues from the neurotic, narcistic, dark side of western civilization's woke culture.

> [Wokeness; "a paranoid delusional hyper-egalitarian mindset that tends to see oppression and injustice where they do not exist or greatly to exaggerate them where they do exist." *Dr. Edward Feser, The Dispatch, March 20, 2023*]

> [Wokeness; "the well-educated, well-fed, well-coddled person with a freakish yearning to be unhappy... about everything." *Me, this book, 2024*]

They base themselves, almost entirely, on capricious emotional feelings, spurious mystical experiences, promises of prosperity and comfort, the social justice issue of the day or a really good praise and worship band. Let's be honest... it's all about the music with these folks.

> [Admission: I have lost count on how many times I have been seduced by this bait (good music) and switch (bad theology) tactic]

Most of these progressive "churches" are led by a single, virtue signaling, performance artist who will say and do anything in their quest to portray Jesus as being a very hip "Spiritual Dude" that would never call out your sinful behavior because he loves you too much (check out S. Furtick, T. White, B. Moore). Some, however, are more mature in their own pride and deceit. To attract their many followers, they tend to be more cunning, subtle and nuanced in their careless rendering of scripture (check out J. Osteen, R. Warren, J. Meyer).

Still, the bottom line is the same – a partial gospel is a false gospel - just as a partial truth is, in part, a lie.

The solution seems clear: read your Bible. Then, if the Sunday morning entertainer on stage is preaching something that doesn't add up – you go back to Scripture. If they appropriate the name of Jesus to conceal or disguise sin, rather than to praise him for the forgiveness of our sins – you walk. Sin, to a progressive Christian, is a "hateful" word that must be buried, marginalized, or preferably, abolished. But know this... God hates sin (Ge 4:7; Ro 6:23).

Then again, I can't help but smile to think how today's progressive Christian must make the once proud atheist absolutely furious. Long has the devil put up with the atheist's ineptitude and countless failures. Atheism, the crown jewel of intellectuals, has utterly failed to rid this world of true peace and true joy and true love that can only be gained by those having faith in Jesus Christ as their personal Savior. Therefore, it was only a matter of time before he (the devil) gave those offering mankind nothing but emptiness and sarcasm (the atheist) a swift boot to the curb.

So, I say to you Mr. and Ms. Atheist, as more and more people are being led astray by "Progressive" Christianity's pleasant sounding and lucrative deceptions, such as;

- the *generous* "Prosperity" Jesus,
- the *maverick* "Social Justice" Jesus,
- the *loving* "Sin-All-You-Want" Jesus,
- the *inclusive* "Not-The-Only-Way-to-Heaven" Jesus, um, well, who needs you?

On a much lighter note, I have yet another struggle. That is, I can't get rid of this subliminal craving to write another book. I find myself wondering what enormous spinning orb has taken hold and compels me to write, like the earth's influence over a compliant moon.

If past experience has anything to say about such a force, it might be that I had overlooked, or perhaps, left out something of importance in a previous story. That is exactly how starting one book back in 2014 ultimately became three books by 2019. This *"excuse me, but I have something else to say"* hypothesis does have some merit given my concerns about the "Progressive" Christianity movement stated above. I do not, however, get the feeling these new concerns of mine were something that was missing from the "Rock Won't Move" series. In my mind, and in my heart, I believe the "Rock" trilogy ended just the way it was supposed to end and I am grateful to the Lord for having given it to me.

If that is true, and there was nothing left unsaid, what is this storytelling affliction of mine all about?

Have I truly become just another hapless writer of paperback novels that dodge popularity?

Being a simple guy with simple ambitions, I tend to think more along the lines of writing as being something that is fun to do. I genuinely miss how new characters seemed to show up at just the right time, thereby, adding their depth and realness to the story. Or when the story itself takes an unexpected turn without warning. That, dear reader, can be pure gold. There was nothing more exhilarating about writing than when the pace of my characters moved so fast, the two fingers I use for typing would race recklessly across the keyboard just to keep up with their action. When the tempo did finally slow once again, it would take me a half an hour or more to correct all the grammatical errors and misspellings.

Then again - along the lines of being a simple guy - rather than taking advantage of an electronic device perfectly suited for saving and retrieving spontaneous ideas, I would scribble random ideas on whatever paper stock was handy. When this ever-increasing pile of meandering thoughts finally became too cumbersome to manage, a decision needed to be made. That is, were all these scraps of paper better served as fireplace tinder on a cold Colorado day or somehow fashioned into another book?

If the answer was another book, do I really want to succumb to the harsh reality of plopping myself down in front of a computer monitor for hours... that turned into days... that turned into months? Or, do I finally begin to enjoy an early retirement unfettered with time commitments. I can tell you the future did not look promising for the aforementioned pile of meandering thoughts.

So, dear reader, you can imagine my dilemma.

At first, I thought it might be fun - and easier - to come up with something along the lines of a "Winnie, the Pooh" type character. You know, like, take the complexities of life down a giant notch or two. More than anything, I wanted to give my grandkids something pleasing to read - before they regressed into video game playing zombies. This style of writing would necessarily include a whole lot of simplicity, innocence, kindness... all the good stuff. Unfortunately, or fortunately, that story never got off the ground. I soon discovered it was neither fun, nor easy, trying to understand the mind of an inanimate stuffed animal. What do they like? What do they want to be when they grow up? How do they handle adversity? Do inanimate stuffed animals go to heaven? When the head of each character in your book is filled with polyester, these kinds of questions require a massive amount of child-like creativity from their creator. That was much more than I was willing, or able, to provide.

Then, there was my passion to understand stuff – how things have come about. Ask anyone who knows me (and willing to be honest) and they will tell you I am not a brilliant man. I know brilliant people... and I am not one of them. I do, however, have an affinity towards looking things up for myself. In fact, I thrive on research. If I find something, anything, the least bit interesting, I will research it to death and somehow find a way to fit it in a book... making me appear brilliant.

Looking back at this process, it could be said that I have squandered vast amounts of time and wasted copious amounts of paper as a direct consequence of doing research for something that went nowhere. But nothing could be further from the truth. I really did enjoy the learning process. I can also say with some assurance that I never once thought of these fits and starts at starting a new book as having experienced a case of "writer's block." That would suggest that I was under some sort of pressure to meet some sort of deadline. Remember, I am a hapless, obscure paperback novel writer... I have no pressure and I have no deadline.

So, all that leads me to this... my fourth book. A book starring Hitch and Wallace as main characters.

OK, I know what you're thinking... why is he bringing back Hitch and Wallace when he just declared that story to have properly ended?

That certainly does sound a bit disingenuous on my part. Some might go so far as to suggest it was simply lazy writing. Was there really nothing else this poor man could write about?

All I can say is that I did try to branch out. Start afresh. Expand my horizon. Except I really and truly enjoyed writing about Hitch and Wallace. This sentiment was especially true of Wallace (the Labra-Skunk). He was the culmination of every dog I ever loved. And Hitch... wow... what can I say about him? Not only did his character appear on the first page of the first book, he also made it to the last page of the third book. His faith in Jesus was slow and methodical, but that is how it works with intellectuals. Unfortunately, when Hitch and Wallace finally did come together (under very sad circumstances), I was running out of book. Again, it was one of those moments when the story itself took an unexpected turn without warning ... pure gold.

So, dear reader, what would you do?

Let me help by sharing a story (cause, that's what I do). Suppose you find yourself panning for gold in the hot desert sun for months. Day after scorching day, you pan that muddy water in hopes of striking it rich. Day after day you pan with nothing to show for it. Day after day nothing but rock and mud and some dweeb's disgustingly inconsiderate trash that floated downstream. Just when you are about to call it quits, hop in your Jeep and ride back into town - two shiny little objects show up in the bottom of your pan. Yes, it's only two small pieces... but it's pure gold!

What do you do now?

Do you stop panning because it's five o'clock somewhere?

To me, Hitch and Wallace are pure gold.

To summarize; this is NOT book #4 in the "Rock Won't Move" series and this is NOT a book intended for young children.

With regards to this NOT being book #4, I would like to think Hitch and Wallace have lived very interesting lives. Their backgrounds have been meticulously crafted and chronicled in "Rock" books #1 ("A Story of Love") and #3 ("The Power of A Cross"). This is especially true for Hitch. Therefore, I do not spend any time rehashing stuff which has already been written. I also bring back a few other lovable characters from those two books, such as; Alex and Francesca, Professor "Jack" Lewis, his wife ("MJ"), their two sons (Jake and Joey), Pamela and Mickey, Charlie (Chief), Monica (Ms. Brown).

The reason for bringing back this small, yet dynamic, group is threefold: First; they provide continuity for those who enjoyed reading the "Rock" series. My fandom (all ten of them) may appreciate knowing what has become of one, or more, of their favorite characters. Second; this particular group of returnees helped advance the new story along at a quicker pace. That is, I did not feel the need to use valuable book space retelling their stories. This leads me to the third reason; I really enjoy the work of creating and developing new characters. That takes time... and I have quite a few of them.

With all that in mind, I would encourage new readers to read the "Rock" trilogy. This can be done either before or after any enjoyment you receive from reading this book.

In regard to this NOT being a children's book - it has adult themes. As a result, my grandchildren will have to wait until their parents deem them ready to understand and handle the mature nature of the content. Still, my intention is to keep these stories clean, lighthearted and fun to read. My hope here is to give my family (and yours) something true, honorable, pure and lovely to dwell upon (Php 4:8). As I am writing this, it is the middle of 2023 and I can't even imagine the filth they will be exposed to as time goes on.

As always, I hope you enjoy this book as much as I enjoyed writing it.

In Him alone,
Hank

Chapter 1

Prophets and Profiteers

It was never in Hitch's nature to leave well enough alone. He was one of those genetic outliers born with an unquenchable spirit of inquiry - along with the brilliant mind to process it all. This innate gift has earned him scholastic success on a global scale, appreciable personal wealth and, until recently, a faultless status in life that was beyond reproach. He remains the same guy for all this time, except he is now a professing Christian and the world around him doesn't exactly know how to handle that ... fault.

Until recently, Hitch had no qualms making people feel uncomfortable. He was, after all, smarter than 99.9% of the people he encountered on a daily basis – including those fine, well-respected folk populating every university campus he stepped foot on. To challenge him on nearly any subject of scientific consequence - or simply a personal interest of his - was a fool's errand. That was then. Now, Hitch will gracefully concede to just about any point of contention if it may lead to a conversation on why a person believes what they believe and where that person believes they may be

1

spending eternity. So, in essence, he is still making people feel uncomfortable.

This concession stuff was not an easy trait for Hitch to adopt. To be clear, he did not, and never would, abandon science, factual and substantiative evidence or independent thought. He simply did not see the correction of others as being the main purpose in this new Christian walk of his. The odd thing about this latest social dynamic is that people found him to be more... approachable. And they did so with tremendous frequency. These abrupt and persistent inter-actions began almost immediately after Hitch's conversion and it was the academic intelligentsia who felt inclined to be first in line. In their own embittered minds, they felt they had been upstaged or embarrassed by Hitch one too many times in the past. Apparently, Hitch's current faith was seen as a weakness and they had a long-awaited score to settle.

Hitch, of course, understood this petty gamesmanship process for what it was – a decoy. It typically occurs in a scholar's life when all its meaning becomes no more pur-poseful than a struggle to extend their Wikipedia bio one more page. What some people will try beyond their initial success in life is anybody's guess. Try as they might, these attempts to remain relevant beyond what God had enabled them to become in the first place were nearly always futile. Not surprisingly, the more intelligent they feel they once were on a certain sliver of life, the more combative and self-de-structive they become.

> [NOTE: the very same fate can be said for those who have more wealth than some

small nations, yet are as smart as a box of rocks. At this very moment, it would not be unusual for you to be thinking of one or more rich Hollywood movie stars, pop chart musicians or professional athletes]

Scripture refers to this human disorder as pride. Or, to its natural conclusion, the pride before the fall (Pr 16:18). Now, unless you lack a shred of decency or compassion for people, the collapse of the proud can be a very unpleasant thing to watch. Ironically, the lives of these people could not be made more comfortable, yet they remain perpetually unfulfilled and ungrateful. How is it that darkness seems to follow the proud regardless of the spotlight they live in?

Then, there was Hitch. He would fit comfortably into both the highly "intelligent" and the relatively "wealthy" categories. It was only a few months ago that you could say Hitch fit comfortably in the extremely "prideful" category as well. Then he did the unthinkable. He invited Jesus Christ to rule over his life. A rather humbling position to take for a rich, self-centered genius, wouldn't you say? Some have suggested, either in jest or in earnest, that becoming Christian would necessarily preclude Hitch from being regarded as a member of the "intelligent" category. Whether in jest or not; amiable or not; open-minded or not, these hapless taunts mattered little to Hitch. If someone felt compelled to share their thoughts on a certain path in which they have chosen to live, Hitch had much to say about the path he has chosen to live.

Unfortunately, his was a much simpler path. It was only considered "unfortunate" because simplicity was not all that appealing to the great many proud geniuses of the world. To them, the appeal... the real challenge... is to turn the simple things upside down so that they become impossible to comprehend. In this way, it would require gifted thinkers like themselves to help everyone else understand it all. Once simplicity is manipulated to incomprehensibility, it must then be tied to some form of business model that typically requires a never-ending complement of "works" or lots of money exchanging hands to fully appreciate.

> [NOTE: This disregard towards simplicity can be applied to the rich as well. In other words, what is so attractive about simplicity if everyone can afford it?]

Christianity is, by nature, a simple path. That is, the Christian believes he or she is a sinner in need of a Savior... and Jesus Christ is that Savior. Not an easy path to follow, but simple enough. The other fairly rigid tenet of Christianity is that it is also dependent on truth. Not just any truth, "absolute" truth. Oh boy, now that really complicates matters.

Enter nihilism... or the art of being "woke."

Truth, formerly a rather simple concept, is now a malleable concept made unrecognizable by the modern-day psychosis of wokeness. In essence, we are all led to believe that, if your feelings are different than my feelings, then your truth must also be different than my truth. Therefore, truth, like feelings, cannot be absolute. Truth becomes relative. Perception is all that is necessary to become a person's truth. Truth belongs to the individual according to their current state of mind and must reign above all other truths.

Of course, if that were true - and today's truth may, or may not, be tomorrow's truth - how are we to have any confidence in either being legitimate? There would be no stopping this meaningless sense of the word from being "refreshed" in perpetuity. Thus, making all relative truth a self-deceiving lie benefitting no one. Most, if not all, of the once great founding church denominations have split over woke ideology.

Hitch was never sympathetic to feelings getting in the way of logic, so this was yet another concession he must endure when receiving the barrage of student activists claiming victimhood by his intolerant, anachronistic, absolute truth, Christian belief system. The "old" Hitch would have taken such derogatory suggestions as fighting words. Without much intellectual effort, he would have demolished the ill-informed, anti-Christian criticisms. But that person was antithetical to whom he is now. The "made new" Hitch (2 Co 5:17) took no pleasure in such battles. When it came to a person's faith in one thing or another, what mattered most was trying desperately to understand how the other person had come to rely on their deeply-rooted convictions and how they benefit by it.

If a person were indeed found to be sane, they would only believe what they believe because the belief was in their best interest, Hitch calmly rationalized.

As confident as Hitch was in his beliefs, he would readily admit there was nothing pleasant about being mocked or ridiculed for those beliefs – even though most of the insults were perpetrated behind his back. On the other hand, nothing would please him more than to engage a "Savior skeptic" and allow the dialog to run its course. Inevitably, the exasperated skeptic would find themselves losing the battle of what is, and what is not, valid logic. Most will give up that fight, but genuinely want to know what could possibly turn the mind of a once revered atheist archetype into a revolting Christian apologist.

"One word," Hitch would offer in all sincerity. "And that word is contentment."

"Surely, contentment, to a great thinker, cannot be found in a dubious God of a dubious Bible," they would ask in some form or fashion.

"At this point, I can only assure you that my contentment is real," Hitch would respond with conciliate gentleness. "Furthermore, the contentment I speak of is only made possible through a faith in Jesus Christ, who I have found to be a reliable God of a reliable historical book, as well as, by many other historical corroborating evidences."

If, by this point, the disgruntled social activist had not yet walked off muttering the customary well-rehearsed inflammatory pejoratives, Hitch would continue with even greater empathy.

"You have explained your position well and I can certainly understand the doubts you may still have about Christianity. I, too, have had similar doubts. In light of our spirited meeting here today, I would enjoy the opportunity to discuss these doubts further. That is, if you can find it in your heart to pursue any future discussion in a respectful manner."

Those closest to Hitch considered this tactical change towards others to be, in some sense, not a change at all. He was still the same hard-wired investigator motivated by matters of consequence. In that sense, he was no different than the man he once was. It was the same man who attempted to astonish the world by proving beyond a shadow of doubt there was never a God. That was to be his "Irrefutability Theory." Unfortunately, to prove God does not exist, the skeptic must temporarily escape time and space... or die. It would be safe to say that the former will not be happening anytime soon... and no one escapes the latter.

For Hitch, it seemed like ages ago that he played the part of atheist bully. That time period has become a cold, dark reminder to him of his new - uniquely Christian - burden. This burden is played out almost every day, on almost every university campus, in almost every free society by faithful Christians. As a result, no matter how many anonymous notes and posters accusing him of being racist, homophobic, transphobic, misogynous or anti-science are attached to his office door overnight or how many vailed attempts to attack him by certain cowardly unidentified faculty members, he remained resolute in the proclamation that Jesus was, and will always be, our only hope for a fulfilled life now and forever.

Hitch could relinquish his title as "Top Dog" at Hillary University anytime he wanted, but never to an individual or group that have abandoned absolute truth, impartial science or a good God to fuel their troubled existence.

The personal check for $1,000 slid across the starched white tablecloth with ease. It was pushed along by a well-manicured hand of medium brown skin tone. The check's forward progress slowed as it approached the dining table's midsection. One could make the case that the arm doing the pushing was simply unable to extend any further, especially since the sleeve of the finely-tailored suit jacket began to pull back slightly from the hand... exposing a magnificent Patek Phillippe watch in the process. Then again, it was not a particularly large dining table. It was no larger than was necessary to seat a party of two comfortably. In any event, without a tape measure of some sort, it would be difficult to say if hand and check did, in fact, make it to midpoint. Whatever the final destination, or motive, it ultimately required the recipient of the generous check to expend at least as much effort to retrieve it.

"There you go, Harvard," prodded the tall, handsomely dressed black man of slender build. "You've remained true to your word. To which I, like many others, am genuinely astonished."

"As I recall, Yale, our little wager does not expire until Easter Sunday," came the swift, yet demurred reply. "Which, if I am not mistaken, leaves you with time enough to profit from the retraction of my pledge."

As you have probably already guessed, "Harvard," is the moniker that "Yale" uses to cordially address the benefactor of the $1,000 check due to his Ivy League alma mater.

Likewise, "Yale," is the moniker that "Harvard" uses to cordially respond to the issuer of the $1,000 check due to his Ivy League alma mater.

Their friendly game of "Posturing for Ivy Leaguers (and other assorted aspersions)" began almost immediately upon the arrival of "Yale" to Hillary University as a professor of music. This came several years after the arrival of "Harvard" to Hillary University as a professor of physics. It was soon after "Yale" arrived at Hillary that "Harvard" begin needling him on how Harvard University exceeded Yale University in almost every meaningful metric known to Institutions of Higher Education.

"The facts speak for themselves when it comes to your university, Yale," Harvard would state proudly. "Harvard was the first to be established (in the year 1636 vs. 1701, respectively); Harvard has produced more Supreme Court Justices (17 vs. 9, respectively); Harvard has produced more Nobel Laureates (161 vs. 65, respectively); Harvard has produced more U.S. Presidents (8 vs. 5, respectively). And, of those U.S. Presidents, it should be noted that Harvard has produced the only "black" U.S. President (1 vs. 0, respectively)."

This peevish game reached its fevered pitch in 2009. That was the year Barak Obama (Harvard Graduate) became the 44th President of the United States... and it was the final straw. "Yale" tried his absolute best to contest this latest setback for his beloved alma mater. Temporarily overlooking the color of his own skin and the socio-political meaning that came with it, he advanced the following hypothetical absurdity:

"Since that Arkansas boy, Bill Clinton (Yale graduate) self-identified himself as a 'black' president (actually coined by Toni Morrison in The New Yorker, 1998), then he (Clinton) created a tie for black U.S. Presidents." Yale postulated. "If that white boy (Clinton) wants to identify as a brother, who are we to judge? Now, if you want to add meat to that bone, since he (Clinton) was elected back in 1993, Yale had the honor of producing the first black man as U.S. President!"

Of course, "Yale" knew the application of identity politics in his facetious scheme was absurd. If taken seriously, it would have diminished Barak Obama's historic accomplishment. That was not his intent and he knew "Harvard" would see it for what it was... pure desperation and nonsense. But "Yale" had nothing else to prove his alma mater was better than Harvard. There was nothing, unless he were to employ the winning record of his Yale Bulldogs over the Harvard Crimson in football (68-60-8). That rivalry dates back to 1875. The problem with being forced to mention Ivy League football at all was the predictably sexist question of whether they still play football in skirts and high heels.

The true identities of these two prominent Hillary University Professors were Edmund "Hitch" Hitchinson of Harvard and Leonard "Leon" Bouchard of Yale (Ph.D. degree in both Music and African American Studies, Yale). The $1,000 bet was the almost certain prediction by Leon that Hitch would not make it to Easter Sunday without somehow renouncing his acceptance of Jesus Christ as Lord and Savior. That was the "pledge" Hitch spoke of and which took place over three months ago.

"I'm not getting the sense that'll be your decision, my man," Leon predicted anew. "I've known you too long to be messing that up twice."

"Careful, Leon," Hitch cautioned as he took a generous sip from his sidecar (also known as "The Professor" at this restaurant – a cocktail using Grand Marnier instead of Cointreau as the liquor). "At this very moment, I can name five once well-esteemed men of faith that have just recently been caught living horribly corrupt double lives."

"We're all born to sin... won't deny that," came Leon's muted reflection on the matter as he, too, took a prolonged hit off his Hennessy XO cognac. "Alright then, if you didn't invite me here to take my money, is this some kind of 'white-guilt' Easter tradition of yours to feed an oppressed African American?"

Leon used to enjoy playing the race card game before critical race theory (CRT) killed its shock value and, therefore, its most humorous quality. That card had been played without any real meaning a thousand times over, but this opportunity was just too irresistible. Since their coming together at Hillary University, these two intellectually powerful men have thoroughly enjoyed the other's spontaneous, uninhibited and tasteless humor (that which makes humor actually funny). This unsophisticated side of their camaraderie was especially gratifying when it came to the pure joy one can receive by ganging up on Hillary University's many other "minor league" Ivy League professors. They were the wannabes from the Princeton on down. The ease with which the unconstrained scoffing flowed upon these lesser Ivy League Universities and their alumnus made a complaisant professor's life worth living. But there was much more to their relationship than the flexing of their academic muscle.

We already know of Hitch's long and winding road back to Christianity. As for Leon, he could say with assurance that he had never once been introduced to a valid argument that would cause him to deviate from the Christian faith of his childhood. A faith that was instilled in him by two loving parents and his own journey to discover if what he was being taught was accurate.

Leon's steadfast "dissension of Darwinism" into adulthood did not come without its trail of critics. This was especially true since the two hostile environments he chose to immerse himself into were Yale - and then Hillary. Both institutions were swarming with the world's most virulent God-hating predators. As if it was incumbent upon intemperate humanist sharks to do, many of his colleagues tried their very best to shame Leon out of his irrational beliefs in a cruel God that would send nice people like them to hell. The push for intellectual conformity on Hillary campus even included a few unflattering remarks at Leon's "jejune" theology from Hitch. That is, of course, whenever Hitch took a break from his unflattering remarks about Yale University.

Surprisingly, there was still quite a collection of underground Christian believers stealthily co-existing with the Godless masses on both campuses. Also surprisingly, were the few believers-in-name-only that wanted Leon to join their trendy Sunday morning "Guilt-Free" church service/party - with live kickass praise music. He soon realized their particular interest in him was for one of two reasons: either they wanted to begin the slow, methodical new-age "deconstruction" of his core beliefs in God and sin, or they wanted a wickedly talented keyboardist to help advance their own music careers. They got neither from Leon.

To be honest, there was never a chance that any of these foolish attempts to marginalize Jesus would have succeeded. Leon knew Scripture as well as he knew the piano. He knew when a church was tinkering with Scripture for nefarious purposes. For example, when asked which is the greatest commandment, Jesus replied, "Love the Lord your God with all your heart and all your soul and all your mind. This is the first and greatest commandment" (Mt 20:37-38). And the second commandment was much like it: "Love your neighbor as yourself" (Mt 20:39). What many new-age and seeker-sensitive movements like to do is morph these two commandments into one meaningless suggestion. That is, they love to love on each other but conveniently forget about the first and greatest commandment altogether... Love the Lord your God.

As for Leon, it was going to be the Gospel message straight-up or go elsewhere.

If not for Leon taking the time to mingle, however, many of these same "believers" would have never known that their sugar-coated version of Christianity was actually keeping them separated from Christ. The "good news" was Jesus' death on the cross and his resurrection three days later (atonement)... not their indiscriminate love making and kick-ass praise music.

Leon never thought it wise to shame or belittle a person for having a different point of view. How and where that person developed their perspective on life and death and God was complicated. That personal experience could never be erased and, therefore, not so easily changed. And rarely did a healthy change come with harsh words and attacks. Besides that, any other treatment would be in violation to what Jesus taught his disciples. According to Scripture, the struggle for the soul of man is spiritual (Eph 6:12). However, like the Apostle Paul, we are to "plant the seed" or introduce Jesus as the God he is. Or, like Apollos, we are to "water it" or share the Bible without making stuff up. That's it. We can do no more than that. Only God can "make it grow" or change a sinner's heart (1 Co 3:5-9).

> [NOTE: many believe Apollos was the author of the Epistle to the Hebrews. If so, he did some pretty good watering of his Hebrew audience]

Leon was a smooth talker, capable of providing a cogent and careful exposition of the core tenets for which he believed, and yet, he preferred being the diligent listener. Instead of a sharp tongue, Leon preferred a softly spoken word offered in gentleness and in patience as if framing his thoughts inside the beauty of a nocturne by Chopin. He was, after all, Hillary University's Music Department Chair now. The care taken to receive, as well as to deliver, information were the qualities that first intrigued Hitch about Leon. Over the years, these two had wrestled many times over their divergent beliefs to a virtual stalemate (or as close to stalemate as Hitch was willing to admit) and, in the process, had become close friends because of it.

"Well, I am not aware of such a tradition," Hitch answered with touch of suspense. "I do believe, however, that your company is always worth the price of a good meal no matter the occasion."

"I'm flattered... I think," Leon replied suspiciously. "But I'm hungry, so this is gonna cost you, my friend."

"I wouldn't have it any other way," Hitch stated as a matter-of-fact and extended his glass for a toast. "To good company."

"To good company," Leon concurred and met Hitch's glass just above the check that still occupied center table.

Both men downed the remainder of their cocktails with zest, sat up tall in the plush upholstered chairs and took a satisfying cleansing breathe in preparation for an explanation as to the true meaning of their little pre-holiday soirée. Hitch was about to speak when Kevin, the proprietor of this upscale restaurant, known as Timothy's, approached their table.

"Gentlemen, may I refresh your drinks, or perhaps I can have one of our dedicated servers come to take your order?" he asked with a cordial tone that suited the surroundings perfectly.

While glancing from one professor to the other, Kevin noticed the check - and the substantial sum it was written for - resting conspicuously on the table. Having a longstanding familiarity with both men (as well as being a fellow Christian himself), he quickly followed up his offer of service with a lighthearted remark of his own.

"Professor (glancing at both), if that is your gratuity for this evening, it is quite generous," he spoke with glib exuberance – knowing full well who the check was made out to. "In fact, it would be my honor to serve you myself tonight... and from this day forward!"

"You wish, brother," Leon snickered as he allowed himself to be drawn back into his seat. "Kevin, my man, that check is the price I pay for opening my big mouth."

"Kevin, allow me to explain," Hitch interjected immediately, concisely and unsympathetically... along with a subtle hint of sarcasm thrown in for good measure. "Our distinguished 'Professor of All Things That Make Sound' sitting across from me made a bet that my conversion and re-generation this past Christmas would not last till this Easter Sunday. And yet here we are – three born-again Christians."

"Well, now, isn't that something?" Kevin feigning some disappointment even though he knew it was an innocent and whimsically proposed gambling bet at best. "I will certainly double check Galatians chapter five again, but I am quite sure wagering large sums of money would not be considered a fruit of the spirit."

"Absolutely, you can imagine my surprise!" Hitch feigned agreement on the biblical impropriety of gambling, or "wealth gained hastily" as Proverbs 13:11 put it. "Being new to my Christian faith, I was terribly shocked. I can assure you that I did not wish to play any part in this, but I am afraid our Christian brother over there will insist on me taking his money."

"Ya'll done chopping me up like I'm a Polk Salad?" Leon feigned remorse as three can play at this game. "Yes, I was wrong and I'm glad I was wrong. And, no, I ain't taking back the money because it was never about the money anyway."

Leon paused a moment for effect, then continued.

"Kevin, I love this place you got here and I feel like celebrating. So, I'll be having the most expensive thing you got on your menu tonight. Don't matter what it is. You fix it up any way you like. You see, my Christian brother over there was once dead in his many sins, but now he is alive in Christ Jesus... hallelujah!"

"Very well stated, my dear friend. And I never once doubted your true concern for my time here on earth and my salvation to come after," Hitch acknowledged gratefully.

Signaling that this particular round of horse-play had played itself out, Hitch posed an entirely off-topic question to their host.

"Kevin, what is the name of that overseas charity you love so much?"

"Compassion International is the overseas ministry we support here at Timothy's," he replied promptly. "Why do you ask, Professor?"

"I would very much like to endorse Professor Bouchard's check over to you with the intention that it will do that ministry some good," came the heartfelt response. "In addition, I will be sending you a check of my own for the same amount and for the same purpose."

"There, that should do it," Hitch reflected for a moment. "Unless, of course, either of you gentlemen would like to add your thoughts to that resolution?"

"I'm cool with it, bro," Leon beamed and looked to Kevin for his response.

"I am extraordinarily cool with it," Kevin answered with gracious appreciation.

After a short pause to appreciate what had just transpired, Kevin took possession of the endorsed check and spoke again.

"Well, what a night it becomes when the two of you dine with us. Professor (speaking to Leon), please let me know if you intend to delight everyone here by playing the piano and I will make the proper arrangements. I will have your server come to refresh your drinks and take your orders at once."

The main attraction of this somewhat out-of-the-way, college town restaurant was the exquisitely prepared food in an aesthetically pleasing environment. Timothy's, perennially earns the coveted Michelin Series Three Star rating for "exceptional cuisine, worth a special journey." Another notable attraction at Timothy's was the immaculate Steinway Model D-274 concert grand piano which occupies a prominent position on the first level dining room. Only the most accomplished musicians were invited to play it... and not once was this offering ever refused by the musician. For those fortunate enough to be dining on the same night an accomplished pianist took the bench, it would be a memorable evening. Therefore, it should go without saying that Timothy's regulars - who recognized Leon's presence - would plan accordingly and request the most expensive bottle of their favorite spirit at once.

"I know exactly where your mind is right now, so before you run off to play that fancy piano, may I commend to you what was on my mind when I invited you here tonight?" Hitch implored, knowing full well of his dining companion's musical inclinations.

"Commend away, my brother," Leon replied without taking his eyes off the Steinway. "You got at least till the nice server gets here to confirm that very expensive dinner order of mine. Then, well, I'm think'n I'm gonna be playing me some Count Basie on that sweet mama over there very soon after that."

This particular meeting with Leon falls back on the premise that Hitch's nature is incapable of leaving well enough alone. By this time, Hitch had been "born again" for a little over three months. There was no new or heightened understanding of Scripture on his part. He grew up in a true Christian household. He understood the meaning of being "born again"... the carefully chosen words spoken by Jesus to

Nicodemus in the Gospel of John (Jn 3:3). It was simply genuine acceptance now.

The season of "Lent" was coming to an end, Easter was fast approaching and the questions mounted. Hitch remembered this Lenten season fondly and reverently, even though Scripture does not provide any record of the Apostles requiring a "40-day fast" in order to replicate the forty days Jesus spent in the desert. Like Easter, it was a man-made obligation and he was comfortable with that. These celebrations were of minor theological consequence and more easily enjoyed than explained.

What concerned Hitch most, since his conversion, were the various assaults on the doctrinal truth of Christianity. This was the faith of his youth. This was the faith he just put all his trust in. So, it did not take him long to notice a change in the way many church leaders were manipulating Scripture to suggest that Jesus himself would fall into line with their modern sensibilities. If Jesus was a good God, he needed to change with the times. If Hitch didn't know better, there appeared to be a concerted effort to destroy the very foundation of the historical church from within the historical church itself.

The devil had been busy while I was away, he thought.

"Leon, I have decided to become a Prophet, or at least, an Apostle," Hitch spoke firmly, and with as much sincerity as he could muster, in order that he might shock his colleague away from thoughts of pianos and Count Basie for a moment. "And I want you to be my fellow sojourner. You and me... like Isiah and Ezekiel, or John and Peter."

"Apostle, huh?" Leon pondered quizzically.

Leon had not fallen for Hitch's absurd opening one-liners for quite some time, but was genuinely intrigued with this one. He continued.

"Gotta say, that's very honorable of you."

"I can't help but feel a moral obligation," Hitch continued on a more revealing note. "You see, in my quest to find a trust-worthy church home, I have come to the unsettling conclusion that I may know more about what Jesus actually says and means than most priests and pastors."

"Well, that ain't too hard, I'll give you that," Leon moaned the words, shook his head and offered the following guidance on becoming an Apostle. "I think I'm smelling what you're cooking here and I agree with you that this is a messed-up world. You won't get an argument from me about needing a couple of righteous men of God right now, but, if you're telling me you want to somehow enter the 'Office of the Apostles' commissioned by Jesus in the Gospels, I'm afraid that door was closed a long time ago."

Leon knew a large number of men - and a few ladies - who have proclaimed themselves to be literal biblical Prophets and/or Apostles. He also knew that at some point, these people will soon prove themselves to be liars, false teachers or just plain creepy. Prior to this evening, Hitch did not show any signs of falling into either of those categories, but Leon now spoke with extreme caution and concern just the same.

"To be an Apostle, you must have seen Christ, or, at least, the resurrected Christ. Kind of like Paul getting called out by Jesus on the road to Damascus (Acts 9). Hitch, please tell me you haven't been called out by the resurrected Christ on some dirt road leading up to Hillary University."

Seeing the worried look on his friend's face, Hitch retracted his glib proposition immediately.

"My apologies. I see where I may have taken this act a bit too far."

It was not Hitch's intention to bring up his brief encounter with Jesus in what appeared to be Eden. That journey, compliments of a "large stone-like object, pure white and without blemish," will forever remain the sole property of himself, Jack, Charlie and Bobbi Lou (who had adopted Wallace as a puppy and was now in the presence of the Lord in Heaven). It's just that Hitch had been out of the Christian loop since his first year at Harvard and all he wanted was to be brought up to speed with the current struggles facing today's church. If anyone knew what was happening here, it would be Leon.

"Let me try this again," Hitch corrected himself. "I believe the focus of my concern can be summed up as 'eisegesis' over 'exegesis.' I cannot help but watch and listen to popular church leaders reading their own biased ideas into sound biblical interpretation (eisegesis). Is it really too much to ask for sound biblical interpretation to stand on its own these days (exegesis)?"

"I can do all things through a Bible verse taken out of context!" Leon exclaimed jovially.

> [Note: the familiar verse from Philippians (4:13) actually reads like this, "I can do all things through Christ who strengthens me"]

The intentional butchering of the verse was Leon's attempt to describe how today's self-proclaimed "spiritual leaders" will take a single Bible verse from over here and a single Bible verse from over there to fashion something the Bible never intended to say.

"I call it discord, Hitch," Leon suggested, now that he was gaining some clarity as to why Hitch invited here tonight. "I like to think of the Bible as a symphony. A Scripture verse taken out of context is like one oboe, or one cello, or one violin playing out of key. To the untrained ear, it may be no big deal because they don't know any better. But, to the trained ear, perfect harmony in music, like context in Scripture, is everything. If that harmony is compromised, it grates, it irritates and it has no place in the world's great concert halls... or in the Christian church."

"So, I'm not dreaming it then," Hitch acknowledged to himself and then began to reminiscence about the good old days. "I remember when these wayward ideas were considered Universalism, or Pluralism, or Perennialism, or Pantheism. What kind of philosophical terms are they using now?"

"Philosophy?" Leon blurted out with a laugh. "There ain't no philosophy other than using the name of Jesus to help build their brand. I got to admit, they do come up with some pretty sexy titles for what they do now. Let me see... you got your New Age, New Thought, New Revelation, Elevation, Oneness, Law of Attraction, Seeker Sensitive, Mystical Miracle... on and on they go. It's impossible to keep up with their vernacular."

Leon paused for a deep, cleansing sigh before continuing.

"I just dump them all in the 'Progressive Christianity' chum bucket and call it a day. Bottom line is these Prophets, Apostles and Wizards are all nothing but purveyors of lies trying to make a fast buck. They love the world and more than happy to perpetuate its darkness. Some folk from the seminaries tried bringing this stuff into our church years ago and our pastor and elders crushed the head of that serpent on sight."

There was defiance in these words, but also acceptance. Leon continued humbly.

"But look here, Hitch. We should all be glad that God is so patient with us, not wishing anyone to perish. I know I am. There will come a day when the Father will clean His house of all these fools."

"So, it's a house divided once again, is it?" Hitch was forced to admit. "Anything I can do?"

"Engage, bro," Leon gently spoke as his attention slowly turned back to the Steinway. "Step out with whoever you can... whenever you can. Remember where you came from, the time it took to bring you back to life, the people along the way ..."

Leon could have gone on, but there were other matters to tend to.

"Take that piano for instance," Leon continued thoughtfully. "She's just sitting over there all by herself, just waiting for someone to step out and engage her... know what I'm saying?"

"I think I do, Professor," Hitch submitted gracefully.

"By the way," Leon muttered nonchalantly. "How's that girl of yours?"

Chapter 2

Bright Eyes and Fang

"You're leading again," Hitch gently reminded his new dance partner.

She was, by far, the more experienced and better dancer of the two. Perhaps that had something to do with the fact that both her parents were professional dancers and that she would learn how to dance soon after learning how to walk. Therefore, she understood perfectly well that when dancing... in general, and ballroom dancing... in particular, the man was to lead and the woman was to follow.

"Sorry," she whispered. "Hold me for a moment or two and then we can begin again, if that's okay?"

"Holding you is my pleasure, Sùilean Soilleir (Scottish Gaelic meaning "Bright Eyes)." The words rolled off his tongue effortlessly as he slowed his pace and brought her into himself gently.

Hitch's dance partner and the object of his affection was Professor Debra Macaulay Shade (A.B., Smith College, M.A., Ph.D., University of Michigan). By some cosmic miracle, these two professing atheists found themselves together in the most unlikely spot on the planet... a Christian church sanctuary just prior to a Sunday service. That was just before Christmas three months ago. Once it became apparent that they were no longer mortal enemies, Hitch was granted permission to call her "Debbie." That name was a slightly less formal name than "Debra" and was used mostly by close friends. Now that he was able to look her way without being accused of one or more forms of harassment, he could not help but notice her eyes. She had the most radiant blue eyes he had ever seen. Shortly thereafter, and in a moment of careless romantic weakness, he referred to her as "Bright Eyes."

To his utter amazement, she smiled at this spur-of-the-moment remark. That was indeed a fortunate reaction because depending on your ideology, that statement - meant as a compliment - could easily be misconstrued as oppressive to a crazed feminist.

Anyway, that was a defining moment in their budding relationship and they have since been upgraded to "couple" status. Recognizing that the use of innocuous pet names such as "Bright Eyes" to address a colleague in the high and mighty halls of Hillary might be frowned upon, Hitch was quick to improvise. Having already shared some of their family's history with each other, Hitch now knew that Debbie's mother was of Scottish Highlander decent. That would also suggest that Debbie spoke some, if not fluent, Gaelic. Since it was unlikely that more than a dozen people walking on American soil today understood the Gaelic language, Hitch began using the phrase "Sùilean Soilleir" in her presence... with no one being the wiser.

She liked his ingenuity even more.

The words spoken by Hitch and Debbie before taking that short break from dancing were few, yet they could not have had more significance. To unpack the full meaning of "you're leading again" and "hold me for a moment," one must take a closer look at "Bright Eyes" growing up. As it is with most of us... the past can explain a lot.

Debra's father was born and raised in America. Debra's mother was born and raised in a small, yet popular, village in the Highlands of Scotland, UK. The village went by the name of Drumnadrochit (Scottish Gaelic: Druim na Drochaid, meaning the "Ridge of the Bridge") This village was not to become popular because of any particular ridge or bridge, but rather by a certain mysterious creature that was spotted in the very long and very deep lake located nearby. The name of the lake was Lock Ness and the first "Nessie" sighting was reported back in 1933.

Debra's middle name, Macaulay, was her maternal grandmother's maiden name. It was an old Scottish tradition for the first-born daughter to take that surname as their middle name. That was done in an effort to keep old family names from disappearing. There was a time when Debra wanted to use this unique sounding middle name instead of her, otherwise, boring American first name. That was until she learned what "Macaulay" translated into (Scottish Gaelic: MacChullach, meaning "Son of a Boar"). Since she considered herself neither a son, nor a boar, she stuck with Debra. From then on, she enjoyed telling all her friends that the name "Debra" was Scottish Gaelic for "daughter of a zebra" (zebra with a "D" instead of the "z"). She liked zebras back then and no one challenged her on its authenticity.

Debra's parents would meet while competing against each other and their respective dance partners. Their first meeting was for the World Ballroom Dance Championship being held in England, UK in 1960. Ballroom dance consisting of the waltz, foxtrot, quickstep, tango and Viennese waltz. Her father (and his female partner) and her mother (and her male partner) were very good individually, but not so good with their current partners. That was a chemistry some dancers never find. As a result, neither couple would place well in competition that year. Her parents would meet again in 1961, only with a new set of dance partners. This time it was for the World Latin Dance Championship, which was also being held in England, UK. Latin dance consisting of the rumba, samba, paso doble and cha-cha. Predictably, neither couple would fare any better than the year before.

It was not until Debra's parents became dance partners in 1962 that they would begin their winning ways. Her father would bring her mother back to America and they would dance. And they danced some more. They would dance 24/7/365 if they could. There was no limit to their passion for dance. They were breathtaking beautiful together and soon became nothing less than poetry in motion. It was virtually impossible to take your eyes off them once they stepped onto the dance floor. The outfits, the makeup, the hair, the facial expressions, the attractiveness, the moves, the eroticism... the ultimate chemistry, all added up to unrivaled perfection.

By 1964, Debra's parents were on top of the world and favored to win both Ballroom and Latin World Dance Championships in England later that year. At the same time, their passion for dance quite naturally became a passion for each other and they became lovers. The result of this romance was Debra. Sadly, it would also result in the end of their life-long dreams to become world dance champions.

Her father's reaction to the pregnancy was utter rage. Their hard work was finally paying off. Everything they had hoped for was within their grasp. He saw no other solution than to have an abortion and to do so without delay. Abortion, other than to save the life of the mother, was an illegal procedure at the time - but it could be done. Her mom, on the other hand, would not submit to such a barbaric procedure and insisted they set their sights on the 1965 championships and beyond.

Unfortunately, Debra's mother would experience sporadic episodes of weakness and intermittent paralysis after giving birth. This left her incapable of competing at such a professional level as quickly as they had hoped. Instead of patience and understanding toward the mother of his baby daughter (they had not yet married), her father became callous and cruel. Then, one day, he was gone. He would attempt several comebacks with several other female partners, but nothing worked. Rumors of other salacious misdeeds spread and he was eventually ostracized by the dance community that once adored him. He would drink himself into oblivion – never to return to dance or to family.

Throughout her adult life, Debra would dream of having short conversations with her mother from within her mom's womb. Part of her would like to think they were actual memories and not some cerebral fabrication. In any case, one of the earliest conversations she remembered having with her mom was this:

"Who are you?"

"I am your mother and you are my daughter"

"Where am I?"

"You are inside of me, m 'ionmhas beag" (Scottish Gaelic: "my little treasure")

"That's strange"

"Yes, it is very strange. You are my first"

"I hear someone else"

"Yes, that is your father"

"Is he angry with me?"

"No, he is angry with me"

"Is he going to hurt you?"

"He may try, but he will not succeed"

"Will he hurt me?"

"I would never allow that"

"Why not?"

"I love you too much, m 'ionmhas beag"

Up until the day she died, Debra's mother never spoke poorly of her father. In fact, she always seemed to make excuses for his many character flaws and failures. The only explanation was that she still loved him. As it was, her mother's beauty never abandoned her and she would eventually regain all her pre-pregnancy strength and endurance. This made her the perfect target for every ambitious wannabe hoping to move up the professional dance ladder. But the obsession to win championships was gone now... single motherhood took care of that. Instead, her mom would open, what was to become, a very successful dance studio in Northeastern Pennsylvania. Mother and daughter would work side by side up until Debra went off to earn her Ph.D.

and then, perhaps, make a name for herself in politics. As a young dance instructor, Debra learned to lead and to follow in order to teach men how to lead and women how to follow. This talent came in handy while living out her adult life as a practicing lesbian because, if she wanted to dance, she was forced into taking the lead. It has been a hard habit to break.

Debra's mother would remarry twice. It did not take long for each stepfather to show up in the middle of night at her bedside. One would leave the room missing his two front teeth and the other found it necessary to crawl out of her room clutching his groin area. Divorce and excommunication came swiftly for these two depraved monsters, but not before adding to Debra's growing contempt of men. Men seemed to take great pleasure in abusing her mom and abusing her. This heinous treatment of women was an all-too-common experience for her. Slowly, but surely, she began to hate everything about men; their deceit, their arrogance, their masculinity, their control... their touch. If she could somehow re-build a man, it would be a strong woman.

That haunting perception of men had followed Debra the majority of her life. Somehow, along the way, she also developed a distain for almost everything a healthy adult would have considered normal, or natural or, God forbid, moral. Even the "barbaric" act her own mother refused to participate in (the abortion that would have taken her own life) was no longer off-limits. In her mind, it was never good enough to simply deflect "some" bad behavior as being somehow good, or "some" wrong behavior as being somehow right. Instead, "all" things bad, wrong, unnatural or unhealthy must be considered normal... so long as they impowered someone. As soon as one mental health issue or cultural norm was attacked and weakened, it was on to the next. Attack, attack, attack was all she knew how to do. It was what she was forced to learn at a young age. It was what she was groomed to do academically as a college student. It had become her purpose in life. Professor Debra Shade was the quintessential feminist "attack dog"... until now.

It wasn't until Debra stopped listening to those people attacking "her feelings," as well as, those people defending "her feelings" that she came to the realization it was "her feelings" that kept betraying her. Feelings, although very human and worthwhile, could easily become self-destructive compulsions and are rarely reliable over time. Feelings are great for the act of falling in love or sensing imminent danger, however, they were never intended to last forever. At some point, reality and absolute truth will find its way back into a fractured life built on feelings. Now knowing this to be true, it would be intellectually dishonest of her to continue this fraudulent and obsessive servitude to deceptive feelings... but what was the alternative?

It was at this pivotal moment in her life that she recalled a very faint, almost forgotten, conversation from within the womb of her mother. Perhaps, it was their very first conversation and became obscured by all the other conversations that would come later. It went something like this:

"Wake up, little one"

(Yawn) "Who are you?"

"I am who I am"

"Am I alive?"

"Oh, yes, little one (laughter). You are very much alive"

"Where am I?"

"You are inside your mother"

"Does that mean mama and I are the same person?"

"Oh, no. You are you and there is no one else like you"

"Does she know I'm here?"

"Not yet, but she will"

"Will she be happy to see me?"

"Oh, yes, little one. You will make her very happy"

"Will you still be with me?"

"I will never leave you"

"Why not?"

"I love you too much, little one"

The way that leads us back to a faith and trust in God is as unique to a person as their fingerprint. Hitch had his testimony and now Debbie had her testimony. Once she accepted that steadfast and imperishable voice that spoke truth, and that it took precedence over her ephemeral and beguiled feelings, everything began to change for the better.

Among other things, Hitch discovered he enjoyed dancing and Debbie enjoyed being led.

Then there was Fang. She was Debbie's four-year-old Belgian Malinois (MAL-in-wah). The "Mal" was first bred as a herding dog near the city of Malines in the northwestern region of Belgium - hence its name. They have a beautiful fawn to mahogany color with a black mask and ears that stood straight up from the crown of the head. Their body is square and muscular. Belgium was also known for three other herding dogs: the Groenendael (aka Belgian Shepherd), the Tervuren and the Laekenois. The Mal shares many of the favorable temperament qualities common to all Belgians, such as being exceptionally smart, relentless at play, and they will do anything you ask in exchange for your approval. Of the four Belgians, however, it was the Mal that has distinguished itself as the go anywhere - do anything - service dog. It might be worth mentioning here that, of the two dozen brave members of SEAL Team Six that took out the notorious terrorist Osama Bin Laden in 2011, one of those SEALs was a dog... a Mal named "Cairo." Over time, the Belgian Malinois has become the much leaner, much faster and much more agile German Shepherd.

> [NOTE: let it be known that there is absolutely no disrespect toward the German Shepherd as a formidable service dog intended here. They make magnificent protectors and family pets]

Debbie bought Fang as a puppy from a well-respected breeder and, in case you are wondering, she came with the name. Fang had four brothers and two sisters. Their names were Slash, Scar, Viper, Stinger, Shredder, Beast and, of course, Fang. These names were in no way a commentary on the mental health of the dog breeder. It was simply the breeder's custom that every new litter be given a new motif, or theme, for which the puppies were to be named. It was generally understood that all of the puppy's names would change anyway, so why not have some fun with it. For example, the names chosen for the previous litter were Twinkie, Cupcake, Ding Dong, Snoball, MoonPie, and Little Debbie.

On the other hand, it may have been a commentary on Debbie's mental health that she kept the name, Fang. It was no coincidence that the dog was acquired at a point in her life when she felt the most bullet proof, the most ruthless and the most out-of-control (even by radical feminist standards). Fang's main purpose was to enhance that image. Debbie now had in her offensive arsenal a supercharged companion used by the US NAVY SEALS, the US Secret Service, the Israeli Defense Forces, et al, for tracking and K9 duty, search and rescue, bomb and narcotic detection and your basic butt stomping. And, the best part was, her new four-legged social justice warrior was only expected to grow into a relatively small, thirty to forty-pound guided missile. Then, on days off, transition to an adorable house pet... or so she thought.

It would take over a year, two timid roommates and most of her belongings ripped to shreds before Debbie realized her Belgian Malinois craved attention - a lot of attention. It soon became apparent that there was never going to be enough hours in the day to fulfil the attention demands of a Mal – unless you also owned a pasture full of sheep, or cattle, or rhinoceros. Which is exactly what Fang needed most. She needed a job. A demanding job. That job not only required the ability to discharge an infinite amount of energy, but it also needed to somehow engage and, hopefully, fatigue Fang's ever vigilant mind.

With those requirements in mind, Debbie knew there were very few things more demanding than two-hour dance practices. At least in the beginning anyway. Everything your body and mind were being asked to do was something new and, therefore, physically and mentally taxing. So, it came quite natural to Debbie that the solution to Fang's atomic energy source was to teach her how to dance.

Canine dancing, in dog training parlance, could best be described as taking both dog and handler to the ultimate limits of "heelwork"... then, add music to it. Their practice sessions began with a few basic moves such as right heel, left heel, face-to-face, face-to-back, back-to-back, and back-to-face movements. When they moved, they were to move together as one. This close-in "heelwork" took a little getting used to, but when the chemistry took hold, the sustained touching soon became automatic. As soon as Fang became proficient with those basic moves (which did not take long), Debbie added spins, turns, and pivots to their repertoire. Thankfully, that made things a little more intellectually challenging and had the intended calming effect on Fang that Debbie was hoping for.

Once those moves were perfected (which, again, did not take long), they had finally developed enough mechanical skills to create a few short routines to music. So, they danced. When these simple routines became too, well... simple, they added distance work, weaves, jumps, send-outs, and they danced some more. Nothing seemed too difficult for Fang to comprehend and she quickly became Debbie's favorite dance partner.

When she was young, Debbie loved watching her mom and dad dance. She had hours upon hours of old video. Her parents were both so beautiful, so graceful, so magical together. She would give up everything to re-live a day watching them dance together. In some ways, she had found that elusive synergy with Fang. On occasion, dancing with Fang would bring back old conversations from inside the womb of her mother. One, in particular, kept coming to her mind:

"What are you doing now (giggle)?"

"I am dancing with your father"

"I thought he was mad at you"

"Not when we are dancing"

"Is daddy different when you dance?"

"Oh, yes. When we dance, there is no one more gentle or kind"

"When you spin, it feels like I'm flying (giggle)"

"Your father is very good at spinning me around and around"

"I can't wait to dance"

"You will be a wonderful dancer"

"But my feet are too small (sigh)"

"Be patient (laughter). You will grow and your time will come"

"Will you teach me?"

"Yes, you will be my dannsair beag bòidheach" (Scottish Gaelic: "beautiful little dancer")

"I love you, mama"

"I love you, m 'ionmhas beag"

Before long, Debbie had completely forgotten about all the nefarious reasons for getting a dog like Fang. Strangely enough, dancing, and the calming effect it was having on Fang, was also having a positive effect on her. When she looked at Fang now, she no longer pictured an attack dog. Just as there was no longer any "attack dog" gazing back at her when she looked in the mirror. What she saw in Fang was a sweet, lovable companion trying to be the best friend a broken and tired girl could ever hope for. What she saw in the mirror was the same girl trying to figure out why she had adopted so many things contrary to what is good, what is pure, what is lovely (Phm 4:8). But if she was no longer the sledgehammer for every supposed victim of a cruel, oppressive world... what, then, was she to do?

Human nature will tell you to resist that feeling. Stay the course. Naturally, you will feel drawn back to the "community" that protected you for so long. That was the dark place where you can hide your hurt because it was a place without self-control or shame or objective truth. That would have been the easy path, but Debbie had come a long way to get to this point. In fact, the decision to finally rid herself of all the hurt and all the pain and all the messed-up feelings of the past, was made as clear as day last fall. It was the day she attended Hitch's lecture to Hillary's incoming freshman class.

"Come alongside us who care about the truth," Hitch invoked at the end of his lecture. "Regardless of where it may take you or who you may shock by it."

Wallace did not like squirrels much. They were small and annoying. Every dog knew that squirrels were nothing more than mischief makers intent on causing trouble wherever they go. Although cats were similar in stature and annoyance, they could, on occasion, be fun to play with (so long as no one was looking). This tolerance did not apply to squirrels, however. Whenever possible, squirrels are to be chased up the nearest tree forthwith. This public service was deemed necessary so that they do not have a chance to congregate in pathways and/or open fields, causing more turmoil and chaos.

Squirrels, on the other hand, believed dogs to be large and clumsy oafs. Every squirrel knew that dogs were lazy behemoths and had a tendency to clutter pathways and/or open fields after only a few minutes of moderate activity. Therefore, it was perfectly acceptable for dogs to be taunted without mercy or remorse. Fortunately, this public service could be accomplished with very little effort because, unlike humans, dogs were so easily triggered.

What do Fang, Wallace and squirrels have in common?

To answer this fascinating question properly, we must go back to when Fang and Wallace first met. That meeting would take place shortly after Hitch and Debbie's meeting in church. Once Hillary University's Spring semester began, these two mismatched canines would be written into Hitch and Debbie's work calendar as "power walks" for one hour. These outdoor ventures were scheduled almost every day, whether school was in session or out, and would take place somewhere along the many miles of serene country footpaths located on university property. Certainly, both human and beast would profit physically from such a commitment, however, that would only be an ancillary benefit. The time spent walking the dogs had more to do with Hitch and Debbie getting to know each other beyond simply sharing the same faith. Fang and Wallace provided the perfect cover to meet on a daily basis without drawing too much attention to themselves. Beyond a few actual emergencies, nothing ever superseded these enjoyable "walk and talk" rendezvous.

From a canine perspective, it was love at first sight... for Wallace anyhow. He had never met anyone like Fang. At almost 27 inches tall, Wallace stood two inches taller than most male Labrador Retrievers. He also weighed in at 75 pounds – which definitely put him in the "big dog" category. Though he was allowed to eat the nutritional equivalent of fat bombs for every meal (the same junk food Bobbi Lou fed him since puppyhood), he was not a fat dog. Because of his size, however, he would experience some trouble finding dog friends that wanted to play rough. Though Fang was average in size for a female Malinois - a smidge over 22 inches tall and not quite 40 pounds - playing rough was never an issue with her.

At first sight, Fang was not overly-impressed with Wallace. He had legs like a giraffe, a big square head with ears that flopped down on either side, a short otter's tail and he was too easily distracted by the silliest things... like squirrels. He was a good swimmer though and she did appreciate his many failed attempts to use his extremely large body to pin her down. She had to admit it - he was fun to have around. More importantly, Fang could sense that Wallace's human dad (Hitch) was having a profoundly positive effect on her human mom (Debbie). That made everything worthwhile.

So, what do squirrels have to do with anything?

Well, as you can imagine, there are quite a few squirrels that consider Hillary University's 10,000 acres of forest their home. Of course, they still believe it is their land and it will be retaken someday, but that is a different story. Now, unless you were a dog, every squirrel looks pretty much the same. It did not take long, however, before Wallace knew the identities of every squirrel in and around the Yard. The Yard was the large, open courtyard behind Turner Hall where Hitch had an office. Most squirrels were hard-working and industrious. They had no problem finishing up whatever activity they were doing before Wallace found it necessary to intervene. Then there was Stache. Stache was the laid-back, fun-loving, live-for-the-moment kind of guy. His ancient name (the name squirrels take on for themselves) was **Wá:nösgai** (i.e., he who likes trouble). He was a Gen Alpha squirrel that never intends on growing up. And, he was Wallace's prime nemesis at the moment. Wallace had many other lesser adversaries in other locations. For example, there was Skeeter, or Yeyano:we (i.e., she who is fast). She was the little speedster at the small park behind Bobbie Lou's office. Then, there were **Ëgadiyóhšö** (i.e., I will fight against all enemies) and Awë:iyo (i.e., the fragrant flower of the field), or Butterbean and Daisy Cup. These two were the inseparable lovebirds at Hitch's weekend cabin in the mountains.

They all had stories to tell, but this particular incident involved Stache. It would be the incident that would help set the tone in Hitch and Debbie's relationship, as well as, initiate the close bond between Wallace and Fang. The day began as any other January day in Pennsylvania... it was cold. The skies were clear and the sun's unhindered rays provided a soothing warmth like that of a softly knitted Afghan throw. It looked to be the perfect morning for Hitch and Wallace's first walk with Debbie and Fang. At this point, both Hitch and Debbie were still a partial mystery to the other.

I can't wait to hear the justification for naming your pet, Fang, Hitch thought, as he patiently waited on the bench in the middle of the Yard for the two to arrive.

It was early and classes had not yet begun, so Wallace was off the leash and allowed to roam the empty Yard doing what he does best… chase squirrels. Leashes were quite unnecessary for Wallace, but Hitch thought it best to have one handy just in case large, unfamiliar canines made another person feel uncomfortable or fearful. He had not been sitting long when Debbie and Fang cleared the wooded trail and entered the open courtyard. Fang was already off the leash, but did not leave Debbie's side. Wallace's moronic behavior could not be more noticeable, and yet Fang remained unaffected and in perfect unison with Debbie's every move. They were an impressive sight to behold. Even Wallace had to stop his squirrel dispersion duties momentarily to watch them glide effortlessly across the field. Hitch stood up as they approached.

"Good morning, Bright Eyes," Hitch spoke in those endearing tones we all save for that one special person in our lives. "So, this is Fang. Not sure why, but I expected more teeth."

"Good morning, Eddie," Debbie replied with a smile and turned her attention to a large yellow Labrador barking at a tree. "So, that is Wallace. Not sure why, but I expected less of a squirrel-o-phobe."

"Well, since you mentioned it, I have been watching these two go at it for some time now," Hitch countered objectively. "I may be over-thinking this, but I get the sense that it is some sort of game they both enjoy playing. In any case, the probability of Wallace ever catching a squirrel is virtually zero. Even if that one-chance-in-a-million day were to arrive,

I doubt he would have the heart to do it any harm. My dog is a very sensitive creature."

Without cause, Fang released a mild, composed bark followed by several other dog utterances.

> [Note: a dog utterance may, or may not, include growls, howls, snorts, whimpers, etc.]

Fang's remark (for lack of a better description) seemed to be directed towards Debbie.

"Very interesting," Debbie responded and immediately sat down.

To whom she was responding, Hitch wasn't quite sure.

"Can we sit for a moment?" she asked politely.

Without really being given the opportunity to acquiesce or not to acquiesce, Hitch sat down. After a long minute of watching Wallace dance and bark feverishly around a tree, Hitch felt compelled to speak.

"I am not one to delve into conspiracy theories, but I honestly believe the squirrel is intentionally provoking the poor dog," Hitch suggested to no one in particular. "Especially this one."

Hitch was now pointing to the squirrel perched on a tree limb that was several feet beyond Wallace's best leap. It was Stache. He was easily recognizable because of the distinct color variation around the muzzle that made it appear as though he had a white mustache. He also appeared to be dumping snow or pelting acorns onto Wallace's head every chance he got.

"Yes, I know," Debbie stated matter-of-factly and without taking her eyes off the activity at the tree.

Again, Fang softly barked something dispassionately towards Debbie. After another brief pause in their sparce conversation, Hitch spoke again.

"You know what exactly?"

"Fang can help if you like," she offered without fully addressing the question being asked.

"Are we talking about a peaceful resolution here?"

"Yes, of course," Debbie replied and smiled. "She does not intend to hurt anyone."

"You know your dog's intentions, do you?"

"I do"

"And how would you know that?' Hitch inquired with a cautious suspicion.

"She told me... more or less."

Debbie was not one to waffle when making her point. She knew what Fang was capable of and she did not try to hide or deny it. She also knew that Hitch must be thinking her a lunatic right about now. And why wouldn't he? They had only been seated for five minutes and she had not given Fang a command to do anything, yet her dog barks twice as if she understands the situation completely and has kindly proposed an amicable resolution... whoa.

Rather than spend an hour attempting to explain Fang's "gift," Debbie took the much quicker "seeing is believing" route. She pivoted her lower body on the bench so that her entire upper body could now face Hitch. With the voice of an angel, she spoke.

"Can you trust me on this?"

"Yes, I suppose I can," Hitch replied hesitantly at first. Then, after seeing the sincerity in her eyes, he firmed up his response. "Yes, I trust you."

Debbie gently took the collar off Fang – who sat patiently. Without giving any specific command or adding any hyped-up inflection, Debbie spoke.

"Go"

Within a matter of seconds, Fang was across the field, used Wallace backside as a springboard and was standing on the same tree limb as the squirrel. In utter shock and horror, Stache momentarily lost all sensation in his legs and fell to ground in front of Wallace. He landed safely on all fours, as squirrels have a natural tendency to do, and for a second, they were face to face. Then, as if neither could believe what just happened, both Stache and Wallace looked up at Fang. By this time, Fang was resting perfectly balanced on the branch and calmly looking down at them both.

Dejected, and not caring if he was to be eaten alive, Stache slowly (for a squirrel) made his way across the thin layer of soft snow and disappeared into the forest. Wallace stood motionless as he watched Stache slink away. It was as if he could not decide whether he just lost a mortal enemy or his best friend. Sensing this might happen, Fang began her decent using Wallace's backside as a cushion before gently hitting the ground running. Instead of heading back to her human mom, however, she swung around and gave Wallace a solid body bump. This was her way of telling him, "Your friend will be alright and so will you."

Chapter 3

The Passion

Christmas and Easter. Have you ever asked yourself which is the more "Christian" of these two epic holidays? One celebrates the birth of Jesus, the earthly son of Joseph and Mary, and the other celebrates the death and resurrection of Jesus, the immaculate son of God. Of course, Jesus was 100% God from day one, but nobody knew that for sure... except for maybe Mary, virgin mother of God. If these were the only two Christian services you go to in the year, and perhaps it is, which makes you feel better about yourself?

Let's take a quick peek at Christmas first.

Both "Christmas" and "Christian" have the word "Christ" in them. That should count for something. The virgin birth itself was clearly a miracle. That's two thumbs up for Christmas. You get toys, clothes and Claxton fruit cake from jolly Ol' Saint Nick. That makes three enthusiastic thumbs up!

Since its inception back in A.D. 336, the time spent examining and giving thanks for the virgin birth on Christmas Day (Old English: Cristes Maesse, meaning "Christ's Mass") was, and continues to be, only a small part within the whole semi-religious extravaganza. The trees, lights, fanfare and camel-loads of gifts being exchanged on Christmas morning are nothing new, but when have you seen a prominent retailer advertising their finest nativity scene being on sale? Heck, even those who mock those who believe that Jesus is the "Christ" (Greek: chrīstós, meaning "anointed one") love getting their fair share of loot on Christ's Mass Day.

And, as miraculous as the virgin birth was, it was only a birthday. In those days, a person's day-of-birth was of less consequence than the day-of-death. If you cared to remember the month of your birth, you cared too much. Even the prominent Christian theologian, Origen (A.D. 185–254), would groan "Sinners, not saints, celebrate birthdays." You could say that Mr. Origen was a bit of a sourpuss, but, if you think about it, that child born in that manger over two thousand years ago did not start proving his divine nature until he was in his thirties (Lk 3:23).

Now, let's take a quick peek at Easter.

Easter is all about how and why Jesus died. Not necessarily a thumbs down, but certainly a buzz-kill if you were a Christian living in the 1st century. The early church referred to this monumental event as the "Passion of Christ" (Latin verb: passio, meaning "to suffer") and is recorded in all four Gospels (Mt 26:36–27:56, Mk 14:32–15:41, Lk 22:39–23:49, Jn 18:1–19:37). The four Gospels also agree that this event occurred on Friday during Passover – which is the "Day of Preparation" for the Jewish Sabbath (Mt 27:62, Mk 15:42, Lk 23:54, Jn 19:42). We can pretty much agree that all living things will die and they will stay dead. If Jesus died on the cross and stayed dead, the whole "Christianity" craze may have dragged on with the support of a few hearty seeker-sensitive types, but its popularity most certainly would have faded in a generation or two - as all empty cults should. Therefore, the resurrection of Jesus from the dead three days after his crucifixion was a big deal... a miracle. So, we now have two miracles; one at birth and one at death. Without the resurrection, however, Jesus would not be the Savior he claimed he was (Jn 14:6). Without the resurrection, there would be no forgiveness of sin (1 Cor 15:17-19).

The great Old Testament Jewish prophet, Isaiah, foretold the "Passion of Christ" 700 years prior to the resurrection (Isaiah 53). On numerous occasions, Jesus himself would attempt to explain these words of Isaiah and the other Prophets to his disciples. He told them he did not come down from heaven to conquer Rome (or to make his believers rich, healthy or equal)... he came to conquer sin... their sin... our sin ... the sins of yesterday... the sins of tomorrow... the sins of the entire world (Jn 16:33). Yet, one after the other, these same disciples freely admitted to the world (in Scripture) they missed this one big, glaring, fundamental lesson... until the resurrection.

Forgiveness of sin – it's the thing. It's the only thing. It is what makes Easter beautiful and rather simple.

I, for one, have come to the conclusion that neither holiday is more Christian than the other. Both were festivals from the beginning, and they remain festivals today. And there is nothing wrong with a good festival. What fascinates me most about Easter, however, is the fact that the word itself does not even make sense as a proper name. That is, the word "Easter" has no Latin, or Greek, or Jewish, or Aramaic root that can be applied to anything biblical or non-biblical. For all intents and purposes, it is a meaningless, made-up word. There are a few theories as to how this word first came into existence. The most plausible "in the ballpark" theory suggests that the word, Easter, was the name of an English goddess, Eostre, that pre-dated Christianity. We are not even sure what she was the goddess of. Apparently, all it took to keep her name around in the history books was a cursory reference by a popular British Monk.

His name was, Venerable Bede, or Saint Bede (c. 673-735 A.D.). This guy was so influential that Pope Leo XIII post-humously declared him a "Doctor of the Church." Bede was, indeed, a brilliant scholar and prolific writer. He is most remembered for a series of books entitled, "Ecclesiastical History of the English People." This body of work is considered one of the best sources for early English history ever written... by anyone. Somewhere in his vast collection of writings, Bede casually observed that the month in which his fellow Christians were celebrating the Passion of Jesus Christ had also been referred to historically as "Eosturmonath" in Old English. This was a small, but clear, reference to Eostre. There was no advocating, no lobbying, no pressure to apply Bede's trivial information to any cause or event. The name, Easter, simply had an appeal with the populace and it stuck... like cold on ice.

While on the topic of making stuff up, Easter falls on a Sunday every year... but what Sunday?

Well, it depends on the moon (here we go again... ugh!).

OK, why?

Because it needed to coincide with the first Sunday after the Paschal Full Moon, which is the first full moon after the vernal equinox. This is a day in spring when night and day are exactly the same length. The date of this equinox can fall on March 19, 20 or 21, but the Roman Catholic Church decided long ago to set that date as March 21.

OK, why?

Because the Roman Catholic Church wanted Easter to coincide with the Jewish holiday of Passover. Passover is based on the Jewish calendar which is tied to lunar cycles. Therefore, the dates of Passover and Easter will fluctuate from year to year.

OK, why?

Because the Roman Catholic Church said so... shut up already!

The same could be said for Lent; Ash Wednesday; Holy Week; Palm Sunday; Spy Wednesday; Maundy Thursday; Holy Saturday. All created for one reason or another by the Roman Catholic Church back in the fourth century. Granted, most of these observances highlight actual events in the Bible, but some do not. Unfortunately, to many non-Christians (and Christians), these minor preoccupations only add to the puzzling quality of Easter... when it should be all about the forgiveness of sin.

Easter, like Christmas, is mostly celebrated as a fun-filled family get-together. Anything that brings a family back together these days is a good thing. As far as the various meanings behind the chocolate bunnies with bow ties, sugar-coated yellow marshmallows in the shape of chickens, multi-color hard-boiled eggs (that require hiding before eating) and wicker baskets filled with green plastic grass... who cares at this point? Some believe that Easter was nothing more than a clever marketing gimmick created by evil confectionery conglomerates to profit off the Christian's gullibility. Then again, the same reverence-diminishing gimmickry could be said of the evil confectionery conglomerate's treatment of Satan's fun-filled holiday - Halloween. Those stupid pagans!

[Note: plenty of sarcasm in both of these illustrations]

In any case, I believe church services being held on these two wonderful holidays are no better, and no worse, than any other Sunday service... as long as the service glorifies God and remains true to Scripture. In other words, I believe Jesus would be more than willing to give us a pass on both Christmas and Easter, if we would just come visit him more often on the many other Sundays of the year.

So long as what is being taught on Sunday is from Scripture, of course.

Ahh... springtime. Snow and ice have melted away, light jackets have replaced Gore-Tex parkas and color has returned to the foothills surrounding Hillary University. Spring training camp is over and baseball is back on the menu. Yes, spring has officially sprung. And in the midst of all this fair weather, All-American pastimes and beauty... is Easter.

For as long as Leon has been alive, he has been celebrating Easter in church... and it never gets old. This was as true today as it was when he was a precocious little prankster. Back then, he and his buddies would use high-profile celebrations, like Christmas and Easter, to race each other from the front of the church to the back. That was no easy task since the rules of the game had to be performed some-time during the service. It also had to be accomplished by crawling the entire way under the pews. That meant in between the multitude of congregant legs. There was no official start time to begin the race. The contestants started when they thought they had the best chance of making it all the way to the finish line. The winner was the first to physi-cally touch the door handles at the church entrance.

Every player knew that the start time was the most important element of the race. If you were to jump the gun and get caught, you would be forced back to your seat and monitored more intently by an embarrassed parent or a jealous sibling eager to rat you out for some past injus-tice you may have done to them. Therefore, patience was key to success. For Leon, that moment came when the choir, the pastor and the entire congregation would be on their feet singing, swaying and lifting both hands and faces to the sky in praises to the Lord. At that precise moment, a small, quick, agile body moving between your feet would hardly be noticed. Having already been classified a music prodigy and having already scanned the bulletin for the songs to be sung at service, Leon knew when a perfectly timed "halle-luiah" take-off would propel him to victory. He rarely lost at this game.

Nowadays, Leon gets his kicks in church by organizing and conducting two mega concerts for the two mega hol-idays - Christmas and Easter. The Christmas offering, was a 90-minute version of George Frederic Handel's three-hour masterpiece "Messiah" with its amazing "Hallelujah" chorus at the end. For Easter, it was Johann Sebastian Bach's complete 45-minute Easter Oratorio: Kommt, eilet und laufet ("Come, hasten and run") BWV 249 with its recitatives and arias in eleven movements. Given the magnitude of these two giant pieces of music, it was just short of a miracle that he has been able to pull it off each and every year for the past ten years. It is true that these two holiday classics are held every year all across the country, but the ones we pay good money to listen to are typically performed by paid professionals. Leon's talented group of singers and musicians, on the other hand, were all volunteers and have always come from local colleges (including Hillary's music department), from local churches (regardless of denomination) or simply everyday people from the area.

This local talent even included a homeless man. He attended every rehearsal, earned the role of the Apostle Peter (tenor) for all the arias and recitations, then, without a word, disappeared into the cold, black night when the whole thing was over. It weighed heavily on Leon's heart long after the various man-hunts failed to turned up anything. In order to make sense of it, some suggested that their amazing tenor was simply an angel doing what angels do.

In any event, not one person has ever been paid a dime for taking part in these two shows, and yet a flood of applications for the Christmas event would begin soon after the Easter event – and vice versa. That enthusiasm should come as no surprise since both concerts are now holiday traditions. Taking part in one, or both, concerts made you an instant celebrity in and around the town of Hillary. It was true that each of these holiday performances has received an immediate, and well-deserved, ten-minute standing ovation upon its conclusion. Still, Leon was understandably anxious because this year was being heavily advertised as the tenth anniversary of these "must-see-to-believe" musical productions.

The venue for both of these nearly-professional level performances has always been the 2,000-seat Walker Auditorium. This acoustically perfect, 160-year-old building is over a mile away from the vastly enlarged modern side of the university. Charlie (aka "Chief") was the person legally mandated to protect and preserve this Civil War landmark, as well as, the three other Civil War buildings at this site.

To refer to Charlie simply by his official title as "Head Groundskeeper and Curator" was to understate his true authority. Legally, "no one" was awarded access to any historical property except that which is granted by the trustee of that historical property. Some of the best lawyers on the planet have attempted to annul or diminish the powers of the trustee, but they have only succeeded in reinforcing the abiding principle that "no one" means "no one." That includes the President of Hillary University and its Board of Directors. For over thirty years, that autonomous position of trustee has been held by Charlie.

Charlie knew the beauty, majesty and meaning of the Handel and Bach compositions. He also knew Leon as the man who could stretch out 10ths on the piano with his left hand as easily as Fats Waller or Oscar Peterson. As soon as Charlie got word that Leon was looking for a new location for these two performances beyond the acoustically-challenged walls of his downtown church sanctuary, he offered Leon the Walker Auditorium. It was a no-brainer actually and the deal was over in the blink of an eye.

"Professor, a little birdie told me that your Christmas concert has become so popular that you will be needing more space soon," Charlie quipped from his side-by-side work vehicle. "Any truth to that rumor?"

"News travels fast around here now, don't it?" Leon replied with a generous smile.

He was just about to step off the curb and into the parking lot outside his office when Charlie pulled up beside him.

"The roses have ears and I tend to them every day," Charlie replied with a sly twitch of the eye.

This was Charlie's patent response whenever he received reliable information that was not meant to be held in confidence. He was not one for gossip. Hillary was also known for its exquisite roses.

"Chief, I'd be lying if I told you I didn't feel Handel's music deserved better. Works like that..." Leon's contagious smile faded slightly as he pressed on with his thoughts, "well, they need a place where the beauty of that sound can bounce and reverberate around the room. A place where that wonderful sound can spread out, come at you from every direction and then, on its own accord, disappear into that space. A place where every listener is held captive for a moment in time by that beautiful, wonderful sound."

"You got it," Charlie responded matter-of-factly.

"Got what?" Leon asked quizzically.

"Walker Auditorium... for your Christmas concert," Charlie answered as if it had already been contemplated and decided.

"And that goes for your Easter program too. Let me know the dates you will be needing them as soon as you can. Gotta run, but we can talk more on this later."

Without waiting to take a question on this generous offer, Charlie was off.

To say this offer was simply "generous" was perhaps the understatement of the year. Charlie had turned down numerus offers in excess of $250,000 from outside organizations for just one 24-hour period of this historic building and use of its pristine surroundings. In other words, Charlie just presented Leon with a gift worth a quarter of a million dollars... per night. This chance meeting of a lifetime took place soon after Christmas break ten years ago.

Of the two great compositions, it was Bach's Easter Oratorio that presented the greatest challenge for Leon. And this year was no exception. On paper, or its handbill, the eleven movements look deceptively plain:

1 **Sinfonia** Instrumental
   Tromba I-III, Tamburi, Oboe I/II, Violino I/II,
   Viola, Fagotto e Continuo

2 **Adagio** Instrumental
   Oboe I, Violino I/II, Viola, Fagotto e Continuo

3 **Aria** (Duet) Tenor (Peter the apostle), Bass (John the apostle) & Chorus
   Tromba I-III, Tamburi, Oboe I/II, Violino I/II,
   Viola, Fagotto e Continuo

Kommt, eilet und laufet, ihr flüchtigen Füße
(Come, hurry and run, you swift feet)
Erreichet die Höhle, die Jesum bedeckt! (Get to
the cave that covers Jesus)
Lachen und Scherzen, (Laughter and jokes)
Begleitet die Herzen (accompany our hearts)
Denn unser Heil ist auferweckt. (For our Saviour
is raised from the dead)

4   **Recitativo**
Fagotto e Continuo

Alto (Mary Magdalene):
O kalter Männer Sinn! (O cold minds of men)
Wo ist die Liebe hin, (Where is the love gone)
Die ihr dem Heiland schuldig seid? (that you
owe to the Saviour

Soprano (Mary, mother of James):
Ein schwaches Weib muss euch beschämen! (A
weak woman puts you to shame)

Tenor (Peter):
Ach, ein betrübtes Grämen (Ah, affliction
and grief)

Bass (John):
Und banges Herzeleid (and fearful
sorrow of heart)

Tenor, Bass (Peter, John):
Hat mit gesalznen Tränen (with salty tears)
Und wehmutsvollem Sehnen, (and melancholy longing)
Ihm eine Salbung zugedacht, (intended an anointing for him)

Soprano, Alto (Mary Magdalene, Mary mother of James):
Die ihr, wie wir, umsonst gemacht (which you, as we, have done in vain)

5 **Aria Soprano** (Mary, mother of James)
Flauto traverso o Violino solo, Fagotto e Continuo

Seele, deine Spezereien (My soul, your spices)
Sollen nicht mehr Myrrhen sein. (should no more be myrrh)

Denn allein (For only)
Mit dem Lorbeerkranze prangen, (with the splendour of the laurel wreath)
Stillt dein ängstliches Verlangen. (will your anxious longing be satisfied)

6 **Recitativo**
Fagotto e Continuo

Tenor (Peter the apostle):

Hier ist die Gruft (Here is the tomb)

Bass (John the apostle):
Und hier der Stein (And here is the stone)
Der solche zugedeckt. (which covered it)
Wo aber wird mein Heiland sein? (But where will my Saviour be)

Alto (Mary Magdalene):
Er ist vom Tode auferweckt! (He has risen from the dead)
Wir trafen einen Engel an, (We met an angel)
Der hat uns solches kundgetan. (who pro-claimed this to us)

Tenor (Peter the apostle):
Hier seh ich mit Vergnügen (I see here with pleasure)
Das Schweißtuch abgewickelt liegen. (the veil lies unwound)

7 **Aria** Tenor (Peter the apostle)
Flauto dolce I/II, Violino I/II, Fagotto e Continuo

Sanfte soll mein Todeskummer, (Gentle should be the sorrow of my death)
Nur ein Schlummer, (only a slumber)
Jesu, durch dein Schweißtuch sein. (Jesus, through your veil)

Ja, das wird mich dort erfrischen (Yes, that will refresh me there)
Und die Zähren meiner Pein (and the tears of my suffering)
Von den Wangen tröstlich wischen. (it will wipe comfortingly from my cheeks)

8 **Recitativo** (Duet) Soprano (Mary, mother of James), Alto (Mary Magdalene)
Fagotto e Continuo

Indessen seufzen wir (Meanwhile we sigh)
Mit brennender Begier: (with fervent yearning)
Ach, könnt es doch nur bald geschehen, (Ah, if only it might soon happen)
Den Heiland selbst zu sehen! (to see the Saviour himself)

9 **Aria** Alto (Mary Magdalene)
Oboe d'amore, Violino I/II, Viola, Fagotto e Continuo

Saget, saget mir geschwinde, (Tell me, tell me quickly)
Saget, wo ich Jesum finde, (Tell, where may I find Jesus)
Welchen meine Seele liebt! (whom my soul loves)
Komm doch, komm, umfasse mich; (Come then, come, embrace me)

Denn mein Herz ist ohne dich (for my heart is without you)
Ganz verwaiset und betrübt. (quite orphaned and distressed)

10 **Recitativo** Bass (John the apostle)
Fagotto e Continuo

Wir sind erfreut, (We are delighted)
Dass unser Jesus wieder lebt, (that our Jesus lives once more)
Und unser Herz, (and our heart)
So erst in Traurigkeit zerflossen und geschwebt (before so dissolved and suspended in sadness)
Vergisst den Schmerz (forgets its sorrow)
Und sinnt auf Freudenlieder; (and thinks of songs of joy)
Denn unser Heiland lebet wieder. (for our Saviour lives once more)

11 **Chorus**
Tromba I-III, Tamburi, Oboe I/II, Violino I/II, Viola, Fagotto e Continuo

Preis und Dank (Praise and thanks)
Bleibe, Herr, dein Lobgesang. (Hell and the devil are overcome)
Höll und Teufel sind bezwungen, (their gates are destroyed)

Ihre Pforten sind zerstört. (remain your song
of praise)
Jauchzet, ihr erlösten Zungen, (Shout and cheer,
you loosened tongues)
Dass man es im Himmel hört. (so that you are
heard in heaven)
Eröffnet, ihr Himmel, die prächtigen Bogen,
(Open up, you heavens, the splendid arches)
Der Löwe von Juda kommt siegend gezogen!
(the Lion of Judah comes drawn in victory)

It was not the music of Johann Sebastian Bach that kept
Leon awake at night. Bach was always a joy to hear and a
blessing to play. There was certainly no shortage of young
and old musical prodigies and their instruments from which
Leon could choose. Nor could his sleepless nights be blamed
on anything having to do with costumes, makeup, wigs, stage
lighting, props or scenic backdrops because this was purely
music - not theater. That is, it was four solo vocalists, backed
by a chorus, backed by an orchestra and guided by a conductor (Leon). They all came appropriately dressed in whatever evening gowns (women) and suits (men) they found to
be the most comfortable. Again, these were unpaid volunteers. Nothing special was required of them other than a
respect for the occasion and their incredible talent.

The scene to be imagined was the grave site where Jesus
was buried. Two of Jesus' disciples (Peter and John) rush to
that place after hearing the news of the resurrection. At the
tomb, they encounter two women (Mary, mother of James
and Mary Magdalene) mourning the death of Jesus. The two

Mary's were there to anoint Jesus' dead body with oil. The two disciples enter the open grave only to find it empty except for the burial cloth that Jesus had been wearing. The two women then speak of an angel who would proclaim that Christ had risen.

Simple enough. It is one of the three main events from Scripture that Christians remember most about Easter: the brutal scourging, the agonizing crucifixion and the empty tomb.

The dialogue (chorus, arias and recitatives), however, was quite a different story for Leon. This musical drama was meant to be sung in Bach's native language – German. Granted, Pennsylvania has always had a large German population. In fact, it was a group of German Quakers and Mennonites from the Krefeld region (western Germany) of the Rhineland that founded the city of Germantown in 1683. William Penn (1644–1718), founder of the "Province of Pennsylvania" (later to be renamed the State of Pennsylvania) was an old English Quaker himself. He eagerly embraced thousands of German immigrants fleeing religious persecution into his new colony. Unfortunately, three hundred years of life in America has taken its toll on those speaking their native language. To find someone who can sing a solo in German, with all the emotion necessary to convey the deepest sorrow and the uttermost jubilation of those present on that day at the empty tomb, was nearly impossible.

If readers recall, it was not long ago that a homeless man was given the opportunity to sing the tenor's solo parts (i.e., Peter). That decision was made, not because it provided a great human-interest story. Rather, it was made because the man was the most deserving of the part.

Four weeks ago, Leon's lead tenor took off for reasons that seemed ambiguous and trivial. It was not the first time Leon had lost a pro-quality tenor and he predicted it would not be the last time. Tenors are most often the superstar (a positive thing)... and the primo uomo (a negative thing). That is why he always had a backup singer for this coveted position. That same safe-guard was true for all his solo vocalists, but it only ever seemed to be applied in the case of the tenor. But backups are backups for a reason. In most cases, these stand-ins only prevented the total collapse of a performance - not enhance it. Leon had been working very hard with this backup tenor for the past three weeks without much to show for it. For better or worse, Leon felt comfortable that this one would not be stolen from him anytime soon. What made Leon drift back into a peaceful sleep after these setbacks was knowing that all the other parts of the Easter oratorio were solid. Leon was enormously grateful for all the dedicated people he was given to work with... that included the imperfect backup tenor.

Why is it always the tenor? Leon asked himself while slowly shaking his head involuntarily. *Must have got a better offer. With so many concerts going on at once, money talks and talent walks.*

It began three weeks ago. The faint echo. It was heard by all and only when the full rehearsals were being held in the Walker Auditorium. The echo mimicked the tenor's solo parts - never the other singers. The echo was clear, strong and always in absolute perfect pitch – just like the original tenor (the guy who left). The diction was flawless German and the delivery was keenly expressive – just like the original tenor (the guy who left). It was as if the imperfect backup tenor was being mocked by the echo.

It happened again tonight. Although this phantom echo was phenomenal, he was starting to become a real distraction. It would come as a complete shock to Leon if he were to discover that the guy who left was capable of such an unethical prank, but the two voices sounded so remarkably identical. Not one to waste valuable time - and wanting to end all speculation quickly - Leon made a respectful call to his previous tenor to subtly confirm his whereabouts. To Leon's great relief, the man and his voice were not in the building. In fact, he was not even in the same state.

This call was made immediately following the seventh movement aria. Not knowing what else to do, Leon resumed the rehearsal with two tenor soloists that evening. One, was not so good... and on stage. The other, was very good... but not on stage.

Leon would have a brief, somewhat cursory, talk with Charlie after this latest intrusive experience. He felt an obligation to say something, but did not want to make a big deal out of it. Charlie, on the other hand, took such news as a serious breach of conduct. If there was a "phantom" in his "opera house" and he was found to be on protected historical property without permission, then trespassing charges might apply should some nefarious motive be uncovered.

This building, along with the other Civil War era buildings, were under constant surveillance. Charlie promised Leon a full investigation.

In any event, Charlie would, from this day forward, have Alex and Francesca on site whenever Leon rehearsed. These two had become Charlie's most trusted **protégés** and had recently proven themselves to be excellent detectives.

The echo had been all but forgotten when Leon began this night's full rehearsal. The important thing now was how to interpret Bach's state of mind when he penned the first two movements of this majestic oratorio. In the opening sinfonia, Leon believed it was all about the race to the Jesus' tomb by the four protagonists (Peter, John and the two Mary's). In the adagio, it was all about the foursome's discovery that the tomb was empty.

"Ladies and gentleman, I thank you all for your faithfulness and your sacrifice," Leon began as he always began, but this time with a gentle reminder of the solemn nature of the great task before them.

"It's up to us now. We are here to tell the story of our Savior's resurrection. We just happen to be using a masterpiece handed down to us three-hundred-years ago. Ya'll know this story. Jesus has already suffered. He has already died on that cross. They carry him away to be buried someplace outside the walls of Jerusalem. It's been three days. That rock blocking the doorway to his tomb has been rolled back."

Leon allowed that imagery to settle in before continuing.

"Folks, what happens next is what Bach focused on. It is where we begin to tell this earth-shattering story. It's the resurrection story. It's the Easter story. It's the story of grace and mercy, of hope and joy, of repentance and forgiveness... of God's patience and his tender love for us. There is no story... there is no music... more powerful than this one right here. You, my sisters and brothers, are now the hands and feet of Christ. For the next forty-five minutes, let nothing else distract you from that purpose... nothing."

While Leon was having his let-us-rise-to-the-occasion moment, Alex and Francesca were having one of their own ... sort of. They were made aware of the unwelcomed "echo" that was presumably coming from within Walker whenever the tenor sang his solo parts. The briefing included a forewarning that the phantom's voice might be faint - almost imperceptible - by the average musically-challenged person. The two were now sitting patiently in the back of the auditorium ready to spring into action. Well, at least Francesca was ready. Alex had already relaxed into a light sleep.

"Wake up, idiot!" Franny snarled and gave her semi-conscious partner a shot in the arm. "Chief says this is important."

"Hey, you're the singer, not me," Alex replied without acknowledging the hit or caring to open his eyes. "I wouldn't know the tenor dude from the tuba dude anyway. Wake me up when you got someone for me to tackle."

"Tuba?" Franny laughed mockingly. "You see a tuba up there?

"Thank you," Alex snickered back. "You just proved my point."

"Really?" Franny huffed in "not-worth-the-effort" defeat.

She knew talking sense with the other gender that has been in a state of relaxation for more than five minutes was futile.

"Keep your eyes closed for all I care, but can you at least keep your ears open? Two short musical parts, then the chorus, then the tenor has a couple short solos. If you hear two tenor voices singing the same thing, we move. Got it?"

"Got it."

"Chief doesn't want us tackling anyone either, okay?" Franny added.

"Why?"

"He doesn't want anyone hurt," Franny calmly stated the obvious. "Why do you think?"

"Who's gonna get hurt. The dude sings the high parts, right?" Alex responded in the way every self-respecting, testosterone-ladened man would respond... with a hefty amount of bravado. "Have you ever seen a jacked singer that, you know, sings the high parts?"

"Alex, no!" Franny barked, now feeling a bit nervous.

Alex was like her brother. They were as close to being family as anyone could be. This was not a request.

"He may have a gun. We get a good look at him. We get height, weight, hair color, tats... that's it. Promise me, you big dope... promise me!"

"OK, OK, I promise."

Just as those reluctant words were released, the music began and Alex was brought to attention. Neither the sinfonia, the adagio nor the aria were very long. So, in less than fifteen minutes, Alex and Francesca heard the tenor sing his first lines... along with his echo. Immediately, both were looking skyward.

"Balconies!" they stated simultaneously.

They had just ten minutes before the tenor sang again and two balcony levels to cover. That was a lot of territory.

Fortunately, they knew this place like the back of their hands and the tenor would be singing by himself for almost ten minutes. That would be the one and only opportunity to track the mysterious voice. From then on, the tenor would sing along with the chorus for the remainder of the concert. They quickly decided to take one level at a time and park themselves in the balconies facing each other on opposite sides of the auditorium.

In a flash they were looking at each other from across the room and stood waiting excitedly. As soon as the first sound emanated from tenor's mouth once again, Francesca pointed to a location above Alex's head and they both took off for the nearest stairway. The second-tier balcony level had a few classrooms along the outside perimeter of the building and was empty of people – as it should be. Once on the second level, the voice and it's hiding place became as clear as a Whippoorwill on a warm summer night.

Alex mouthed the words "ready in three" silently. With one hand he reached for the door handle and with the other he started finger counting. Francesca immediately put her hand on top of his counting hand and slowly pushed it down to stop the count. With pleading eyes, she mouthed the words "let him sing."

"What are you doing?" he mouthed back impatiently and moved his hand away from the door.

"It's too beautiful," she mouthed. "Let him sing... please."

Chapter 4

Enchanted Forest

Did Debbie and her Malinois, Fang, really have some sort of verbal conversation just now?

There were many other questions to be answered when you are on your first date, but that one went straight to the top of Hitch's list while sitting on that bench three months ago. Normally, the pet owner will command their pet to do a certain thing; like sit, stay, rollover, etc. and their pet will react. The pet does not ask why or offer any alternatives. If the pet knows the word and its meaning they will comply – not a conversation. In this case, however, Hitch witnessed Fang barking (speaking) and Debbie actively listening and understanding. Then, Debbie spoke and Fang appeared to be actively listening and understanding. The argument that, just because Hitch did not comprehend one side of this exchange, therefore, a conversation did not take place, was invalid reasoning. So, it might just fall somewhere in the grey areas that define what it means to have a "conversation" – if the only rule to having a conversation is an oral exchange of sentiments, observations or ideas.

After giving it some serious consideration, Hitch came to the conclusion that Debbie was not crazy... at least not in this instance anyway. Perhaps they do communicate on a higher level than most pet owners and it approaches that of an oral exchange. So what? It is not that much different than his familiarity with Wallace. Since they first teamed up, it always seemed to Hitch that Wallace had something to say when the situation dictated it. Wallace certainly let it be known when someone was lying through their teeth. That would be his malodorous sixth sense. Indeed, Hitch would be hard pressed to deny having observed Bobbi Lou and Wallace communicate with each other. It could be said that anyone's communication with their beloved pet could – on some basic level – border on conversation.

That hypothesis might even have merit if the attempted communication was between an adult and an infant. One having highly advanced aptitude skills and the other having only rudimentary aptitude skills. The incoherent chattering of the infant might seem to be an awkward stab at conversation, but I'm guessing many people would put conversations with Brittany Spears (pop singer) into this category as well. She has, after all, become just as famous for her incoherent chattering as she has for her ability to sing. Take, for example, her interview for Blender Magazine (April 2004) in which she exclaimed, "I get to go to a lot of overseas places, like Canada"... it's a classic. The point being, conversations take effort on the side of the recipient.

So, now that Fang's mind-blowing display of mental acuity and athleticism was over, Hitch and Debbie were off to a great start. On the other hand (or paw, in this case), it took a while for Wallace to forgive Fang for sticking her long, perfectly contoured snout into his personal business. For weeks afterwards, when Debbie and Fang came to visit, Wallace would head straight to the foot of the tree, lie down and wait. This was normally where he and Stache would begin their daily obsession of being two opposing combatants on a field of battle when, in fact, they were just two dudes playing a stupidly fun game. Only, now, Stache never showed up. This was not supposed to be how it ended. If it ever did end, it was to share a few laughs, a few tears, a few cigars and a few beers... metaphorically speaking... then, go back home to be with family.

This mood swing of Wallace's did not go unnoticed. Even Fang was moved by it.

As was the custom for these early morning get-togethers, Hitch and Debbie would meet at the bench in the Yard to plan out their walk. This also gave the dogs an opportunity to pal around and stretch their legs in a wide-open field. After being rebuffed by Wallace for a second day, Fang walked slowly back to the bench, sat by Debbie's side and let out a short, forlorn whine followed by a series of growls and whimpers. Now knowing the drill, Hitch spoke first.

"I believe Fang has something to tell you."

"I'm sorry. It's got something to do with Wallace," Debbie responded graciously to Hitch and then turned to Fang.

"Be his friend and give him time," Debbie responded encouragingly to Fang and turned back to Hitch.

"Just a little squabble," Debbie wrapped things nicely up for Hitch. "Now, where were we?"

This melancholy mood of Wallace's lasted about two weeks when all of the sudden he felt a little something hit his head. Several days ago, he stopped looking up after every little disturbance - only to find the trees above without a squirrel in sight. This latest incident had minimal hope attached to it and Wallace barely flinched. Shortly thereafter, he took another hit to the head. This time he noticed it was an acorn. An acorn is the fruit of an oak tree. An acorn just dropped on his head from an evergreen tree. That was strange. As soon as he looked up, he was hit square in the face with a good size mixture of snow and pine needles. That was followed, almost immediately, by a good size pinecone. Stache was back. Let the stupid games begin!

This brought the world, according to Wallace, back into alignment and an end to his grievances with Fang. The resolution came with the understanding that Fang, although beautiful in every other way, must stay out of his police work... or soldiering duties... dude time... or whatever you want to call it. She readily agreed to these terms and began playing chase-and-be-chased with Wallace around the Yard. Whereas, Wallace had the disposition to make many new friends easily, Fang did not. This made time with Wallace very special. Debbie was her human mom... Wallace had become her best buddy.

Springtime was slowly making its presence known and unless you were an avid snowboarder, skier or Alaskan Malamute, this would be considered the true beginning of the new year. Both Wallace and Fang had sensed the change coming for a while and there was no lack of excitement. To them, springtime provided the perfect conditions for deeper exploration and, therefore, a higher adventure value. While their human parents traversed the miles of pathways agonizingly slow and seemingly oblivious to what was going on around them, Fang and Wallace began to expand their knowledge of the boundless territory presented to them. The trees that lined these campus pathways were old and young, straight and bowed, strong and broken. They zigged when the trail zigged and zagged when the trail zagged. The conflation of tress, shrubbery and underbrush created a never-ending, living, breathing curtain which kept the timid passersby on the trail. Occasionally, an inquisitive soul would stray off the path, but never too long or too far. Stragglers would soon discover that on one side of this natural curtain was the security of the pathway, but on the other side – thousands of acres of dense forest teaming with all manner of uncivilized life. The laws of man no longer applied beyond the curtain. There were no rich or poor, no woke or traditional, no artificially prescribed equity-of-outcomes out here. There was you, your family (herd, brood, scurry, etc.), maybe a friend or two, and nature. For the most part, the various species of wilderness animals lived their lives in harmony.

It was not unusual for Fang and Wallace to make several crossings into that great unknown beyond the natural curtain. The forest had a rejuvenating effect on their mind, body and soul. For Wallace, it presented many more opportunities to interact (chase) with the indigenous population. For Fang, it presented many more obstacles to leap over (canine version of "parkour"). After several minutes of unfettered fun and recreation, their human parents would notice them missing and summon them back. On this one particular morning, however, time stood still.

The adventures began a month ago. Adventures; plural, meaning there were others that came after, but the first of its kind was always the best. University classes were on hold for a day and the skies were bluer than blue. There was no better invitation to come play outside than that. And, without hesitation, Hitch and Debbie did just that. Their short, early morning jaunts were not only having a positive effect on their relationship, it was also having a positive effect on their cardiovascular endurance (along with all the dancing). They had been discussing the possibility of tackling a much longer, more challenging trek as soon as the weather broke. That break in the weather had arrived and the trail was set. It was a lesser traveled, five-mile loop with an elevation rise in excess of one-thousand feet with more than a few challenging switchbacks. This was not a trail for those weak in the knees. About midway on the map, there was a large rock formation that presented a panoramic view of the valley below. It was said to be a breathtaking place to dwell and look out over God's untouched handiwork. That made it all the more appealing for Hitch and Debbie.

The morning weather was crisp and cool and perfect for an exhilarating romp through the woods. They made the pinnacle in good time, but were looking forward to a nice relaxing lunch break. With no cell phone service and no other person within miles, Hitch and Debbie knew they had found their new favorite getaway spot. Wallace and Fang, on the other hand, were just getting started. After a snack or two, and once their human parents began their long-winded chirping about this and that, they set off. Whereas, there were no other human-sized trails to be found besides the loop, the animal-sized trails were plentiful and provided easy access to destinations in any direction they wanted to go. They were sure to take a sip from every small stream they crossed because each had its own impact on the palate – like a fine wine.

As usual, the minutes slipped by unnoticed as both dogs wandered through the maze of trails - precipitated by Wallace's need to chase anything that crossed their path... big or small. They were not lost. They never got lost. Both had a keen sense of time and direction, but they had traveled a bit farther away from their human parents than on a typical morning walk. At this point, they had not yet been called back. Still, they both sensed it was time to return and decided to take one last look around for future reference before leaving. Just then, Wallace caught a glimpse of something very strange looking cross an intersection of two trails up ahead. If it was a deer, it was smaller than most and it had a bulging waist line – like that of a donkey. There was also some question about the animal's front legs - which seemed to want to buckle at any moment.

"No chase," Fang communicated in canine-speak. "Go time."

"No chase," Wallace agreed, but could not resist taking one more look. "Look, smell, go time."

Not quite sure what to expect, Wallace's approach to the intersection was quiet and cautious. Evidently, not silent enough because now facing him on the adjacent path was perhaps the oddest four-legged creature he had ever laid eyes on – except for that porcupine that got him good once as a pup. Even its scent was unfamiliar and clearly not born from out of the wilderness. Wallace was not mistaken about the legs being ill-fitted and the bloated belly. What made this walking anomaly even more fascinating was its face. It had a long, shaggy beard that hung from the chin like stringy moss from a tree limb, offset eyes that looked to the left and to the right at the same time, and rabbit ears that popped out of the head horizontally. To make matters worse for the poor mixed-up beast, were the two short spikes coming out of his head that aimed backwards. This made the barbs somewhat useless as an offensive weapon. In other words, Wallace had met his first goat.

Not overly impressed by what he saw, it was Wallace's intention to leave peacefully and so he began to inch his way backwards. This movement, although non-combative, caused the goat to drop its head and charge... only to stop a foot in front of Wallace. After bracing himself for the blow that did not come, Wallace took up an offensive position. He then unleashed a series of loud, commanding barks meant to clarify the rules of engagement. Undaunted by the blustering, the goat took two steps backwards and charged again. Coming no closer to hitting Wallace than last time. The bizarre animal then turned and calmly began walking in the direction it was headed in the first place. This was, of course, unacceptable behavior and Wallace had no choice but to chase this thing down the road a bit... which is exactly what happened.

"No chase!" Fang screamed, but it was too late.

Instead of putting up a proper fight, the goat took off with Wallace in hot pursuit. Much to Wallace's surprise, the ill-mannered creature was very fast and very agile for something with so many anatomical deficiencies. In fact, using a series of carefully timed, back-to-back, zig-zag maneuvers, the goat was able to lose him momentarily. It wasn't until Wallace heard the laughable bleating sound that goats make, followed by another laughable bleating sound in response to the first laughable bleating sound. Assuming one of the two laughable bleating sounds came from his fleet-footed adversary, he slowly rounded a thick copse of trees from where the sounds emanated. Now, standing rather nonchalantly before him, was his adversary. Standing next to him was another animal with similar quirky qualities - presumably his mate. And, standing next to her was a much smaller version of the two – presumably their offspring.

Wallace froze for a moment with indecision. At the same time, the "smaller version" slowly walked up to Wallace, bleated something indistinguishable and then head-butted him in the knee cap. Seeing how the little guy stood no more than a foot off the ground, the blow was hardly felt by Wallace. Having successfully proven his point, the young goat boldly walked back to mom and dad's side. Everyone found this display of budding masculinity amusing... including Wallace. While Wallace contemplated the idea of becoming a dad someday, Fang rolled up in a huff.

"Fang angry!" she bristled with a slight growl. "Wallace annoy much!"

"Wallace sorry," was all Wallace could ever say. He was genuinely sorry and Fang knew this to be true – which annoyed her even more.

Is this my life with him? She asked herself. *Is he really worth this much trouble*?

This was a question she has been asking over and over again since they met. Quite by surprise, there came a women's voice through the tress. It was as clear as if she were standing in front of them, and yet, it came from far away.

"Wallace, Fang, can you two come over here?" the voice asked politely. "I have a favor to ask."

The three goats immediately turned and headed in the direction of the voice.

"You can follow my goats, if you wish," the voice added. "Your human dad and mom won't mind, I'm quite sure."

Wallace and Fang looked at each other curiously. They understood every word. It was a soft-spoken and pleasing voice, without being hypnotical. That is, they could follow the goats or turn around and leave if they wished. There was no deceit in the claims being made or Wallace's "sixth sense" would be kicking in right about now. Fang also sensed no trap being set and even thought she heard a mother's plea in the woman's voice.

"Yes go?" Fang asked in a manner that suggested she would be willing to go if he was.

"Yes go," Wallace replied.

The path widened and, in the distance, they could see a beautiful two-story farmhouse with three chimneys puffing out white smoke and a wide inviting porch. The front yard was not manicured by any stretch of the imagination, but appeared to be kept in fairly decent shape considering it was presently occupied by a few dozen goats and twice as many chickens. The perimeter of the yard, however, was taken up by pumphouses, springhouses, chicken coops, animal-pow-ered agricultural equipment, hand-drawn water pumps and wood piles. Off to the side of the house was a stable with two horses in a corral. Seated on the bottom porch step was a lovely, middle-aged black woman providing first aid to the leg of an injured barnyard cat.

"Well, thank goodness you two made it. I was beginning to worry," the woman commented unceremoniously as Wallace and Fang made their way across the front yard. It was as if this meeting was all part of a plan.

"My name is Miss Rosie and, as you can see, I am needed here. But I am told there is trouble brewing down by the stream. Be a dear and check it out for me. It shouldn't take you long."

Again, Wallace and Fang looked at each other curiously.

"The stream is that way," she stated with a little more urgency and pointed to her left. "Please hurry."

They could hear the soft bleating before they got to the water. It was a kid (i.e., a baby goat) and he, or she, was on the other side of a fast-moving stream at least ten yards in width. Apparently, how to get a stranded kid back on this side of that water must have been the trouble that Miss Rosie was talking about. As close as a hundred yards to their left, was a gently sloping waterfall. The water surged over the top edge of the falls with great force. As the water fell, however, it was forced to slow its momentum somewhat as it passed between the various rock formations below. This created several smaller cascading waterfalls. It was most likely here that the baby goat passed over to the other side because, to their right, the stream remained wide and steady-paced as far as the eye could see.

No sooner had they decided to walk the hundred yards, find a path across the waterfall, grab the kid, cross back over the waterfall and go home, Fang thought she saw something move along a small wooded ridge not far from the kid. If something was out there, it was moving intermittently and with precision, so not to be seen.

"Enemy close," she whispered to Wallace.

"Where enemy?" Wallace responded intently as he moved in close to Fang.

"Hiding there," she was now looking directly into the eyes that betrayed its owner by reflecting the least bit of light in darkness. A cat's eyes. A very big cat. A bobcat. "Goat baby danger."

"Save goat baby," Wallace growled, leaped into the water and paddled as hard as he had ever paddled before. Unfortunately, for every foot forward, the swift current was taking him two feet downstream. Now knowing he had been detected, the bobcat made his move.

"Save goat baby," Fang growled, took a few steps backwards and ran as fast as she could go to the stream's edge before leaping into the air. She did not come down until she had crossed the entire thirty-foot span of water. Hitting the ground running, Fang immediately took a defensive position just in front of the kid – who seemed oblivious to the peril.

"Go now!" she barked furiously at the big cat.

A male bobcat making Pennsylvania its home can weigh as much as 40 pounds and this boy was all of that... plus some. Fang weighed a little less than the cat did, but all of it was determination... plus some. Momentarily stunned by this dog's amazing leaping ability, the bobcat stopped, crouched low and reassessed the changing conditions. He had tangled with dogs before and did not particularly like the idea, but he was hungry. This would be the second time in two days that his dinner plans had been interrupted; first, by two humans and now by two dogs. If he had any chance of satisfying his hunger, it had to come before the bigger dog arrived.

Everyone knew that the urban dog's most useful flaw was its desire to chase things – especially when it comes to cats. If he could draw this smaller dog towards himself just far enough, he could use his own speed and misdirection to slip by, grab lunch and not look back. Even if it did come to blows, he carried more muscle and stood a good chance of slashing his way passed her. It was a calculated risk he was willing to take.

The plan seemed to be working. He slowly paced back and forth, while, at the same time, getting closer and closer. When he got too close, Fang would show some teeth and advance a few inches each time. With each advancement, he would put what little tail he had between his hind legs to show weakness and back pedal a step or two in feigned submission. This was in hopes that she would finally give chase. He was close to success. He could feel her frustration. He could see it in her eyes. Just one more lame attempt should do it.

Bam... ugh... the next thing the bobcat saw after regaining his senses from the direct hit that took him by surprise was 75 pounds of angry, snarling Yellow Retriever looking down upon him. Fang took the opportunity to start the kid back across the waterfall and to safety. When it became apparent that there was no more fight left in the wounded bobcat, Wallace issued a final warning should they ever meet again.

"Bobcat come back, Wallace hurt you... Fang kill you!"

The long hike to the overlook was as rewarding as Hitch and Debbie had hoped. They were certainly tired, but nowhere near exhaustion. The daily walks from one side of the Hillary's campus to the other paid off. Hitch was ten pounds lighter and Debbie discovered the outdoors to be an irresistible diversion now. They had everything they needed: they had each other, they had Wallace and Fang, they had sunshine, they had food and water, they both wore hiking boots that were properly broken in and they each carried a compact Bible. This was not the average hiker's "How to Survive in The Wilderness" kind of bible. This one was so much better because it contained information on how to survive in the fallen world. Until recently, they were both deeply rooted in that fallen world. The enchantment of looking out over the pristine countryside from above seemed like an appropriate place to allow God's word to refresh their jaded 21st century minds.

The day had warmed up quite nicely. They had no intention of moving anytime soon, so the boots came off – giving them an opportunity to dry on the inside. They were immediately replaced with warm fuzzy slippers. To suggest that experienced hikers must never weigh themselves down with non-essentials is absolute nonsense. Unless you wanted your hike to be more like a death march, comfort had tremendous value. Take warm fuzzy slippers for example. They might be considered hiking luxuries by many, yet they weigh next to nothing and feel oh-so-good on the tootsies. The lightweight camp chairs were worth their weight in gold at the moment as well.

"Eddie?" Debbie spoke first once they had settled in. "Do I make you happy?"

"You make me very happy, Sùilean Soilleir," Hitch replied lovingly and took her hand in his. "If I ever fail to show you how much you make me happy, tell me, and I will do my best to make the necessary corrections."

"On a scale of one to ten, how much would you say I make you happy," she continued, while showing all the signs that this was to be considered as a legitimate question.

To Hitch, this latest query sounded ominously like trying to answer the question "Do these pants make me look fat?" The important thing to remember in these situations is to answer without delay. Do not waste time and effort responding poetically – it will only be misconstrued as indecision in the mind of the inquirer.

"Ten," Hitch stated definitively.

"How about on a scale of one to a hundred?"

"One hundred."

"How about on a scale of one to a thousand?"

Okay, so, now Hitch knew this was never going to stop until he stepped into the bear trap being set for him. Bear traps hurt, but if it helped to advance the conversation, he would have to man up. Debbie was not a child, playing a child's game. She was intelligent, rational, strong, savvy... and, at this point in life, vulnerable. These were all positive character traits Debbie shared with her mom. So far in life, she had perfected all of them except for the latter. Yes, vulnerability can be a good thing, but it takes trusting others. Besides her mom, the only trust she had ever known came from within an insulated, like-minded "community" that demanded conformity. Trust in a group, however, is not the same as trust in another person. That takes a little more courage. It was obvious that she needed to resolve something and this line of questioning was a means to an end. The unsophisticated approach was as good as any.

"Nine Hundred and Ninety-Nine." Hitch replied in the same calm, matter-of-fact, manner as the other two answers.

"Why not one thousand?"

"Because the law of large numbers, my sweet Bright Eyes," Hitch answered with as much authoritative prowess as he could evoke. "The greater the number of possible outcomes, the more accurate its actual probability. In theory, when relating marginal probabilities to conditional probabilities, the total probability of an outcome must account for every distinct variable. Those tangible and intangible variables lessen the likelihood of any specific outcome coming to pass unchanged or immutable. Therefore, the idea of someone making someone else happy all the time is highly improbable... theoretically. So, you see, it would be unethical for me to say otherwise, even though every bone in my body would say 'yes' to you making me one thousand percent happy. Does that answer your question?"

There, that should do it, Hitch thought, with the hope of dodging the bear trap.

"Yes, I suppose... but why not one thousand?" Debbie sighed, appearing to accept the heart-felt last part, but rejecting the lengthy reiteration of the word "probability" part.

"I cherish these moments when you make me work for an answer," Hitch countered tenderly and flashed a big smile her way. "Can you remind me when I have ever given you the impression that I was unhappy?"

"No," she replied as if finally satisfied, then.... "What is it like to be married?"

There it is, Hitch told himself. *Now it makes some sort of sense. Her mom and dad never married, her mom also had two failed marriages, and Debbie never married – although, for a time, her feelings and the laws of man told her the definition of marriage applied to homosexual partners. Evidently, she has begun contemplating the whole meaning of that, supposedly everlasting, institution between a man and a woman once again. Didn't see that coming.*

"Sùilean Soilleir," Hitch breathed out her name affectionately. "Are you asking me to marry you?"

Hitch's playful inference was stated in jest, but along with it, total empathy for the woman seated next to him... with whom he was falling, if not already, in love with.

"I recall asking you what marriage was like, not what marriage would be like with you," Debbie clarified, though she knew he was toying with her.

These two share things about themselves every morning. So far, all Debbie knew about Hitch's marriages was what everyone else knew about Hitch's marriages. He had been married to three different women; Sunshine, with whom he had a son (Jimi); Aubrey, an agnostic turned Christian; and Gloria, whom she knew and associated with during her angry "pro-abortion" years. It was not Debbie's intention to delve into these personal matters. He was a new creation, just as she was a new creation (2 Co 5:17). She considered Hitch to be a kind and thoughtful man with a remarkable ability to look at, and decipher the many nuances of a complex issue - without necessarily taking a side. She was simply looking for some insight on marriage from the man seated next to her... with whom she was falling, if not already, in love with.

It was times such as these that Hitch wished Wallace were by his side. There was never a time he truly did not want to know the truth of the matter. There have been many times, however, when he did not speak the truth. In other words, he knew himself to be so intelligent and clever that he could lie to himself and be fooled by it. With Wallace's unique ability to sense a lie, he had been caught more than once doing this very thing. He promised himself never to lie to Debbie.

"Well, I will not bore you with the details of just how absolutely abysmal a husband I was. I did not treat marriage with the respect it deserved and I am not proud of my behavior," Hitch began introspectively. "If you still wish to know my thoughts on marriage, I can say with some certainty that my feelings of happiness, my feelings of love, my feelings of intimacy, can all take a backseat to the longing for trustworthiness. It is something I have lacked and now committed to improve upon."

He went on. "As the dominant species on this planet, we humans have developed a morbid attraction to trusting those least worthy of our trust. As I see it, the evolution of mankind is less from ape to man, than it is from truth to lie."

Hoping to keep the conversation as uplifting as the beautiful environment that surrounded them, Hitch added a final caveat.

"Oh, and having one spouse or the other who can cook is good too."

Just then, Wallace and Fang reappeared from the density of the woods and collapsed in front of the chairs. They seemed fatigued for some reason, and yet, they had only been gone a few minutes – according to Hitch and Debbie's reckoning.

"What is with you two lazybones?" Debbie quipped. "Go, play, find something to do."

Fang made several dog utterances, then gently rolled onto her side.

"Oh," Debbie replied somewhat intrigued. "No kidding?"

Chapter 5

That Wiccan Boy Can Sing

"Now?" Alex mouthed silently and impatiently. The tenor's solo had been over for seconds, which seemed like minutes, and Frannie had not moved.

"OK, now," Francesca answered without making a sound. She had been so immersed in the voice that it took her a little longer to re-engage.

How could a voice that beautiful, belong to someone mean, she thought, then leaned into her partner.

"No fighting," she whispered in his ear. "You promised."

"If he comes at me... self-defense," he acknowledged in a whisper and put his hand on the door knob. "If he comes at you... he goes down fast and hard."

They already knew the contents of the room. It was one of six small rooms on the second level that contained old workhorse pianos for students to use. Since the music department now had its own facility on the other side of campus, these rooms were rarely used. Alex opened the door with no additional force that might provoke a negative reaction. They both entered the room as if in the middle of a conversation.

"So, I said, 'hey, man, just because I can't spell Tchaikovsky, doesn't mean I can't play his stuff' right?" Alex moaned.

"Yeah, right, I don't know anyone who can spell Tchaikovsky," Francesca replied with a reasonably believable laugh.

Once all the way inside the room, Alex and Francesca paused as if startled that another person was present.

"Whoa... hey, how ya doing?" Alex asked rhetorically of the dude sitting calmly on the piano bench. Without taking his eyes off the guy, he shot Frannie another phony question. "Thought you said we had this room?"

"I'm sure they said it was this room," Francesca replied without taking her eyes off the dude sitting at the piano. In a very conversational manner, she attempted to get the stranger to speak. "Are you a student here?"

This brief exchange gave them all the time they needed to help identify this guy later on; 6 foot tall (though he was still sitting), twenty something (about their age), 170/180 pounds, slim to muscular frame, spiked black hair (cut to perfection), full dark beard (trimmed to perfection), bright clear green eyes, white teeth (perfectly straight), random tattoos running up both arms (but no tats on neck or face), dressed in black head to toe (more grunge than gothic). Generally speaking - a clean dude with no offensive body odor.

He also had a sick looking bass guitar resting on his lap.

No worries here, Alex thought. *Just a harmless rocker with a fine bass guitar.*

For some reason, both the rocker and his bass seemed familiar to him.

You can relax now, girl, Francesca thought and then thought some more. *I never dated a guy with a full beard before.*

89

"T-C-H-A-I-K-O-V-S-K-Y," the stranger methodically spelled out the Russian composer's name for Francesca.

"What? Oh... that... thanks... for spelling that... um, name... yup, that's some name..." Francesca rambled on sheepishly. "I definitely would have butchered that one... name."

Alex was now staring at his partner in disbelief. He had seen that "hot-for-dude" look in Frannie's eyes before and, once again, he would have to become her protective older brother.

"Where did you pick up that bass, man?" Alex redirected the conversation back to gathering information and why the guitar and the stranger seemed familiar to him. "You don't see many like that one."

"It's a Le Fay's Herr Schwarz Grant Stinnett with the D-Tuner on each string," the stranger replied with a distinctly German accent this time.

The inflection in his voice made it seem as though he had answered that same question a hundred times before, and yet he was still very appreciative. As if switching off the German accent and turning on the Pennsylvanian accent, he continued.

"They allow me to alternate tunings on the fly. I can move to another room if you like, but they are all about the same."

"Well, that's kind of why we're here, actually," Francesca spoke almost apologetically, "I love your voice, I really do. The way you sing Bach in German is so beautiful. We have a pretty good Easter concert happening at our church right now and I'm singing mezzo-soprano, three octaves, close to four, but not in German... "

"Frannie," Alex butted in and gave her a "move it along" hand gesture.

"Oh, right. Yes, um, they can hear you downstairs," she continued. "Alex and I work for the university. We were asked to find you and then ask you to leave. I am so sorry."

"Yeah, apparently, you're making the new guy look bad," Alex added with as much tact as a 900-pound polar bear asking a 90-pound penguin where he could grab a bite to eat.

"Man, I am so sorry. I had no idea my voice carried that far," the stranger uttered regretfully. "That was wrong and I apologize. I hate it when the psychos interrupt the music."

"That's it!" Alex exclaimed in amazement.

 Now realizing where he had met this guy. He began to rattle off as many bits of information as he could.

"I've seen you guys play a couple times. In that little club downtown. Alternative to heavy metal stuff? Yeah, yeah, yeah, you were at the outdoor festival last summer too. Makes sense why you do the singing – phenomenal voice. I'm guessing they wish you were downstairs right now, bro. Honestly, when you hang around the front of the stage and start two-hand tapping those bass riffs – it is mind-blowing. Fastest stuff I've ever seen or heard on a bass. Everyone goes crazy. I am not joking. We actually had some serious conversations about that bass after the show - it's legend. And the hot chick on drums..."

"Hot chick?" Francesca asked rhetorically. She took no offense, but wanted Alex to know his statement lacked considerate thought... again.

"You know what I mean… great drummer," Alex replied with mediocre contrition. "Anyway, how did you get in here? We have alarms on every door and window."

"I have a key card," the, now, somewhat more familiar, stranger replied without any noticeable sense of wrongdoing. "And Jen could play drums for any band, anywhere, anytime. We are lucky to have her."

"Um, should you have a key card?" Francesca asked the question that she hoped would not result in theft charges in addition to trespassing charges.

"My mother is a professor here. Music department," the, now, charming hard rocking bassist explained. "I have access to certain buildings and the Walker is one of them. If you still want me to leave, I will go. I never meant to cause any trouble."

"Let's see; he's got a card, he's more than happy to stop singing and he has a bass… without an amp. That's kinda odd, but I'm good with him staying if he wants to," Alex passed his judgment, but looked to Frannie to make the decision.

"Of course," Francesca readily agreed with the resolution, but found it hard to say goodbye to this guy. "If I could just take a peek at that key card first, I guess we will just, I don't know, get out of your hair. And, by the way, that short, textured thing you got going on up top of your head with the Viking beard on the face looks, just, kind of nice. It goes along with your voice, just, kind of nice."

"Thank you, Frannie," the charming bassist said, gracefully accepting the compliment. He was now facing her directly and smiling. "Maybe I could come hear you sing sometime. What church do you go to?"

"Fellowship Bible Church," Francesca offered excitedly. "What church do you go to?"

"Oh, that, well, I really don't belong to a church necessarily. We meet in covens," the young man replied nervously.

It was obvious that he was trying to make a good first impression... until this bombshell.

"I'm a Wiccan."

"Wiccan," Francesca repeated the word curiously. "What denomination is a Wiccan?"

Uh, oh, here comes goodbye, Alex thought.

Ask a hundred Wiccans (always capitalized) what being a "Wiccan" means and you will get a hundred different answers. All of them, however, will begin their assorted explanations of what a Wiccan is or isn't, by first disassociating their non-threatening religion from the other guys – the blood-thirsty "Church of Satan." Yes, if you haven't heard, Satan has himself a church. It was founded in 1966, by Anton Szandor LaVey (1930–1997) and was officially given 501(c)(3) tax exempt status by those wonderful little devils at the Internal Revenue Service in 2019. So, let us be clear, Wiccans do not worship Satan, or Jesus, or Allah, or Buddha, or Oprah. Of course, they can if they want to. There is nothing in their sacred text that says they can't. That is because they do not have a sacred text. That is how loosely organized the Wiccans are.

You could say that the modern Wiccan movement began with the English author and witchfather, Gerald B. Gardner

(1884-1964). His Book of Shadows (BoS), published in 1954, became the first detailed instruction manual for some (not all) witchcraft practices. It created the popular "Wheel of the Year" calendar, whereby some (not all) Wiccans celebrate up to 8 festivals according to the rhythm of nature. For example; Imbolc, celebrates the turning of winter to spring, while Beltane, celebrates the turning of spring to summer and so on. These seasonal get-togethers are known as "Sabbats."

The second thing to come out of a Wiccan's mouth will be their motto (the Wiccan Rede): "Harm none, do what ye will." This pithy little adage seems harmless enough, except that, it too, is malleable. For example, you may hear a few of the more highly-strung Wiccans say to you, "harm none, lest it be for thy defense or for the greater good." That seems to fit the narrative of the young, abrasive "rage-against-the-machine," social justice warriors in their ranks.

Some (not all) Wiccans are polytheists and have a tendency to borrow their gods and goddesses from other religions and cultures. Therefore, if you feel "in tune" with water – you would most likely lean towards an "ocean faring" god or goddess to worship and vilify a "fire breathing" god or goddess. If you feel "in tune" with trees – you would more than likely choose a "forest dwelling" god or goddess to worship. If you like things made of wood, the "fire breathing" god or goddess would not be a good choice for you either. See how that works?

Some (not all) Wiccans like to practice magic, but it is imperative to spell magic with a "k" at the end, as in, "magick." It is not Wiccan approved magic without the "k" at the end. Some (not all) Wiccans like to think of themselves as being witches. Both men and women can identify as being a witch (the term is gender fluid). Never, I mean never, compare Wiccan witches to Harry Potter witches. They hate that. They consider it blasphemy and they will put a hex on you if you ever make that mistake.

Speaking of hexes and spells, get it out of your mind that Wiccan witches sacrifice animals. They are not into sacrificing anything... except maybe mental health. Nor can Wiccans turn themselves, or you, into an animal... unless, of course, you already identify as an animal. However, there are guidelines when casting spells. It is called the "Threefold Return" rule and goes something like this: good magick benefits the sender three times the good; bad magick harms the sender three times the bad. So, apparently, there is a need for some form of self-monitoring... at least for those that believe in the veracity of magick.

Let's see, what else captures the essence of being Wiccan? Oh, yes, the charming bassist (we will soon discover his name to be, Everett Albrecht Wagner-Weiß) mentioned the term "coven" as a place where he meets other like-minded people. That is true. These gatherings can be anywhere and anytime, but are preferably held outside - if weather permits. Unlike traditional religions, covens have no central leadership that holds them all together. Most (not all) will, however, have a "High Priest" or a "High Priestess" at the local level. It is in these small group settings that most (not all) Wiccans feel comfortable conducting their Sabbats, Esbats (lunar holidays) and other useful rituals that will rid themselves of any negative energetic contamination. Some (not all) just come to learn magick, practice witchcraft, dabble in herbs for their potions and crystals for their spells, seek balance and unity with the natural world, tap into the spirit world, perhaps meet a god, pursue self-growth, feel self-empowered, blah, blah, blah. The sky is the limit when Wiccans gather together.

Oh, and it just so happens that Everett's mother, Professor Gretchen Wagner (faculty member at Hillary University since 2020; chamber music and strings), is a 3rd degree Gardnerian Wicca High Priestess and local coven leader.

How do I tell him without breaking the poor guy's spirit? Leon thought. *He must know. Everyone knows.*

Not only was his new solo tenor not improving, he was getting markedly worse. In the back of his mind, Leon knew this day would come. He had let this go on for too long. After this poor guy's demotion, however, Leon would have to go out into the marketplace of vocalists and rent himself another tenor. It was always the tenor. The idea was appalling to him, but he had no other choice. Next week would be their last full rehearsal and Leon now felt that overwhelming burden to do what was right, and yet, it was the very last thing he wanted to do. It was a difficult decision entrusted to him and to him alone. He owed it to the ensemble as a whole, he owed it to the people in the audience and he owed it to J.S. Bach.

"Carl, can we talk?" Leon spoke directly, yet discreetly, into his tenor's ear.

To Leon's surprise and relief, his tenor was overjoyed at the prospect of going back to his comfortable position in the chorus. The guy had already admitted to himself that he was way over his head. In fact, he was being made painfully aware of his limitations and insecurities with every rehearsal. If Leon had not come to him, he would have gone to Leon. Unfortunately, with that mutually acceptable resolution, Leon was still without a tenor capable of singing this challenging solo. In an attempt to find a replacement for his replacement, he knew he would be cashing in every favor ever owed him. His phone would be smoking after tonight.

Unless..., he began to wonder as his attention turned towards the balconies.

"So, Everett, how do you play a bass without an amp?" Alex intruded in on the painfully sweet, non-essential conversation between the bass player and Frannie.

[NOTE: Having inspected Everett's key card with name and a facial imprint clipped in the corner, they all now knew each other's names]

Alex knew it would be one of those sappy conversations that had the potential to go on forever. He was already getting the sense that these two talented singers were having some sort of spontaneous neurological attraction to each other. As big brother, he felt an obligation to slow things down a bit. Alex had a pretty good idea of what Wiccans claim to be. He had researched their eclectic beliefs while on his own journey of faith. They had their kooks just like Christianity have their kooks, but bottom line, they were deeply and unashamedly pagan. Frannie was new to her faith in Jesus Christ. She didn't need a deluded "sorcerer wannabe" filling her mind with sweet smelling potions, magical rocks and mystical incantations right now... no matter how good he looks and sings.

"I don't really need an amp," Everett stated without ego.

Everett and Francesca were still facing each other. It took him a second or two to actually face Alex and reply.

"When I play the classical stuff, I actually prefer to feel the sound of the notes rather than to hear them.

"Classical stuff?" Francesca asked, finding the answer to this question more interesting than the answer to the "what is a Wiccan" question at the moment.

"Yup, not only was I singing the tenor lines... much too loud obviously," Everett jokingly admitted as his attention turned back towards Francesca. "I was also playing the first violin part on the Le Fay. You know, without the amplification. My Hartke LX8500 Tone Stack EQ preamp and HyDrive HD410 cabinets stay at home when I travel light. Sorry, couldn't help squeezing those names in there. It took me forever to find my sound... if you know what I mean?"

"Wait a second. You're telling me, you can play a violin riff on a bass guitar?" Alex cut in, not knowing one preamp from another. "How is that even possible?"

"I tap a lot. I slap, I pop, sweep, harmonics, teeth... whatever it takes to get the sound, you know," Everett replied humorously. This answer was in response to Alex's question, but his attention never turned away from Francesca. "Would you like to hear something?"

"How?" Francesca replied with anticipation, but unsure of what to do. "I don't think I can feel sound the way you do."

"That is why I never travel far without my Sennheiser's," Everett declared, as he rifled through his backpack. In no time, he produced an audio interface and a set of the headphones. "The HD 650 Open Back's to be exact. May I?"

Francesca wagged her head yes and he carefully placed the headphones over her ears. After taking a moment to play with the dials on his bass, Everett slowly, softly, began playing Beethoven's Für Elise (i.e., for Elise). She noticed he did this by tapping the strings up and down the long Rosewood fretboard of his bass guitar with both hands. Francesca recognized this beautiful song and slowly took a seat on the piano bench next to Everett. Within a matter of seconds, her eyes had closed involuntarily and she could sense the emotion, the tenderness... the sadness... that poured out from the notes being played with exquisite sensitivity. Within a matter of minutes, each rising crescendo that faded into the much gentler decrescendo caused her to tremble a little. She felt like a feather or a leaf being picked up by the wind, tossed about and then allowed to fall - only to be scooped up again... and then again.

Could anyone love a person more than Beethoven loved Elise? she thought.

So lost in the music was she, that by song's end Francesca found herself with a lone tear in the corner of each eye... one for Beethoven and one for Elise.

"Thank you for that," was all Francesca could come up with after Everett gently removed the headphones.

"My mother likes to think Beethoven is my kindred spirit." Everett spoke lightheartedly as he started packing up his gear. "When I play the classics like this without using an amp, she believes the old guy is channeling his deafness into me even though my hearing is perfectly fine. Wiccan moms like to say wild ass stuff like that all the time."

"Do Wiccans believe in Jesus?" she inquired earnestly, now that the mystery of playing classical music on a bass without an amp was solved.

"Some do, but not the same way Christians believe in Jesus," he continued. "Wiccans can pick and choose whoever or whatever they want to worship; one god, multiple gods, the moon, the sun, water, a rock formation... goddesses, whatever appeals to them. Very pro-choice you might say. Never a dull moment."

"Goddesses?" she asked and frowned in mild disbelief.

"Frannie, you are obviously Christian and believe there is no other God in the heavens or on earth except Jesus Christ. I applaud your belief," Everett stated quite convincingly. "Every Wiccan I know would applaud that belief. Wiccans are taught from birth to err on the side of tolerance. There is no other religion on earth that wants to coexist more than a Wiccan. That has its advantages and its faults."

Everett had cleverly answered each one of Francesca's questions with a subtle detachment that suggested he was not totally on board with the whole Wiccan "open borders" policy. Alex picked up on this wavering nuance quickly. Still, this was text-book Wiccan strategy when engaging a woman. That is, throw out the instant appeal of worshiping a goddess and not another dude. Since 99 % of Wiccan practitioners are women - or so it seemed to him - this ploy had a much higher batting average.

"They practice witchcraft, Frannie," Alex chimed in.

Let's see him spin his way out of that one, Alex thought.

"Witchcraft?" Francesca exclaimed as the fragile smile began to dissipate from her face.

Francesca had heard enough. Screwed up, New Age, mommy-boys were immediately scratched off her list. Everett was masculine and attractive in her eyes – without a doubt. She had not met a more likable person with as much musical talent than Everett – also, without a doubt. She might even be able to mold him into whatever she wanted him to be (even a Christian believer) over time – at least temporarily. But changing another person to suit her whims did not interest Francesca anymore. That maxim was especially true when it came to something as important as her own salvation. She will find a real man to share a lifetime with... and he will be 100 % Christian already.

"We can go now," Frannie stated with the satisfaction that she did not fall into another dead-end relationship. She gave Everett one last sweet, sincere, fare-thee-well smile and walked slowly towards the door.

"It's not what you think, Frannie," Everett spoke with affection, but without pleading.

Alex didn't know it yet, but he was right. Everett was not buying what the Wiccan culture was selling. Naivety was never Everett's strong suit. As with all families, however, a child's upbringing is thrust upon them. There is no escaping it. And at the top of the list of family traditions, is religion... or having no religion (which is still a religion)... or, in his case, Wicca. When Everett was small, these strange people amused him. As he grew older, these strange people bewildered him. As an adult, these strange people unnerved him. Nothing scary. The people in his mother's coven were all very sweet and very gentle... just a little wacked. He kept a fire extinguisher handy, just in case a concoction requiring heat went awry. For the most part, no one got hurt. They would come from all over, practice their peculiar art of deception (i.e., witchcraft, magick, reiki, tarot cards, psychics, mediums, etc.) and go home happy. As the adorable son of the coven leader, Everett would stay and help his mother clean up afterwards. He had his music, so very little of this was of interest to him.

Growing up Wiccan gave Everett great insight on what it really means to be tolerant – the true meaning of the word. That is, he did not believe a word of Wiccan gibberish, but accepted the fact that each and every person in his mother's coven truly did believe in their supernatural powers. As long as no one forced their fringy behaviors onto another's fringy behaviors – who cares? That blissful tolerance was especially true of his mother. At times, when she dwelled too long among the witches, his mother could be as crazy as a loon. At other times, when she held a stringed instrument in her hands, his mother became a musical virtuoso. At all times, she was a loving mother to him, a devoted wife to his father and a caring professor to her students. In every way that mattered to the world, their family and the life they led was normal and healthy.

Given the fact that, by adulthood, every person on the planet has a belief system (whether they know it or not), what exactly did Everett believe in?

If Everett could not find refuge, or truth, in Wicca, can music alone satisfy that emptiness?

Few people are born with perfect pitch. It is said that Mozart, Beethoven, Chopin and Liszt had absolute perfect pitch, whereas, Tchaikovsky and Wagner did not. Everett has it. So, it would be quite natural for him to think that music was something a person could believe in - and draw from it, happiness and fulfilment. Then, one day, he noticed the words "Music is my religion" written on a wall somewhere. It was not an uplifting memory. Perhaps it was in some rank-smelling night club bathroom or a grossed-out New York City subway station. In any case, it was attributed to Jimi Hendrix. Hendrix was the iconic rocker of a long-ago generation who died of a drug overdose at the age of 27. To Everett, that seemed more like music at the expense of happiness and fulfilment. After seeing what that belief system got poor Jimi, Everett decided it was best to leave the worship of music to others.

Maybe it was alignment of the stars that led Everett straight to the Unitarian's door. Unitarians are basically Wiccans that baked cookies instead of casting spells. They also had the good sense to meet indoors. Like Wiccans, they have no problem with any one religion. In their "judge not, lest thee be judged" mindset, all religions can and should lead to the eternal progress of the soul... even if they all contradict each other. This convoluted attempt to appease everyone by helping no one sounded familiar to him. It reminded him of a book his mother read to him as a child:

`Cheshire Puss,' [Alice] began, rather timidly, as she did not at all know whether it would like the name: however, it only grinned a little wider.

`Come, it's pleased so far,' thought Alice, and she went on. `Would you tell me, please, which way I ought to go from here?'

"That depends a good deal on where you want to get to," said the Cat.

"I don't much care where--" said Alice.

"Then it doesn't matter which way you go," said the Cat.

"-so long as I get SOMEWHERE," Alice added as an explanation.

"Oh, you're sure to do that," said the Cat, "if you only walk long enough."

[excerpt from Lewis Carroll's classic children's tale,
Alice's Adventures in Wonderland]

Unfortunately, this "If you don't know where you're going, any road will take you there" methodology summed up the whole Unitarian Universalism experience for Everett and his fascination with their happy-talk faded quickly. He certainly learned a lot from these pointless quests for purpose in his life, but that still left him with a huge void in his heart.

If you do exist, I want to know you, Everett thought in terms of a person and not a long walk to "SOMEWHERE."

Alex and Francesca slowly wandered down onto the balcony overlooking the stage. The music had ended, the instruments that produced all that beautiful sound were carefully being stored in their protective cases, and what musicians and stage hands remained, were chatting among themselves. Leon was nowhere in sight.

"You, OK?" Alex asked his partner once they were back in the hallway again.

"I'll get over it... as usual," Francesca sighed. "For once, could I just meet a strong guy that isn't a fricking nut job?"

"There is something else about him," Alex replied unconvinced that "nut job" accurately defined who Everett was. "I'm not defending him or anything. I mean, I don't know the dude. But, as smooth as the guy pretended to be on the outside, there was something else going on inside. You probably didn't see it because you were, like, fantasizing on him."

"Was not, you jerk!" she screeched. "Maybe I got caught up in that pretty voice, but that's all."

"You just said you wished you could meet a guy that... oh, forget it," Alex began to try to rationalize the conversation, but why bother. "You want to call Chief, or should I?"

"You can, I'm tired of talking... and listening," Francesca now spoke with a sadness in her voice. "I guess we should let Professor Bouchard know what is going on too."

Just then, they both noticed the professor walking the perimeter of their level in long, determined strides. It did not take long for the three to make eye contact and they closed in on one another outside the room that Everett, presumably, still occupied. Before coming to complete stop, Leon spoke quietly.

"There you are. And, how are my house detectives doing tonight?"

"He's in there, Professor," Francesca faked a smile and pointed towards the room.

"He promised us he wouldn't sing again," Alex added proudly.

"Well, I hope I can talk him out of that," Leon spoke without elaborating. "Thank you both. I think I can handle it from here."

"He's not in trouble, is he? I mean, he has a key card," Francesca stated in remorseful tones. "Please, Professor, he didn't know his voice carried that far. He said he was sorry, didn't he?"

Francesca glanced momentarily at Alex, but not long enough for him to nod one way or the other.

"Having a beautiful voice isn't a crime," Francesca's voice had a stern quality to it now. "He has every right to be in there. He has a key card, doesn't he?"

She momentarily glanced at Alex again, but could have cared less for an answer.

"Everett might look strange to you and have strange ideas," she continued as if trying to convince herself rather than to anyone else. "But he is sweet... gentle... beautiful... "

Francesca had included a few other adjectives to describe the charming bassist that stole her heart, but her voice had trailed off so softly that those words became unintelligible.

"Alex thinks he is nice too and..." she suddenly began again with more vigor.

"I what?" Alex exclaimed at the mention of his name.

"It's OK, Francesca. I'm not here to punish anyone," Leon promised her. "Did you say this guy's name was, Everett?"

"Yes, Everett."

"Let me guess," Leon replied with a sly smile. "He plays a mean bass?"

Chapter 6

Cabin In the Woods

While most urban, office dwelling couples will end up in front of a bar after a hard day, Hitch and Debbie preferred a nice long dance session to unwind, as well as, the potential for cuddling that comes with it. Like their morning walks, dancing had become an almost daily routine. It could take place in a dance club, if they both had energy to burn, or at home, if one or the other was running close to "on empty."

Hillary University's spring break had finally arrived and it had been a long, busy work week for both professors. The decision to relax in the comfort of Hitch's backcountry cabin for an entire week was unanimous. It should be noted here that this cabin was no squalid, single room hunter's shack with a Franklin stove for heat and cooking indoors. Nope. This was a two story, 2,800 sq/ft, 3 bedroom, 3 ½ bath, 2 fireplace, 5kW solar assist, cabin made of 13" Montana Western Pine Logs. It was once an intimate "Bed and Breakfast" retreat until the aging proprietors decided it was time to sell. Soon after Hitch realized just how much he enjoyed dancing with Debbie, he took it upon himself to redecorate the entire 18' x 21' (380sq/ft) grand living room to create a generous dance floor in a moment's notice. This project included removing several pieces of furniture with no real purpose other than to create a certain ambiance and rearranging the rest. Afterwards, the room maintained its country charm without all the clutter.

Some time ago, it also dawned on Hitch that there were really only two categories of dancers; the ones who like to talk while dancing and those who don't. His sweet Sùilean Soilleir was a talker and he was not. "Dancing and talking" was akin to "walking and talking" with her. He was the noob. Dance or talk – not both. As Hitch's mastery of dance progressed, Debbie's extemporaneous verbal conveyances became somewhat less disruptive. He still found it necessary to save all difficult maneuvers for the quiet interludes. Fortunately, the vast majority of these verbal distractions were only fleeting monologues concerning the day's most compelling or amusing events. In other words, Hitch was expected to listen, but was also given the option to respond – or not to respond. Every so often, like tonight, Debbie would begin in the emotional realm... a realm that required his full attention and a thoughtful response.

"What do you find most attractive about me?" Debbie asked Hitch soon after beginning their first dance of the evening. "And eyes don't count."

Hitch quickly determined this would not be the time for dipping or spinning his partner.

The evening dance began (as their dances often did) with Hitch approaching Debbie in a confident and respectful manner. He would offer his hand for Debbie to take, then politely ask if he could have this dance. It worked every time. Her question to Hitch occurred about halfway down the hallway that led into the kitchen. Every now and again, Hitch would lead Debbie into the lavish kitchen when he had his fill of dancing in circles in the grand living room. From the kitchen, he would take her out another doorway, through the spacious dining area and back into the grand living room. This path was fun, but complex. It would test the lead dancer's skill at dodging lots of hard, immovable objects and, therefore, require additional concentration on Hitch's part. For this reason, Debbie did not get her response from him until they had safely danced their way back into the grand living room.

"That's easy," Hitch finally replied after successfully maneuvering through the ground floor obstacle course. "That silky smooth hair of yours is a close second to those beautiful blue eyes. I like running a hand through it - when you permit me. If you were asking about an intangible attraction, then it would be your courage and self-control in the face of all the attacks."

The attacks he was referring to were on Debbie's character and came as a result of her decision to become a Christian. Many of those attacks came from people she once considered friends. She did not respond to the attacks in kind (a natural reaction given her past)... but preferred to discuss any opposing worldviews with truth and kindness (a reaction she is still working on).

Debbie's question to Hitch this evening was not meant to elicit a host of superficial compliments to boost a fragile self-image. Her place and purpose in this mixed-up world could not be more rock solid. She did, however, have some deep emotional scars that needed tending to. Occasionally, she would allow herself to become absolutely vulnerable with Hitch.

"Fang is jealous that I dance with you more than I dance with her," Debbie stated as a way of saying she was gratified by Hitch's reply and could move on.

"I suppose she told you that?" he replied.

"She did," she replied unequivocally.

Fang and Wallace were parked side-by-side in front of the fireplace. They were inseparable now. Wallace was sound asleep and snoring, while Fang was wide awake and looking intently at Hitch and her human mom dance.

"Fang gave me you, and I gave her Wallace," Hitch submitted to both Debbie and Fang. "In my estimation, a fair trade was offered and accepted."

This caused Fang to snort something indistinguishable to Hitch, then laid her head gently onto Wallace's tummy - which ebbed and flowed with each breath.

Juliet:

O Romeo, Romeo, wherefore art thou Romeo?
Deny thy father and refuse thy name;
Or if thou wilt not, be but sworn my love
And I'll no longer be a Capulet.

Romeo:

[Aside] Shall I hear more, or shall I speak at this?

Juliet:

'Tis but thy name that is my enemy:
Thou art thyself, though not a Montague.
What's Montague? It is nor hand nor foot,
Nor arm nor face, nor any other part
Belonging to a man. O be some other name!
What's in a name? That which we call a rose
By any other word would smell as sweet;
So Romeo would, were he not Romeo call'd,
Retain that dear perfection which he owes
Without that title. Romeo, doff thy name,
and for thy name, which is no part of thee,
Take all myself.

[*the 'balcony scene' from Romeo and Juliet, Act 2 Scene 2*]

To be Romeo was to be a Montague. To be Juliet was to be a Capulet. Montagues and Capulets were sworn to be rivals. To meet the other in a public square by chance was unbearable, to love the other was unthinkable. Yet, there was nothing, other than the name, that kept these two lovers apart. And, so it was for Ëgadiyóhšö and Awë:iyo.

These were the ancient squirrel names taken by Butterbean and Daisy Cup. Butterbean was a large "gray" squirrel measuring 20" in length, including a 10" tail, and a weight that fluctuated around the two-pound mark. Like most new dads, he had a tendency to gain a little extra weight around the middle during the winter months. He had every intention to turn that extra padding back into muscle now that spring had arrived. Daisy Cup, on the other hand, was a diminutive "red" squirrel measuring not much more than a foot and a half from her nose to the tip of her rusty-red tail and would normally weigh less than a pound. She had also pick up a few ounces during the winter months, but much of that was due to her pregnancy. It was their first litter. She delivered six weeks ago, but forty days of carrying three kittens (baby squirrels) took its toll on her, otherwise, athletic body.

To be Butterbean was to be a "gray" squirrel. To be Daisy Cup was to be a "red" squirrel. Like the Montagues and the Capulets, gray and red squirrels were expected to remain separate and distinct. Grays were big; Reds were small. Grays prefer a deciduous forest of mixed maples, oaks and hickories to live; Reds prefer a coniferous forest of evergreens in which to live. Grays prefer living in tree "nests" built of twigs, leaves, and bark; Reds prefer to live in tree "dens" built into the cavities where a limb has broken off or in a deserted woodpecker hole. Grays prefer to eat mast (acorns, hickory nuts, walnuts); Reds enjoyed the mast, but nibbled on immature, green cones off the white pine from time to time. Grays prefer to bury each nut they saved individually; Reds prefer storing nuts in large caches - often inside a hollow log. The list of entrenched family differences facing Butterbean and Daisy Cup went on and on. Having been born a gray or a red squirrel was who they were to their family name. Their unbridled love was who they were to each other.

> What's in a name? That which we call a rose
> By any other word would smell as sweet;

Against all odds, they were now **ganöhgwa** (a married couple). Butterbean was **gonöhgwa** (her husband) and Daisy Cup was **honöhgwa** (his wife). Like all grays, Butterbean built a sturdy nest out of twigs and bark in the deciduous trees that surrounded Hitch's cabin. This seemed like the perfect location to start a family since it was half way between their respective relatives and there was hardly ever any activity in the human's gigantic "nest" made of wood. The lights inside the human nest would come on at night and go off in the morning, but that was the only thing they considered annoying about their absentee neighbors. Like all reds, Daisy Cup collected and stored, large caches of food in hollow logs and deserted woodpecker holes close to home. Living on love in a quiet neighborhood looked promising for these two newlyweds... until Wallace showed up. That was three months ago.

It was dead of winter when Wallace first appeared. Christmas had come and gone and Hitch decided to make better use of his cabin in the woods. He often wondered why he had bought the property in the first place. Hitch had become very accustomed to living the life of ease in his luxury apartment on the outskirts of Hillary. Driving his luxury sedan back and forth to the university was so habitual – he could make the trip in his sleep. For the life of him, Hitch could not remember which mid-life crisis took possession of his mind to the point where he would ever consider the purchase of nearly 100 acres of wood, water and clean air in the middle of Pennsylvania's South Mountains. That buying decision was made five years ago. At first glance, the acquisition of so much beauty and serenity seemed in preparation for some future, less-complicated life. Perhaps it was to be the place he could go to retire and die quickly. The acquisition of Wallace changed all that. Hitch may retire here, but there was a lot of living to do before death ushered him into the presence of the Lord (2 Co 5:8). That reason for living has since been expanded to include Debbie and Fang. To put icing on the cake, Hitch also traded in his plush domesticated-man vehicle for a trail-rated Jeep Gladiator pickup - with the limited-edition Rubicon Launch Edition package... no less.

No sooner had Hitch and Wallace pulled up to the picture perfect, yet woefully underused, cabin, that Wallace and Butterbean locked eyes onto each other. As notated earlier, Butterbean was not used to receiving uninvited guests – and certainly not one that would have ever noticed his presence right off the bat. For Wallace, he had never seen a squirrel so large as Butterbean. The potential for conflict over such things as; property rights, food "supply and demand" issues, as well as, basic "how to be a good neighbor" guidelines was to be anticipated. These issues, among others, demanded further investigation on both sides. With that in mind, Wallace was on a tightrope and headed in the beefy squirrel's direction as soon as the Jeep's door opened. Butterbean, meanwhile, held his ground. If you recall, in the ancient dialect, his name means: "I will fight against all enemies." This "stand and fight" attitude by a squirrel presented a unique set of circumstances for Wallace.

At 75 pounds, Wallace towered over Butterbean's two-pound frame, yet the two now stood face to face. There were no antagonizing barks or "chucks" (as squirrels like to call their barking) to project dominance. There were no quick, unpredictable movements to gain a competitive advantage (although it was quite natural for Butterbean's long, bushy tail to twitch involuntarily). When Wallace tentatively moved in, Butterbean countered. When Butterbean tentatively moved in, Wallace countered. At this point, the idea suddenly crossed Wallace's mind that he was being set up for an ambush. Perhaps, there were many more of these giant squirrels lurking in the trees ready to pounce on him at any moment. A quick scan of the leafless trees, however, detected only one, much smaller, squirrel having any interest in the outcome of this stalemate. Still unclear as to whether he might be the bait for some sort of squirrel trap, Wallace erred on the side of caution (not his strong suit). He had every intention of allowing the intrepid squirrel to make the first move – until he got called away.

"Wallace, let's go, buddy," Hitch called out from the front porch. "We have work to do and will be running out of daylight soon. You have all weekend to make new friends."

That sounded reasonable and Wallace started back to the cabin, but not before emitting a cautionary "bark and growl" to let his new "friend" know this first test was not going to be the last. Butterbean emitted a casual "chuck and snarl" of his own to let the new "intruder" know that he too was looking forward to their next meeting. In the months that followed, these two would square-off every chance they got. Nothing too serious mind you. In fact, to say they "battled" each other, would be to overstate the utility of these contests. Then again, to say they were just "messing around" would understate their exhaustive efforts. It was more like... tangling. They tangled. So long as they did not hurt each other too badly, Fang and

Daisy Cup were, more or less, comfortable in letting their men do their man thing.

The cabin in the woods was, without a doubt, the definition of picturesque. That country charm was especially true in winter. The only thing missing was a one-horse open sleigh parked out in front. Seated comfortably under a large woolen blanket would be a guy in a top hat and a woman donning a fluffy hand mitt that went from elbow to elbow. Add this nineteenth century image to the cabin and you got yourself the perfect print for the month of December inside your kitchen's hanging wall calendar. Regardless of the beauty, there were certain absolute truths that must be taken seriously when dealing with such remote, mountainous terrain beyond the cabin. For example, there is no cell phone service in the woods... so you carry a map and a compass. There are no first responders just waiting to bail you out of the life-threatening situation you put yourself into... at least, not until they are made aware of your foolishness. So, you carry food, water and first aid. And forget virtue signaling your way out of a confrontation with a mother bear or a pack of wolves... so you carry a weapon. That's how it is with life: there can be danger in beauty.

There were many unmarked, dirt roads on the property that go this way and that way. Some roads (the goat trails) extended out beyond the property line. These paths were extremely hazardous and would necessitate a true rock climbing, four-wheel drive vehicle to navigate. Some roads (the horse trails) were somewhat wider and easier on the four-wheel vehicle. They would take the experienced recreational hiker a little closer to some spectacular natural formations like cliffs, waterfalls and open fields of wildflower. Then there were the two roads (the human trails) paved with stone or gravel that would take the curious weekend novice to the ruins of two man-made stone structures.

Prior to the construction of the new cabin, this area was farm land. The closest of the two stone structures was the original house and barn. Everything made of wood was long gone. All that remained were the 3' tall foundational walls and two tall, but slowly deteriorating, stone fireplaces. The other abandoned stone structure was, most likely, a rye whiskey producing gristmill. It had the three things essential for making good booze close by: water, wood and grain. The perpetually flowing, fresh mountain stream provided the water. There was American oak as far as the eye could see to provide the wood for cooking the mash and barrel making. Finally, acres of farm land provided the fertile soil for growing the grain. Another proof this might be a stillhouse was the old, worn-down mill stone that laid half buried nearby.

Why rye?

Because the favorable Pennsylvania weather provided the perfect conditions for growing the rye grain... and Germans loved their rye. When the Revolutionary War ended, a third of Pennsylvania's population was German. Nothing was more complimentary than rye whiskey and rye bread (pumpernickel). Whenever rye whiskey was present, you might hear something like;

"Ich hab voll Bock auf bauernbrot!" (German translation: "I'm in the mood for farmer's bread!")

In the year 1788, "A. Traveller" (this was a real person - not sure this was a real name) wrote this in the Pennsylvania Gazette;

> "In the neighborhood of Pittsburg almost every other farm has a still-house on it. All the rye made in those parts is distilled in to whiskey. I was surprised to find some German farmers infected with the pernicious custom of using whiskey in their families. Every morning a dram was handed round to each man, woman and child in the house, and so much have some of them become attached to it, that they mix it with cucumbers for their breakfast."

Neither Wallace, nor Fang, were German, but they could not believe their good luck. Except for a few close calls (to be described soon enough), the cabin in the woods had become a winter wonderland and they were given free rein to explore it. With the arrival of Spring, the woods, and all who lived in it, had awakened from their slumber. For Wallace, the fair weather seemed to produce many more friendly adversaries. That is, there were a multitude of gray squirrels, red squirrels, fox squirrels, flying squirrels and woodchucks all willing and able to be chased. None, however, would come close to the kind of rapport he had developed with Butterbean.

For Fang, less snow allowed for greater PRs (personal records). A PR is the maximum effort given to a particular exercise or movement. It is intended to evaluate how fast, strong, or explosive an athlete you have become. There was the fun stuff, like the jump, climb, crawl and swim training. Then, there was the hard-core stuff, like the strength, speed, agility and quickness drills. There was also the mental stuff, like toughness, fortitude, willpower and courage building. For the first time in her life, Fang felt like she could actually take a day off from all the activity... or, at least, sleep in late once in a while.

As for the close calls, springtime also brought with it some corresponding danger. One such danger comes as a direct result of everyone being extremely hungry when they wake from a long winter's nap. It just so happens that early spring is also the time when most squirrels are having their litters. With three little ones in the nest, this "natural order" vs. "defending the family" dynamic, kept Daisy Cup and Butterbean on their toes.

Wallace and Fang did their part by keeping the fox, coyote and other large, predatorial animals away. Wallace did this by making as much "un-wilderness-like" noise as possible. There was no stealth involved. If you were within a mile of the cabin - and Wallace was home - you knew it. Fang took it upon herself to provide a more personal "hedge of protection" around Daisy Cup and the kittens. Very little escaped her attention when the kids were out of the nest playing. Like the men folk, Fang and Daisy Cup developed a high regard and fondness for the other. In addition to her own vigilance, Fang could tell from Daisey Cup's warning chucks, when and where present danger existed.

There was one sound that Daisy Cup made that Fang did not quite understand. Fang knew it meant trouble and she would immediately go into DEFCON 2 mode (DEFense CONdition). That elevated her senses to slightly less than maximum readiness. It wasn't a fox or a coyote or a snake. She knew the meaning to those sounds. Whatever it was, it was different. It was something more ominous. She got the sense it was not extremely large or brutish. It did have more evil attached to its meaning than these other predators – if that was even possible. No matter how hard Fang concentrated on the threat, she could not see it, hear it or smell it before Daisy Cup gave the "all clear" and "thank you" signals.

What was she missing? Fang could not help but feel she was running out of time. Daisy Cup's cryptic signals for this mysterious creature were becoming more frequent – like the enemy was planning to strike soon. What was she missing? To help narrow down the flood of sensory information that only caused more inaction, Fang decided to turn off, or lessen to some degree, two of her more acute senses: sight and smell. She wasn't exactly sure what was going to be accomplished by doing this, but she had to try something before it was too late.

Just before dawn the next morning, Fang was at Hitch's bedside. Hitch was usually the first one up in the morning and, therefore, the one to make coffee and let both dogs outside … just never this early. When the staring and heavy breathing in close proximity to the face failed to wake Hitch, Fang released one soft whimper and gave his exposed cheek a soft, moist lick. That did the trick, and within minutes

Wallace and Fang were outside the cabin. This was business and Fang let Wallace know it.

"No bark, no chase, listen," she insisted.

So, there they were, laying side by side on the front porch as the dawn provided just enough light to differentiate the darker tree tops from the, barely much lighter, sky in the distance. While Wallace immediately rolled over and fell back asleep, Fang laid herself down into a relaxed, but ready, state of repose. Then, she closed her eyes and simply listened. Within seconds, she was listening in on the hundreds of constant and repetitive sounds that only dense woods could make. There were also the familiar sounds of nocturnal animals lumbering about making their last-ditch effort to snag more food before disappearing for the day. Daisy Cup and the kids would still be in the nest.

Then, suddenly, she heard it. It was a very unique sound... soft and pleasing to the ear. She had heard it before, but thought nothing of it since there was no anger or hostility in the making of the sound. Maybe that is why she misunderstood Daisy Cup's warnings.

Hoo-hoohoo hoo

There it was again. But this was a slightly different sound. *It was a reply*, she thought. *There must be two.*

Fang gently put a paw onto Wallace's side so as to wake him - but not to startle him. When she had his attention, she spoke in hushed tones.

"Enemy close."

"Who enemy?" Wallace asked in whispers as he gradually took a defensive position next to Fang.

He was aware of her concern for Butterbean's kids, but did not know to what extent she was involved.

"Flyer," Fang replied.

Flyers were anything with wings.

"Where?"

"Hidden," she answered with what information she had so far. "Listen."

The "Great Horned" owl was affectionately known as the "Hoot Owl" for its delightful "hoo-hoo" hoots that can resonate great distances through the night air. On the other hand, it was also named the "Tiger of the Air" because it was also known to be a ferocious, aerial, meat eater. Armed with powerful talons and a hooked beak, it was capable of crushing the spinal column and tearing the meat off of prey much larger than itself... and it can weigh up to 3 ½ pounds. It has a rust-colored face and soft brown plumage mottled with grayish-white on the upper body that would blend in naturally with any forest. The owl's so-called "great horns" are actually prominent ear tufts that extend up and out from its forehead two or more inches. With an enormous wingspan approaching 5 feet, the great horned owl is considered a "Perch and Pounce" hunter. That is, it will sit in a tree or tall post and wait patiently for the opportune moment to swoop down on their prey undetected. And their choice of prey included rats, mice, voles, heron, grouse, chicken, fox, skunk, weasel, muskrat, rabbit... and squirrel.

Hoo-hoohoo hoo

"Two enemy," Fang whispered and scanned the trees in hopes that the flyers would give themselves away by moving just a tiny bit. "Protect squirrel baby."

"Protect squirrel baby," Wallace concurred with a semi-controlled snarl.

After a while, the skies turned from a charcoal grey to a dark shade of blue and Wallace could smell the coffee brewing. This, of course, meant their breakfast would be waiting for them in bowls on the kitchen floor. When the front door finally did open, Wallace's attempt to get to his feet and to his bowl in haste, appeared as if he wore hockey skates on all four paws and the porch were made of ice. After regaining traction, he quickly disappeared into the cabin. Fang, on the other hand, did not move. Again, she hoped Wallace's mealtime acrobatics would disturb the enemy enough for her to catch a glimpse – but there was nothing to see.

It was Debbie who opened the door.

"What is it, Sweetie?" Debbie asked Fang, to which she responded in a series of barks, whines and growls.

"Well, I know you will do your best to help them," Debbie replied with empathy. "I'm sure Wallace's dad would want him to join you. Come in and eat now. It sounds like you will both need your strength."

Let's be clear. Debbie did not speak the canine language and Fang did not speak the human language, but they both interpreted each other's sound and body language very well. This helped them to understand the elemental morphology, syntax, semantics, pragmatics and phonology being used. That is, they inferred things with surprising accuracy. This gave Debbie some idea what Fang and Wallace were up against and that these two would need to be outside for most of the day.

To live in constant fear is no way to live, and so it was with squirrels. As soon as the sun came out, so did Daisy Cup and the three kids. To live without enjoying every waking minute of every day is no way to live, and so it was with Wallace. As soon as he was awake and fed, it was off to the races. To live in relative safety and not help those who's safety might be put in jeopardy, is no way to live (with yourself), and so it was with Fang. As long as Daisy Cup's kids were outside the nest, she would not allow herself to become distracted from that mission. The cabin porch provided the best over-all picture of the danger field, so that is where Fang sat at attention. Defeating a flyer would not be easy because they definitely had air superiority, but she had Wallace.

Hoo-hoohoo hoo

There it was. The sound she was waiting for. Wallace heard it as well and took his position close to the tree where Butterbean and Daisy Cup had built their nest. As expected, Daisy Cup chucked her alert – which now made perfect sense to Fang. Daisy Cup had scooped up the kitten closest to her and scurried up the tree and into the nest. Butterbean came out of nowhere, grabbed the kitten closest to him without slowing down and ran as fast as he could towards the nest. The plan was for Wallace to protect the squirrels retreat across the yard and, if given the chance, Fang would get a shot at the winged killers. Unfortunately, that left one kitten momentarily alone and unprotected.

That is when Fang saw them both... in the same tree. In an instant, both owls had moved to the outer branches, spread open their wings and dove one after the other.

"Flyer!" Fang barked at Wallace and flew off the porch. "Save squirrel baby!"

"Save squirrel baby!" Wallace replied and bolted towards the stranded kitten.

By this time, Butterbean had handed off his kitten to Daisy Cup and was already heading back towards the one spot that two dogs and two owls were now converging. The first to reach the defenseless squirrel baby was Wallace. If he had not arrived when he did, it would have been too late. In fact, the race between Wallace and the first incoming owl was so close, that the owl's talons unintentionally dug into Wallace's side instead of the kitten. Due to the unavoidable collision that ensued, the talons did not go deep. Wallace took the painful opportunity to body-slam the owl into the ground with such force, that it took several seconds for the dazed bird to get airborne again. This miscalculation caused the second owl to pull up and circle back around.

In the meantime, Butterbean had gathered up the last of his kittens and started back towards the nest. Unable to run as fast with this added weight clinging to him, Butterbean knew they would become an easy target for the circling owl. At exactly the right moment, Butterbean set the kitten down, turned and leapt bravely into claws of the swooping owl. Seconds later, however, he was tumbling on the ground – along with the owl and Fang. Unable to gain altitude as fast with a two-pound, Butterbean sandwich in its claws, the owl became an easy target for Fang. She skillfully made the six-foot vertical leap to catch the struggling owl by the tail feathers and dragged him and Butterbean back down to earth.

That was last anybody ever saw of those two great horned owls. Not all of Wallace's and Fang's adventures were matters of life or death. In fact, the vast majority were simply the absurd situations they get themselves in and out of. Well, um, I suppose it could be said that Wallace was the one to get them into most predicaments and Fang the one to get them out... but who's counting, right?

Chapter 7

In God's Hand

It was as *if the rug was pulled out from under his feet.*

It was an old expression, but Leon could not think of a more appropriate visual than that. He knew all about Everett – except for the golden voice. The young man was just like his mother in one respect – both were instrumental virtuosos. Pick any instrument, put it in a room with Everett for an hour and out pops a virtuoso. This would, however, be the first time Leon heard the boy sing.

Big oversight on my part, Leon thought with a sigh.

It was a voice that made you stop whatever you were doing and savor it while it lasted. None of that mattered now. Leon had been after Everett for years, but he was his mom's prodigy and no one else's. Whenever she had an opening in her stringed ensembles, she filled it with Everett. At the age of ten, the kid had started his own jazz quartet (i.e., piano, horn, drums, double bass). Everett preferred the double bass, even though Leon remembers the little guy having to stand on a box to play it. At the age of sixteen, Everett had his own jazz fusion band and it was back then that Leon got his first glimpse of the prodigy's extraordinary talent.

This kid plays that stand-up like Big 'Un, Leon remembered thinking.

Big 'Un, or Walter Sylvester Page (1900–1957), was the accomplished African American jazz bandleader for "Walter Page and the Blue Devils." He would later become the legendary double bass playing sensation with the Count Basie Orchestra from 1935-1948. It was Big 'Un who some would say revolutionized the "slap bass" (alternate between slapping and aggressively plucking the strings) and the "walking bass" (the steady expression of all four beats in a bar, rather than two).

Leon was never one to exaggerate much (except when it came to his Yale University), so Everett was that good. In an effort to help advance this gifted teenager's career, Leon made several attempts to make contact with him through his mother. Even at Everett's young age, Leon was more than willing to introduce the boy to some of the most powerful and influential people in the philharmonic universe. Again, Everett was that good. Leon would have pulled the same strings for anyone with that much raw talent. Unfortunately, Leon found it impossible to wrest the youth away from his mother and their preoccupation with voodoo and palm readers.

Everett was no longer a kid under his mother's wing, but it was too late for Leon to bring him back from so much influence and distraction. The last he heard, an electric bass took over where the mother left off and Everett was into the mind-numbing heavy metal tripe that passed for music. It was music, of course, but it was pathetically simple rhythms with abominably vulgar lyrics attached to it.

Such a waste of God-given talent, Leon thought before entering the room where Everett was discovered.

Leon had not seen Everett in years, but always remembered him as a polite young man. Perhaps it would be a chance to reminisce for a minute or two and get a feel for what the bass playing tenor was up to these days. Maybe he would invite him to the concert if he didn't already have a ticket. If anyone could appreciate Bach's Easter Oratorio, it would be Everett. Maybe not the message, but the music anyway.

I'm here. He's here. Let's go in, Leon thought.

Leon knocked before entering. Everett was on his cell phone.

"Zeke, Zeke, got to stop you here, bro. We can discuss the tour later," Everett replied in an obvious attempt to end a business call quickly once he noticed the head of the entire music department had just entered the room. "Zeke, later... Zeke, no... Zeke, shut up... no, I said later... no... later doesn't mean keep talking... Zeke... bye."

"Very good, you're still here," Leon was the first to speak once the call ended and the cell phone tossed into a gym bag.

"Professor Bouchard. I'm honored, sir. I was on my way down to apologize when Zeke... when our business manager called. He's a phenomenal guy, watches out for us, but it's hard to turn him off sometimes," Everett spoke energetically. "But, let me start by saying how sorry I am. I never meant to be heard, sir. The acoustics in this place are just better than I thought possible. I have been listening in on your rehearsals for months and know how hard you have been working on this piece. I hope you will forgive me, sir."

"No harm, no foul," Leon responded calmly. "So, you know this piece?"

"Of course, yes, sir," Everett shot back enthusiastically. "It's the Oster-Oratorium BWV 249 (German: "Easter Oratorio") by Johann Sebastian Bach. One of my all-time favorites around this time of year. I like his Weihnachtsoratorium BWV 248 (German: "Christmas Oratorio") around Christmas. I know you like to perform George Frederic Handel's Messiah Oratorio HWV 56 for Christmas, but either one is good."

[NOTE FOR THE CURIOUS: "BWV" stands for Bach-Werke-Verzeichnis (German: "Bach Works Catalog"). In 1950, Wolfgang Schmieder assigned numbers to J.S. Bach's compositions. The numbers are assigned thematically, not chronologically. "HWV" (Händel-Werke-Verzeichnis) is the catalog of Handel's compositions. It was published in three volumes by Bernd Baselt between 1978 and 1986]

"If you have been listening for months, why did you wait until now to start singing?" Leon inquired, as he earnestly tried to fill in the blanks with this complex young man.

"When you swapped out the tenors, I couldn't help singing the part properly. If you don't mind my saying, the German is not what it once was with the other guy. And, in the sixth movement recitative, the contrast of Peter's joy at Christ being risen to the music in b minor was completely missing. Then, in the seventh movement aria in g major, where Peter accepts the resurrection of Christ, his voice should flow with the flutes and violins... like this."

At this point, Everett sang the verse he had in mind ("Sanfte soll mein Todeskummer... Gentle should be the sorrow of my death")... in perfect German, in perfect cadence, in perfect pitch.

"I'm sure you are looking forward to having your first tenor back soon." Everett stated in less critical terms, then it suddenly dawned on him who he was talking to. "I'll shut up now, sir."

"So, if I hear you correctly, you believe you could do a better job singing Peter's aria?" Leon asked with all sincerity and effectively nullifying Everett's comment about shutting up.

"I do, or did, enjoy listening to the first guy," Everett admitted. "But, this new guy? Not really feeling it... to be honest."

"You didn't answer my question, Everett," Leon replied stoically. "You know what you are capable of, young man. Do you believe you could do a better job singing Peter's aria... yes or no?"

"Yes"

"I agree," Leon replied without hesitation.

Then, he sat down at the old, industrial-strength upright piano, lifted the fallboard and began to play. The piano was woefully out of tune and each key felt like a brick to the touch. He had played on worse growing up.

"Let me tell you a story," Leon spoke as he tinkered around on the piano. "It won't take long."

The story Leon shared was a true story. It was a reoccurring story. It happened twice a year - every year. To put it very simply, Leon gathered a group of extremely talented musicians and vocalists to play and sing two extremely difficult masterpieces; one by Handel and one by Bach. These were regular people. No one was considered famous – except within their own circle of family and friends. These were moms and dads, sons and daughters, young and old, reserved and flamboyant, well-liked and misfits, over-worked and out of work. Most were Christian, but not all. They flocked to him. There were so many, Leon had to find some polite way of telling nine out of ten candidates to try again next year. For most of those being chosen, it would be a once-in-a-lifetime experience... a long-awaited dream that has finally come true. For others, it was the profound satisfaction that comes from being part of something great for one more year. As promised, this story did not take long.

"Everett, would you like to be part of something great?" Leon asked while seeming to enjoy the imperfect sound being produced by the beaten-up old piano.

"What are you asking, Professor?" Everett inquired with a sheepish grin.

At this point, Leon stopped playing the piano, gently lowered the fallboard and turned to face Everett.

"The tenor you enjoyed listening to so much, has left us for good... and you summed up the flaws of his stand-in pretty well," Leon verbalized his dilemma in as few words as possible to get to the point. "You now know that everyone in the Walker has heard you sing. So, I am asking you to be our soloist tenor."

"I, I, don't know what to say, Professor," Everett replied, as he was momentarily stunned by the offer.

"I do not ask this lightly, young man. Peter's aria has always been the centerpiece of Bach's Easter oratorio and deserves the best performance possible. We've got one full week till opening night. That gives us one more full rehearsal," Leon concluded. "It seems to me to be the perfect solution."

"Can I have some time to think about it?" Everett replied tentatively in an effort to fully comprehend such a prestigious offer. This was not some hollowed out, sound-sucking sports arena converted into a concert venue filled with half drunk, half pharmaceutically-infused metal head bangers.

"Of course, son," Leon responded with father-like empathy. "How does thirty minutes sound? That should give you plenty of time to call Zeke. Or, perhaps you should call your attorney back in here. She did an excellent job of defending you a few minutes ago."

"My who did what?"

"Francesca... she is your attorney, isn't she?" Leon mused as he walked over to the felt-lined guitar case that held the distinctive bass. "I have to say, she was rather convincing of your innocence. Nice Le Fay. I am also certain she would be in favor of you accepting this important role."

"Frannie?"

"Yes, Frannie," Leon answered candidly, then casually moved to the door. "Everett, I do not believe our meeting was by accident."

Leon paused at the door, not sure if what he was about to say next would benefit his cause or send a Wiccan flying off the broomstick. Only one way to find out.

"I do not particularly enjoy adversities, but when they come, I look first to see God's hand in them. Not that he sets these hardships, but I do understand that he will allow them to happen. I then look to see how many different paths I am given that will help me get out of the mess I'm in. I am always given a path to lie, or to cheat, or to somehow sin my way out. Here's the thing, Everett. There is always a path that glorifies God. I just need to be patient enough to see it. I believe God allowed this meeting. I believe we have both been patient. You decide if God is glorified."

There. He said what he said. Everett said nothing, but was clearly moved by the words. Before leaving the room completely, Leon turned, offered up a great big smile and spoke cheerfully.

"I will be downstairs for the next half an hour... should I send in your attorney?"

Debbie and Fang lived in the heart of downtown Hillary. It was within walking distance of everything necessary for a single, progressive woman to survive: the office, trendy shoe and purse shops, trendy bakeries and tea rooms, trendy health clubs and late-night party bars... Planned Parenthood. It was the true narcissist's utopia – a pint-sized San Francisco. Debbie was once well known and idolized here. That ended with her regeneration from being a sinner with an axe to grind, to being a sinner with a Savior. She was now considered "persona non grata" (Latin: "person not welcome"). Soon after it was learned she had "defected" to the Christian side, there were many overt confrontations with foul language being tossed her way. These were groundless expressions out of anger by those that are hurting inside and she knew it. She would be the worst kind of liar if she said she did not share these same feelings not long ago. It was a constant reminder of God's hand lifting her up out of the darkness. When it was clear she was not going to retaliate or leave downtown Hillary, most simply sneered at her as they walked by. Debbie loved her cute little townhouse in town. Then again, nothing seemed to measure up to a day spent outside with Hitch and Wallace.

It had been a dreary "crawl back under the covers if you could" kind of work week. Spring break was over and the time spent at the cabin with the boys (Hitch and Wallace) were just fond memories at this point. Easter was something to look forward to, but currently, the winds had picked up significantly and it had been raining relentlessly. This abysmal combination of mother nature's wrath turned the leisurely morning walks into a race from one make-shift shelter to the next. These fits and starts made going outside for any length of time dreadful rather than pleasurable.

If rain hitting the face sideways weren't enough, Wallace – having healed quickly from the wound given to him by a bloodthirsty Hoot Owl - found it necessary to submerge himself in every mud puddle he could find. And no one; not Hitch, not Debbie, not Fang could persuade him otherwise. To make matters even worse for Debbie and Fang, their afternoon dance lessons were limited to simplistic close-in heel-work inside the confines of a small townhouse. By mid-week Debbie had had enough.

"That's it, let's go," Debbie snapped and reached into the closet hastily to retrieve her rain gear.

All of it to Fang's great delight.

This was not their first rodeo when the rains came and Fang knew exactly where they were going and why. The Hillary Commons Dog Park was a 5-minute walk from the townhouse. It was a five acre, off-the-leash, well maintained playground for dogs. The majority of that area was fenced and dedicated to the large dogs. Another, much smaller section was fenced and dedicated to the smaller, more fragile, breeds. The entire property was wooded, except that each section had its own open space. The open space in the large dog section was graded, drained water well and about the size of a football field. Half of that open space was filled with various obstacles for dogs to climb, jump or pass through. The other half was a grassy field. The park was the "Gem" of Hillary since it seemed everyone in town owned a dog or two. It was so popular that, on occasion, the town would find it necessary to limit admission so as not to exceed the legal capacity and to help maintain the peace. This overcrowding was especially true on the weekends or on a beautiful clear day. On rainy days - like today – it would be empty.

Fortunately for them, the winds had subsided and only a steady light sprinkle from the dark foreboding cloud cover persisted. To no one's surprise, the place was empty. Debbie and Fang agreed (intuitively speaking) this trip to the park (although wet) was for one necessary (although fun) purpose. That purpose was to take advantage of that empty wide-open space to practice their musical freestyle dance routine. More specifically, to practice the distance work; such as the weaves, the jumps and the send-outs. This required space... lots of space... and practice... lots of practice. Debbie and Fang were in the big leagues now. Gone were the days of simple heelwork routines with noticeable hand cues and minimal amounts of precision. These advanced routines were expected to be technically and artistically flawless. That is, there was to be no noticeable hand or verbal cues between the handler and the dog. If that were not enough, these routines were also twice as long (i.e., 3 minutes verses 1.5 minutes). That was a very long time to fill in "dog" minutes.

From a technical standpoint, Debbie and Fang could hardly get any better than they were. They were currently holding on to an average Technical Merit (TM) score of 9.8 - with 10.0 being the highest. This number makes up 50% of their total score. TM scores are based on the variety and difficulty of the routine's movements, as well as, the flow and accuracy. With Debbie's dance background and Fang's tremendous athleticism, they would consistently rack up perfect scores for technical merit. If they had a weakness, it was in the more subjective aspect of canine dancing, or Artistic Impression (AI).

Again, Debbie was born to dance. It was in her nature to make every intricate movement that seemed impossible... seem effortless. Every choreographed dance step she took was made to appear graceful, fluid and natural. She knew what it took to make a dance routine sizzle with emotion. Fang, not so much. In canine dancing, the one thing to keep in mind at all times was the judge's eyes were mainly focused on the dog... not the handler. If the handler were to overshadow the dog in any way, points would be deducted. So, that was a problem. Complexity and precision did not confuse Fang. Fang never faltered, never wavered, never showed her feminine side. In other words, Fang lacked balance in dance and in life... until she met Wallace.

Debbie recognized this attitude change in her canine daughter early on and they talked about it (intuitively speaking). This new freedom to be less than perfect in life actually had a positive side effect on their dancing. There was a new level of cohesiveness, or synchronicity, in their presentation. If ever there was a time to prove something, it was now. So, into the annoying dense mist they went.

They were deep into their routine. It was a point where they were standing twenty feet apart from each other and yet mirroring the other's dance steps. Suddenly, Fang stopped. Her complete focus of attention was now on the obstacle course at the other end of the open field. There was no need for Debbie to call out to her. She knew Fang was not one to become easily distracted unless it was for some significant reason. So, instead of yelling something pointless, which would only cause more delay, Debbie walked purposefully up to Fang's side and stood there looking out over an empty park. Seeing and hearing nothing unusual, Debbie simply waited patiently for the explanation she knew would be forthcoming. Without moving a muscle or turning her attention away from the obstacle course, Fang let out a brief distinguishable pattern of soft whines.

As close as Debbie could tell, Fang heard a soft sound in the direction she was now looking. It would normally have no meaning, except the inflection in Fang's whimpering made it seem as though the sound was a cry for help. But the sound was now gone.

"Go," Debbie stated in a manner that was intended to give permission to investigate, but to do so with caution.

It didn't help matters much that the mist turned back into a light rain and the darkening sky above decided to emit a deep, threatening rumble. It was the ominous sound that thunder will make - somewhere far off in the heavens - just before the lightning bolt came crashing down to earth. There were at least a dozen agility stations in the park. Most of those were narrow, slightly elevated dog walks, bar jumps, weave poles and cones that provided no protection from the elements or from sight. There were four stations, however, that a dog – or a person – could go to get out of the rain. One was a large A-Frame and the other three were tunnels of various sizes. The A-Frame was open on the sides and, therefore, easily inspected from a distance. The largest of the three tunnels was only 6' long and yet 3' in diameter. It was obviously intended for the larger dogs to pass through with ease and, therefore, easy to inspect from a distance. That left two smaller tunnels that required a closer look. The medium size tunnel was 10' to 12' long, 2' in diameter and curved softly into a half-moon shape. If she wanted to, Fang could pass through this tunnel at half speed in seconds. The smaller of the three tunnels was slightly shorter than the last, but had a more abrupt zig-zag in the middle. The diameter was also slightly smaller and, therefore, may force a dog of medium build or larger to crawl through it. It was these last two tunnels that Fang set all of her attention.

Since these two tunnels were on opposite sides of the field from each other, Fang approached the closer of the two. This would be the C-shaped tunnel and it was cleared with military precision in less than a minute. That left the crawling tunnel. This outcome allowed Debbie to relax somewhat knowing that, if something... or someone... were to pop out of this remaining tunnel, it should be smaller than her. Again, she would allow Fang do her "Malinois" thing.

The rain, of course, decided to do its "add water" thing.

Fang entered the tunnel without a sound and on all fours. It was a long minute before Debbie saw Fang's backside slowly emerge from the same side as she entered. In her mouth was a small object – a kitten. The little guy was perhaps a day or two old and making a barely audible squeaky "feed me" noise. Debbie took the kitten and carefully placed it into the large duffel bag that was used to carry canine dance paraphernalia, treats and lots of big fluffy beach towels (for rainy days).

"What was she thinking?" Debbie asked out loud.

While Debbie gave thought to all the stupid reasons why a mom cat would choose a dog park to start a family, Fang went back into the tunnel. She repeated this meticulous rescue process three more times – producing a final tally of four squealing kittens. The fourth and final kitten was brought out through the opposite end of the tunnel. This was to ensure there were no stragglers left behind.

Now what to do?

"Let's go," Debbie said after giving the saturated dog park one more 360° scan for the mom cat.

Unable to see much of anything now that the incessant rain began to inhibit visibility, Debbie pulled the hood of her rain jacket as far forward as it would go and headed for the exit gates. That's how it is with rain. It is as if some ill-mannered Greek god, or goddess, stood high upon on a mountain top somewhere and in the palm of their hand they possessed a device that would control whatever inclement weather condition their meddling hearts desired (i.e., wind, snow, ice, rain). The dial would be turned down low - to lull you outside. Then, slowly but surely, they would turn it up until you are standing outside in the pouring rain asking yourself why.

They had not yet reached the gates of the park when Fang turned and barked once. Debbie immediately turned around and gently raised her head enough to peer out from under her hood. There, standing on top of the tunnel, was a soaking wet and clearly upset mom cat.

"You want'em, come get'em," she yelled unsympathetically before turning back towards the gates.

And so it was, as if in formation and with Fang in the lead... then Debbie, with the kittens safely tucked away in the duffel bag... then mom cat, they came walking through the center of downtown Hillary. It was understood between Debbie and Fang that their stride would be cut in half and they would slow down even more whenever mom cat fell behind. Debbie kept the duffel bag opened wide enough to let air in, but also wide enough to let the cries of the hungry kittens out. This kept mom cat engaged and it only took a couple of complete stops before they all arrived safely back at the townhouse. Debbie opened the garage door.

"Welcome home, kids," she said joyfully as they all walked in out of the rain... all except for mom cat, of course.

Debbie popped open the rear trunk of her Tesla and set the duffel bag down inside. The trunk was deep and, by and large, empty. It provided some additional protection from the elements while they went inside to dry off and to change clothes. The duffel bag was unzipped to expose the four exhausted rug-rats, fast asleep and nestled in thick pile of warm, dry towels. It continued to rain, but not driven sideways by the wind, so the garage door was left up in case mom cat wanted to join the dry snooze-fest.

At the park, Debbie had noticed that, although each kitten was having their own little temper tantrum, none of them had yet opened their eyes. They did seem well fed however. This bought some time. That is, there was no need to rush out to buy kitten formula. Hopefully, mom cat will accept the idea that "living" in a garage was a more suitable environment for her kittens than "not living" very long in the middle of a dog park. Debbie would give mom cat an hour without interruption to make up her mind. In the meantime, she would watch events unfold inside and outside the garage by way of a smart video doorbell security system.

Wallace stared out over the rain-drenched "Yard" from the large windows in Hitch's office. Every so often he would let out an elongated "ro, ro, ro, ro" followed by an accentuated "whine/sneeze" and then look sullenly towards Hitch seated at his desk. Unmoved by this blatant attempt to evoke some sort of sympathy for his plight at being stuck indoors, Hitch spoke without raising his head from the papers he was reading.

"See those?" Hitch stated rather testily and pointed to the significant pile of soggy, mud-caked towels lying beside the door. "You have already used up your daily allotment of clean towels due to your complete inability to sidestep even the slightest accumulation of water and mud. Therefore, unless this is a bathroom emergency - in which case you will be on a short leash the entire time we are outside - please keep your thoughts to yourself."

It was not necessary for Wallace to understand all that was said. It was only necessary to understand that the culmination of all those big human words meant "no." Then again, "no" did not always mean "no." Occasionally, if he stared long enough and dialed in the right telepathic mind control frequency, his human dad would change all those big words to mean "yes." All he had to do... now... is... keep... concentrating... on... the... mind... control...

"Not working," Hitch stated emphatically as he continued reading his papers.

Oh well, Wallace thought as he trudged back to his favorite napping spot on the expensive hand-tufted Persian rug in the middle of the room. *If his human dad could not see the pleasure and therapeutic benefits in a soothing mud bath, it was his loss.*

It wasn't long before Wallace heard a soft knock at the door. He knew who it was even before the knock occurred because of her graceful footstep patterns. She was the human person with two names. That is, Wallace's human dad (Hitch) would refer to her as either Monica or Ms. Brown. The name usually depended on who she brought into the office with her. Wallace would also sense that Hitch preferred the name

"Monica" over "Ms. Brown" when addressing her. To Wallace's trained ear, "Monica" was clearly more personal in nature, whereas, "Ms. Brown" was the stand-offish business application. Monica (or Ms. Brown) was Hitch's long-time office manager, but sometimes it was hard for Wallace to tell who exactly was in charge.

Wallace loved Monica. Two things could happen when Monica walked into the room. If she said nothing, Wallace would rise from his favorite spot in the middle of the room and she would give him one heck of a good, strong body rub and pet before conducting the business she came in for. This would, of course, force her to use some sticky paper roller thingy to remove all of his yellow dog hair from her clothes. Or, she would immediately say "Not now, Wallace" and he would remain parked in the middle of the room – until given specific orders to move out of everyone's way. Wallace was provided a large, plush dog bed that was located in the corner of the office, but he chose not to use it unless ordered to move out of everyone's way.

"Not now, Wallace," Monica declared as soon as she opened the door.

She casually walking around Wallace's sprawled body and stood in front of Hitch's desk until they made eye contact. Monica was currently engaged to Hitch's son, Jimi, and a fall wedding was in the works. That blessed event, however, did not change the well-established, professional courtesy these two shared while at work.

"Your two o'clock appointment has arrived, Professor," she pleasantly reminded him. "Are you available?"

Hitch vaguely remembered something about an after-noon appointment from this morning's briefing with Ms. Brown. The fact that she asked if he was available told him it was a meeting that could be rescheduled if he needed the time.

"I'm sorry, Monica, who did I agree to meet with?" Hitch admitted dispassionately.

"She… is your new representative from your publishing company," Monica stated objectively, with emphasis on the pronoun "she" at the start. "Apparently, you have broken off one too many scheduled appointments with your previous representative. All having been at the last minute, I might add. So, evidently, he… has decided to turn you over to the sales office noob. A rather prudently decision on his part, in my opinion."

"So, good ole 'what's his name' cancelled me, huh?" Hitch feigned regret and overlooking her sarcasm. "I believe I have a few minutes to spare. Please, send her in."

Before turning to leave, Monica gave her future father-in-law an uncomfortably long "you had better be nice… or else" look.

"What?" Hitch countered, as if insulted by the unspoken accusation.

"You know what," she replied sharply and turned to leave.

Then, without subtlety, "Please, move your butt out of the way" as she passed Wallace.

"Ro, ro, ro," Wallace countered before taking his time getting up and moving to the bed in the corner.

Monica returned moments later with the rookie sales-person and the two stood quietly in front of Hitch's desk for a second or two before he looked up from his papers.

"Professor, this is Annastasia Grecu, your new pub-lishing coordinator. Did I get that right?" Monica asked her guest politely.

"Yes, thank you," the young lady replied anxiously. "You can call me Ana if you like."

Ana knew Professor Hitchinson had made her company millions of dollars over the years. One book sale and she could easily pay off her considerably large college debt. A new car that would run more often than not would be nice too.

"Great, Ana. I'll leave you two to talk business," Monica said. "Can I get you something to drink before I go; water, tea, coffee?"

"No, thank you," Ana replied gratefully, feeling a little more at ease now.

"So, Annastasia, you have a very unusual surname," Hitch began, preferring not to shorten such a beautiful first name. "It means Greek, I believe. A very common name in Romania, is that right?"

"Yes, my grandparents and many other relatives still live in Romania," she replied with a generous smile and continued. "I was warned... oops, I'm so sorry... I was informed that you're an extremely busy person and I'm not to waste your time. So, in the few moments I have with you, I'd like to demonstrate to you just how important you are to our company."

With that introduction, she began to open up the pain-fully ostentatious company portfolio. The last thing Hitch wanted to sit through again was that utterly monotonous sales pitch. He would much rather understand the content of character of the young woman sitting in front of him. Having a fundamental understanding on just about everything on the planet, he knew Romania to be a very religious country.

"The warning you were given was accurate. I am a very busy man, Annastasia," Hitch began unapologetically. "So, if you don't mind, I would like to spend what little time we have getting to know a little more about the person I am dealing with."

Assuming consent, Hitch continued.

"Correct me if I am wrong, but would you say that the predominate faith in Romania is Christianity?" Hitch asked cordially, but already knowing the answer. "You do not need to answer, if that makes you uncomfortable."

At this point, Wallace was sitting up with ears at full attention and looking directly at Ana. This was his "Labra-Skunk" sixth sense kicking in. This was his innate ability to sense that a material lie was about to be told. It was a familiar reaction. Hitch was taught his lesson on honesty back when Bobbi Lou owned Wallace and he told a lie in their presence. Once a lie was told, Wallace would emit an odor (let's just say from the "caboose side" of things) that would instantly cause the surrounding air to become unbreathable. Hitch would have his answer on Ana's character within minutes.

Ana also sensed this was a test. She had been forewarned about the professor's atheistic views and to avoid talk of religion at all costs. This information was obviously outdated, but even if it were still true, the question was about a country – not about her.

"Yes, I'm pretty sure it is," she answered truthfully.

"So, do you consider yourself to be a Christian?" Hitch inquired with the greatest gentleness.

Not wishing to bulldoze this young lady off a cliff of regret, Hitch added an incentive to be honest.

"Annastasia, I do not know all you have been told about me, but let me assure you of one thing. I place honesty above all other human characteristics and interaction. I will not knowingly work with someone I cannot trust to speak the truth."

"Professor," Ana softly spoke as a tear slowly made its way down her cheek. "I accepted Jesus Christ as my personal Savior when I was twelve. I won't ever deny him because I know he wouldn't ever deny me before the Father in heaven."

Ana knew what she had just confessed would cost her more money than she could possibly imagine, but that did not matter. These tests of faith always made her stronger, not weaker. As she began to pack up her things to go, Hitch extended a box of tissue across the desk. This caused her to stop packing and regain her composure. Wallace - unfazed by the truth - rose from his seated position, yawned widely, stretched extensively, shook robustly, made two circles in his rarely used bed, then plopped down in a heap.

"I am putting the final touches on a book that I would like you to manage from start to finish," Hitch stated with confidence. "Ms. Brown is my right arm. She will provide you with everything you need. Do we have a deal, Ms. Grecu?"

Finding it hard to talk and hold back tears of joy at the same time, Ana dabbed her eyes, wiped her nose and wagged her head in agreement.

Chapter 8

Palm Sunday – Part I

Passion Week, also known as Holy Week, begins on Palm Sunday. It would become the Sunday before Jesus' crucifixion on Good Friday. It is best remembered as the day Jesus rode into Jerusalem on a donkey and it is recorded in all four Gospels (Mt 21:1-11, Mk 11:1-11, Lk 19:28-44, and Jn 12:12-19). Of course, back then, no one knew Jesus would lay down his life for our sins five days later. Not even his disciples truly understood that part. The day created quite a stir nonetheless. On this particular Sunday, half of the crowd wanted nothing more than to see the Jewish healer credited with raising a man (Lazarus) from the dead. The other half hungered for the "Triumphal Entry" of their long-awaited Jewish king into Jerusalem. To them, it was the fulfillment of a few more Jewish prophecies (Zec 9:9; Ps 118:25-26).

"Hosanna! Blessed is he who comes in the name of the Lord!" they all shouted on Palm Sunday.

"Crucify him!" they all shouted on Good Friday.

Good grief, just when you think a situation could not get any better... or worse!

It was Palm Sunday and Everett found himself in a most unlikely conundrum. First of all, he had not been inside a true Christian church since his paternal grandparents took him to their Sunday service at the age of four. His parents never left him alone with them on a Sunday again after that. Second of all, he was just about to walk into another Christian church. He was not there to see Jesus. He was there to see Frannie. That's all. Nothing more. Or, so he thought.

Granted, there was nothing complicated about sitting in a non-denominational church where the teaching was predicated on scripture. In the same way, there was nothing complicated about hoping for a second chance to impress a very attractive young lady - who just happens to be a Christian. Nothing complicated about any of that... unless, of course, you have been identifying yourself as being a Wiccan your entire life!

If that contradiction were not enough, you (Everett) were just caught singing Bach's Easter Oratorio too well and too loud. This was not any oratorio. This was the lead soloist part of a large-scale musical composition based on the death and resurrection of Jesus Christ just before Easter. Not only was that transgression blatantly incongruent to the Wiccan code, the whole singing misunderstanding came about BEFORE meeting the Christian girl... that you can't seem to get off your mind!

If that yummy layer of sweet truth on top of the complexity cake you call a life were not enough, you (Everett) were already having some doubt as to why your life as a

Godless wanderer was not as liberating as your generation's "culture of conformity or be cancelled" advertised it to be.

Why can't it be as simple as two people getting together and sharing an extreme love of music? he thought emotively... yet unconvincingly.

Having already discarded the whole metaphysical nonsense of "music is my religion" years ago and being the frequent target for every horny psychopathic groupie, Everett could only hope there was more at play here than what first meets the eye. He held on to the belief that there was so much more to him than his association with a pagan religion and amplified music.

She did invite me to come listen to her sing? he thought again.

Everett would stick with that. It was simple, it was truthful and it helped to placate the dogmatic part of himself that opposed all forms of organized religion. Since their initial meeting a couple days ago, Frannie had now become his situation. Up to that point, his life had never been easier and he never intended to add drama to it. In a manner of speaking, he had no problem with skating through life for the time being. Yes, he found himself actively looking for something (or someone). But that something (or someone) was to add clarity and honorable meaning to his life – not more dopey escape routes from the expectations of others that went nowhere. That something (or someone) was also far greater than simply meeting a girl he liked. Yet, there was a uniqueness about Frannie that seemed to be playing a part in his puzzling quest for purpose... and it was tugging unmistakably at his heart.

As anticipated around this time of year, Everett found Frannie's church bustling with the holiday spirit. Lots of people were coming and lots of people were going and lots of people just milling around outside... but no Frannie. A quick glance to the grassy area on the right side of the building he spotted a large holding pen that had attracted a small crowd. Inside the pen was at least one donkey and one person dressed in an ancient peasant's robe. Assuming Frannie would be gearing up for the next performance, or the first performance, or any performance, he headed across the parking lot to the front door.

Once inside, Everett recognized no one and no one recognized him. Those that did make eye contact, simply flashed him a welcoming smile and went about their business. Not wishing to be the cause of any distraction for Frannie, he would refrain from actively seeking her out and quickly find a spot in the auditorium/sanctuary where he would become as inconspicuous as possible. As it turned out, stealth was completely unnecessary due to the fact that there was no evidence to suggest that there ever was, or would be anytime soon, a musical event in this place. The stage was decked out to mimic first century Jerusalem, but the only musical instrument in sight was a baby grand piano, covered and pushed off to the side of the room. Just when he thought there might be more than one Fellowship Bible Church in town, he recognized Alex walking across the stage with a cordless drill in his hand. He was being followed by two young boys and a shaggy dog with a yellow tennis ball in his mouth.

It only took a matter of seconds for Everett to reach the stage.

"Hey, Alex," Everett called out over the familiar sound of heavy objects being dragged across a stage.

"Everett?" Alex replied as if Everett was the last person he would expect to see standing before him.

But, then again, not that unexpected.

"Hi, Mister Everett. My name is Jake and this is my brother, Joey," Jake interjected.

"Hi, Mister Everett. This is Lucky. He's our dog," Joey added.

"We're helping Mr. Alex build stuff," Jake stated proudly and showed Everett the box of screws he was carrying.

Joey showed his involvement by extending the tape measure and pencil he held in his hands. Lucky took the opportunity to drop the ball he was carrying in hopes that the new guy would throw it. No one ever threw the ball for him inside, but this was a new guy. Perhaps, no one explained the rules to him. When Everett did not react the way Lucky had hoped, he gladly scooped the ball back into his mouth. Hey, it was worth a try.

"Hi guys," Everett replied with a smile. "Nice job so far."

"Do me a favor," Alex said while turning the drill over to Jake. "Put these back in the tool box where we found them and come back here. We have one more project before next service. Don't run with tools, we have plenty of time, OK?

"Sure!" they both responded excitedly.

"Bye, Mister Everett. It was nice meeting you," Jake said jovially.

"Yeah, bye, Mister Everett, see you later," Joey added.

"See ya," Everett replied cheerfully.

"Professor Lewis' boys," Alex stated, now knowing that Everett's mother was also a professor. "He teaches English. You might have met him on campus."

"I've read some of his poetry," Everett replied and pressed on before the kids came back. "Want to guess why I'm here?"

"We don't need a bass player, so I'm guessing it has something to do with Frannie," Alex answered as if he expected Everett to have shown up sooner.

"I really only wanted to hear her sing... really," Everett lied in a way that, if you knew anything about him, you would immediately know it was a lie. He never found it easy to lie.

"Really?" Alex replied in a way that suggested if he doesn't hear the truth, and soon, he had a hundred better things to do with his time.

"Alright, I made a mistake," Everett confessed. "Look... I'm not Wiccan. I'm not anything. I put that out there because that is what people expect me to say. It shuts them up quicker, so I can get back to the things I enjoy quicker. I should not have said that to Frannie. That's the truth."

"She isn't here," Alex replied, feeling a little more comfortable with being told the truth.

Having already got the feeling these two were destined to meet again anyway, he continued.

"The choir will usually go out to other locations before the big event here at home. They like to go to the smaller churches and the older churches and sometimes the public places will let them sing. Not everyone from the cantata goes out on these side trips, just some singers and Miss Jillian, the pastor's wife, on the piano. The little churches love hearing them sing... everyone loves hearing them sing."

"Does 'everyone' include me?" Everett asked politely.

"Sorry man. I'm pretty sure you missed their performances for today," Alex stated with some empathy.

Seeing the effects of dashed hopes on Everett's face, he decided to throw this poor dog a bone.

"I'm pretty sure that most of them will come back here after their performance if you decide to stay... including Frannie.

Everyone seemed to be adjusting nicely to their new situation. The four kittens were three, maybe four, days old and living inside the townhouse now. Their eyes were open, but actual vision was spotty, so they would roam the room until they hit something that would stop all forward progress. Not seeing the wall or counter in front of them, they would stay there making a fuss until mom cat, Fang or Debbie turned them around. Mom cat made it very clear that she was no feral cat. In fact, how she managed to survive outdoors for any length of time was anyone's guess because she had little, to no, survival instinct. Capturing her inside the garage was as easy as lowering the garage door the final foot as she was napping and nursing her kittens inside the trunk of the car. Capturing her inside the townhouse was as easy as moving the kittens inside, then closing the door leading from the garage into the townhouse while she napped and nursed her kittens in the kitchen. She also seemed to appreciate Fang's willingness to help out a tired single mom by keeping the young ones occupied after feeding time. Debbie was also struck by the loving attention Fang was giving to the kittens and her acceptance, albeit a rather tepid acceptance, of mom cat.

"You know, maybe we should give mom cat a name," Debbie asked whimsically. "Let her know we care."

Fang responded with a series of utterances that might have equated to naming her something like "empty-head."

"Be nice," Debbie quipped in a manner that may not have disagreed with the choice of names.

It should be noted that Debbie took them all in to see the vet the day after they were found. Once it was determined that all were healthy a follow up visit for shots was scheduled.

It was a beautiful Palm Sunday. The rain was gone – thank goodness - and a warm, soft breeze delivered the most wonderful array of fragrances depending on which patch of flora it had recently passed over. The plan had been to head out to the cabin after church and stay there for a few days... or the entire week. Once there, the decision to stay or leave was to be made entirely on a day-to-day basis, since neither professor encountered any resistance from their students or faculty by going remote for Holy Week. The question of where they would be worshipping for Easter was also a non-issue. It was the same church they were both baptized in and located just about as far away from the town of Hillary as it was from the cabin in the woods.

That was the plan. It was the plan before Debbie's five feline houseguests arrived. It was agreed by all that the kittens were too young to be left alone for days at a time or to travel such long distances. So, the new plan was for Debbie and Hitch to go to the early service, drive back to Hillary (instead of the cabin), check on mom cat and the kittens, pick up Fang and Wallace and then spend the remainder of the afternoon hiking back out to their new favorite scenic overlook on university property. Unfortunately, this trek had been planned and cancelled twice (for good reasons), but now the tables have turned. It may have been unfortunate that their planned visit to the cabin had to be cancelled (for a good reason), but that only opened up this opportunity for a nice day-hike.

These long periods of time spent away from the university have not gone unnoticed by many on campus. It has become a paradox even. The daily walks, the long hikes, the dancing, the cabin, the church have all gobbled up tons of time. Time that Debbie and Hitch would have thought impossible to make available only a year ago. And yet, here they are - both happier and more fulfilled at work than they have ever been. Of course, much of the recaptured hours came as a result of Debbie stepping down as chairperson for Hillary's history department and all her arbitrary social justice commitments. For Hitch, it was stepping away from all the media appearances and limiting the speaking tours to locations that only Ms. Brown had any interest in going – preferably with a warm, sunny beach nearby. The most unexpected consequence of making themselves scarce on campus, however, was the reaction of their critics. These people seemed to have become even more upset at them for finding true happiness outside the university's "I-must-be-offended-by-everything" bubble.

Oh, well. No pleasing everyone.

Like clockwork, they were on the trail by noon and made the 2.5 mile half way mark to the rocky summit in a little over an hour. They passed no one along the way and the large, accommodating rock that looked out over the university's expansive countryside seemed untouched since their last visit. Whereas, they would fill a small bag or two of litter on their daily walks on campus, they had not yet come across one empty plastic water bottle or carelessly disposed granola bar wrapper on this trail. After setting up the comfy chairs and donning the fuzzy slippers, they started their peaceful escape by coming up with an appropriate name for this little slice of heaven. There was no name on any map for this trail or the rock formation at its half way point, therefore, in effect, the name was up for grabs. At the top of that list of names was, "Bethphage" (Hebrew: meaning "house of unripe figs"). It was the small village on top of the Mount of Olives where Jesus began his triumphal entry into Jerusalem on Palm Sunday. Also making the list was, "Gethsemane" (Hebrew: meaning "oil press"). It was the olive garden on the lower slopes of the Mount of Olives where Jesus prayed "Abba, Father,... take this cup from me..." and where he would be betrayed by Judas. Honorable mentions included some of the old favorites, like "Lover's Leap" and "Billy Goat" trail.

They would eventually settle on "Urquhart" (pronounced: ur-kert). This name was based on Urquhart Castle (Scottish Gaelic: Caisteal na Sròine) and a stone's throw from where Debbie's mom grew up in Drumnadrochit, Scotland. The popular ruins of that once fortified medieval residence, turned medieval fortress, sits on a rocky promontory with a commanding view along the Loch Ness. It was said that St. Columba (521–597 AD), a Catholic Saint and one of the "Twelve Apostles of Ireland," visited this residence sometime around the year 580 AD. At that time, the castle was owned and occupied by an elderly "Pict" nobleman (people who lived in what is now northern and eastern Scotland). His name was Emchath. The highly regarded missionary was credited with converting Emchath and his entire household to Christianity. Debbie related a few more heartwarming stories about her mom and how she would play and dance among these ruins as a child.

"This spot shall forever be remembered as Urquhart, then," Hitch agreed upon hearing these endearing tales about life along the Lock Ness. "Have you seen the dogs?"

"Fang said something about a visit and not to worry," Debbie replied calmly.

"She said that?" Hitch asked automatically.

He was quite used to asking the question and receiving the obligatory response of...

"She did," Debbie responded on cue.

Wallace and Fang knew the way back to Miss Rosie's farmhouse and wasted no time heading in that direction. They were met by the same goat and at the same trail inter-section as the first time they all met - only this time, they were all generally happy to see each other. Just as before, the goat took off running with Wallace in hot pursuit. Fang followed in less dramatic fashion.

Once Wallace had reached the farm yard, he was imme-diately surrounded by a half-dozen baby goats that hopped and danced excitedly around the big, yellow "bobcat-slayer" that saved their friend. The jubilation quickly transformed into a "bump and run" game, whereby, the kids would try to headbutt Wallace and then run away. Wallace would either, allow this to happen and then give chase, or he would leap over the attacker at the last second – causing the baby goat to headbutt nothing but air - and then give chase. In either case, Wallace and the kids got their fair share of chasing and being chased.

"There you are," came a man's voice from inside the farmhouse. "I do believe my Rosie said something about the two of you showing up today."

Again, as it was with Miss Rosie, Wallace and Fang understood every word being spoken and looked in the direction from where the new voice came. After a brief pause, the man spoke again. This time his comment was intended for the baby goats.

"Children, you done showed enough appreciation for one day, so please find something else to do and leave poor Wallace and Fang be. Go on, now."

When Wallace and Fang returned to the farmhouse after the altercation with the bobcat, Miss Rosie thanked them both for their heroic deeds. They were both given a quick, but thorough, physical examination to be sure they were not seriously harmed. They were also given as many freshly baked biscuits – like large, crunchy animal crackers – as they wanted. There was no request for details about the incident and Miss Rosie shared no other details about herself... or anyone else. After a long, refreshing rest lying in the soft grass under the warm afternoon sun, she suggested it was time they return to their human parents. That was the full account of their last visit here.

Presently, the kids scattered as they were told and Wallace and Fang walked up to the porch unhindered – at which point, Fang released a lively bark of greeting.

"Yes, yes, yes, I'm coming. Just as soon...," the man in the house said politely, but not quite finishing that thought. "Oh, boy."

A second or two later, out of the house popped a tall, handsome, middle-aged black man wearing a ladies kitchen apron over his blue jean pants and shirt. On both hands he wore oven mitts. In one hand he held a large sheet pan that left a trail of smoke behind it. Whatever it was that he was carrying, it had obviously been in the oven way too long.

"Hello there. You can call me, Samuel, if you like and only by God's grace did my darling Rosie agree to marry me ... a long, long time ago," he began his touching introduction as being Rosie's husband. "Soooo, I heard all about you two."

He glanced down at the smoking sheet pan with a hint of embarrassment, scratched his head (with oven mitt on) and continued.

"I was asked to make some more of them biscuits you liked so much, but, dang if I ever was much good at cooking."

Wallace was clearly disappointed, but more than willing to sample the biscuits anyway. Fang sensed there was something else that needed to be said and barked her curiosity.

"Of course, of course, right you are, Miss Fang. I was supposed to tell you something," Samuel replied forthrightly. "Right after the biscuits I was to... tell... you... that ..."

The tempo of Samuel's words slowed and his voice drifted off as he desperately tried to recall the message that was entrusted to him to tell. He set the hot, smokey tray on the porch swing to cool and walked down the porch steps. Upon reaching the bottom step, he looked to his right and then to his left.

"Let's see now. Rosie and Tilly went that way to handle some kind of mess going on," Samuel stated definitively and pointed to his left (with oven mitt on). "Tilly girl is her horse. A mighty fine horse she is too."

"And you two were to go that way," Samuel stated just as definitively and pointed to his right (with oven mitt on). "Because Rosie thought you were better able to handle the mess up that way... just can't remember exactly what kind of mess it was. It was a tricky one, I can tell you that. Not too clear on the specifics though. Too many messes out here in the forest for Rosie and me to handle all by ourselves. Thank goodness you two came along when you did because..."

Fang stopped listening at this point. These ruminations of Samuel's were taking longer than they had time for, so she turned to ask Wallace his thoughts on heading out on their own... except he wasn't there. A quick scan of the front yard produced nothing but goats and chickens. It wasn't until she turned her attention back towards the porch that she saw movement beyond Samuel's tall, slender body. There, parked in front of the porch bench, sat Wallace happily chowing down on burnt biscuits.

"Go, now!" she barked impatiently and began walking in the general direction that Samuel pointed.

This declaration stopped Samuel from talking mid-sentence and Wallace from chomping mid-biscuit.

"Yes, yes, my apologies for rambling on so," Samuel stated. "I'm sure Rosie would not have placed this burden on you if she didn't think you were up to it, so off you go."

Wallace caught up to Fang easily and carefully set a burnt biscuit on the ground a foot or two in front of her which caused her to stop. She took one look at the charred, dried-out biscuit and sighed. Then she looked up to see Wallace's cheerful face smiling at her. She smiled back. Even though his head was big and blocky, with ears that flopped down at the side, he was the most ruggedly handsome guy she ever knew. He was her "knight in yellow armor" and she would do anything for him - even eat a tasteless charcoal briquette... which she did.

"Go, now!" Wallace barked happily and took the lead.

They did not go far, or so it seemed, when the skies darkened somewhat and a warm, moist wind began to pick up. The wind bent the fields of grass in waves - like that of an ocean, and filled the leaves of a tree - like the sails on a boat. This analogy was not by accident because as they looked ahead, a dense fog rolled in over the open field and the solid ground beneath their feet turned to a granular sand. From somewhere in the mist there came a raspy old voice.

"If it's treasure ye be after, ye won't be find'n it 'ere. This be the 'Port of Demise.' We don't give back anything 'ere. We be keep'n it all."

Soon after the ominous verbal warning was given there came, from out of the mist, a longboat - along with the water it floated in on. Both the sea and the boat came to a halt several yards from where Wallace and Fang stood on the beach.

Standing with one foot inside the boat and one foot on its bow, was a very large, burly man with a thick, dark beard. Atop his head he wore a wide-brimmed hat over a red head scarf. At his waist he wore a wide sash belt with cutlass on one side and flintlock pistol on the other. On his feet he wore tall black cavalier boots. In other words, Wallace and Fang met their first ghost pirate.

For as big as he was, the pirate easily leaped the distance from the boat to a mark even with Wallace and Fang. But, then again, he was a ghost and evidently gravity made little difference to them. Once he nailed his dismount, the fog dissipated exposing a harbor large enough to accommodate the pirate's massive four masted, 74-cannon Man-O-War; a three masted, 12-cannon Cromster and a single masted, 4-cannon sloop built for speed – all flying the infamous Jolly Roger. Regardless of what realm you find yourself in (living or non-living), if the size of a man's fleet was any indication of a man's success, this ghost was at the top of his game.

"The name be Captain Goodfellow. How's that fer irony?" the hulking pirate spoke again in a crotchety hoarseness that pirates are known for. "Never did like that name. Ye can call me Captain G and I own all o' them ships, this 'ere port, this 'ere island… and ye too!"

This blustery introduction did not sit well with Fang, but she accepted the pirate's candor. After introducing herself as a simple "peacemaker," she politely explained to the ghost captain that his ships, his port and his island were having a negative impact on the "real world" property, or at least, the "enchanted forest" property and that they must leave... forever.

"Well, lassie, I never was good at be'n the one to bear bad news, but it appears ye be the one do'n the trespass'n," Captain G replied with a crocodile smile. "If I was in yer position... and I'm not ye... but, if I was ye... I'd be a wee bit more concerned about how to get off me property – not the other way round."

Looking around and seeing nothing but ocean and sand, this last point made a lot of sense to Wallace. After introducing himself as a simple dog that likes to eat and chase stuff, he politely asked the ghost captain in what direction was the exit and they would be out of his life... forever.

"I supposed ye be want'n to leave this nice place – like all the others." The not-so-good-fellow Captain snarled. "Well, ye can't. Not only that, ye and yer charm'n bonnie lass will be eat'n hardtack and swab'n the poop deck of that ship out thar soon enough."

By this time, the beach had filled up with every kind of pirate. They included pirates by choice and pirates that were given no other option. There were men pirates, women pirates, child pirates, bear pirates, fox pirates, squirrel pirates, fieldmouse pirates... if they ended up in the "Port of Demise" somehow... they became Captain G's captive pirates.

"Take'm away!" Captain G yelled.

"The Code!" Wallace barked loudly.

This outburst caused everyone to stop what they were doing. Wallace was not exactly sure why he yelled that particular word, except that he knew everyone had a code of conduct they lived by. His human dad had a code, dogs had a code, his squirrel friends had a code and maybe there was a code that even pirates must abide by. If so, hopefully, somewhere in that code was their way off this island.

"What about the Code, lad?" Captain G muttered in annoyance.

"The Code, the Code, the Code," the crowd began to chant.

"I heard him... shut yer filthy bilge-rat yaps!" Captain G hollered to the crowd.

"No offense intended," he stated remorsefully to the bilge-rat pirate in the crowd.

"None take'n, sir," the bilge-rat replied.

"Yea, we have a Code," Captain G grumbled. "Ye are, no doubt, refer'n to article two, section four, clause six that let's ye go free... on one condition. Ye must beat me at any contest I be choose'n."

Let it be food, let it be food, let it be food, Wallace wished with all his might it would be an eating contest.

"We win. We go home. You go away?" Fang barked above the cheers of the crowd.

The crowd was not cheering for Wallace and Fang necessarily. They knew these two would lose to Captain G – just like everyone else in the Port of Demise lost to him. They were cheering mainly because they were all pirates now and pirates love their games and every game was a betting game. It gave them something to do with all their ill-gotten loot. Everyone knew the answer to Fang's question as well. The Code was clear enough: "The Captain can do anything he or she wants to do that isn't specifically restricted elsewhere in the Code." And, there was nothing in the Code that said you couldn't abdicate the position of Captain once you have earned it... or go back to the world of the living whenever you wanted... or take with you whoever wanted to go. Captain G won his position fair and square and, for the most part, his fellow ghost sailors liked him. He was rough on the outside, but he was always fair, almost kind - for a pirate.

"Little lass, if ye were to beat me, then, I suppose, the Port of Demise and all them ships would have a new captain," Captain G explained cordially. "But I don't feel like retire'n anytime soon, if ye don't mind. So, I be choose'n muskets at twenty paces."

These contests never involved killing your opponent – that would be against the Code. Besides, a dead ghost was not much good at looting or swabbing. Therefore, the use of firearms to settle matters such as these, were always held at the local PRA (Pirate Rifle Association) approved shooting range. Since this was a reoccurring event and news travels fast on the island, the tables were already prepared when the contestants and the crowd arrived. Two loaded pistols (aimed safely down-range) were placed upon Wallace and Fang's table. Each would be given an opportunity to win their freedom. Large targets were set at 20 paces. The rules were simple: on the count of three, pick up your pistol, aim and shoot. First to hit the bull's eye wins.

Wallace and Fang looked at the pistols on the table and then to each other. How, exactly, were they supposed to lift a gun, aim it and pull a trigger?

"I know what ye be think'n," Captain G bellowed and looked directly at Wallace. "But, a pie-eating contest wouldn't be all that fair to me now, would it?"

Wallace responded to the accusation with an aggrieved "ro, ro, ro" followed by a subtle moan.

"Thank ye all for come'n out 'ere today," Captain G began the festivity. "Remember, we still got a pot-luck set for tonight, so bring out yer favorite dishes. Without further ado, place yer bets and may the best man... or dog... win."

"Ladies first," he added courteously while looking at Fang. "It's really not that bad 'ere. Ye get used to it."

Fang leaped up on the table as the range master began the countdown. When the count reached three, Captain G calmly raised his non-shooting arm up to cover his eyes – as if this gesture made things fair – and blindly picked his pistol up off the table. He gave the weapon a clockwise turn in his hand and back again to check the balance, pointed it at the target and slowly squeezed the trigger. What Captain G did not know was, after he blinded himself with his arm, he also lost sight of Wallace – who leaped in front of the Captain's target just as he pulled the trigger. This produced an immediate collective gasp of horror from the crowd.

"What be this?" Captain G shouted as he dropped his arm from his face and saw Wallace's motionless body at the foot of his target.

"No, my love!" Fang cried out in agony and rushed to Wallace's side.

"Ye killed him," someone called out.

"I meant him no harm," the Captain answered sorrowfully and rushed to Wallace's side.

"T'was an accident, Captain," another called out.

"He threw himself in front of yer shot, Captain. I saw it," another called out.

"Quiet, all ye!" Captain G yelled out furiously as he checked the body for any sign of life.

"No die, my love. No leave me," Fang spoke in breathless whispers as she paced back and forth not knowing what else to do.

"Tragedy it is, sir, but yer not to be blamed for this," another called out.

"Quiet, I say!" Captain G repeated himself angrily.

Not a sound could be heard after that... except for Fang's pleading whispers. Now knowing his fate, the Captain rose and turned towards the stunned crowd. The air around him darkened, his features had turned an ashen grey and he grew twice his normal size. He spoke only once in this condition and his words shook the ground.

"The Code be clear. There be no kill'n!"

He turned himself around and now faced Fang. The air cleared and his physical attributes returned to normal as he spoke to her in gentle tones.

"Fang, the Code be clear and I will abide by it. Kill'n, no matter how it be done, be against the Code. I killed Wallace and I be forever sorry for that. His death, while I be in contest with ye, makes ye Captain now. Give me yer order and I will see that it gets done."

This proclamation drew many protests from those close by, but Captain G paid no attention to their arguments.

"Fang, be our Captain now and I won't be repeat'n me self," Captain G addressed the anxious crowd. "Anyone who be oppose'n her will be join'n the rest of the scallywag mutineers in Davy Jones Locker before nightfall."

It took every ounce of energy for Fang to end her vigil over Wallace's body, but she was still in too much pain and sorrow to speak. She did not hate this man kneeling in front of her. She just wanted her sweet, lovable Wallace back. Salty tears kept her eyes from seeing clearly and she began to tremble involuntarily, but she was able to make out these soft-spoken words being whispered in her ear.

"Fang, if ye be want'n to go home with Wallace and fer the Port of Demise to leave this forest forever... say 'aye.'"

"Aye"

Chapter 9

Palm Sunday – Part II

The next moment, Fang and Wallace were standing in the same grassy spot they were standing just before the fog rolled in. Wallace showed no signs of being shot, although he had zero recollection of the events that occurred after the count of three. They were surrounded by a small group of other animals that were also captured against their will. The spell was over. The pirates were gone. They were all back home.

"Fang so angry!" Fang barked as she and Wallace danced excitedly around each other.

Fang could never stay angry at Wallace for long. The dancing and sheer joy of being together did not stop until they were back on the rock formation with their human parents. Once again, time had stood still. That is, Debbie and Hitch had just named the rock "Urquhart" and Hitch asked about the dog's whereabouts. They were about to conclude an earlier discussion they were having on the trail about mom cat and her kittens, when the two panting soulmates tumbled their way back onto the scene. After a short cooling down period and a few dog treats, Debbie received a dog's perspective of the pirate adventure in dog utterances from Fang.

"Amazing!" was all Debbie could think to say.

For obvious reasons, a dog's perspective in dog utterances would have to be communicated in inexact, low resolution, conceptually abstract terms. For example, Debbie understood that these two visited the same place as last time. It was a good place and a peaceful place. The person that greeted them was a man - not the woman. He was a good man and good husband to the good woman. In addition to the good man, there was another large man. He was both real and not real, bad and good, was here and is now gone. In other words, there was no exact translation in dog parlance for a ghost pirate. This strange man did something to hurt Wallace badly, but was sorry for what he had done. In the end, he would bring Wallace back to health... or life(?). There were other shadowy terms being mentioned by Fang; like floating houses (ships) on water that extended as far as the eye can see (oceans) in every direction (islands) and animals speaking words like a human. Debbie got the gist.

As always, Hitch took the information in stride. These highly improbable events did, however, raise some serious questions. But what was he to do? Wallace did nothing to suggest what was being relayed from Fang to Debbie was a lie. The veracity of these fanciful stories has been proven over and over again. And, other than his natural instinct for things to make perfect sense, what difference does it make whether or not there is a nice family living in a farm house located deep in the woods on university property? Trespassing laws may apply, but he was most certainly not going to mention any of these events to Charlie. That would only bring university attention and university people to their serene getaway spot. As long as everyone returned safely, he felt no inclination or obligation to go traipsing through unchartered forest to find anything... or nothing.

And why did Fang get to do all the talking? he thought. *Why should we not be asking to hear Wallace's side of these stories?*

Hitch knew these were not questions that a rational mind should be thinking - much less asking out loud. However, in light of this most recent experience, and the last experience, and the experience before that, perhaps it was time to explore the possibility that he and Wallace could communicate more effectively. Perhaps, it was time to speak "outside the box"... so to speak. After taking some time to conclude that mom cat and the kittens will be staying indoors at Debbie's place for at least six weeks, Hitch turned to face Debbie.

"Sùilean Soilleir, would the ability to understand Wallace the way you understand Fang be something that is teachable?" he asked in all sincerity.

This line of questioning was not on any list for discussion today and it temporarily threw Debbie for a loop. It was not as if she had not tried to understand Wallace herself. She did try. Wallace was sweet, gentle, lovable... even thoughtful. These were all the things you look for in a pet ... or a friend. But it was plain as day that Wallace preferred to work things out physically - rather than mentally. He was an "action figure" – not a smooth talker. If she had to guess, Hitch would have his work cut out for him with the end result being very short conversations.

"Mo luaidh (Scottish Gaelic meaning "my darling"), I really don't think Fang, or I, planned this thing we have. The understanding part sort of happened at a time when we both just wanted someone to listen to us. There were no attempts to try to teach the other," Debbie stated in an attempt to explain the unexplainable. "Mostly, it took a lot of patience... from both of us."

This was the best advice she could offer at the present time. Well, maybe one more thing.

"Oh, and Wallace has got to want to say something."

Hitch loved how Debbie started referring to him as "mo luaidh," or its English equivalent, "my darling" this past Valentine's Day. The day was a lover's holiday he once looked upon as inhibiting a person's maturity and only the foolish would celebrate it. Having now been on the receiving end of endearing names and included in these silly nonsensical holidays, he had come to appreciate how important they can be for a relationship to flourish. Therefore, Valentine cards, chocolates and flowers were added to Christmas cards, gifts and tree ornaments as pleasurable items that had eluded him for far too long. He took Debbie's hand in his and contemplated her words of advice.

"Can I try?" he asked Debbie in a manner that suggested she was free to offer any helpful tips along the way.

"Of course," she replied. "I'll be right here."

This should be fun, she thought.

"Wallace come over here, buddy," Hitch called out.

Wallace dropped the stick he was gnawing to pieces and walked happily over to where his human dad sat. Hitch brushed the small bits of clinging bark from Wallace's face and gave him a good strong hug to set the mood.

"Wallace, you and I have been together for quite a while now and I believe it's time we had a talk. A 'father-to-his-son' talk, if you will," Hitch began warmly and glanced at Debbie for the approval of a good start. "So, to begin, then, I would like for you to know that I love you very much and I am truly grateful for your companionship."

There was so much more to be said, but Hitch thought it best to keep things simple for now. One concept at a time. He continued.

"Is there anything you would like to say?"

Wallace barked once and sat down.

"Did you catch that?" Hitch asked Debbie enthusiastically.

"Yup, yup, I sure did," Debbie replied with an encouraging smile, but did not elaborate.

After a long moment of silence, Hitch spoke again.

"Is there anything you would like to add to that?" he asked Wallace patiently.

Wallace barked once and put a paw on Hitch's knee. The bark sounded identical to the first bark.

"Yes, I got that part and thank you," Hitch acknowledging the second bark. "Was there anything else you would like to say to me?"

Wallace barked once more and laid down. Hitch bent over and patted Wallace on the side.

"You are a good boy," he stated lovingly and then turned to Debbie. "I thought that went well. What do you think?"

"That was... a good start, my darling," she addressed his optimism with the utmost compassion. "It may even be helpful if you were to ask closed-ended questions for a 'yes' or 'no' response. At least in the beginning. You know, give Wallace time to build up his vocabulary."

"Great point," he agreed excitedly.

Everett decided to wait for Frannie inside FBC, which would involve sitting through their Palm Sunday service. He could have waited comfortably outside in his truck, but he thought that might give Frannie the wrong signal - like he was accepting of her, but not her faith or her church. He had already blown Frannie's first impression of him. He was not going to let this opportunity slip away. In fact, when Everett mentioned this decision to stay to Alex, he was immediately invited to sit with him. He had only been in a Christian church once before and that was a long time ago, so the invitation was greatly appreciated and accepted.

It just so happened that the seating arrangements meant he would be sitting with Professor Lewis (Jack) and his two boys - Jake and Joey. The professor's wife, MJ, would not be joining them until later because she was out singing with Frannie, Jillian (the pastor's wife) and the choir. It was early and Alex rarely ever gets the chance to sit down prior to a service because of some emergency. Today was no exception. That left Everett, Jack and the boys sitting together for a while. The two grown-ups talked a little about Jack's poetry and Everett's music. This naturally led to a conversation about collaborating on a song or two sometime in the near future. Given the huge divide in religious beliefs and the subtle differences between the millennial (Jack) and the Gen Z (Everett) generational concerns, that idea might have sounded untenable. The particulars were just about to get interesting when Jack was called away himself. That left Everett and the boys to hold down the seats.

"Mister Everett, if you know Mister Alex you must be really cool," Jake stated as a matter of fact.

"Yeah, because Mister Alex is super, really cool," Joey added.

"I don't know if I will ever be that cool," Everett replied unselfishly. "And you guys can call me just plain Everett if you want."

"We can't," Joey grumbled.

"Oh... why not?" Everett asked politely.

"That's what mom and dad say we have to call old people," Jake answered respectfully. "Do you know Miss Frannie too."

"I guess I know her a little bit," Everett replied discreetly while getting a chuckle from being labeled old.

"They are always together," Joey added. "We thought they were brothers and sisters."

"We thought they were married too," Jake asserted and started giggling - which caused Joey to start giggling. "But mom says they are just friends."

"Frannie sings here, right?" Everett inquired as a nice way to make small-talk.

"Yup, she's got a pretty voice too," Joey added.

"Mom and Miss Frannie sing together," Jake declared. "You should come back next week when they sing here."

"Yeah, that's Easter," Joey added.

"Ooo, I already have something planned, but thanks for asking," Everett answered gratefully. "So, if Easter is next week, what are all those decorations on stage for?"

"This is Palm Sunday," Jake began.

The "decorations" Everett spoke of were actually three separate and distinct theatrical scenes constructed side-by-side. To the audience's left (stage right), there was a floor-to-ceiling backdrop depicting a stone wall with several three dimensional stage props placed in front of it; in the middle (center stage), there was a floor-to-ceiling backdrop depicting an ancient indoor dining room with a large wooden table stage prop in front of it; to the audiences right (stage left), there was a floor-to-ceiling backdrop depicting a barren hilltop with a large wooden cross stage prop in front of it. During the service, stage lights would illuminate one scene at a time – from left (stone wall) to center (empty room) to right (barren hilltop). The actors and actresses would then play out their parts in each scene as Pastor Steve narrated the action.

At this point, Jake and Joey took turns describing the three different scenes on stage as best as a six and eight-year-old could hope to do. From what Everett gathered, the section on the left told the story of Jesus entering Jerusalem on Palm Sunday. There was to be a donkey involved in that one. The section in the middle represented the last supper by Jesus and his disciples. This event would have taken place on the Thursday after Palm Sunday. Everett had a basic understanding of this scene because it was one of the most famous paintings in the world. "The Last Supper" by Leonardo da Vinci (1452 - 1519) was painted sometime between 1494 and 1498. The section on the right represented the crucifixion and burial of Jesus. This event would have taken place on Good Friday.

Everett could not believe how well Jake and Joey knew their Christian lore... at least the days leading up to Easter Sunday.

"How do you guys know all of that?" he asked in amazement.

"Everybody knows that stuff," Jake replied nonchalantly.

"Yeah, and we get to play shepherds for Christmas," Joey added excitedly.

This special performance had already been acted out once – for the first service. That was a packed house and, with ten minutes to go before the second service was to start, the house was packed once more. Unless they had invited guests, it was understood that the regular church attendees would temporarily give up their prime locations in the sanctuary for these kinds of events. This was to allow the newcomers a chance to claim the better view and, hopefully, a better understanding of what Jesus had accomplished here on earth. Therefore, Alex, Everett, Jack and the boys were all seated in the very last row and off to the side now. As a newcomer, Everett was given the option to move forward, but he had graciously declined the offer.

As the service progressed, Everett appreciated what the Professor's boys had shared with him. As elemental as it was, their insight did help to open his mind for what was to come. In fact, he was so engrossed in the story being told on stage that he hardly noticed when Alex got up from his seat. Soon afterwards, however, he could not help but notice a distinct change in the air he was breathing. It quickly turned from an everyday dude's cologne to an intoxicating woman's perfume.

When he looked up, there was Frannie inching her way down the row. She took the empty seat next to him and opened up her Bible.

"What did I miss?" she whispered into Everett's ear.

If asked, Leon would never admit to being a cat person. Until a few weeks ago, two of these capricious little furballs had resided in the same household as he. One of those two having recently passed away. When both were alive, he fed them, he cleaned their litter box, he let them lay in his lap, he would pet them, he gave them treats, he took them to the vet for their annual checkups, but he was not a cat person... crazy or otherwise. Leon would bristle at the notion that owning a cat or two could earn him such an epithet. To such a charge, he would offer the following rebuttal.

"It has been my experience that folks having one or two opinionated stickers attached to the bumpers of their cars have been fairly decent human beings. You know, they tend to exhibit relatively normal social behaviors in group settings. As the bumper stickers meet and exceed the number of three, however, the more delusional the messages become and the more certifiably insane these folk are likely to be," Leon would state as if everyone knew this to be true. "My experience with cat owners has been the same. One or two cats in the same household should be no cause for concern. However, as these furry, self-absorbed freeloaders meet and exceed the number of three, the crazier the cat owner is likely to be."

The only woman he had ever loved was a cat person... and that beautiful woman was now gone. Leon and Ruthie were married for 34 years before the stroke (aka transient ischemic attack), took her from him two years, nine months and eleven days ago. It was the same disease that took one of her two sisters before her. Unchecked heart disease and high blood pressure ran in her family. He thanked God for their time together. Ruthie made him a better person in this life and he took comfort in knowing they will be reunited again when Jesus calls him home.

Leon also thanked God for his two daughters, Billie and Ella. Without them, he could have easily slipped into a much deeper, much longer depression. If truth be told, he would even have to say his two cats played a positive role during this grieving period... but that did not make him a cat person. Leon was happy to see that both his girls were taking their family's history of poor health seriously. They ate right, exercised and monitored the four primary vital signs closely. Those vital signs were body temperature, blood pressure, pulse (heart rate), and breathing rate (respiratory rate). Conspicuously missing from their meal planning was anything fried or high in saturated fat, refined sugar or salt (sodium). In other words, no matter how hungry they were, fast food joints were to be avoided like the plague. They were also aware that pain spreading to the shoulder, neck, or arms was a potential heart attack sign and must never be kept a secret or downplayed.

When Chief offered Leon the Walker Auditorium for his Easter and Christmas Cantatas ten years ago, Palm Sunday became the special day that was set aside for the Bouchard family to relax and spend time together. Ruthie understood how gifted her husband was. She was as grateful for that opportunity as anyone, but she also noticed the enormous toll these two colossal endeavors were taking on her husband – especially the Easter Cantata. Palm Sunday was to be the quiet before the storm. After Ruthie's death, Billie and Ella (both married to strong, Christian men now) were eager to take over all the planning, preparation and presentation for this pre-concert family tradition. Daddy was their hero and momma would have wanted it that way.

After church, Leon was made to feel "King for The Day." He could do what he wanted, when he wanted and he would not be bothered until dinner time - if that was his wish. Most of the cooking was done at Billie and Ella's homes and brought back to the house they grew up in for final preparation. Even though this time together was supposed to be a small, calm, personal affair, it had grown to more than a dozen people. The attendee's included Leon's daughters, their husbands, the grandchildren, an occasional brother, and an occasional sister-in-law. Leon learned over the years that it was best just to stay out of everyone's way until called. And that hiding place was his studio with a 5'1" Bösendorfer baby grand piano, recliner and 65-inch 4K big-screen TV. On occasions such as these, it was the man cave where he could enjoy watching his beloved, 1980 and 2008 World Series Champion, Philadelphia Phillies play until he dozed off.

"Bye, Daddy," Ella stated lovingly as she saw him walking in the direction of the studio with that 'if I can only make it to my chair' look on his face. "See you in a couple hours."

"Love you, Daddy," Billie called out from the kitchen.

It wasn't long after the TV was set to the Phillies (vs. Reds) game and Leon had sunk comfortably into the recliner that he thought he had heard his name being mentioned.

"Ah, good, you're up," the voice from inside the room continued. "We need to talk."

It took a second or two for Leon to regain clarity of mind. He looked around, but the only things capable of making sound were the piano, the TV, and Pumpkin Puss (the family cat). Pumpkin Puss, or Punkin', was named for the dark orange color of her fur. That was two inanimate objects and a cat.

Punkin' was an old cat. Her sibling, Bear, died peacefully in his sleep three weeks ago. Before he passed away, they flipped a cat toy to see who was going to have this conversation with Leon. Bear lost the toss. That made him responsible for this important talk, but he was always a procrastinator. So, it was up to her now.

"Over here," Punkin' stated as she barely managed to leap from the floor, to the piano bench, to the top of the piano, whereupon she sat on the edge closest to Leon. "Oh my, that's getting hard to do nowadays."

As astonished as Leon was, he did not say a word. All the questions he thought to ask had the same conclusion – none of this makes any sense. If he had to guess, he would have to say he was in some sort of dream ... a very realistic dream. The house was quiet, the game on TV was stuck on "pause" without him pausing it and a cat he had known for fifteen years was now talking to him. What else could it be?

"I know this must be weird for you, Mister Leon," she spoke softly as if to conserve the air it took to deliver each word. "You and Miss Ruthie have been very good to Bear and to me, but every bone in my body is hurting me right now. I'm afraid I do not have much time left."

Leon had yet to say a thing, but remained attentive. He could tell it took a great amount of effort for Punkin' to speak as she did. Since it made no sense, why torture the poor apparition by forcing her to answer superfluous questions?

This is what Punkin' and Bear agreed must be said because it was what Miss Ruthie spoke about most often when they were together. Punkin' started by pointing out that people will say the strangest – and most honest – things to their pets.

First and most importantly, Miss Ruthie loved Leon. She told them this all the time. Because of her family medical history, Miss Ruthie knew she was running out of time. So as not to worry Leon, Miss Ruthie would never mention to him any of the mini-strokes she had been experiencing over the years. Miss Ruthie would tell Billie and Ella, but she made them promise not to tell their Daddy.

Secondly, Miss Ruthie was proud of Leon. She told them this all the time. Miss Ruthie knew how many people Leon had introduced to the Lord through his music – especially the cantatas. It never crossed Miss Ruthie's mind to ask Leon to stop this good work. But a large, "selfish" part of her wanted her simple, piano-play'n man back – all to herself. Miss Ruthie would tell her brother-in-law about these feelings, but made him promise not to tell anyone.

Thirdly, Miss Ruthie wanted Leon to be happy. She told them this all the time. Miss Ruthie knew there was a shortage of good men out there. It was Miss Ruthie's opinion that this day and age was producing far too many weak men afraid to stand up and speak out against evil – especially the insidious attacks on the family. Leon was a good, strong man and deserved a good woman. After an appropriate grieving period, Miss Ruthie wanted him to marry again. Miss Ruthie would tell her sister about these feelings, but made her promise not to speak of this until after she was gone.

Finally, on a lighter note, Miss Ruthie loved baseball. She loved the Philadelphia Phillies baseball team and loved listening to Leon call the televised ballgames from his recliner. She told them this all the time. Miss Ruthie would turn down the volume on the tv just so she could hear Leon provide the color commentary for his beloved Phillies. If it were not for music, she thought her husband would have made a brilliant sportscaster. Leon probably did not notice, but Punkin' and Bear would curl up next to Miss Ruthie on the couch and watch every Phillies game with them. When the Phillies games were on, Miss Ruthie considered it "family night" at the Bouchard's.

When Punkin' had finished talking, she slowly laid herself down. Normally, the cats were not permitted on the piano, but she had no strength left to climb back down. With tears in his eyes, Leon walked over to the frail and faithful pet and stroked her thin, soft body gently.

"Thank you, Punkin," Leon spoke tenderly. "Can I help you down or would you like to stay up here?"

"Down, please," were the last words she would ever speak to him again.

One by one, throughout the day, Leon would have an opportunity to speak with both his daughters, his sister-in-law and his brother about these secret conversations with his wife. One by one, the secrets were reluctantly - and tearfully - confirmed. These were very serious matters of the heart and he would have preferred knowing about them while his beloved wife was still alive. Then again, would he have listened to her with as much compassion back then as he did with their cat today?

Neither did Leon hold anything against his loved ones for not speaking up. They were made to promise to hold something very personal in confidence and they kept their word. Neither did he think twice about staying put while listening to his elderly cat speak about his beloved wife. His only desire going forward was to love on his family like never before... and that included Punkin' Puss.

That "surprise" encounter between Everett and Frannie in the sanctuary of FBC was, in actuality, all pre-planned. As soon as Everett let it be known he was going to stay in church and wait for Frannie, Alex texted her. When quizzed by Frannie, that was all Alex would say on the matter. He knew if he were to say too much, he would get in trouble later. He also knew that if he were to say too little, he would get in trouble later. Either way, he would get in trouble later. History has proven that saying too little produced the least amount of trouble later.

After the service, Frannie and Everett remained seated and talked. Oddly enough, the first thing that Everett wanted to know was Frannie's thoughts on the three different scenes on stage. He seemed genuinely interested and sincere. She wished she knew more than what he already seemed to know.

Frannie admitted to being new to the Christian faith and that some of the biblical references in today's performance were still a bit fuzzy. What she did know – with every fiber in her body - was that God is good. He was never not good and she was living proof of that. Instead of leaving things unresolved, however, they agreed to list a number of questions that both had in common and, together, they would seek the answers. More importantly, they would seek the truth.

Every so often, someone would recognize Frannie sitting with someone - who was not Alex - and swing by to say hi. The list of after-service visitors included MJ, Jillian, Pamela, Mickey and half the women in the choir. These introductions were all rather short and sweet, except for Pamela and Mickey.

"Hi, my name is Pamela," she said unreservedly and for-mally offered her hand for Everett to shake. "And this is Mickey, my best friend. We sing with Frannie. Well, I sing and Mickey plays the piano and..."

"It's nice to meet you, Pamela," Everett replied the first chance he got and they shook hands. "And you too, Mickey."

Mickey smile generously, but before she could formulate a response, Pamela turned to Frannie and spoke... again... unreservedly.

"So, Mickey and I were wondering what it feels like to kiss a guy with a beard."

"Pam!" Mickey screamed in horror. "You didn't have to say it like that."

"How else am I supposed to say it?" Pamela asked as she turned to face Mickey.

"I don't know. Not like that."

"I wouldn't know, Pam," Frannie interjected with a slightly embarrassed grin.

Having had enough of the serious church talk, Frannie felt in the mood for some fun.

"I'm guessing kissing through a beard is like kissing something on the other side of a big, leafy shrub," Frannie added.

"When Daddy doesn't shave his face for a couple days, it's like kissing a hairbrush," Pamela replied with an agreeable laugh. "After he goes out hunting for a week, he comes home looking like a mister porcupine face. Smells like one too."

"It looks like it would tickle my nose," Mickey observed while making her nose twitch side to side. "And besides, who knows what crawls up in there. Good hiding place for bugs if you ask me. I mean, how would you know, right?"

All at once, the three girls grimaced and looked intently at Everett's beard for signs of any teeny-weeny intruders. It had been a while since Everett had been the target for such playful taunts. He discovered early on that the ladies either loved the full beard or hated the full beard. Most loved it, but there were a few that said it was going to be the beard or them – not both. He did end up shaving it off for one special person, but she dumped him anyway. Lesson learned. If nothing else, the beard was the perfect icebreaker. It was kind of like a guy walking a cute puppy.

"You have nothing to worry about because I had it fumigated last week," Everett responded boldly to ease their fears. "I was given a written guarantee saying the termites and leeches will not return for ninety days."

"So, you're saying the termites and leeches are gone, huh?" Frannie asked skeptically.

"That's right," he replied and stroked his beard proudly. "The chemicals caused me to go blind for two days, but I'd say it was worth it."

"I suppose I'm cool with it," Frannie stated and looked to the girls for confirmation. "At least for the next ninety days."

"OK, I think I'm good, too," Pamela agreed happily and glanced Everett's way to be sure he was paying attention to her words of advice. "As long as he keeps it neat and clean."

"I kind of like the short scruffy look better, like Aragorn in The Lord of the Rings," Mickey stated and glanced over at Everett to be sure he was paying attention to what women really liked. "Or Legolas in real life."

"Orlando Bloom," Pamela added for clarification. "But Everett is not your boyfriend, Mickey."

"I know that," Mickey shot back. "I'm just saying, Pamela."

"Fine, have your face all scratched up every time you kiss a guy," Pamela stated calmly.

"Fine, I will, if I want, which I don't, yet," Mickey countered calmly.

"We're just friends," Frannie interjected... again.

With a not-so-stealthy wink in Pamela's direction, she continued.

"Pam, don't you guys have something to do?"

"Got to go," Pamela declared in a way that indicated she understood the meaning of the wink. "It was nice to meet you, Everett."

"Go where?" Mickey asked in a way that indicated she had totally missed the wink.

"Go," Pamela stated with several winks and head movements until Mickey got the hint. "You know, right?"

"Right, got to go," Mickey agreed awkwardly. "Do those things we need to do. It was nice to meet you, Everett."

"It was nice meeting you both," Everett stated pleasantly as the girls slipped away.

"They are both very talented and have a song for the Easter Cantata," Frannie said with a smile. "Can you come next week?"

"Well, there is something you should know," Everett uttered and flashed her a coy smile.

Chapter 10

Say You Love Me

Palm Sunday was the turning point. Prior to that day, Jesus would travel around Galilee and Judea healing people and teaching them to be nicer to one another. Along the way, he would intimate that he was God ("Son of Man") without coming right out and saying it. He would keep saying it was not yet his time (Jn. 7:6). After Palm Sunday, however, there was no going back to the way things were. In other words, his time had come (Jn. 12:23). Every morning after that, Jesus would walk the two miles from Bethany into Jerusalem with his disciples, make his presence known in town and then go back to Bethany for the evening. On Monday morning he was back in town overturning tables at the Jewish Temple and referring to it as a "den of thieves." On Tuesday morning, Jesus was back in Jerusalem, openly challenging the Jewish priests on their understanding of their own scripture and branding them as hypocrites, blind guides, fools, whitewashed tombs and snakes. On Wednesday morning, the Bible is silent on where Jesus spent the day. Given the excitement he created over the past two days, he was most likely praying to the Father to keep his earthly body strong - for he knew

191

what was to come. On Thursday morning, Jesus sends Peter and John into Jerusalem to book the "upper room" where they would all eat the Jewish Passover meal that evening. That last meal would be known forevermore as the "Lord's Supper." Later that same night, Jesus would leave Jerusalem, but instead of going back to Bethany, he would head over to the Garden of Gethsemane. In fact, Jesus would never make it back to Bethany. It was at Gethsemane that he would be betrayed by Judas, arrested and brought back to Jerusalem. On Friday morning, Jesus was standing before Pilate as a condemned man.

He would not leave Jerusalem alive... but his encounter with death was not over.

There comes a time when we all must put up or shut up. A time to show who you really are and what you are really up to. A time to come clean. This week was God's designed plan for coming clean. Not that he had to, but it was his design. It was the way God chose to show his great and unconditional love for us.

In the Gospel of John, Jesus commands us to "love one another, even as I loved you, that you also love one another" (Jn 13:34). After all Jesus has done for us, or, in the case of Holy Week, what he was about to do, how is that kind of love even possible?

In his letter to the Ephesian church, the apostle Paul encourages husbands to "love your wives, just as *Christ also loved the church* and gave himself up for her" (Eph 5:25). Paul uses the same ancient Greek word for "love" as Jesus uses... the word "agape" (pronounced "uh-ga-pay"). When even the best Christian on his, or her, best day is still quite capable of sinning, how is that kind of love for a spouse even possible?

For Hitch, it was time to put up or shut up... he was in love.

Love, and its usage, had been suppressed long enough. Hitch rarely ever used the "L" word. It never seemed to meet, much less exceed, the bar he set for its proper application. He would readily admit to loving his parents, but could not say he truly loved the three women he was once married to. That love, those feelings, were pure "eros" (the ancient Greek god of love and sex). It was sexual, passionate, addictive, fleeting in nature, where the element of lust far exceeded the element of love. Hitch also believed true love had some element of time attached to it. Love should last through "thick and thin" as they say.

It could be said that Hitch loved Wallace, but that kind of "love" was a pet owners' adaptation of the ancient Greek word, "storge" (pronounced "stor-gay"). It was a love that a parent would have for their child and vice versa. Wallace had found some way to fulfill that natural human condition inside Hitch to be wanted or needed... regardless of how many mud puddles he laid himself down in. Then there was his biological son, Jimi, with whom he shared DNA but hardly knew. Musashi and Sunshine did a fine job of parenting him. The more he and Jimi talked, the more Hitch came to the conclusion that they did a far better job than he would have done. Instead of feeling hurt or jealous, he looked back upon this whole family dynamic with gratitude. And when speaking of extended family, Hitch would have to include Monica (aka Ms. Brown) in that category. Even before Jimi showed up, she had become like a daughter to him.

That leaves Debbie.

Was Hitch capable of loving her like Jesus loved the church?

Holy Week was a normal work week at Hillary University. Both Hitch and Debbie had given fair notice to their students and faculty that classes for the week would be little more than an opportunity for students to catch up on their lessons or earn extra credit. All correspondence deemed essential would be handled remotely. In other words, their students were free to enjoy Easter as they saw fit. The plans to spend Easter at the cabin had been postponed due to the concern for the kittens, but the status of the online class work remained the same. Monica was given the week off to spend Easter with Jimi's family in California. The office phones would remain silenced, but not turned off. All calls coming into the office would still be monitored by Monica from a California beach somewhere. Nothing would reach Hitch's desk unless it was an emergency.

With one thing leading to another, the Monday following Palm Sunday found Hitch and Debbie sitting on the bench in the middle of the Yard in preparation for their morning walk with Wallace and Fang. Mondays like these were the best. It was their chance to reflect on the joys of being together over the weekend and anticipate the joys of working with students during the week. Yes, they discovered joy in both.

This Monday morning, however, would start off a bit more "open" than most mornings... and Hitch would do the opening first.

"Madainn mhath, Sùilean Soilleir."

"Madainn mhath, Mo luaidh."

[Madainn mhath, Scottish Gaelic meaning "Good morning" and pronounced "Ma-ten va"]

"Hey, I want to thank you for sharing your memories of your mom and her life on the Lock Ness yesterday. I know how much you miss her and the naming of the rock 'Urquhart' was absolutely fitting. Perhaps you can take me over there someday," Hitch began in unrushed tones. "I can see it now. It's as clear as that bright blue sky up there. The more I learn about you... the more I learn from you... the more I fall in love with you. You have lived an extraordinary life, Sùilean Soilleir. This world, and those in it, may not have treated you kindly, yet you have overcome all of that. There is so much beauty inside you that..."

"Um, wait!" Debbie interjected suddenly. "Can you repeat that?"

"You have lived an extraordinary life?" Hitch asked.

"No, before that!" Debbie countered.

"You take me to see Scotland someday?" Hitch asked.

"No, after that!" Debbie snapped.

"Oh, that I am madly in love with you?" Hitch asked innocently.

"Yes, that!" Debbie huffed.

"Oh, I haven't mentioned that before now?" Hitch responded with a perplexed look on his face. "I'm sure I must have. It's been on my mind for months now."

"No, I think I would have remembered that conversation," Debbie responded with the same perplexed look on her face. "Yep, I'm positively sure you didn't mention that."

"Well, I sure hope we can remain friends now that you know I'd rather arm wrestle a grizzly than to go on living without you," Hitch continued. He could easily come up with a few more analogies if they were to become necessary.

"You're being serious?" Debbie stated in a way that suggested she wanted it to be true, yet it was a guarded response... fearful, in a way. It brought back memories of those rotten games devious men like to play on women.

"Debbie, I have never been more serious than now," Hitch replied fast and true.

He did not reach out to touch her. He did not add subtext. He did not look away. He simply gave her as much time as she needed to read his face for whatever it is she needed to see.

"Eddie, are you sure about this? she asked both suspiciously and lovingly.

Debbie had come a long way and processed a lot of hurt till now. But she would be lying to herself if she thought their relationship had not progressed beyond mere friendship. She had hoped and prayed for this day to arrive.

"I love you Debra Macaulay Shade. All of you," Hitch assured her. "I just wanted you to know what is on my mind and in my heart."

"But I'm the psychotic radical lesbian, remember?"

"Yes, and I'm the contemptuous non-romantic sociopath, remember?"

"My, aren't we a pair?" Debbie stated rhetorically as she wrapped her arm around his arm tightly and rested her head comfortably on his shoulder.

It was an exceptional day to fall in love. The sky was as blue as Hitch claimed it to be and they had the entire court-yard to themselves. The warm breeze at sea-level kept the cool mountain air at the perfect temperature for warding off the tens of thousands of thoughts that raced across their mind at once. Without lifting her head off Hitch's shoulder, Debbie spoke.

"Now what?"

"I suppose we go for a walk," Hitch stated without moving from his spot.

"Yes, my darling," Debbie agreed without moving from her spot. "In a bit."

Meanwhile, Wallace and Fang spent the first ten min-utes roughhousing in the open field until Stache showed up, whereby, Wallace politely excused himself to give chase. Watching these two play their silly games has become sort of an amusing pastime for Fang. Nothing says entertain-ment quite like two meatheads going at each other hard with nothing ever accomplished or gained. She slowly came to the realization that Wallace was never going to be like her brothers – or her sisters for that matter. And she was fine with that. Fang was not alone in her amusement. The other squirrels were finding Wallace and Stache's rough and tumble antics hard to ignore as well. After a few minutes, however, they would all go about their business as if nothing unusual was happening. But something was happening - at least for Fang.

After Wallace was accidentally shot by Captain G, Fang had to explain to him what had happened because... well, in his deceased condition, Wallace had no recollection of it. What she failed to mention in these eyewitness accounts was her repetitive use of the canine phrase for "my love" as she stood tearfully over Wallace's lifeless body. Those impassioned statements came out of a place within Fang that she never knew existed... until now. The emotion was as strong, if not stronger, as her love for her human mom. But this felt altogether different. It was not long ago that her Belgian herding dog pride had brainwashed her into believing that he needed her more than she needed him. She was obviously the smart one. She was the one that everyone looked to when things needed to get done right the first time. There was nothing she could not do all by herself, except to love someone else more than she loved herself. Wallace's latest selfless and heroic actions only confirmed the suspicions she had already arrived at... she needed him more than he would ever know.

Of course, how would he ever know unless she told him?

That was not going to be as easy as it sounded.

Wallace was a warm and fuzzy kind of guy with a heart of gold. Those qualities were the good stuff and they ranked at the top of Fang's list of things she loved about him. But he was still a guy loaded with all the flaws you come to expect in a guy. Not a brute. He was never a brute. Instead, he rolled as the masculine, but kind-hearted, take-charge kind of guy.

In other words, this made him the good kind of guy - for the most part. For better or worse, whenever Wallace was present, he controlled the circumstances. It could be said that Wallace's penchant to "take the tiger by the tail" has gotten them into more trouble than out of trouble, but Fang has become used to that. In fact, that impetuous "good guy" spirit combined with his "always looking to do the right thing" nature, have slowly moved up a few notches on the list of things she loved.

Fang also knew that Wallace loved her. He showed all the signs of instant infatuation as soon as they met. That affectionate behavior has not subsided, but the way in which they are conveyed have certainly matured a great deal since then. Even still, having a meaningful dialogue about love - with the intention of "settling down" one day - was not something Fang could just blurt out with Wallace. That talk would need to occur in the right place and at the right time in order for any hope of complete comprehension to settle in. Until then, she just needed to keep him from killing himself.

Fang knew in advance that the morning walk would not allow her the time or the environment to say what was on her mind. She was right. Apparently, today was "Mess with Wallace Day" on the University trails and it seemed like every woodland creature got the flyer. As soon as one trail interloper was chased back deep into the woods, another would pop up a little further down the way. This was a clear violation of the "no loitering" rules which state that all well-defined human trails were to be crossed without delay unless, of course, animal children were involved... and bears. Bears, big and small, were given the right-of-way at all times.

Immediately following the walk, it was "Introduce the Kittens to Wallace Day." Fang thought this might finally provide her the quiet time she was hoping for. She was wrong. This would be Wallace's first opportunity to meet mom cat and her kittens. By this time, all their little eyes were wide open and functioning properly. The motor skills in their tiny legs had improved dramatically as well. Since the kittens didn't know a dog from a cat, Wallace instantly became the focus of their insatiable attention. Mom cat could not be happier. This attention would normally be welcomed, but after an exhaustive day of keeping the trails clear, all Wallace really wanted to do was lie down someplace and take a rejuvenating power nap. Unfortunately, not only was it impossible to lie down, it was virtually impossible to take a step without coming close to stepping on a kitten. There were only four of them and yet they were everywhere at once. It took several minutes and several evasive maneuvers before Wallace found an open spot to lie down. He was thankful to be off his feet, but soon afterwards he became nothing more than a big, yellow mountain for the kittens to play on. Eventually, the kittens wore themselves out and, one by one, began to camp out at the base of the big, yellow snoring mountain.

The plan for the day going forward was to split up. Debbie would stay at home, take care of a few school-related issues remotely and then head outside for dance practice with Fang. Hitch would go back to the office in Turner Hall and read until it was time to sign a few papers with his new book publishing company representative, Annastasia. They would all meet back at Debbie's for a quiet dinner. It was a well-planned day full of gainful activity that would culminate in an evening full of solitude and relaxation. This should turn out to be the golden opportunity that Fang was looking for to express her love and devotion to Wallace.

The only glitch in this busy day was the appointment with Annastasia. Hitch was to sign a few documents that would begin the process of publishing another book. That was simple enough. Since Monica was out of town, Hitch's only condition was that Annastasia bring along another associate so that they would not be alone in the office together. When the time had come for the meeting, it was not Annastasia and her associate at the door, but rather, the fellow who had ghosted him. Hitch held no grudge against the man. How could Hitch be offended when he had ghosted this guy countless times over the years? Even Monica felt sorry for the poor man. Therefore, Hitch saw no problem in Annastasia and this charming fellow sharing the wealth on this new book deal... until the big lie.

The outright lie came after their initial greetings and mutual apologies over past transgressions. When asked why Annastasia was not present, the guy began to weave a convoluted story about her leaving the company abruptly and voluntarily. Hitch immediately noticed Wallace pop up from his bedding and begin to grumble and howl. Soon after that, the air within the office became unbearable. Windows were opened, documents were torn in half, and the charming liar was summarily dismissed without much ado.

Like Bobbi Lou before him, Hitch had become somewhat immune to the lingering odor beyond the first malodorous blast. This lie, however, must have been the king of all lies. If you have ever been pepper sprayed directly in the face, you might understand what Hitch was experiencing. Regardless of how ineffective his auto-immune tearing response mechanism was at handling the situation, Hitch walked over to where Wallace was now curled up in a ball and comforted him. These lie-detecting episodes took a lot out of Wallace. It normally took a great deal of fresh air, socialization and snacks for Wallace to return to normal. So, out the door they went with a pocket full of dog biscuits.

Once Hitch was outside and seated on the bench in the Yard, he would text Monica about what was said at the meeting. He impressed upon her the seriousness with which he was taking the matter and asked that she investigate as soon as possible. Not only did he want Annastasia back, but if it was discovered that the publishing company had anything to do with her not attending today's scheduled appointment, he would find another publisher.

The remainder of the day went according to plan and, when they were all back together again that evening, Hitch and Debbie had a few more things to talk about. After a fine meal and playtime with the kittens was over, they all retired to the living room. The lights were turned down low, which enhanced the beautiful crackling orange glow being produced by the artificial logs in gas fireplace. The choice of music was soft and romantic. The collective sighs were irrepressible once all activity ended. Wallace could be oblivious to certain things going on around him, but he knew Fang wanted to talk. She did not come right out and tell him this - he just knew. Unfortunately, it was an extraordinarily rough day for him. Not that it was a great excuse, but he was never given the chance to lie down long enough to recharge and his batteries were nearly spent. He wanted to hear what she had to say. All he needed to do now was to concentrate whatever remaining energy he had left on keeping his head from touching the floor. If that were to happen, it would be lights out.

After sharing each other's stories for the day and seeing Wallace struggle to stay upright, Fang accepted the fact that her man was in no condition to talk. There was always tomorrow. With that in mind, she curled up beside his exhausted body and told him everything was OK. At this point, Wallace slowly allowed his head to fall onto the floor. After a minute or two, and thinking Wallace asleep, Fang spoke again.

"Fang love Wallace"

"Wallace love Fang," Wallace replied as if in a wonderful dream.

Love at first sight. What a wonderful idea... rarely. We have all fallen for it. We have all soared above the clouds when its influence is upon us and then crashed and burned when its influence wears off. Both Everett and Francesca fell for it last Wednesday night in the Walker Auditorium. They gained a little speed yesterday at church and it could be said that they were way beyond the clouds because of it today. It was that euphoric feeling that is never discussed in practical terms. Today's "date" was intended to fill in some of the blanks that two strangers would have when they meet and are instantly attracted to each other. And there were a lot of blanks to fill.

Monday was still a work day for Francesca, so they agreed to purchase their meal at Hillary University's massive, multi-million dollar food court and then meet on one of the many outdoor terraces. Everett had just come from a band recording and photo shoot. It was also considered a work day for him.

"You're wearing black again," Francesca stated as she approached the table where Everett sat while waiting for her to arrive.

This comment was in reference to what he was wearing the first time they had met in the Walker Auditorium.

"Had to. I wore everything I owned that wasn't black to church yesterday," Everett replied jokingly as he stood from the table and waited for Francesca to have a seat.

Didn't expect that, she thought. *How could he not know that thoughtful mannerisms like standing at the table or opening doors were only used by men to oppress women... at Hillary anyway. I like him even more now.*

"I sure wish I could be there to see Professor Bouchard's face when you walk on stage wearing that ensemble," Francesca continued sarcastically.

"I'm sure I can upgrade to something less gothic by then," Everett responded in kind. "Maybe something from the Jonas Brothers' collection."

"Watch what you say, Bass Man," Francesca barked while feigning the regrets of a heart that was broken. "I was in love with Nick once."

"I read you," Everett sympathized and wiped a non-existent tear from his eye. "I was very into Priyanka."

Neither could sustain their charade long and awarded each other's acting skills with a broad smile. For one reason or another, Everett and Francesca's time together in church yesterday lasted only about as long as their time together in the Walker on Wednesday - which is to say - not very long. There was no real expectation in Everett's mind that a longer, more meaningful date would have resulted just by him showing up to hear Francesca sing. But he would be content to learn a little more about her with each brief encounter – if that is what it would take. In fact, it was yesterday that Everett learned Francesca was new to the Christian faith. It was also yesterday that Francesca learned Everett had accepted Leon's offer to sing tenor in the Easter Cantata. Both were extremely and genuinely happy for the other. Not only that, but yesterday's meeting provided them with some positive ideas to build on today - besides Gen Z 's favorite dating topics like global warming and gender fluidity... ugh!

They had both sat through that "date" from hell before... never again!

To their dismay, they also discovered that their Cantata's were on the same day (i.e., Saturday) and at the same time (i.e., 6:00 pm). On the other hand, and to their delight, their final full rehearsals fell on different days. That is, Everett's rehearsal was this Wednesday and Francesca's rehearsal was this Thursday. So, if there was no "love at first sight" crashing and burning today, they would still get to see and hear each other sing this week.

"Honestly, I thought it was just band practice today, but our manager threw in a photo shoot at the last minute," Everett continued apologetically. "Franny, I promise you black isn't my favorite color. It's business, this is my business suit and I have to go back after lunch. Trust me, I prefer the comfortable slob look. What are you eating?"

"Chef Anabella makes the best Brazilian shrimp pastel. She told me once that the best kept secret about making it was the vodka. It makes the dough really crispy... oh, and any leftover vodka makes a great sea breeze too," Francesca replied as she folded back the lid of the container. "I'm just playing with you about your clothes. I am wrong half the time I judge people by how they look. So, I try not to do that anymore. What are you eating?"

"Baked chicken à la carte from the Asian Bistro and a whole lemon **méringue** pie from the bakery," Everett stated as he unpacked the chicken dish. "The pie is for later. I don't do drugs or alcohol, so the occasional sugar blast helps keep me going during the long recording sessions. None of my band mates do the drugs either, so I bring a whole pie just in case we all tank."

"Very thoughtful of you," Francesca remarked candidly.

"Seth, our lead guitarist, gets anything left over. Seth and I go way back. He has a beautiful wife and a new baby," Everett added some band trivia. "If we are cranking on all cylinders, the pie gets forgotten sometimes and he'll take the whole thing home with him."

What is going on here? Francesca thought. *Can this guy be more based... more nice... more attractive in every freaking way?*

As one might expect, their time together started out with the many musical activities they were currently involved in. Everett has a rewarding music career, but he was excited and honored to be a part of the hugely popular Easter Cantata at Hillary. Francesca was enrolled in Hillary as a freshman studying law, but she was excited and honored about performing, once again, with the FBC choir and on such a special occasion. The difference in scale between the two Cantatas was extreme, but that didn't matter much to either one. Francesca would casually make the point that Jesus would enjoy one just as much as the other.

Could such a statement about Jesus be true? Everett thought. *Could less than absolute perfection satisfy an all-powerful "God"?*

It was surprising how much music Everett and Francesca had in common. Most of it was not necessarily great music that would ever stand the test of time, but it allowed them to sing a couple ultramodern, and relatively unknown, songs a cappella... right there... where they sat... between bites of lunch. No rehearsal. No amplification. No holding back.

The blending of their voices created a beautiful melody in perfect harmony. Their control was flawless and the projection was powerful on each song. Needless to say, these two spontaneous duets attracted quite a few captivated onlookers. Once the captives understood what was happening, both songs received an enthusiastic round of applause. It was not Everett and Francesca's intention to put on a show or to show off. They were just doing what singers enjoy doing.

No one was more stunned with their performance than Everett.

"Frannie, that was outrageous!" Everett exclaimed as he tried to find the right combination of superlatives to describe what he had just heard. "Your voice, I can't, there's nothing, it was, let me, the thing is... ah, forget this. Thank you."

"Oh, sure, yeah, you're welcome," Francesca replied quizzically. "For what?"

"For letting me sing with you," he replied in all sincerity.

"Oh, that, sure, no problem," she replied as if uncertain where this conversation was going. "But it was your idea."

"Yeah, I know, but that was before I knew how good you were," he admitted. "Frannie, can I ask you something?"

"Ummm, Oooh-K," she replied cautiously.

"How long have you been singing?"

"All my life," she stated joyfully. "As long as I can remember anyhow."

"No, I mean singing in a structured or formal setting," he clarified. "Like your choir or maybe in school or a band?"

"Since Christmas, I guess," she replied truthfully. "Since FBC choir let me sing with them."

"That is hard to believe because you have such an extraordinarily balanced voice, but if you say so," he began patiently. "Frannie, do you know why people were clapping for us?"

"They liked us," she responded with some assurance.

"Not exactly," he stated with conviction. "They liked you."

Everett proceeded to explain his understanding of music and the "Francesca" factor. That factor went something like this. Some songs were written to be sung as a duet – especially when it involved the love story between a man and a woman. Some songs were originally written for one voice, but later adapted for two. Sometimes they work and sometimes they don't. It mostly depends on the vocalists. The two songs Everett and Francesca ended up singing today were not written with two voices in mind... ever. They fell into a fringe category of music that created a great innovative sound, but are loaded with highly enigmatic lyrics that help to disguise the torment and self-loathing of the person doing the singing. The emotionally tortured vocalist could be male or female – but not both. When understood in their proper context, these eerie songs were not the kind to get applause from the firmly entrenched, three chord progression, pop song enthusiast that surrounded them on the terrace. Even with Everett's perfect pitch, no one would have reacted the way they did if he had sung those songs by himself.

"In other words, Frannie," Everett concluded affectionately. "It was your beautiful voice that made those songs a privilege to listen to."

"Shut up… don't tease," Francesca stated as if embarrassed by the compliment.

And you are beautiful in more ways than one, Everett thought.

"Does Professor Bouchard know you can sing like this?"

Chapter 11

It's Hard to Explain

Sunday may have all been a dream. Maybe it was a simple case of temporary insanity, but Leon was now - officially - a cat person. He felt no need to explain this new affinity towards cats. He simply found himself talking to Punkin' more now than before. These extemporaneous moments were not intended to be dialogs. He did not expect Punkin' to respond. He just made casual small talk whenever she was in the room or curled up in his lap. In the beginning, Leon would reminisce mostly about his late wife, Ruthie. They shared a wonderful life together and he felt as though Punkin' would understand that. When it finally dawned on him that Punkin' just recently lost the love of her life and was most likely going through the same early stages of grief that he once experienced, Leon made it a point to include Bear in his recollections.

"Miss Punkin', I know you must be missing Bear terribly. I hope you will pardon me for not comforting you sooner," he began with the best of intentions. "If you don't mind my saying, I thought it funny when he would sit on the windowsill for hours and give those trash-talking Blue Jays what for.

Bear would have made a magnificent Serengeti chieftain so long as you were by his side."

Although these intimate little encounters were not perfect, they were from the heart now that Leon was more aware of Punkin's age related health issues. She was always the affectionate cat when compared to Bear, but there was also a spunkiness to her to go along with it. To be on the safe side, he scheduled another appointment with the vet to get blood work done. Hopefully, they would provide him with a medication mild enough to help ease the joint pain without all the harmful side effects. Time was taking its toll on her. He would not leave the house in the morning without saying goodbye to her, and more often than not, he would come home in the afternoon for lunch to make sure she was safe, eating normally and moving around some. They would end the day in the recliner with Leon doing most of the talking and Punkin' doing most of the listening. As fate would have it, baseball season was now in full swing and the past three evenings have become "family baseball night" at the Bouchard's house once again.

Since Ruthie's passing from this world into the next, Leon had continued his habit of calling the Philadelphia Phillies games out loud from his recliner. Even though Ruthie was no longer beside him, Punkin' and Bear were... for every one of these games. The two of them would curl up on the couch together and listened to Leon call out every batter's name along with their statistics and a hope that they would come through in the end - as if Miss Ruthie were still with them.

It just so happened that the Phillies started a three-game series with the Reds on Palm Sunday and it was now Tuesday.

"Miss Punkin', did I ever tell you that the Phillies are the oldest continuous franchise in all of American professional sports?" Leon gently spoke as his hand glided effortlessly along her soft fur in long, rhythmic strokes from head to tail. "Yes ma'am, they have had the same name (Phillies) and been located in the same city (Philadelphia) since 1883."

"Meow," she replied faintly.

Every once in a while, Punkin' had enough breath to cause a sound when attempting a response. More often than not, however, it was simply the mouth opening and then closing again.

"I know, I know. We were the last National League baseball team to put a black man in uniform back in '57. John Irvin Kennedy (1926–1998) was his name and they would find every which way not to play him," he admitted with some deep-seated feelings about the past. "But I never was much interested in blaming the son (Phillies today) for the wrongdoing of the father (Phillies racism of the past). We can't change our past, we just got to find a better way to learn from it."

"Meow," she replied, only there was no sound this time.

"Content of character, Miss Punkin'. That's what I base my opinions on… content of character. That's my answer to all this racial tension we got going on these days," Leon exclaimed as if asked for a comment to back his reasoning. "Now, we also got ourselves a low scoring ballgame here. That's because we got a good, old-fashioned pitching duel so far. The pitch count is getting high for both those fellas on the mound, so can we just enjoy the ballgame without trying to fix a world that don't want to be fixed, please?"

"Meow." (inaudible)

"Thank you," he said just as the Phillies batter swatted a deep fly ball to left center for a double. "See there, see there? Now we got one out, the tying run on second, the go ahead run at the plate and an opposing pitcher who is getting sloppy with that slider of his!"

"Meow." (inaudible)

"That's right, Punkin'. That is so right," he agreed with what he believed any devoted lover of baseball would say at this moment. "With Bryce (Harper) up to bat next, why in the world are they letting this guy pitch to him? Harper is one of the best designated hitters in the league and he is already 1 for 2 today. Oh, would you look at that. The Reds manager is going to leave that boy in to pitch. I can't believe my eyes. A line drive in the gap and this ballgame is all tied up. We can take the lead here if Bryce was to go deep. Reds messing with fire here."

Over the course of two and a half games, Leon noticed there were only two reasons Punkin' would rise from her comfortable semi-napping, prone position. She would stand and stretch for the 7th inning stretch and she would rise to a sitting position whenever Bryce Harper came up to bat. Once Leon announced who the next batter was, up popped Punkin'. Of course, "popped" is a relative term. There was no time limit for Punkin' to "pop up" into her sitting position.

As expected, the pitcher threw nothing but low and outside – being content with walking Bryce unless he felt the need to chase after garbage. Unfortunately for the Reds, the 3-0 count sloppy slider came in right over the plate like a big ham sandwich. Bryce took the opportunity to smack a high, fly ball off the left field wall for a stand up double and chalk up another RBI. The home crowd went crazy and so did Leon and Punkin'.

"Meow," she screamed audibly and immediately stood up in Leon's lap.

Leon scooped her up securely into his arms and they both danced slowly, but excitedly, around the room.

"You play with fire long enough... you gonna get burnt," he quipped joyously. "Ain't that right, Miss Punkin'?"

"Meow." (inaudible)

The text from Monica to Hitch read like this:

> Annastasia is still your book coordinator. She did not leave nor was she ever asked to leave by her publishing company. This incident came as a complete shock to her. Surprisingly, she asked me to ask you not to pursue a grievance against this guy. She confided in me that her colleague has experienced a few professional and personal setbacks recently - that she knew of. She would not elaborate. Also, she described him as a devoted family man with a wife and kids at home. It would "devastate" Annastasia should he lose his job over this matter – her words.
>
> I reminded Annastasia that she had a written agreement to split all commissions 60/40 for

taking your book to market - with 60% going to him and 40% going to her. As crazy as it sounds, she requested that we honor that agreement and that split. Any change now would only attract suspicion and "not end well" – her words.

Professor, from what I could tell on the phone, she was very upset by this and may have been in tears at this point. How would you like to proceed?

The immediate reply from Hitch back to Monica read like this:

You may tell Annastasia that I will yield to her request – this one time. Please explain to her that it is times such as these that put me to the test. Should God's policy on forgiveness take precedence here or should my policy on working with those I cannot trust supersede? I think we all know the answer to that one. However, I cannot find anything in my heart or in Scripture that requires me to continue working with this, otherwise, fine husband and father in the future.

Monica, it is my opinion that Annastasia should say nothing to her colleague about this. You can assure her that once this man realizes he has not lost everything – which is what I told him - he will be as silent as a door mouse. If, for any reason, he should display even the slightest amount of obstructive or uncooperative behavior with regards to this project, simply have her suggest to him to contact me directly... which, of course, means you. I doubt it will ever come to that.

Now then, Debbie and I will be at the cabin for the remainder of Holy Week. Contact me if you must. I hope you and Jimi are enjoying your stay in California.

The resolution to this book dilemma was not a contributing factor to spend the remainder of the week at the cabin. This text messaging could have been handled from any place just as easily. Leaving town had more to do with the fact that both Hitch's students and Debbie's students were taking full advantage of having no physical classes for the week and the kittens were able to travel now. As long as they had mom cat for their main source of nourishment and Wallace to climb all over, they could be happy anywhere. And let us not forget that love was in the air. What better place to express that love, than a mountain hide-away in need of continuous "spring cleaning" and 100 acres of unexplored mountainous terrain?

Thank goodness for the Jeep. It does not fit in very well with all the compact, hybrid, electric, smooth-road, urban-dependent cars that occupied the majority of the parking spaces in and around Hillary, but it has become essential for the rest of life. When heading out to the cabin, the luxury high-capacity 4x4 was never not fully loaded with people, animals, clothing, food and the things that made them feel un-plugged from Hillary's "matrix." For instance, owning a cabin in the woods meant owning every kind of landscape and gardening tool known to mankind and a pair of gloves to go along with each one. Sharp knives, from the largest bush-whacker to the smallest pen knife, also seemed to come in handy... all the time. Unfortunately, regardless of how many you own, hand tools were often the least effective and the most time-consuming alternatives. Therefore, it was Hitch's intention to purchase a tractor someday. That useful piece of machinery will come once he can process the mental image of himself wearing baggy overalls and a wide-brimmed straw hat.

Also going with them on each trip to the cabin were the guns of various kinds and calibers. It was Jimi and Monica who got them started with owning and shooting guns. The large and extremely heavy gun vault for their safekeeping had already been delivered to the cabin. Neither Hitch, nor Debbie, were ever going to become game hunters. Rather, the guns were intended for their enjoyment and personal protection. Safety was a priority when living in relative seclusion and these powerful firearms provided that peace of mind. They were not paranoid, but they were also not stupid enough to become a victim. With Wallace and Fang as natural born sentinels, the chances of not being fully prepared to greet a stranger on their property at any moment would be slim to none.

When choosing to become a gun owner - proficiency mattered. Therefore, they brought with them plenty of ammo for target practice. The site of the original farm house became the perfect location for a live-fire practice range. It was far enough away from the cabin to be considered outlying and yet easily accessible by gravel road. When covered in thick blankets, the ruin's 3' tall stone walls provided the perfect firing line and ledge for resting unloaded firearms when their makeshift range was declared "cold." The reusable, ricochet-free targets were placed out in the "backyard" of the ruins. It was an open field and 100 yards down range before it started sloping uphill. The stone ruins were never used to set physical targets on and be shot at. In their minds, damaging these walls would be equivalent to spray painting graffiti on a person's home. The area would be swept clean of the spent brass casings and restored to its original condition before calling it quits for the day. Hitch and Debbie loved to shoot. Even Wallace and Fang were getting used to the blasts and would wait patiently in the Jeep bed until they heard the word "cold."

On the topic of security, the cabin came with a mishmash of security cameras and surveillance systems monitored by various commercial security firms in the past. It was a private bed and breakfast out in the middle of nowhere owned and operated by an elderly couple, so that was to be expected. Because of his steadfast beliefs concerning privacy, all of those devices located inside the cabin were professionally removed as soon as Hitch took possession of the property. The exterior cameras were allowed to stay. A couple years back, however, those ancient exterior security devices were replaced with the latest surveillance camera systems using sophisticated motion sensing software that would trigger an email or text a message to a cell phone whenever activated. A series of strategically placed and remotely controlled cameras would then pan, tilt, zoom in on and record any guest, invited or uninvited, from the entrance gate all the way up to the cabin. So far, the only vandalism caught on tape was the destruction of the flimsier birdfeeders and the toppling of trash cans by a pair of mischievous racoons – who have subsequently been nicknamed, Bonnie and Clyde. Otherwise, it was amazing to see just how many animals stop by the cabin on a daily – and nightly - basis.

It was on their spring break visit two weeks ago that Hitch and Debbie decided to stop off at the charming country store nearest the cabin for a few forgotten supplies. This stop had actually become pretty much routine because there was almost always a useful tool to be found. They would also fill a large produce carton with locally grown fruit and veggies. On this particular visit, however, they could not help but notice a wide selection of motion activated game and trail cameras commonly used by hunters. The curiosity was almost instantaneous.

"I wonder who else lives on the property?" Debbie asked rhetorically as she gazed wide-eyed at the life-sized still photo of a mountain lion, seemingly, taken by one of the cameras for sale.

"I agree. We should know who is roaming around out there," Hitch replied playfully as he carefully inspected one of the boxes. "We may very well have flesh-eating zombies for neighbors. In which case, more ammunition would be warranted."

"Don't be silly," Debbie proclaimed dismissively. "A Yeti maybe. They seem to like mountainous areas and, fortunately for us, there is no reason to believe they are flesh eating."

"Your feet's too big," Hitch replied suddenly as if it was the beginning of a song.

"Pardon me, my..." Debbie exclaimed, but was cut off before she could finish her thought.

"Don't want you 'cause you feet's too big," Hitch continued and began to sing and sway to what appeared to be the next lyric to a song.

"Excuse me, my...?" Debbie interjected while taking a quick glance down at her feet, but was again cut off.

"From your ankle up, I'll say you sure are sweet... from there down, there's just too much feet." Hitch sang and swayed to what was obviously more lyrics to a song. "Can't use you 'cause you feet's too big ... don't want you 'cause you feet's too big."

Then, as abruptly as he began, he went silent and motionless.

"Are you finished?"

"Unless you want to hear the rest of the song."

"What song?"

"Fats Waller's 'Your Feet's Too Big', of course," Hitch answered as if everyone had heard of the old jazz tune. "According to Professor Bouchard, it is one of his most requested songs when dining at Timothy's."

"Oh, I see now, yes, so, you decided to sing that funny little song in this adorable little country store knowing full-well that everyone is listening to you and looking at me because...?" Debbie asked with a 'can't wait to hear this one' smile.

She left the sentence open-ended for Hitch to complete.

"Oh, that, well, I was simply trying to clarify a minor distinction between the Yeti and a Bigfoot," Hitch began innocently. "It is true that both are mysterious and elusive creatures. Both have been depicted in the wild as mis-appropriating that unmistakable 'Neanderthal' look. And more to the point, they both have disproportionately large 'feet's' attached to their lower limbs. With that being said, the Yeti, or as they are sometimes referred to in the movies as an 'Abominable Snowman' or a 'Sasquatch,' primarily habitate the Himalayan Mountain range in Asia. Therefore, it is more likely we would have a Pennsylvania version of Bigfoot and not a Himalayan Yeti. As I said, it is a minor distinction."

"So, what I hear you saying... or singing... or whatever that was you were doing, is that I needn't worry that my 'feet's' are too big?" Debbie responded with a fake sigh of relief.

"Exactly. Your feet's are neither too big... nor are they too small... they are just right," Hitch declared as he took her in his arms. "In essence, my sweet Sùilean Soilleir, everything about Yeti and Bigfoot has been proven false - or at least questionable – including those gunboats they call feet's. You, on the other hand, are fearfully and wonderfully made (Ps 139:13-14). If I had any less self-control, I'd ask you to dance here and now."

"I think we've attracted enough attention here and now," she suggested happily. "But tonight, my feet's are all yours."

With great anticipation, they walked out of that country store carrying two solar powered trail cameras with built-in WIFI signal, 4K@30fps video resolution and dual day and night vision lenses to capture the action 24/7/365 in the greatest possible detail. These devices were installed and tested two weeks ago. One camera was attached to a tree overlooking the open field beyond the ruins of the original house (the firing range). The other camera was attached to a tree overlooking the mountain stream that flowed near the ruins of the original millhouse. Both locations were in areas off to themselves and provided adequate sunlight for power, yet, easily accessible by Jeep. Since their property shared its boundary lines with back-to-back-to-back State parks, both Hitch and Debbie were looking forward to seeing what might wander in and out of the distance.

It was late afternoon on Tuesday by the time they got rolling. The packing had begun in the morning, but contemplating and satisfying the needs of two adults, two dogs, one mom cat and four kittens for a five-day stay at the cabin took more time and effort than expected. Even still, things were forgotten and a stop at their favorite country store was necessary. The store's supply of game and trail cameras had dwindled significantly in the two weeks since they purchased theirs and had been relocated to a less prominent area towards the back. The large picture of the mountain lion could still be seen and it re-ignited the curiosity and excitement which caused Hitch and Debbie to buy their cameras in the first place. They couldn't wait to get to the cabin and see what these "private eyes" had captured in their absence.

The country store was very good at capturing the imagination of their customers. In the first place, its full name was "Huskey Brufus' Country Store." But no one could adequately explain who Huskey Brufus was. Was Huskey Brufus a dog with a strange name? Was Huskey Brufus a big, burly guy with a strange name? Rusty Turner bought the store 25 years ago. He was born and raised here. He grew up knowing the family who owned the store before him. If anyone would know the origin of Huskey Brufus' Country Store, it would be Rusty. Yet, even he can't – or won't - tell you where the name came from. All he would ever say when pressed about the name of his store was this:

"As far as I know, it has been Huskey Brufus' Country Store for a hundred years. Now, give me one good reason to go messing around with a name like that?"

Of course, the locals simply call it the store, as in "going to the store, need anything?" If they are talking to out-of-towners, the locals might be a little more specific, as in "I'm sure the Huskey Brufus has what you're looking for and it's just down the road a ways." In any case, the country store also seemed to be experts at keeping things fresh, exciting and fun without having to sacrifice traditional boundaries, thoughtfulness and reverence. Take Easter for instance. The store tastefully promoted the wonderfully fragrant, white, trumpet-shaped Easter Lily for the occasion. They even referenced the "Sermon on the Mount" discourse where Jesus said,"And why are you anxious concerning raiment (clothing)? Consider the *lilies of the field*, how they grow; they toil not, neither do they spin. Yet I say unto you, that even Solomon in all his glory was not arrayed like one of these" (Mt 6:28-29).

The Easter lily, *Lilium Longiflorum*, has long been an American tradition at this time of year because it so beautifully symbolizes the purity, rebirth, new beginnings and hope that comes with the resurrection of Jesus Christ. The flower itself, however, was native to three small southern islands of Japan. It was discovered by Swedish naturalist, Carl Peter Thunberg (1743 - 1828) back in 1777. Over forty years later, in 1819, he would ship the flower to England. By the 1880's, the 'Trimphator' white flower with its rosy pink centers, were being imported to the US from Japan (which was under imperial rule at this time) or Bermuda. It is rumored that an American soldier by the name of Louis Houghton was stationed in Japan towards the end of WWII and he returned to his home in the Pacific Northwest with a suitcase full of these lily bulbs. That explanation was as good as any because by 1945, there were over 1,000 Easter Lily growers from California to Canada. Today, virtually all of the potted Easter lilies are produced by less than a dozen growers located in a narrow coastal region along the border of California and Oregon – otherwise known as the "Easter Lily Capital of the World." Interestingly, the majority of Easter lilies grown in the US are of the variety called "Nellie White." This was a popular selection by grower James White who fondly named it after his wife.

No where to be found in Huskey Brufus' Country Store were the shelf upon shelf of cheap, cellophane draped, Easter baskets from China full of garbage up to the bend in its tall plastic handle. They were perfectly content with the larger food chains setting these tacky Easter offerings at their entranceway - right next to the absolutely antithetical, yet cleverly stacked, mountains of cheap beer sold in "suit-cases" that screamed "let's get trashed for Easter!" Yes, the Huskey Brufus carried Easter baskets. These were, however, sturdy hand-crafted baskets made by local artisans. The baskets were sold empty in hopes that they might be filled with locally grown confections, honey, jellies, etc. for the holidays. And, yes, the Huskey Brufus sold alcohol. Hey, the country store owner was in business - to stay in business - for Pete's sake. The beer was mostly craft beer made by Pennsylvania micro-breweries and remained available, but not overtly promoted during the two Christian holidays. There were many other dissimilarities between this simple country store and the big box stores, but you get the point.

Needless to say, they now had to find room in the Jeep - already filled to the brim - for the fragile Easter lilies and two Easter baskets full of assorted locally-produced edibles. The sun was still above the tree tops when they finally did reach the cabin, but the eastern sky had darkened several shades of blue. By this time, Hitch and Debbie were both feeling a bit cranky from packing, driving and general self-pity for arriving so late in the day. Wallace and Fang, on the other hand, were just getting started. They had been relegated to being passive bystanders for most of the day and their restlessness could not be more noticeable.

"Away with you both!" Hitch exclaimed as he opened the Jeep door for them to escape.

In their lethargic condition, it seemed to take Hitch and Debbie just as long to unpack as it did to pack. It was unanimous. There would be no additional cleaning, no unnecessary straightening and no impromptu dancing tonight. When the least that was required of them was said and done, they filled a colander with some of the local produce that had just been purchased, applied a quick rinse to it and headed outside to the cushioned porch swing. Once seated, they cuddled, swung, ate and allowed several minutes to pass by without a word being spoken.

The sun had at last disappeared beyond the trees which left the western sky awash in soft, warm color... so, there was that. The distinct, intermingled chatter of life in the forest replaced the easily disregarded, droning noise of life in the city... so, there was that. The fruit tasted especially sweet when eaten so soon after being taken from the tree or vine... so, there was that. This would be their first Easter as born-again Christians and they were together... so, there was that. From time to time, Wallace and Fang would appear from the woods - then disappear as if called back by the woods... so, there was that. They had only scratched the surface with the questions about their love for each other... so, there was that.

Debbie spoke first. She opted to start the conversation with a softball.

"Mom cat and kittens seem to be happy campers."

"Yes, they do," Hitch replied tenderly. "You and Fang did a wonderful thing bringing them home. They are very lucky to be alive."

On its face, there was no doubting that. So many circumstances had to come together at just the right time in order to save the lives of those kittens. What else could it be, but luck? The word seemed innocuous enough, but it stirred something else inside of Debbie. There was a time when she would have accepted that catch-all explanation and move on... that time was not now apparently.

"Are you and I lucky?" Debbie asked as if she were still contemplating the answer to her own question.

It never fails. Just when Hitch thought he might be able to keep his thinking cap off for a while, Debbie would cause him to put it back on – and always for good reason. It was a fair and brilliant question.

"No, my love, we are not," Hitch replied earnestly.

Hitch knew better than to say things like the kittens were, "very lucky to be alive." The remark was intended to be nothing more than a ubiquitous expression being applied to an unknown statistic, but it was not biblical. The Bible says that all things have been ordained by God (Eph 1:11). That is, all (not some) things are known, beforehand, by God and for his purpose. Luck, by secular definition, is a "force" that causes good or bad things to happen to people. Therefore, non-Christians consider that "force" to be "chance" or "luck." Things that happen without any discernable cause. They have no other explanation. In other words, it was "good" luck that Debbie and Fang came along when they did... or, it would have been "bad" luck had they not come along when they did. The deciding luck was merely by chance.

Luck, or chance, however, are not concepts Christians should believe in. The most conspicuous example of this would be the non-Christian's belief that the universe was formed by chance and aren't we so lucky to be living on a planet that supports life. To hold this opinion you must, of course, disregard the fact that creating something out of nothing breaks every law in every scientific instruction manual on every university bookshelf in every multi-universe they have concocted. Christians, on the other hand, believe that a Sovereign and Almighty God, existing outside of time and space, created the heavens and the earth (Gen 1:1). To hold this opinion, of course, you simply disregard chance, or luck.

Dr. R.C. Sproul (1939–2017), reminds us why there can be no such thing as chance. In his book, "Chosen by God: Know God's Perfect Plan for His Glory and His Children" he writes this about chance and the "maverick molecule:"

> "What I tried to get these young people to see was this, very simply that if God is not sovereign, God is not God. If there is one *maverick molecule* in the universe, one molecule running loose outside the scope of God's sovereign ordination, then ladies and gentlemen, there is not the slightest confidence that you can have that any promise that God has ever made about the future will come to pass."

With any luck (just kidding), Hitch could explain to Debbie what he really meant by luck. He continued with a bit less sentimentality and a bit more clarity of thought.

"What I meant to say is that I am very happy that mom cat and her kittens are sleeping safe and sound inside the cabin right now. Luck had absolutely nothing to do with you finding them and saving them. Just as luck had nothing to do with our coming to faith in Jesus Christ or our coming together as we have. I believe that was all predetermined before the creation of the world and is in accordance with God's perfect plan for us."

"I was thinking the same thing, only I like the way you say it better," Debbie responded sweetly and stood up. "I'm going in. I'm dying to see what's on those trail cameras. You coming?"

"If you've seen one Yeti, you've seen them all," Hitch answered while remaining seated and slowly allowing her hand to slip away from his. "I'll give Wallace and Fang a few more minutes to discharge more energy, then I'll be in."

Several minutes had ticked away when Wallace and Fang finally made their reappearance. There was no need to call them in because they were running full-throttle across the front yard and towards the porch. Hitch was about to lift himself off the swing to see if they were being chased when Debbie came charging out the front door and stood in front of him excitedly.

"Eddie, you need to come inside," she stammered.

"Is everything alright?" he replied and immediately stood up.

"The cameras. They caught something."

"What?"

"Well, it's hard to explain."

Chapter 12

Music to My Ears

It was now Wednesday. A day like any other day. It will come and it will go. Most people will neither rejoice in it nor regret it. What's the difference when there will always be a tomorrow. Some may even include it in a week full of minor toils and randomness that will also come and go without much fanfare. But for Jesus, it was the day before he would be betrayed by Judas Iscariot in the Garden of Gethsemane. Judas would kiss Jesus on the cheek and address him as "master" (Mt 26:49-50)... that took guts. Oddly enough, as important as every minute of every hour was on this particular day, Scripture is silent on what Jesus said or did. What? Why?

Jesus knew he was running out of time. There must be something else he wanted all of us to know. So, why the silence? It harkens us back to the time where Scripture was silent when Jesus ominously started scribbling something in the dirt when the Pharisees brought to him a woman caught in adultery (Jn 8:1-11). The Jewish priests wanted nothing more than to throw lots of rocks at her, but for some unknown reason they all scattered... one at a time. What did Jesus write?

Why the silence at Gethsemane?

Why the silence at the Mount of Olives?

Why the silence on this Wednesday before his crucifixion? Don't know.

What we do know is that the silence was intended. That is, if we were supposed to know, then Scripture would have included it. We can say that Jesus preserved that woman's life at least one more day. We can also say with certainty that Jesus knew all along that the "cup" he was born into this world to drink from – a metaphor for our sin - would soon be emptied on the cross (Isa 51:17; Eze 23:33; Mt 26:39; Mk 14:36; Lk 22:42; Jn 18:11).

Silence can say a lot. It forces us to contemplate our own tendencies and desires. Evil will use it for evil, good will use it for good. It should make us think twice for being silent about telling those you love - that you love them. Could there be anything worse than to hear someone you love say "don't know" should they be asked if you loved them?

"I love you" spoken tenderly and honestly is music to the ear.

Everett was up to bat first. Francesca's final rehearsal would come tomorrow. They would both sing in their respective Easter Cantatas on Saturday evening. This debut appearance as lead tenor for Bach's Easter Oratorio was challenging, but nothing Everett could not handle. Even at such a young age, Everett was a seasoned professional. In fact, the Walker auditorium was like a second home to him since his mother joined Hillary University as a professor of music back in 2020. Still, there was another dynamic going on with this concert. There was a significance... a relevance... a closeness to his participation with this one that he had not experienced before. His initial inkling that something extraordinary was happening occurred when he first accepted the tenor role. His bass-guitar-dominate, alternative rock band, "Barely Famous Pirates," preferred the outdoor festivals that exploded on the scene this time of year.

> [Note: Praises like "Blackbeard's riffs will stay the hand of a hangman" by Beautiful Rockers Magazine were everywhere now. Everett was Blackbeard, of course. He was "Blackbeard... the bass-slinger!" That was his stage name. It was his professional identity. Very few people knew (nor cared) that Blackbeard was born Everett Albrecht Wagner-Weiß and he pre-ferred it that way]

As usual, they were getting peppered with new invita-tions every week in addition to what was already on their schedule. Yet, with all that going on, there was very little hesitation on acceptance when Leon made his offer. If the offer were anything other than Bach's Easter Cantata, Everett would have graciously declined.

When Everett informed his band mates of this unique opportunity, they were all excited for him. First and fore-most, they were not losing their front man because it was just one gig. Secondly, they were all best of friends. At one time or another, every core member of the group had been given the freedom to go out and explore something new with the understanding that they would be welcomed back with open arms. This friendship-before-fealty attitude has produced some of their best music and why they try very hard not to think of themselves as having a single-minded loyalty to a band, a sound or a leader.

The next substantive inkling that something was different about the Bach Cantata came from the most unlikely of sources – Jake and Joey. Believe it or not, Everett had found their charmingly simplistic, yet keenly illuminating, explanations of the long-ago events that preceded Easter genuinely compelling. Up to this point, Everett knew nearly nothing about the life of Jesus Christ except that which came to him unsolicited and in dismissive terms. That brief encounter with Professor Lewis' two boys inside FBC even brought back fond memories of the time when he was their age and in church with his grandparents.

The final inkling that some strange new fascination, or transformation, might be at work came when he began reading the Bible for himself. More specifically, reading the four Gospels (Greek word for "Gospel" is **"Euangélion"** which literally means "good news"). These Gospels according to Matthew, Mark, Luke and John are the first four books of the New Testament. Even more specifically than that was what these four first-hand perspectives had to say about Holy Week. Everett knew the lyrics to Bach's work like he knew the back of his own hand. He also knew the kinds of deep-seated emotions the main characters would have felt finding an empty tomb where Jesus, their "Savior," should have been.

What Everett did not know was what this man did that was so astonishing to cause all these people to believe he was a God... a God that wanted to redeem them all by giving up his own life... a God these people would willingly die for. This kind of understanding would, of course, necessitate him going out and actually purchase a Bible.

And, then there was Frannie.

When their conversations turned from music to religion, it was Francesca who recommended Everett purchase the New American Standard Bible (NASB). It was not the best-selling Bible version on the market. That honor would go to the New International Version (NIV). Unfortunately, the NIV's more reliable 1984 version (taken out of print) was replaced with a lesser reliable "gender-neutral" version in 2011 (the only version available in stores today). This arbitrary change-of-lanes by the translation team at NIV has subsequently made other versions, like the NASB, better options for those looking for the best literal translation from the original texts. The NASB was also the Bible version that she was reading and studying from. They agreed that the use of the same Bible version would allow their chats on Christianity to flow much easier.

Although the mystery of the faint echo had been solved, Francesca and Alex were asked by Chief to continue checking all visitors at the door. Everyone affiliated with the concert in some fashion had been given a special pass. That has always been the case. All others - even if they have a valid university pass - must now be approved by Leon to gain entry to the Walker on rehearsal nights. With everyone's consent, Francesca was given permission to sit and enjoy Everett sing.

The rehearsal had not yet begun when Francesca took a seat in the back of the Walker.

The majority of the musicians and choir had taken their seats on stage by now. Leon stood alone on his raised podium looking down intently at the large music stand containing the full musical notations for all instruments and voices. The four SATB (soprano, alto, tenor, bass) soloists, including Everett (tenor), were all standing patiently in front of their preferential seating just to Leon's right. Everett's back was to Francesca and he was having a conversation with a tall, slender woman.

It was plain to Francesca that the woman was not part of the choir, yet Leon paid her no attention. Francesca could also tell Everett was the one doing most of the speaking because the woman's lips never seemed to move beyond a slight pursing. The woman's face remained stoic and expressionless as she listened. Then, suddenly, without any movement of the head, the woman's eyes locked onto Francesca's eyes. The look was only a short glance, but seemed to last forever and it sent a cold shiver up Francesca's spine. There was no malice, no anger, no squinting intimidation in the look. It was more like "I see you. I know who you are" look.

Satisfied with what he saw before him, Leon looked up from the music and asked for everyone's attention. It was hard to believe he had been doing this for ten years. For ten glorious years he had been given the privilege to worship the King of kings and Lord of lords while playing some of the greatest music ever written... all at the same time. It was an intensely humbling experience that he felt needed a contemplative moment of silence. A moment that a few of the impatient newcomers thought might have been better spent sharing some special insight. But, what could he say that he hasn't already said. And so, he took his time scanning the faces hoping to make eye contact with each and every one of these talented performers. In so doing, silently thanking them for their service to the Lord and making the last ten years some of the best years of his life.

They would understand in time, Leon thought as he would dwell on the familiar faces of those who had been with him the longest.

"Ladies and gentlemen...my friends," Leon began solemnly. "This will be my last performance as your conductor..."

He had more to say, but was unable to do so because of the immediate, knee-jerk reactions to this shocking news. In a split second, it seemed everyone had formed an opinion – and they all wished to express it at the same time. Above the mingling clamor, Leon could hear the unsettled pleas of "no" and "you can't" and "you mustn't" along with the more accepting chants of "we love you" and "thank you" and "God bless you." The one outburst that shook his soul the most was the man who calmly, yet with the commanding power of a strong baritone chest voice, say "you done good, brother. Go in peace."

After the "go in peace" comment, they were all on their feet. The impassioned cries of support and adoration slowly turned to simple appreciative clapping with a few "bravos" mixed in. Leon said nothing except for an inaudible "thank you" over and over again as he scanned the room. It took several minutes for him to quell the applause and to get everyone back in their seats with the downward motioning of his hands. Slowly, but surely, the exuberant noise subsided. This return to normalcy began with the orchestra - who found it difficult to clap with instruments in hand anyway. Leon allowed the dust to settle before finishing his thoughts.

"Well done, that concludes our cardio workout for the day," Leon said with a sheepish grin as he tapped his baton on the music stand.

This joke, at the opportune moment, brought with it a much-needed, stress-settling laughter to the room. Leon was not going off to war, but it was a lot to handle for most of the performers after ten years of pulling off the unimaginable in a small college town like Hillary. Leon knew the feeling. It was a decision that forced him to wrestle with his mind, his body and his soul. A large part of him wanted to continue. After all, who could possibly fill his shoes? But, then, who would want to fill his shoes? The instinct to take on any challenge and exceed all expectations went all the way back to when he was that kid in church. Who could possibly beat him in a race to the church doors during a holiday service? But that was then. This is now. Now, all he kept thinking about was what Punkin' had to say about Ruthie and her unspoken desire to have her "piano-play'n man" back... all to herself. Sadly, it was too late to give all of himself to the woman he loved and adored, but it was not too late to give more of himself to his family. It only took a day to make up his mind.

"First, let me thank you all for the hard work and dedication to your training, to the demands of this crazy production of ours and for putting up with me every year around this time," Leon continued in an effort to give credit where credit was due. "If you think about it – as I have – without all of you,

I am nothing more than a tall, very handsome, black man with a short stick in his hand."

This endearing quip about being handsome, along with the "raise the roof" motion with his hands, brought another round of tension-relieving laughter and more applause. He continued.

"Now, as sure as I'm standing here, I'm not gonna rest until I find you another person, man or woman, black or white or green, tall or short, handsome as me or funny looking that will be capable to lead this talented ensemble for the next ten years, because at the end of the day... it's night."

It took a few seconds for the group to separate the trustworthy promise of finding a qualified replacement from the humorous closing punch line. Once that happened, you could sense all remaining tension had evaporated and it was time to get down to business. Without further ado, Leon put on his game face which caused the singers and musicians to do the same. Leon gently tapped his baton on the music stand once more to bring everyone's attention to him and then he spoke from his heart.

"Let us not forget that it is our Lord and Savior, Jesus Christ, who we honor and glorify here tonight."

Meanwhile, as Leon was announcing his retirement, the lady that had been talking to Everett on stage was now walking up the center aisle and towards the exits in the back of the auditorium. And, not so coincidentally, this just happened to be the same aisle closest to where Francesca was sitting. Not wishing to be the cause of any trouble on Everett's first rehearsal night, she tried to make herself as small as possible for some strange reason. The mystery lady continued walking at a comfortable pace and seemed to have no interest other than to make it to the exit doors. A few discrete glances, without a turn of the head, seemed to confirm this belief. Oddly enough, the woman's departure gave Francesca a comforting feeling. That feeling was short-lived, however, because, without a sound, the woman had taken the seat next to her.

"Slouching is not good for the posture, sweetheart," the woman said pleasantly.

"Thank you," Francesca replied respectfully and sat up straighter.

Why would I do that? Francesca thought. *She's not my mom!*

Francesca thought about slouching back down, but something told her that the move would be exactly what the woman would want her to do. She stayed where she was.

"So, you are the Christian who is after my son?" the woman asked rhetorically. "You are very lovely though, my dear."

"Thank you," Francesca replied graciously, but soon realized there were two parts to the woman's comment. "Wait, I'm not after your son."

"But you are a Christian?" the woman inquired calmly.

"Yes," Francesca answered almost apologetically.

"So, what you are telling me is that my son is not good enough for you?" the woman stated with a satisfying smile. "Well, that is good to hear."

"I didn't say that!" Francesca snapped.

"What did you say, darling?" the woman asked innocently.

"I don't know, but not that," Francesca responded defensively. "Why are you trying to confuse me?"

"I'm sorry you are confused," the woman continued sweetly. "But, why else would you be sitting here? Shouldn't you be helping your friend guard the doors?"

"I have permission to sit here," Francesca replied as if being falsely accused.

"Of course you do, sweetheart. You must really love Bach to abandon your friend at the doors?" the woman observed politely, but there was now a taunting quality to her words. "Can you name any other masterpiece written by Bach or the name of any person up on stage other than my son?"

"Why are you doing this?" Francesca asked in hopes of ending this cat and mouse game.

"What am I doing?" the woman replied as if legitimately curious. "You say you are not after my son, yet you can give no other reason for slouching where you are."

"I enjoy listening to Everett sing," Francesca stated honestly. "He has a beautiful voice."

"Yes, he does," the woman stated with a sigh. "Well, I am glad to hear you have no intention of pursuing a relationship with my son. I will let him know."

"I didn't say that!" Francesca snapped... again.

"What did you say, darling?" the woman asked innocently... again.

"I enjoy being with Everett," Francesca replied earnestly. "He is a beautiful person."

"Well, now we are getting somewhere," the woman replied smugly. "But my son is a heathen according to your sacred scriptures. That makes him an enemy of your god. Isn't there some rule against being "unequally yoked" to an unbeliever?"

"I don't know everything the Bible says," Francesca freely admitted. "But we are working on it."

"We?" the woman countered forcefully. "Now I am confused. One minute ago, you simply enjoyed listening to Everett sing. Now you are proselytizing my son into your corrupt religion. Do you think you are the first pretty face or the first pretty voice that tried to change Everett into something he is not?"

Francesca said nothing. Why should she continue talking when everything she said so far had been twisted and used against her. The "pretty face" and "pretty voice" remark was the last straw. The inferences hit home. It saddened her, when she should be feeling only gladness for Everett tonight. The commotion on stage about Leon's retirement that had been going on since Everett's mother took her seat next to Francesca seemed to have been resolved. At this point, if this woman uttered one more inflammatory comment to trick her into saying something hurtful or stupid, Francesca would quietly move to another seat in another row.

Everett's mother took Francesca's silence as a win for reason and understanding. She stood and spoke once more before turning to leave.

"I knew you would see it my way. You are smarter than you look."

It was now Thursday and Francesca's turn to sing. As far as last night was concerned, Francesca had been on the wrong end of a "helicopter" mom before. This over-protective parent appeared to be the common denominator for the immature "mommy's boy" syndrome. She had dated a few of these adult "boys" prior to becoming a Christian. Fortunately, immaturity did not appear to be the case with Everett. She was no longer angry with Everett's mother. In fact, Francesca forgave her. Her only wish was that she could have had a little more warning, so that she didn't come across as such a bubble-headed pushover. In any case, once the first movement of Bach's Cantata started, Francesca had forgotten most of what was said between them. Once Everett started singing, bombs could have been exploding all around her and it would not have mattered.

Everett, on the other hand, was incensed and would apologize profusely to Francesca. He knew what his mother was capable of. That is why he did not tell her about accepting the role of tenor - much less, inviting her to the rehearsal. She just showed up... like she always does. There were times when Everett thought his mother had powers beyond heightened intuition. That was because very few things occurred in his life - and in the lives of many others - that his mother did not already know about or predict with incredible accuracy. Everett took some comfort in knowing that his mother would have already predicted the consequence of her callous behavior last night.

That consequence was for Everett to put his mother on restriction. That's right. Just as we all have been put on restriction for misbehaving as a child, Everett would impose restrictions on his mom for interfering in his adult life. Even his father was in agreement that some form of justice was appropriate for his wife's more egregious intrusions into his son's life. The restrictions included, but were not limited to; no personal visits and no response to her many phone calls, texts or messages. Everett felt a week was appropriate for yesterday's transgression. Since these two would normally meet and/or speak multiple times on a daily basis, a week was tantamount to being shipped to Siberia for a determined "helicopter" mom.

The Easter preparations were in full swing at FBC. The final full orchestra and choir rehearsal was just one of many events being tended to in the building this night. The songs chosen for the Easter Cantata were:

> "Kyrie Eleison" Christian litany
> (Francesca: soloist)
>
> "Our Hope Is Alive" written by Zach and
> Josh Sparkman (full orchestra and choir)
>
> "Lead Me to The Cross" written by Brooke
> Fraser (Pamela and Mickey: duet)
>
> "Can It Be" written by Adam Morgan
> (full orchestra and choir)
>
> "Living Hope" written by Phil Wickman
> (FBC male soloist)
>
> "Nearer, Still Nearer" written by Lelia N. Morris
> (full orchestra and choir)

This program would be followed by an Easter Hymn sing-along with the audience.

The last time Everett was in FBC, he was literally an unknown. As soon as he stepped into the building this evening, he was immediately recognized and acknowledged by his first name. And the spotters and greeters just happened to be Pamela and Mickey. These two were sent out to usher all Cantata participants back into the sanctuary for rehearsal. They would inform him that the whole thing would begin as soon after everyone was accounted for. It was also made perfectly clear to him that, not only was Francesca here, but if he did not find her to be the most beautiful girl in the world, then he was just stupid... or something to that effect.

Before reaching the sanctuary, he would also run into Jack shepherding a large group of children - which included his two boys, Jake and Joey. The group carried with them several basketballs and were heading for the doors.

"Hi, Mister Everett. Check this out," Jake yelled and did his best to spin the ball on the tips of a couple fingers.

"Hi, Mister Everett. Watch this," Joey echoed and did his best to dribble the ball between his legs.

Everett gave them both a thumbs up for their solid efforts and gave Jack a wave.

"Shooting hoops," Jack called out.

It was all he could fit in without falling too far behind the anxious group.

Having already experienced Francesca's vocal richness and skill, Everett was really looking forward to tonight. He was also made aware of the church's fashionably conscious, yet appropriately reserved, ways of dress. Therefore, he was very intentional about wearing something other than all black. The last thing he wanted to do was to take the slightest attention away from Francesca or the Cantata. In fact, he was only admitted to the rehearsal by exception. You should not have to be Leonard Bernstein to know that Christmas and Easter Cantatas were two very unique endeavors that required every person's absolute concentration and attention to detail. So, it made perfect sense to limit unnecessary distractions by implementing a reasonable policy that prohibited guests - other than a quiet spouse - from entering the sanctuary during rehearsal. Even more reasonable would be for that policy to be more rigidly enforced as the weeks and days got closer to game day. Rules were meant to be broken, of course. However, all exceptions to the rules must have been granted by Pastor Steve in advance and the circumstances must be extraordinary. Since Everett was starring in the Town of Hillary's famed annual Easter Cantata and he came pre-approved by Jack and Alex, his request to sit quietly in the back was granted without a fuss. Francesca would add her stamp-of-approval for Everett as well - but girlfriend (boyfriend) votes don't count for much.

There were a handful of empty chairs on stage that needed to be filled before final rehearsal could begin. Pamela and Mickey had not yet returned, but every few minutes another performer would show up and take one of those empty chairs. Everett took a seat in the back and marveled at how relaxed everyone seemed to be. Francesca had given him the weekly bulletin detailing the songs chosen for the Cantata. He was not familiar with the music, but had an opportunity to look over an easily accessible published score with both instrumental or vocal parts included. In his humble opinion, the Easter Cantata would definitively be a challenge for one mid-sized church's congregation to perform with some degree of proficiency. This conclusion would be especially true if the conductor was also the pastor!

Francesca and MJ were seated next to each other having an animated conversation. MJ spied Everett first and evidently passed this new information on to Francesca, who waited for Pastor Steve to look away before surreptitiously leaving her seat. Everett stood up as she approached.

"About time you got here," she grumbled with a smidgeon of fake annoyance. "Did Hillary's latest celebrity have a rough night?"

"You wouldn't believe what my driver had to do to lose that army of paparazzi tailing us," Everett exclaimed with an equal measure of mock annoyance. "How are you feeling?"

"I'm OK, I suppose," she replied hesitantly. "I really enjoy singing these Christian songs, but they are all new to me. They are fun to sing, but sometimes I don't get the meaning. MJ has been helping me out with how they relate back to the Bible. Sort of what you and I are doing. Sometimes that will change the way I sing the song too."

"That's such a good point," Everett agreed.

There was no need for Everett to offer any advice. He knew Francesca was the real deal with near flawless control over her voice. He was, however, going to add a few words of encouragement. Heck, even he responded well to encouragement. Then, they both watched as Pamela and Mickey strolled back in to the room.

"Oops, got to go," Francesca said excitedly. "Wish me luck."

"Hey, you got this, Frannie," he stated with assurance... and gentleness. "No need for luck."

Instead of parting – which would have been the natural next move for an excited person to do – Francesca stood there. The second or two that followed had them gazing intently into the other's eyes for something unstated... a connection. Someone needed to break the spell and fast. It would be Everett this time.

"Did you know that hugs are the preferred way for professional singers to show their respect and encouragement for other professional singers just before a performance?" he lied and took a half step closer to Francesca.

"Never heard that," Francesca replied and took a half step closer to Everett.

The resulting embrace was momentary, but was viewed by just about everyone in the room. The entire choir could not help but notice because they were elevated and already facing in that direction. It could be said that the choir - especially the ladies - had collectively adopted Francesca as their own. She was their present-day, Oliver Twist. Francesca had lived a hard life and they were willing to do almost anything to keep her safe and away from the 21st century version of bad guys like Fagin. As a consequence, they had all been kept up to date with the cute little stories about her and Everett since the incident in the Walker. Most of these stories have been corroborated by Alex, but he also thought it was comical to see Francesca's brash demeanor backslide into a cringe-worthy scatterbrain whenever Everett was around. Rarely did Alex get the opportunity to needle her the way she would needle him. This fast-tracked relationship that

Francesca and Everett were on has quickly become the perfect ammunition for some long-overdue paybacks.

Pastor Steve turned around just in time to see "the hug" only because he could not help being curious as to what everyone in the choir was so pre-occupied with behind his back. Unfortunately, most of the musicians missed the now infamous embrace because they were at floor level and facing neither the front nor the back. By the time they got to their feet and made the quarter turn, the PDA (Public Display of Affection) was over. Francesca smiled uncomfortably at all the happy faces that were now staring at her and marched quietly back to her seat. Once there, she would immediately bury her face in the singer's music folder. Everett, having accomplished exactly what he told himself he would never do, sat quietly and waited for someone to come and throw him out.

"I knew it. I knew it!" Pamela declared boldly.

"Stop having a cow, Pam," Mickey interrupted her loud friend. "Everyone knew it."

"Alright, thank you two," Pastor Steve began jokingly as he looked directly at Francesca and Everett individually and then returned his attention back to the choir. "Well, now that these two young people have formally announced their engagement to be married, can we all get back to this little ditty we call our Easter Cantata?"

"Daddy!" Pamela exclaimed harshly, taking exception to her father's apparent male insensitivity.

"I'm sorry, Cupcake, but Pastors get to tease people every once in a while," Pastor Steve replied. "It's one of the benefits to the job."

"We just want you to be safe and happy, that's all," MJ whispered in Francesca's ear. "Are you OK? I can ask for a short break."

"I am happy, MJ," Francesca replied gratefully. "God is good and all I really feel like doing right now is sing... for Jesus."

Chapter 13

Good Friday

Is Jesus God?

None, zero, zilch, nada, big goose egg... no legitimate scholar can deny this one absolute truth... Jesus lived. When applying the term "legitimate scholar" to a person in this regard, I am referring to a relatively intelligent academic willing to overlook their religious bias to accept that Jesus walked this earth some 2000 years ago. Simple enough. For example, Origen (c. 184–c. 253), Augustine of Hippo (354–430), Thomas Aquinas (1224–1274), and C. S. Lewis (1898 – 1963) would fit nicely into the definition of "legitimate scholar" on the Christian side. I suppose Karl Marx (1818–1883), Friedrich Nietzsche (1844–1900), and Bertrand Russell (1872–1970) would represent the atheist side well enough. I would also have to throw into this pile of savvy atheists, "Theophrastus Redivivus." Not the Greek philosopher, Theophrastus (c. 371–c. 287 BC), who lived and died long before Jesus Christ walked the earth and, therefore, would not have had an opinion on the matter. "Theophrastus Redivivus" (Latin: The Revived Theophrastus), on the other hand, was actually a book published anonymously sometime around 1650 AD. This was during the "Age of Enlightenment" period when atheism, and its long-bearded apologists, grew exponentially. The premise of the book was basically this: only atheists can be great scholars.

Pretty unenlightened if you ask me.

Anyhoo, a legitimate scholar can say what they want about Jesus being God, but to say that he never lived is nothing more than wishful thinking and a deliberate fabrication. There is just too much historical documentation and archaeological evidence that says otherwise. Something the "illegitimate scholar" would rather you not fact-check them on. Likewise, the legitimate scholar cannot deny that Jesus performed some pretty incredible acts of wonder while he was alive. Since Jesus was neither king nor wealthy aristocrat, it stands to reason that it was only because of his actions (miracles) that we have all the historical data on him today. Again, they can say his actions (miracles) were just smoke and mirrors. They can suggest it was all some phenomenal group hypnosis (which has never been replicated). However (and this a big HOWEVER), what they cannot deny, is that Jesus made such a big splash... in such a short period of time... only because he pulled off some pretty cool tricks!

The legitimate scholar must also accept the truth about Good Friday as well. That is, Jesus died that day. He succumbed to an excruciating death on the cross outside of Jerusalem by Roman decree that day. The Romans did not dream up the cruel art of crucifixion, they just perfected it. No one ever survived the cross. That is how Jesus died on Good Friday.

Having said all that, I would agree that this factual evidence alone does not prove Jesus is God. That evidence is coming soon enough.

What would the Easter season be without the chance of a spring rain disrupting all the carefully planned outdoor events like egg hunts, the overcooking of hamburgers and hot dogs on a barbie and the spitting of watermelon seeds for distance competitions? And, so it begins. Fortunately, the rain was a light, comfortable and constant sprinkle that gave everything it touched that glossy, polyurethane look. It was nothing the flimsiest umbrella could not handle if you needed to stay absolutely bone dry. Then again, if you were Wallace, it meant the prospect of more mud. And more mud, more fun. Wallace had become somewhat of a connoisseur of mud. He felt the hills of South Mountain produced a heavier, stickier mud capable of massaging those deep, hard to get at, muscle fibers, whereas, the mud in and around Hillary University produced a much thinner, soupy consistency that felt better the longer you laid in it... much like an artesian bath.

If you were Hitch and Debbie, there were just as many things to do inside the cabin as there were outside. In fact, these inside chores had been neglected over the last two days because of their preoccupation with the moose... or what appeared to be a moose anyway. It all started the night they arrived at the cabin. Debbie caught something on one of the two trail cameras that took her breathe away. Her investigation commenced the morning following their arrival.

"So, we agree that was a moose in the pictures, right?" Debbie asked enthusiastically while sipping at her morning cup of hot ginger turmeric tea with honey. "Even Fang said they sensed something very large out there last night."

"She told you that?" Hitch auto-responded.

"She did," Debbie auto-replied.

The pictures that Debbie spoke of were taken by the trail camera set furthest away from the cabin and it overlooked the wide, clear mountain stream by the old millhouse ruins. The images were somewhat fuzzy due to the "subject-in-question" being at the far end of the camera's range of focus. The dense early morning fog didn't help the camera optics, either. In fact, if not for the presence of a few white-tail deer in the foreground, the motion detection sensor might not have been triggered at all. Still, it was one unmistakably massive animal with an impressive set of antlers attached to its large, woolly head. Unfortunately, the beast was gone by the time another deer triggered the motion sensor almost an hour later.

Hitch did find it strange that Wallace and Fang would be so eager to get back to the cabin last night without being called multiple times to do so. But a moose on the loose in their backyard? Granted, a bull moose can grow to be 6' to 7' in height at the shoulders and weigh more than 1,000 pounds. The only problem with this hypothesis was... there are no moose in Pennsylvania. The last known native "black" moose was killed near the Juniata River, a tributary of the Susquehanna River in central Pennsylvania around

1790. They were supposed to be all gone. Mostly true. There was that one, lone, misguided moose spotted and photographed foraging in the Delaware Water Gap along the Pennsylvania-New Jersey border back in 1996 (The Express-Times; Sept. 26, 1996 edition; photo by Joe Songer).

Can't blame the poor beast for wanting to leave New Jersey.

If not a moose, what else could it be?

At less than 200 pounds and only 3' to 4' in height at the shoulders, the northern white-tail deer does not come close to the measurements of the "subject-in-question" in the pictures. With that being the case, the only other alternative to the moose would be an elk. Large herds of "Eastern" elk (which the native American Indian called "wapiti") once roamed wild and free in the Pennsylvania countryside, but had been wiped out by the mid 1800's. It is believed that the last known native Eastern elk was killed by Jim Jacobs (a full-blooded American Indian) back in 1867 on the headwaters of the Clarion River, a tributary of the Allegheny River in west central Pennsylvania.

In 1913, 177 "Yellowstone" Elk were re-introduced back into Pennsylvania. Today, that number has grown to over 1,000 in a safe haven known as "Elk Range." This isolated, well-managed, area includes portions of Cameron, Clinton, Clearfield, Centre and Elk counties. Ironically, that was the same area where the last native elk was killed by Mr. Jacobs. Those north central counties are not exactly around the corner from South Mountain, but at 600 pounds and 4' to 5' in height at the shoulders, the elk was certainly closer to the stature of the "subject in question" than the white-tail deer.

"Yes, Sùilean Soilleir, I would have to agree," Hitch admitted after having had a peaceful night's sleep, his first cup of morning joe and seeing the glow of amazement in her sparkling eyes. "These are not the best pictures from which to draw an absolute conclusion, but the animal's size, the paddle shape of the antlers and the fullness of the nose certainly differentiate it from a deer or elk."

"Good, then we can take the Jeep out for a spin sometime today. You know, do a little exploring of our own. That kind of thing," Debbie stated excitedly. "It's been two weeks. The memory cards in the cameras must be full by now. At least we can bring those back here to download."

"Agreed... and what are Jeeps if not for doing a little poking around in the woods," Hitch replied with an uncontainable smile. "I must admit to being a bit curious myself. Then again, I would be most grateful not to see a mountain lion or a pack of wolves on those memory cards."

The rains had not yet begun – which made their exploration a beautiful experience. The fair weather also allowed the Jeep to take them as far into the forest as they wanted to go. There was much to be said about owing a Jeep, but being quite was not one of them. If they were to come across a moose undetected, that would have to be one stupid, or totally deaf, moose. To ensure a safe trip out, they stocked the Jeep for every emergency that had the potential to stop their fun. To ensure a safe return, they did not attempt to climb rocks too steep or traverse streams too deep. To ensure they could find their way back, they would blaze their trails at constant intervals with spray paint on live trees at eye level. Unfortunately, or fortunately, no deaf moose was spotted. It was late afternoon by the time they returned to the cabin with the SD memory cards.

Cleaning everyone up, making and enjoying a delightful dinner, cleaning up after a delightful dinner, playing with the kittens, this, that and the other, took precedence over the viewing of the contents of the memory cards once they were downloaded to the laptop. By following that order, it was late in the evening before Debbie began to look at pictures once again. She did so by starting where she left off - at the old millhouse ruins. It did not take long for her to call out to Hitch.

"Eddie, it's him again," she announced with a tad less shock and awe as the first time she looked upon the extraordinarily large animal. "And he has company."

Apparently, later in the evening that same day, a second time-stamped series of pictures captured the "subject-in-question" once again. Whether it was intentional or not, the animal was now standing inches away and staring directly into the camera's lens. This time, the images were a bit clearer, but somewhat distorted due to such close proximity to the lens. All that could be seen now was the top portion of a furry brown snout – which seemed like it was a mile long due to the optical distortion. At the other end of that elongated honker were two large inquisitive eyeballs strategically placed on each side of a large head and just below the base of two thick antlers. Because the head took up so much of the picture frame space, little else about the animal was visible.

To add some intrigue to the whole affair, there, standing boldly between the base of the two antlers, was a squirrel. It seemed equally fascinated by the camera. Now, assuming the "subject-in-question" was not standing on a rock or a box or a ladder, that would mean the enormous head - and the squirrel on top of it - were close to 8' off the ground. That was the height at which Hitch set the camera on the tree.

"May I be the first to state the obvious?" Hitch asked politely.

"Please do," Debbie replied sweetly.

"That is definitely a moose... and definitely a squirrel," he stated as if the combination were something one might see any day of the week.

"Nothing more unusual than that, huh?" Debbie asked in a manner than suggested she was a bit "under" whelmed by his response.

"You and Fang talk to each other," he replied thoughtfully. "Am I supposed to see something more unusual in this picture other than a moose and a squirrel?"

"Hmm... I see your point, mo luaidh," she admitted and leaned upwards for a kiss to signal the end of his need to stay. "I will call for you if I come across anything unusual."

It was now Good Friday. This was two days after Hitch and Debbie first discovered they had a moose roaming around the fields and streams beyond the cabin. Oh, and his cute traveling companion - the squirrel. It took Debbie all day yesterday to go through the rest of the pictures taken by the two trail cameras. The cameras were set to take pictures having a whopping 22 megapixels. That setting provided the best picture quality and, thankfully, kept the total number of pictures down to a reasonable quantity of about a 1,000, or so. Regardless of whether it was day (vibrant color) or night (black and white), the images were sharp and crystal clear as long as the subject was within the detection range of 60 feet. As one might expect, there were all kinds of wildlife out there: beaver, bear, bobcat, coyote, deer, fox, opossum, otter, porcupine, raccoon, skunk – just to name those that were the largest and easiest to identify. To their relief, there were no mountain lions or wolves. Sadly, however, there were no additional pictures of the moose and squirrel duo.

The steady rain began overnight and there appeared to be no end in sight. If you were the two-legged type that liked to stay dry and clean, it was the perfect day to play a "best two out of three" game of chess, or team up and put together a challenging 1,000-piece puzzle, or finish reading that light-hearted, un-scholarly, "take-you-far-away" book you started a month ago. If you were the four-legged type that preferred being wet and muddy, it was the perfect day to be outside. Which is why Wallace was standing impatiently at the door after inhaling breakfast. He always finished his meal - every meal - before Fang. She was one of those who took an aggravatingly long time to enjoy every delightful morsel. The fact that he had to wait until she finished to go outside was a huge sacrifice that he was willing to endure... for love. Not that he had any choice really, but he would do that for her even if he were not forced to... probably. Fang was not completely finished with her meal when Hitch approached Wallace at the front door. It was not yet time to go out, but he simply wanted to attempt another "conversation" with his beloved pet. Misunderstanding this awkward moment without Fang by his side, Wallace took his normal position just slightly out of the path that the door would take when it was opened.

"Wallace, good boy. Not yet," Hitch spoke in that half-hearted voice one uses before having their morning coffee. "Can we talk before you go out today?"

He waited momentarily for a response that would indicate Wallace was half listening. Per Debbie's recommendation, whenever Hitch wanted to communicate with Wallace, he would phrase the question to elicit a "yes or no" response. To Wallace, it was as plain as day. This was a loaded question that had nothing whatsoever to do with opening the door, therefore, it only caused him to shift his stance in a more animated fashion. That was not exactly the response Hitch was looking for. Not wishing to belabor that point, Hitch continued.

"OK, good boy. Not yet," Hitch uttered patiently. "It is raining today. Rain creates mud. We both know you have no self-control in the presence of mud. That mud – which will soon cover 90% of your body's surface area - must be removed before re-entering the cabin. We also know whose job it is to remove it... yes or no?"

Wallace let out a muffled bark appropriate for the time of day, followed by a fairly testy "ro, ro, ro" and heavy breathing before returning his undivided attention back to the door. Hitch was not quite sure if the bark was a "yes," or a "no." They still sounded too much alike to him. He continued.

"Yes, good boy. Not yet," Hitch replied gently. "Let me re-phrase the question..."

Just when Hitch was going to ask a less verbose "yes" or "no" question, Fang showed up. Now, he had both Wallace and Fang standing in front of the door and looking up at him with rapt anticipation of the door being opened. For a brief moment, Hitch felt as if he were Abraham Lincoln and this was going to be the Gettysburg Address. Hitch was never one to back away from delivering a good speech. He had been doing that sort of thing for years with Hillary University's Freshman class. The bottom line was always the same; if all you want is affirmation, give them what they want to hear. Hitch was not looking for affirmation necessarily, but the time for a reasoned dialogue had passed. And, hey, it was Good Friday... give them what they want.

"Go," Hitch stated genially as he opened the door.

As soon as Wallace's front feet touched wet grass, his head lowered and he performed the perfect "motorboat." This maneuver was aptly named because - when the grass was at the right height and saturation point – you could plow yourself forward by using the hind legs only. When done properly, it created a wake of displaced water beside you as you advanced. After five feet or so, Wallace allowed his hind legs to catch up with his front legs in order to complete a forward roll into a standing position.

After a good shake from head to tail, he noticed Butterbean off in the distance. Daisy Cup and the kids were also up and going about their morning rituals. When guy dog and guy squirrel locked eyes, they rushed towards each other at full-throttle. They called this game "professional soccer" for some reason. The object of the game was to come as close to the other without making full contact. The only two options available for Butterbean to pass close enough to make the move appear dangerous was to go under or over Wallace. In either case, once they passed, Wallace would flop down on the ground and pretend to writhe in pain. Butterbean's job was to vehemently deny any wrongdoing and, in a matter of seconds, both were ready to play some more.

Fang, on the other hand, would say her "good mornings" to Daisy Cup and play tag with the kids. Occasionally, she would pick one up with her nose and toss them in the air a few feet. They loved that. Fang was now the "very odd-looking favorite aunt" for both the baby squirrels and mom-cat's kittens. She was still the hard-bodied athlete she always was, but her heart had been gently re-made. She loved that. After ten or fifteen minutes, it would be Daisy Cup that would call for an end to the horseplay.

Wallace and Fang could not think of a better way to kick off a wet morning than that... but that did not stop them from trying. Just as the winter snowfall brought with it new adventures, so did the spring rainfall. One thing rain did well was to expose, or open up, trails though the forest that would normally be hidden by low lying broad-leaved plants when they are dry. Rain brought these big leaves sagging, limp and lifeless, to the ground. Rain also kept tracks from disappearing longer or it could erase them in an instant. It took a while, but Wallace and Fang finally stumbled upon one of those "hidden" trails.

The discovery of this trail came after following a large "known" trail, which led to a "known" mud hole. After messaging his tight muscles in the reddish-brown goo, they both followed another smaller "known" trail, which led to a "known" clear mountain pond. By this time, it had exceeded its banks to the point where it put the bottoms of the wild berry bushes that surrounded it under water. After a few mud cleansing laps by Wallace, they followed an even smaller "known" trail, which would have led them to another "known" mud hole. Instead, they came across the "hidden" trail. There were many other "hidden" trails, but what made this one impossible to resist were the animal tracks that sunk deep into the soggy ground. The tracks were unfamiliar to Wallace and Fang... and they were huge!

"No chase. Tracks too big," Fang barked her objections after seeing the tracks. "Go time."

"Tracks slow," Wallace replied. "Look, smell, go time."

Of course, "look, smell, go time" was the same line Wallace always used just before the inevitable chase, but he was right. The tracks did show a heavy four-legged animal with a slow, lumbering gait. Whatever it was, there was little doubt in Fang's mind that they could outrun it. Maybe, just maybe, this adventure might end without bumps, bruises or bullet wounds.

"Look, smell, go time," she repeated his words as if they were a legally binding verbal agreement.

"Look, smell, go time," he immediately agreed to the terms.

"No chase," she added hastily.

"No chase," he grumbled.

The tracks were fresh and deep. That made them easy to follow despite the soft rain. Wallace led the way. They were venturing into unfamiliar territory, but the large animal seemed to be happy following a well-defined animal path that stayed close to a narrow, but fast-paced mountain stream.

This was the same stream that fed the refreshing pond they just left. The animal's tracks and path crossed the stream at the bottom of a waterfall that cascaded over a 20' cliff with terrific force. The water's force was greatly diminished once it hit the rocks and pile of dead timber below. The path crossed the stream again above the waterfall and that is where the tracks appeared to end. The stream was much wider above the falls than below the falls, making it difficult to know for sure whether the animal crossed here or decided to walk up the stream itself. There was one way to find out. Wallace was the better swimmer, but Fang jumped the 20' span with ease.

"No thing," Fang barked after finding no tracks on the other side.

"Go time," Wallace replied after looking up-stream, then down-stream towards the falls.

The leap coming back over the stream should have been a piece of cake. Instead, upon takeoff, Fang twisted her front paw in a pocket of loose mud and tumbled head over heels into the deep rolling water. By the time she resurfaced and started paddling with the three good feet she had left, the current had swept her into the stream's fast lane – heading directly for the waterfall. Watching all this unfold, Wallace instinctively jumped in after her. Instantly, two thoughts came to mind; one, he was not doing any good being in the water with her and, two, he quickly recalled seeing a large rock formation in the middle of the stream just before the waterfall. Wallace paddled frantically close to the stream's bank and barked directions.

"Rock in water. Go to rock!' He barked over and over again. "Rock in water. Go to rock!"

It worked. Fang turned her attention down-stream - instead of up-stream - and corrected her course just in time to crawl up onto the rock. Fortunately, it was a large, smooth flat rock that jutted out of the water high enough to allow her to lie safely without any fear of being washed away. That was the good news. The bad news was - she was still in the middle of a fast-paced stream close to a 20' waterfall with a twisted ankle. Wallace climbed out of the water another 10 yards up-stream from where Fang was resting on the rock. It was the last opportunity he had to save himself before going over the waterfall.

"Fang hurt?" he asked.

This was more of an observation than a question. It was obvious that Fang was struggling to swim after failing to get a good launch off the opposite bank. He just needed to know how bad.

"Foot hurt," she replied. "No swim."

"Wallace go," he stated without hesitation. "Bring help."

In a flash, Wallace had his whole body turned in the direction of the path and was about to make his first explosive leap to get help when he noticed something that froze him in his tracks. He could honestly say, it was the largest animal he had ever set eyes on. The hairy beast was not just large... it was monstrously large with antlers that were no less than 6 feet in width. It was standing just up-stream from where he and Fang entered the water moments ago. It did not move. It did not speak. It just stood there... watching. In other words, Wallace had met his first moose.

Not only did the moose surprise him, but perched on the very top of one of its antlers stood a very small squirrel.

Comparatively speaking, that is. The squirrel was actually a large grey squirrel and almost the size of Butterbean. It, too, just stood there watching the events that led to Fang being hurt and stranded on a rock. Perhaps it was the presence of the squirrel that made Wallace less fearful of the massive creature. Not that the moose did anything to be fearful of. It was just shockingly big... that thought nothing about strolling through a raging stream... with big strong antlers... capable of carrying another injured animal to safety. Wallace could not have hoped for more.

"Fang hurt," Wallace pleaded softly. "Help Fang."

The moose and squirrel seemed to give it some thought, but said nothing. The moose turned slowly to walk back up-stream.

"Please!" Wallace barked at the top of his lungs.

This emotional plea for help did not seem to faze either the moose or the squirrel as they started their slow progress back up-stream.

"Ëgadiyóhšö friend!" Wallace called out Butterbean's ancient squirrel name.

This latest outburst caused the moose to stop and turn its head slightly as if it wanted to hear more about what was being said. The squirrel immediately raced down the antler and then to the moose's rump. He stood on his hind legs and stared back at Wallace intently. After a brief pause, the squirrel spoke.

"Speak name."

"Ëgadiyóhšö and Awë:iyo friend," Wallace replied. "Wallace squirrel name, O'tsögwasnye, (ancient squirrel name meaning, "he took care of us"). Fang squirrel name, O'töwödisnye, (ancient squirrel name meaning, "she took care of us").

These were the names given to them by Butterbean and Daisey Cup. At this point, Wallace took the time to explain how they met, the ordeal with the flyers (horned owls) and a brief description on how he and Butterbean played the game of "professional soccer" this morning. When Wallace had finished speaking, the squirrel turned and serpentined his way back up to the head of the moose with a few hops and bounces - as squirrels like to do... saying nothing. Wallace's heart sank.

Suddenly, the moose turned and began to trudge slowly through the water down-stream towards Wallace. It took all the bravery he could manage not to run for dear life, but Wallace stood his ground. The giant moose stopped directly in front of Wallace, but kept his huge body in the water and pointed down-stream towards Fang. After two acrobatic leaps, the squirrel was standing in the middle of the moose's back and facing Wallace.

"Hodí:wade:nyö (ancient squirrel name meaning, "he's got things to do"), my name," the squirrel offered with some formality.

"Hakowanëh (ancient squirrel name meaning "the boy can eat"), my friend," he spoke again and took one vertical hop to indicate he was speaking about the moose he was riding.

"We take O'töwödisnye home now," the squirrel stated unceremoniously.

The moose walked slowly over to the rock without much trouble. He stopped in front of the rock, his enormous body preventing the rushing water from hitting it directly. Then, positioning himself with great care, he lowered his head and angled his antler so that Fang could maneuver herself safely into its wide, thick palm.

"O'töwödisnye ready?" the squirrel asked Fang politely.

"Ready," Fang replied gratefully.

The moose and squirrel were true to their word. Not only were they going to bring Fang safely out of the water, they were going to carry her all the way back to the cabin. It would be a different path – a much wider path – to allow for a more comfortable ride. Along the way, the squirrel would talk with the moose and Wallace would talk with Fang. Occasionally, Wallace and Fang would hear the squirrel call the moose "Bruce," but mostly just, bro this and bro that. The moose (who did not do much talking) would call the squirrel "Flea," but mostly just "li'l bro." Fang's foot throbbed, but it was not broken and she predicted it would heal quickly. Nonetheless, it would have been a long, painful trip back to the cabin if not for the generosity of Bruce and Flea. Showing little concern about being seen, Bruce exited the forest and walked casually into the front yard. He did not stop until he was almost to the cabin's porch steps.

Fang had not yet been lowered to the ground when Hitch and Debbie walked out the front door and onto the porch. Not only that, Butterbean, Daisy Cup and the kids came from all directions and were now huddled together in the front yard. So, for an instant, there they all were in the light rain - both motionless and speechless. Bruce gently lowered Fang to the ground, but instead of leaving, he walked slowly over to where Butterbean, Daisy Cup and the kids gathered. Apparently, Flea and Butterbean were related somehow. So, while Flea would hang out with family in the front yard, Bruce went about eating everything in sight, including the beautiful Easter lilies that were left outside. After a half hour or so, moose and squirrel said their goodbyes to the family and left.

Meanwhile, Debbie carried Fang to the porch, dried her off and wrapped her paw. The injury was confirmed to be a painful sprain only and would heal in a couple days. Hitch washed the remaining glops of red mud from Wallace's body, dried him and offered him a few extra dog biscuits. Wallace would accept them all gratefully.

What else are you supposed to do in circumstances like this?

Run around like a chicken with its head cut off?

It's a moose. It's a squirrel. It's a family reunion in your front yard. It's life at the cabin in the woods... for Pete's sake.

Get over it!

Chapter 14

Dueling Cantatas

It was now Saturday, April 4, AD 33 in Jerusalem, Judaea. If the majority of biblical number-crunching scholars were accurate in their calculations, Jesus would have died the day before, on (Good) Friday, April 3, AD 33. It would have been about 3 pm and a few hours before the beginning of the Jewish Passover and Sabbath. Most Christians have since referred to this day as Holy Saturday. Jesus has been crucified and his body was now resting peacefully behind a rock somewhere in a garden tomb near Golgotha (Jn 19:17-18, Jn 19:41-42). Because Passover was to be a day of rest for the Jewish population, not much was going on in town or at the tomb. The only biblical account of what took place on Holy Saturday comes to us from Matthew's gospel (Mt 27:62-66). In it he states that Pilate (in office 26–36 AD) had agreed to post a Roman guard at Jesus' tomb to prevent anyone from stealing the body.

That, of course, begs the question; what difference should that make to a Roman? The man is dead. Let the thieves or the crows have the body. Good riddance!

Not so fast. Didn't Jesus say something about returning to life three days after death... like a resurrection of some sort? Yup!

After all his wonderous acts (miracles) early on, Jesus finally began to explain to his disciples what was really going on. That is, he must die and on the third day be raised to life (Mt 17:23, Mk 8:31, Lk 9:22, Jn 2:19).

It is kind of ironic that no one, not even Jesus' own disciples, totally grasped the whole "raised to life" part... except the Jewish chief priests and Pharisees!

"So, Pilate, bro, thanks for taking care of our little problem yesterday. Man, even I had trouble watching that go down," the chief priest stated squeamishly. "Got one more favor to ask."

"What now Caiaphas?" the Roman prefect (governor) asked with some annoyance. "And stop calling me bro."

"Well, I could use a couple of your best guys to protect the tomb where Jesus is buried," Caiaphas asked straight up.

"He's dead," Pilate answered bluntly and with even more annoyance.

"I know, I know, that's the tricky part," Caiaphas replied nervously. "As crazy as this might sound, Jesus said he would rise from the dead three days after you, um, I mean, we killed him."

"And you believed him?" the Roman politician asked.

It was hard to tell if what he was being asked was just another one of those prophesy pranks that Jews liked to play on him.

"Dude, we know how to kill people.", Pilate snarled. "It's what we do."

"Yes, yes, I know that. But, it's not me, it's the people who believe this resurrection thing," the priest whined.

The chief priest knew he was between a rock and hard place, but it was best to be safe than sorry.

"Look, we both know people are stupid. You should understand that. We are both politicians now. We deal with stupid people all day, every day. It's what you and I must do," Caiaphas groaned. "A couple of guards for today and through the night is all I am asking. After that, we are golden. You got to trust me on this one, man."

"Caiaphas, if you weren't such a useful puppet, I'd have you flogged just for grins and giggles," Pilate snorted, but relented. "Take a guard. Make the tomb secure. Now, go away before I raise your taxes."

OK, dear reader, I know what you're thinking, "Kinda funny spin on things, but you're fairly sure that is not what happened back then."

Fair enough. Now, in a hundred words or less (and preferably funny), you tell me how Caiaphas convinced Pilate – a ruthless soldier turned ruthless politician, that Jesus - a man he just crucified, will be returning from the dead.

Yeah, right?

It was now Holy Saturday in Hillary, Pennsylvania.

"The day we have all been waiting for... well, besides Easter itself," the enthusiastic broadcaster proclaimed to his radio co-host. "It's the day we get to watch the battle for Easter Cantata supremacy in this relatively small college town called Hillary. Will it be the heavily-favored, defending champion's masterpiece by J. S. Bach in the Walker Auditorium or the much smaller, but highly entertaining, underdog offerings from Fellowship Bible Church? I won't lie to you - it looks like it will be another uphill battle for FBC this year. What may make this contest much too close to call, however, is the addition of that dazzling rookie mezzo-soprano, Francesca. She certainly does bring a lot to that talented FBC lineup.

"That's true, Bud," the equally-enthusiastic co-host exclaimed. "But the reigning champs have not been idle in the offseason either. For the past ten years, this group has been brilliantly coached by Professor Leon Bouchard. And, not to be outdone, he has just recently acquired the phenomenally talented free agent tenor, Everett. I don't know about you, but I am super excited about this year's competition. We haven't seen this kind of matchup in years, folks. It is not something you will want to miss. So, buckle up Hillary... 'cause its show time!"

OK, dear reader, I know what you are thinking, "Kinda funny spin on things, but you're fairly sure that was a fake competition announced by a couple of fake broadcasters. That would never happen between two Christian organizations."

Fair enough. Still, you can bet your bottom dollar that everyone involved in these two Easter super-charged events was feeling some heat.

The stubborn weather pattern of relentless drizzle had finally passed through, leaving behind only a few puffy white clouds in its wake. Not that fair weather had anything to do with it, but Everett and Francesca decided to meet early for breakfast at the small, family-owned French bakery in town. Of course, "early" for young adults on their day off meant some time just before noon and "breakfast" was, more or less, a croissant au chocolat et **café** (chocolate croissant and coffee).

Everett placed their order in French.

Oddly enough, the conversation that followed had little to do with music.

"So, you speak French too, huh?" Francesca asked as if not surprised.

"Oui," Everett replied without explanation and took his first sip of hot coffee cautiously.

"Figures," Francesca retorted as she inspected her chocolate croissant on the plate in front of her. "Italian?"

"Sì," Everett replied just before taking a bite out of his croissant that a Jurassic T-Rex would be proud of.

"Figures," she retorted while using a fork to carefully tear off a portion of her pastry.

Francesca already knew Everett spoke German and almost everyone knew that most operas were sung in Italian, so his answer did not come as a surprise to her when she popped the question. Spanish was another language he would most likely know. Even she knew a little Spanish. So, why ask?

She took some delight in watching Everett attempt to clean the numerous croissant crumbs from his well-maintained beard. This gave Francesca enough time to enjoy a bite of her own French croissant and contemplate the next major language that would actually surprise her if he knew how to speak it.

"Russian?"

"Нет (pronounced "nyet")," he replied using the only Russian word he knew.

Slightly embarrassed, Everett collected the crumbs that did not make it into his mouth into a pile on the table. This pile was then swept off the table and into a napkin. He was about to speak when Francesca smiled affectionately, leaned forward and brushed away one missed crumb from his beard with her napkin. Then, as if acting out a silent tutorial, she slowly sat back, paused, tore another bite-size portion off the croissant with her fork - paused - carefully picked it up with her finger tips - paused - gently placed it onto her tongue - paused - then allowed it to disappear into her mouth without a trace. Softly chewing the tasty French creation, she gazed down at the table as if looking for something. This caused Everett to look down at the table. Satisfied there was not one errant crumb to be found, she returned her attention back to Everett.

"You were about to say..." Francesca spoke kindly.

Let's face it. The only good way for a good man with a good beard to eat a good croissant was to make it quick and messy!

"Comment appelez-vous votre tante française en colère?" Everett asked while choosing to accept the cute little jab at his table manners without comment.

"What?" she grunted – not understanding a single French word being spoken.

"What do you call your angry French aunt?" he translated.

"What?" she asked with a hint of anticipation – now understanding she was about to hear the punch line of a joke.

"A cross-aunt," Everett stated – barely able to keep a straight face. "Cross aunt... croissant... cross-aunt."

"Good one," Francesca admitted with a chuckle.

Appreciating a good joke, but only able to remember the corny ones, she continued.

"What do you get when you cross a shark with a snowball?"

"What?" he asked after thinking about it for a second or two.

"Frostbite," she answered tentatively.

"Nice," Everett stated after a hearty laugh. "Cross joke too. Funny and genius."

They would share a few more silly jokes until the topic turned to Easter... and more specifically, Jesus. It was part of the reason they were sitting across from each other. Both Everett and Francesca agreed that for someone to rise from the dead it would have to be considered a miracle. So, a brief conversation on miracles followed. A supernatural event such as that must stand in total contrast to a magician's trick or the power of hypnosis on a weak mind.

All of that naturally led to a brief conversation on the trustworthiness of Scripture. That controversial topic not only touched on the part that said Jesus was raised from the dead, but also the part that said "All Scripture is God-breathed..." (2 Tim 3:16). They could not deny that it would be the epitome of hypocrisy to believe only those parts of the Bible that made you feel happy about yourself and disregard, or claim falsehood, the stuff that made you feel unhappy about yourself. That meant you were either in – or you were out. Fence-sitting was not an option.

They also agreed that if Jesus claimed to be God - and, yet, was not truly God - then he must be considered some kind of delusional nut-job. Lots of those people running around these days claiming to be something they are not. The strange thing is that lots of people are believing everything these nut-jobs say. Of course, virtue-signaling is a twisted twenty-first century phenomenon. It was doubtful that very many people would still agree to such nonsense if their lives were at stake.

It was getting deep now.

Too deep... and time was zipping by - as it often does when two battered hearts longing for true love finally meet.

So, did Jesus rise from the dead 2,000 years ago the way Scripture says he did?

At this point in their journey together, Everett and Francesca both agreed that Easter... heck, Christianity itself, should probably stand or fall on the answer to that question. Regardless of his strong feelings towards Frannie, Everett freely admitted to her that that was a giant leap of faith he was not prepared to make right now. Francesca understood, but claimed it was faith that grounded her decision to follow Jesus. Faith did not stop her from asking tough questions about the unfashionable biblical doctrines like sin, repentance and hell. Faith did, however, give her someone perfect to talk to, someone perfect to pray to, someone perfect to surrender her circumstances to... and not expect perfection in return.

Without being preachy, Francesca explained it this way. It was her opinion that faith gets short-changed and misrepresented way too often. To some, faith is simply having a belief in something despite there being no evidence to prove it. OK, but that seemed too wishy-washy and unconvincing to her. She much preferred how the writer of Hebrews put it;

"Now faith is the assurance of things hoped for and the conviction of things not seen" (Heb 11:1).

To Francesca, that definition of faith had power and was worth checking out.

"Faith is also a gift, Everett," Francesca wrapped up her thoughts. "It is a free gift. It is a free gift from God."

"Frannie, I hear you," Everett replied earnestly. "I think my hang up with Christianity, till now, has been the Christian, not the Christ."

"Um, can you unpack that for me, please?" Francesca asked politely.

"'Don't bother looking to the man who calls himself a Christian, my boy, you will only find corruption and deceit. Look to Jesus. No one else,'" Everett stated as if reading it off a Carolina billboard. "My grandfather told me that when I was four years old. I didn't even know what corruption and deceit meant back then, but I think he knew that statement was going to be his only shot to plant a seed somewhere in the back of my mind."

"I see what you mean," Francesca moaned, then lit up like a Christmas tree. "I got an idea. I'll sing for Jesus tonight and you sing for your grandpa tonight. He would go for that, right?"

"Now that you mention it, I'm thinking it would blow his mind hearing me sing tonight!" Everett agreed wholeheartedly. "Frannie, if I was given one wish, it would be to have my grandparents at the Walker tonight. If I was given a second wish, it would be to hear you sing."

"But you did hear me sing," she replied softly.

"Yes, I did. And you were magnificent," he said gratefully. "But that was just a rehearsal and your next Cantata isn't until Christmas, right?"

"True," she confirmed with some hopefulness. "But I sing with the rest of the choir almost every Sunday, you know."

"I heard about that!" Everett exclaimed as if that was new news. "I'm almost positive Jake and Joey will allow me to join their 'Francesca for President of the Whole World' fan club. Man, I hope they have a tree fort with secret passwords and stuff."

"Shut up," Francesca quipped with a bright, beautiful smile. "Besides, I would be more worried about what Pamela and Mickey think of you hanging around."

"Good point," he stated nervously. "I better keep the beard products handy."

It was an hour before the show was to begin and the Walker was filling up fast... God is good. Everett was so at ease with his role in this Cantata that he treated the whole event like any other gig. The "chill" factor was so low that when Leon casually asked how he was feeling, Everett answered by belting out his part (Peter the apostle) in the third movement aria, "Kommt, eilet und laufet" (come, hurry and run), on the spot. After a few verses, Leon held both hands up and gently motioned for him to put a cork in it. "Save it for later," Leon would say before smiling and walking off.

There would be no hiding out in a back stage dressing room until the last minute either. When his spontaneous "sound check" with Leon was over, Everett would spend the next several minutes walking among the many wonderfully talented and pleasantly down-to-earth people in the choir and orchestra. He would say hello to those he knew and introduce himself to those he did not. This special rapport was no different than being on tour with his band. He and his bandmates enjoyed the, almost familial, interaction between musicians from other rock bands before and between sets. If there was a difference, it would be that tonight's musicians were not high as a kite.

With a half hour before he was to take his place on stage, Everett stepped out into the seating area and continued to speak with those people closest to the stage. This venturing out into the audience was not something he would ever do at a rock concert. The open area just off stage was considered the "mosh pit" and it can get plenty dicey down in there - to put it mildly. In fact, it was considered his job - the ultimate goal as a rock performer - to whip that particular group of party animals into a frenzy. Of course, he never wanted anyone to get hurt, but it was inevitable.

Everett felt no such reservation in mingling here since those having front seat tickets were much older and a whole lot wiser. They were patrons of the arts. He liked the fact that not one of the patrons he greeted recognized him as being the lead tenor. They all thought he was just some nice young fellow hired by the university to make them feel a little more welcomed on this very special evening. Won't they be surprised?

Everett was about to return to the stage when a very old gentleman in a space reserved for those with disabilities requiring wheelchairs waved him over. The time was getting short, but Everett felt compelled to assist in getting the help he needed. The shortness of time was confirmed when a woman on stage announced the doors would be closed in ten minutes and asked all those standing to please find their seats. This prompted Everett to hasten his pace.

"Sir, I have ten minutes," Everett stated politely, but firmly. "Can I find you some help?"

"I heard you sing the aria just now," the elderly man spoke with a distinct German accent. It was a hoarse, breathless voice that matched his frail body perfectly. "You are the tenor. You are Peter."

"Yes, but are you hurting? Do you need medical assistance?" Everett asked nervously as he looked around the room for someone in uniform to take over or, at least, call 911 if necessary.

"I have prayed for you," the old man said.

There was a sadness in the old man's words now. This added a raspy quality to his already weakened voice.

"Do I know you, sir?" Everett asked as curiosity replaced his nervousness. "Why would you pray for me?"

"My grandson was the tenor before you," the sad man replied. "I prayed you would come to make everything right again."

"Your grandson has a wonderful voice," Everett reassured the man who obviously felt some deep regret for what occurred. "Honestly, I was happy to step in."

"What my grandson did to everybody here was wrong," the broken man stated tearfully now. "He waited so long because it got him more money. He knows it was wrong and he did it anyway."

If Everett didn't know better, it sounded as if this poor man was blaming himself for the actions of his grandson. He watched carefully as the old man took a moment to wipe his eyes and nose with a clothe handkerchief in trembling hands. This man's contrition was certainly misguided, but it was having a profound effect on Everett.

"Really, it's OK," Everett spoke kindly. He slowly squatted down so that the old man was now at eye level. "It will all work out for good. You'll see. Are you alright?"

"My grandson... I tell him all the money in the world won't bring him happiness. I tell him only Jesus will bring the kind of happiness we all want and need so desperately," the old man spoke softly while allowing his head to droop forward. "I talk and I pray he will one day know this joy I have had in Jesus. I love my grandson, but my time here is almost up."

"Sir," Everett spoke pointedly which caused the old man to raise his head and look him square in the eye. "I need to go now, but you did everything Jesus asked of you. Let him take over now. You go and rest."

Everett wasn't exactly sure where that mouthful came from, but it was sincere. He stood up to leave, but then immediately squatted back down again and spoke once more.

"It may seem to you that your grandson wasn't listening, but he will remember."

This meeting in the center aisle did not go unnoticed. Leon knew the man Everett was speaking to and had some idea what was being discussed. He knew the man because he had come to Leon last week asking for forgiveness for what his grandson had done. Jesus had been mocked and the burden on this old man's heart had become too great for him carry. Once he was told by Leon that his grandson had already been forgiven by him, the old man burst into tears. "Thank you" was all the man would keep repeating until he was assisted out of the room by a slightly younger, older gentleman – both being Army veterans. Leon would stall long enough for Everett to make it back on stage without anyone being the wiser.

What had just taken place in the seats could not have set a better stage for Bach's first movement instrumental sinfonia. With a wave of the hand, Leon let loose the strings, continuo (pipe organ and bass), oboes, bassoons, flutes, three trumpets and timpani in triple meter. It would proclaim the pure joy of the Easter miracle to all in attendance.

Meanwhile, on the other side of town, Francesca was back at FBC spending her first Easter weekend as a born-again Christian with her new born-again friends. It had been quite a week... or two... or three. FBC was not a mega-church where the hundreds of minor tasks could be contracted out so the congregation did not have to get their hands dirty. It functioned like most households, if something needed to get cleaned or the grass needed to be mowed, then someone in the family would take care of it. So, there she was – FBC's newest shining star – out in the open field helping Alex clean up after the popular kid's Easter egg hunt that morning. This was no easy task. There were over a hundred kids looking for over a thousand plastic Easter eggs filled with wrapped candy. And, well, kids will be kids. Who among them could resist breaking open an egg or three and enjoy the fruits of their labor – right there in the field - leaving behind hundreds of tiny wrappers?

Actually, the clean-up was not so bad. Alex, Francesca, and a few other adult volunteers were given permission to eat the contents of any over-looked egg they may come across – if they wished. The plan, otherwise known as a sweep, was to spread out in a line across the field, start walking towards the opposite side of the field picking up any trash along the way. Then, walk back again for good measure. Francesca started on the far end closest to the tree line, with Alex two sweepers to her right. Among the debris and assorted kid's clothing left behind (socks, shoes, hats, sunglasses, etc.), Alex found three filled eggs and Francesca found ten. She had always been good at this game. They were all about half way up the field when Francesca noticed a colorful egg that had been opened, surrounded by several wrappers and close to one of the wide trails leading into the trees. The large wooded area was also owned by the church. It was not necessarily a dense forest, but it was full of nice hardwoods that gave each other plenty of room to grow tall and strong. This made it great for hiking around in, overnight camping and hunting deer - when in season. The woods seemed to go on forever, but that was mainly because the church property was adjacent to other private property with even more acres of unimproved wooded terrain.

The wooded area was not supposed to be used to hide Easter eggs and it concerned Francesca when she spotted another opened egg and trash further down the path. The church was extremely diligent when it came to the safety and wellbeing of its children. As far as kids go, she knew everyone had been safely guarded during the event and meticulously accounted for after the event. If not, all heck would have broken loose. It was most likely one of those thoughtless "prodigal" sons and daughters she heard about in church. The ones that torment their parents and wreak havoc - and litter without thinking - wherever they go. In any case, she followed the path down to the trash and picked it up. Of course, what did she see even further down the path?

That's right. More trash. Oh boy, now Francesca was getting a little upset. Not only was this slob unconcerned about the mess they were making, they had no qualms stealing candy intended for the kids. If Francesca were to meet up with the thoughtless punk, he or she would get an earful. This would be the last candy wrapper she would pick up. If she were to see more further down the path, she would rejoin the others back on the field and organize a cleaning project for the woods after the holidays.

Well, wouldn't you know it, more discarded plastic eggs, wrappers... and a bike. The bicycle was leaning up against a tall, wooden structure several yards off the hiking path. As she got closer to the structure, she noticed an identical structure on the other side of the wide, shallow ravine that separated them. They were both walled towers on top of 10' posts. There were also several short 3' x 3' wooden fence panels placed randomly in between.

Cool. FBC has a paintball or airsoft course, she thought. *Will definitely check that out later.*

"You up there?" Francesca called out from a safe distance.

"Who wants to know?" a woman's voice replied as if someone had just interrupted their nap.

"The person who just cleaned up the mess you made. That's who!" Francesca barked, feeling a little better about the voice being female.

"Thanks, princess," the voice said. "Now go away unless you have something besides candy to eat."

"Sorry, it's all I got," Francesca replied sarcastically.

"I'll take it," the woman replied as she popped up and leaned her elbows on the 3' wall of the tower.

It was hard to tell the woman's age from her smoker's voice and disheveled appearance. It seemed to Francesca that the woman could be much younger than she looked. From the evidence that presented itself, she was most likely homeless. There was also something else about the woman that made her less angry. It was not the compassion one feels for the homeless and their troubles. It was more than that. It was something in the woman's eyes. They were empty of feeling and stared back at Francesca blankly, but they seemed... familiar. Did she know this woman?

"Here, catch," Francesca stated pleasantly and tossed her bag of unopened Easter eggs up to the lady. "I'm sure our church has some real food. Want to follow me back?"

"No thanks, sweetie. The demons inside me might start rebelling. It wouldn't be pretty," the old, young woman quipped and chuckled at herself. "You could be a sport and go get me something. Bring it back here and we can have a nice picnic. Just you and me. Sound good?"

"I'm not sure they would allow me to do that," Francesca responded politely.

"Then shut up and go away, princess!" the old, young woman snapped angrily. "Like you have ever been hungry in your life."

"I know hunger. I know abandonment, witch!" Francesca snarled, unable to contain the deep, dark emotions about her own past in which she lived from one bad foster home to another, even worse, foster home.

This brief, but heated, exchange caused both ladies to stare more intently at the other. After what seemed like forever, the woman slowly stood upright. She did not take her eyes off Francesca, but the bitterness and the emptiness disappeared from them. If Francesca didn't know better, she thought she saw the woman's eyes soften and turn moist.

"How old are you, child?" the woman asked tenderly.

Before Francesca could answer, Alex came running up.

"Are you OK?" Alex huffed as he took turns looking from Francesca to the lady in the tree stand.

Alex knew Francesca. He could tell from the expression on her face that something was going on, but uncertain just what. He even sensed something odd in the way the old lady looked at Francesca. Having only one "X" chromosome, Alex believed it would be over his head to presume he could possibly understand these matters and waited patiently for further instruction.

"I'm OK. I need you to bring me some food," Francesca stated without any emotion that would add clarity to Alex's doubts or concerns.

"I'm not sure they have anything left," he replied naively.

Francesca turned slowly in order to face Alex directly. With what seemed to be great restraint, she spoke so that each word was clearly annunciated.

"I need you... to bring me... some food... for two... now... please."

"I'm on it," Alex answered and was gone.

"Why did you ask me my age?" Francesca inquired.

"You remind me of someone, is all," the woman stated as if she had changed her mind about something.

Francesca was invited to join the woman in the tree stand and they enjoyed conversing in generalities before and after Alex brought enough food to feed a small army. It was easy to see there was going to be a lot left unsaid. The obfuscation began as soon as Francesca asked for a name. The woman gave her a first name, but not a last name. And that name was "Gypsy." There was a distinct hesitation, as if the woman could not decide on which alias to use for this occasion, but Francesca did not press. They each sang a few songs, but not together. Francesca could tell Gypsy loved to sing and had a beautiful voice once - before all the smoking. After an hour or so, Alex returned.

"Frannie, it's three o'clock," Alex gently reminded her.

"OK, thanks," she replied sadly and he left.

"I have to go now," she said having already explained her role in the church cantata. "I wish you would come tonight... please."

"Maybe I will, Frannie. Maybe," Gypsy stated kindly, yet unconvincingly. "But you best be going now, sweetie. I would feel horrible if anyone missed out on hearing you sing. You sing like an angel. Just like an angel you sing."

"Yeah, OK. I'll see you later then, maybe," Francesca replied hopefully, then tentatively gave her a hug. "Hey, maybe we can do this again next weekend. You know... picnic in the tree stand. You know... same time. I'll be here... same time. Every Sunday. I'll be here. OK?"

"OK, that sounds good too," Gypsy replied a little more convincingly.

"OK," Francesca replied and smiled.

"OK," Gypsy replied and smiled.

Alex was waiting at the door. Without a word, Francesca hugged him. She hugged with all her might. While still clinging to him, she tearfully whispered in his ear.

"Pray for her, Alex. Pray God will protect her from evil."

"I will," he promised.

Chapter 15

You're Just Who I Needed

"Faith is to believe what we do not see; and the reward
of this faith is to see what we believe"
Saint Augustine of Hippo

Easter, or Resurrection Day, or the essence of the
Christian faith, or the reason for the season, or the one day
out of the year we should all stop putting ourselves first, or
the... oh, heck, you get the point (Lk 24: 37-40). On this day,
Leon preferred the 6:45 am sunrise service his church offered.
These services were usually held in some reserved location
outdoors that best captured the gradual rising of the sun
in all its splendid glory. The unique time and place - which
naturally attracted fewer attendees than the 9:00 and 11:00
services inside the church – provided the perfect tranquil
environment for worshiping that Leon appreciated. It had
become another rejuvenating Sunday tradition for him and
Ruthie after the demands of a Saturday Cantata were over.
Early morning, or "while it was still dark" (Jn 20:1), was also
the time when Mary Magdalene, Mary (mother of James) and
Salome (Mk 15:40-41, Mk 16:1) went to the tomb to find it open

and Jesus missing. If you were to add to that beautiful back-drop a simple hymn from days gone by, well, now you have got yourself one phenomenal start to Easter. That is, unless dark clouds covered all that splendidness and heavy rains drove everyone back inside.

Fortunately, the only clouds in the sky were few and harm-less, thus assuring Leon's presence at this outdoor service. It was touch and go when his alarm went off this morning, however. The problem was sleep, or lack thereof. As it turned out, Leon had a late night. An unexpected late night. And the night was courtesy of everyone associated with the Easter Cantata, both past and present. If Leon thought he would serve Hillary's Christian community faithfully for ten years and disappear without some sort of grateful recognition for his selfless efforts, he was gravely mistaken. That recogni-tion took the form of a surprise party held in the Walker after everyone not associated with the Cantata had gone home for the evening.

As a matter of fact, that entire enterprise was the Chief's brainchild from its inception. He would get a call from Leon on Wednesday informing him that Saturday's performance was to be his last. That shocking news gave Chief Thursday and Good Friday to make good on his idea. There was no time to lose. The only way a project of this magnitude had any chance of succeeding on such short notice would be with help... lots of help. The first two names on Chief's list of contacts were Leon's daughters, Billie and Ella. Since their father had already spoken to them about his plans to retire, they were not surprised by the news, but they were overjoyed to hear Chief's plans to honor their dad. Billie and Ella would spend Thursday and

Friday on the phone contacting past members... who would then contact past members they knew... who would then contact past members they knew... and on and on it went. Even though time was short and Easter plans had been set by many, the number of people grateful for having performed with Leon would be in the hundreds.

Billie and Ella discovered early in the phone calling process that the same people willing and able to come also offered to bring something to eat. That prompted Chief to make the kitchen and dining hall in the Sanctuary available on Friday and Saturday to begin the staging of food. The non-alcoholic drinks, beer, wine, and one massive cake would be compliments of the university. Needless to say, paid entertainment was unnecessary since all but a handful of the invited guests were very nearly professional musicians or vocalists. There was nary a moment when music or a cappella did not break out from somewhere inside the auditorium that night.

For Leon not to get wind of this large gathering in his honor was truly a miracle. Since he was toasted more times than he could count, as well as being one of the last to leave the party, it was just as miraculous that he did not roll over in bed this morning and fall back asleep. And yet, here he was, sitting patiently in the semidarkness. The folding chairs faced southeast so that he and the others were not staring directly into the ascending morning sun. They were into the third hymn when the bright yellow orb finally crested the tree line. Leon could think of no better metaphor than that for Easter.

"For since the creation of the world God's invisible qualities—his eternal power and divine nature—have been clearly seen, being understood from what has been made, so that men are without excuse."

Romans 1:20

He has risen. Where, O death, is your sting?

Jesus rose from the dead that beautiful day long ago to conquer sin and death. For those who believe in him and obey his commands, their everlasting life will be free of all things evil. That truth - born of suffering – hasn't changed and never will. Last night's celebration was exactly why Leon needed to get out bed this morning. Yes, he was made to feel like the G.O.A.T. (Greatest of All Time) last night. So, why should he not sleep as long as he wanted? Why not blow off church entirely if he wanted? Why not walk around in nothing but underwear all day if he wanted? No one would have to know. No one would care. And if anyone deserved time off – it would have to be Leon... the Great Conductor.

Don't misunderstand. Last night's celebration was greatly appreciated. Leon was humbled by all the time and effort his friends and family put into its making. The adoration he received, however, was misplaced. It was easy to see why exceptionally talented people love it when their admirers put them up onto pedestals. Once elevated on their tem-poral pedestals and thrones, they would rather not think about who it was that gave them their talent. Leon was a very talented, well respected and truly loved individual... who was also a sinner in need of a Savior. Jesus was just who he needed right now. Otherwise, the intrinsic beauty of that sunrise was nothing more than a 10,000° ball of hot plasma making its rounds.

As usual, Leon's relatively small church shared this particularly large location with another relatively small church on Easter. The pastors of both churches would share the pulpit and the service was as good as it gets. It was gratifying for Leon to see a few of the talented people that performed with him last night also in attendance. Just as he did not expect to see any of them so early, they did not expect to see him. Leon would soon discover there were many more at the sunrise service that were also in the audience last night. They would all gather around him after the service to wish him a wonderful Easter.

Then she appeared.

"Good Easter morning, Professor," she said politely. "I'm a little surprised to see you up and so chipper... after such a long night."

Leon did not recognize her as being one of his musicians or vocalists from last night. Nor could he place her from a previous performance, but he had been doing this for ten years. He was also quite certain this very fit, middle-aged, brown-skinned beauty standing before him was not a member of his church. He would have remembered that. By the way she tilted her head and raised an eyebrow, he assumed she was referring to the late-night party.

"Good morning... and it's Leon," he replied politely. "Please forgive me if I have forgotten your name."

"It's Hélène (French: pronounced "ā·lěn") and you don't know me," she offered candidly.

"French?" Leon inquired.

"The name... yes," she replied.

All the while Hélène was talking, she also allowed Leon to view her cell phone. On it was a picture of himself standing next to a very pretty twenty-something holding a violin. It was obviously a selfie that was taken last night.

"This is my daughter and she is very upset with you," Hélène stated in a lighthearted manner.

There was no aggravation in her voice. In fact, the words spoken seemed to contradict the happy faces in the picture. The playful inconsistency was immediately followed up with the point she was trying to make.

"Her heart was set on playing second violin in Handel's Messiah Oratorio this Christmas... with you as its conductor."

"Shhh," he whispered and put his pointing finger up to his lips. "That is still classified information right now, but you can tell Georgy there will be a Christmas Cantata. I already have my replacement in mind."

"Ooo, sorry," she whispered back.

"It's all good," Leon joyfully exclaimed and acknowledged his young second violinist. "It is Georgy, right?"

"Yes," she stated, a bit surprised that he would remember her daughter.

"French?" he inquired... again.

"The name... yes," she replied. "Georgette was her French great grandmother's name."

"Hélène, let me tell you something you probably already know," Leon began earnestly. "Your daughter is an excellent musician. In fact, she was one of the easiest choices for second violin I have ever made. I suspect she will only get better and not have to worry about making the Christmas squad."

"Thank you for those kind words. I know that will mean a lot to her when I see her later today. When she gets up, that is. It was a late night, you know," Hélène replied with a mischievous half-smile. "I doubt she told you this, but her father was a first chair violinist and concertmaster in Philadelphia. He would have been very proud to see his 'little girl' perform last night."

"Hmm... I don't remember her sharing that little piece of very impressive information," Leon remarked curiously. "He was unable to attend?"

"The Lord called him home unexpectedly three years ago," she sighed through the words.

"I am truly sorry to hear that," Leon offered tenderly. "Had I known, I would not have been so hard on her."

"No, no, no," Hélène declared. "My husband and I love Georgy and our two boys very much. That is why we would never allow them to slip slide aimlessly through life. It was God, lots of love and an appropriate amount of discipline that has made our daughter the strong and confident young lady she is today."

"I got no argument with that," Leon agreed. "Well, Hélène , since the Lord intended for us to meet on this glorious morning, is there anything I can do to help advance your daughter's love of music?"

"I appreciate the offer, Leon, but I doubt yours is the expertise Georgy needs right now," she muttered under her breath.

This was not the response Leon had expected. The voice that was once cheerful, was now shaded in sadness. Not wishing to intrude into the personal life of someone he just met, yet feeling an obligation to help in any way he could, he would try one more time before changing the subject.

"Maybe, maybe not," he replied with kindness. "Don't know for sure unless you ask."

"That's true, but it's a woman thing," she quipped. "You wouldn't be interested."

"I helped my wife raise two daughters," Leon countered without trying to claim too much of the credit. "Both happily married now."

"Hmm... that is a pretty good resume," Hélène admitted and a wide smile returned to her face, but only briefly. "It's a long story."

"I got the time if you got the time," Leon stated emphatically, then casually dropped the name of a small, but very popular, coffee shop nearby.

So, with a tall Americano for him and a medium regular with almond milk for her, Hélène began sharing her family's dilemma. It was a story of a single mom living in the same house with a respectful, yet headstrong, young adult daughter. Her husband of thirty years died suddenly three years ago and her daughter was not handling the loss very well. That was not unexpected. Georgy was "daddy's little girl" after all. Her brothers were adjusting to their loss much better, but they were both much older than their little sister. To make this long story short, mother and daughter butted heads over just about everything now... especially when men entered into their lives.

Hélène went on to explain that her late husband had a very successful career in Philly, but she found the city too violent and decided to move back to Hillary last year. Unfortunately, the transition was too late for Georgy to audition for the past Christmas Cantata. That is when she noticed a positive change in her daughter's behavior. Georgy began playing the violin with greater passion and, slowly but surely, her joy returned. Hélène had not seen that kind of happiness in her daughter since her father passed away. Making second violin in Bach's Easter Oratorio was a dream come true.

"I'm not asking for any special favors for Georgy. I'm not sure what I'm asking," Hélène finalized her thoughts. "But you did ask."

"I did ask and consider it done," Leon replied happily and raised his coffee cup to toast the occasion.

"I hope your wife doesn't mind you paying attention to a widow's daughter," Hélène asked with some reservation as she gently touched her cup to his.

"It will be three years ago this July that my wife passed away. Ruthie was the love of my life," Leon spoke affectionately about his wife. "She was also a kind and selfless person. I think she would approve of my helping another talented young musician."

"Oh, my. I am so sorry about your wife," Hélène stated compassionately. "Maybe after church next Sunday, I buy the coffee and you can go on about your girls."

"You got yourself a deal," Leon accepted the invite without hesitation. "By the way, do you like cats?"

"Why, yes. Julius," **Hélène** replied curiously. "He keeps me company while I'm watching my '83 NBA Champion Sixers play."

Debbie was able to get from Fang the significance of what the moose and squirrel did for Fang. After hearing Debbie's interpretations, Hitch had to wonder how in the world they could have rescued Fang from a rock in the middle of a deep, fast-moving stream without everyone being swept over the edge of a waterfall. Even if the Jeep had been equipped with a winch, it would still need to be in the water and, most likely, submerged up to the doors for an extended period of time. The only rescue strategies that made sense involved equipment and manpower they did not possess. There was no getting around it, the moose and squirrel were heroes. Debbie only wished she had purchased more Easter lilies for Bruce to munch on.

That incredible story did not change their plans for getting a good night's sleep so they could attend Easter sunrise service this morning. Having to wait for a later service would push their return back to Hillary late into the evening – which they would rather not do. And skipping church on Easter was not an option. Both Hitch and Debbie loved their church. The sermons were based on Scripture and truth uncorrupted by societal pressure. The life lessons being taught were becoming indispensable for helping them navigate through today's dysfunctional world where wrong was right and fallacy was truth. No one knew modern nihilism better than they did. God's word was exactly what they needed. Their church may have been considered far away from the cabin in the woods and their permanent residences in Hillary, but the reward was well worth a scenic drive.

There was definitely a heightened sense of anticipation on this trip to church today. It wasn't so much that they had to start off in the dark in order to reach their destination... still in the dark. Rather, it had more to do with where they were relationally. How things have evolved between themselves and with Jesus Christ. They met at this particular church just before Christmas four months ago. Since they were both unrepentant sinners at the time, that unforeseen meeting in church was as shocking as it gets. Nothing could have been more out of character for both. Uncharacteristic, except for the day they found themselves back in church... two weeks later... on Christmas... being baptized. Today, they would once again be together in church for Easter service. Of course, they are still sinners, but repentance has taken on a whole new meaning.

How could they criticize, or want to circumvent, repentance when they were experiencing life with more abundant joy than either had known for a long time?

Hitch and Debbie were more excited than ever to be praising the only one who could have made that joy possible. They would arrive, park the Jeep and walk out to the church's outdoor chapel and pavilion in plenty of time. It was not long ago that these two high-profile professors were treated like Hollywood celebrities by awestruck parishioners. That was then. Now they were just plain Hitch and Debbie. Both would take their time before service talking to others about basic family stuff...the good stuff.

On any given Sunday, the church could summon up a sizable orchestra and choir. For this hour of the day, however, the number had been whittled down to just three stringed instruments; violin, viola and cello – along with a handful of singers. Whereas the sky was once black, it was now a deep dark blue without many people taking notice of the change. The stringed trio, on the other hand, did take notice and began playing Beethoven's String Trio No. 1 in Eb major, op. 3, mvt. 1. This was a short, beautiful allegro con brio (Italian meaning "fast tempo with spirit") sonata that was also the signal for everyone to find a seat. With impeccable timing, the music director welcomed everyone, announced the name and the page number of first hymn to begin this special celebration, and prompted the stringed trio to begin playing just as the sun peaked over the tree tops.

When the service had ended, Hitch and Debbie hopped back in the Jeep and headed to the Springhouse Restaurant for breakfast. Apparently, this cozy, family-owned establishment was the place to go after church on Sunday. The restaurant's hours on the Lord's Day were a tight window between 7:00am and 2:00pm. These were, more or less, the perfect hours for capturing the hungry mob that went without breakfast before leaving the house for church. It could seat well over two hundred people comfortably, but no matter what time you arrived - if it was on Sunday - the line was out the door. Regardless of your status in life, you waited patiently knowing the chocolate-chip pancakes with bacon on the side or the waffle with scrapple on the side were going to hit the spot. So, there they were... waiting patiently outside.

Fortunately, the owners knew their business and the line to get in advanced quickly. After ten minutes of smelling freshly brewed coffee and hyper-palatable breakfast options walk by them, Hitch and Debbie were seated. Their breakfast table conversation would be kept light, carefree and local. That is, topics and discussions would not stray too far off from the here and now. They would have plenty of time to discuss work-related obligations on the ride home. It was never a dreary ride back home. In fact, the only conundrum between the time spent away from the university and the time spent at the university was that they both enjoyed the getting away and the coming back. As long as they were together, life was good.

Still, it seemed to Debbie that Hitch was on edge about something. The moment he sat down, Debbie could not help but notice his eyes begin to scan the room. She knew it was a natural tendency for Hitch to take a moment to become aware of new surroundings, but they had eaten here before. If she was not mistaken, the curious behavior was more like Hitch was looking for someone... in particular.

"Fang seems to be healing nicely," Debbie stated as a subtle means of bringing Hitch's attention back to the table. "I know she will want to dance in a couple days, but I'll give her a week."

"She is a genetically-gifted sweetheart, isn't she?" Hitch replied with a sudden burst of energy. "I am going to use the men's room... be back... soon. Don't go away."

Don't go away, Debbie thought. *What a strange thing to say.*

It was a somewhat long bathroom break, but Debbie said nothing when Hitch returned to the table. Really. What could she say? Instead, she would just watch him for a little bit. The only thing she found different upon Hitch's return was his fascination with the surroundings was over. He seemed to be back to his old attentive self once again. Breakfast was ordered and the leisurely conversation began anew. Shortly thereafter, breakfast was served. The conversation ebbed and flowed to allow for the enjoyment of good food and Debbie soon forgot all about her concerns.

About half way through their meal a well-dressed gentleman walked up to the table. He looked familiar, so Debbie assumed he was from their church having breakfast – just as they were doing.

"Good morning," he stated pleasantly, but awkwardly. "I'm Bill from church… this morning."

"Good morning, Bill… from church," Hitch replied pleasantly, but awkwardly. "How nice to see you again."

"Yes, it is nice to see you both… again… from church," Bill stated as if reading from a script.

Bill then extended his arm towards Hitch. In his hand was a "doggie" bag. He continued.

"I think you left this bag at church… this morning."

"Thank you, Bill," Hitch replied with as much sincerity as he could muster and pointed towards Debbie.

"I think you left this bag at church… this morning," Bill repeated himself and now extended the arm holding the bag towards Debbie.

"It's a Springhouse Restaurant doggie bag for leftovers, Bill," Debbie replied back to Bill suspiciously, but she was looking at Hitch all the while.

"Well, thank you again, Bill," Hitch stated gratefully. "We are in your debt for returning whatever it is that you found of ours this morning at church and put into a doggie bag for safe keeping until we were to meet again... which is now... at Springhouse Restaurant... after church... this morning."

Debbie took the bag from Bill and thanked him. It was evident that all the gratitude being extended was meant for Bill's acting skills rather than for him finding a bag that did not fit too well in the charade's timeline.

"It's at the bottom," Bill whispered to Debbie and gave Hitch a thumbs up before leaving.

"So, did you cook this little scheme at church or here?" Debbie asked calmly.

She had not yet looked inside the bag.

"Here," Hitch replied without further explanation.

"Hmm," she exhaled. "And Bill?"

"They came into the restaurant after we sat down," he admitted. "I recognized him from church. A very nice fellow. Not the best actor it turns out, but my options were limited."

"Hmm," she exhaled. "Anything you want to say?"

"Not this second," Hitch stated candidly and sat up straight. "You going to look inside?"

"Yes, I think I will," she replied tentatively. "Here goes nothing."

The bag was full. The first items removed and put to the side were two complete sets of plastic utensils. Then, out came a fist full of napkins. That left a small carton at the bottom of the bag that would normally be used to take home a half-eaten hamburger or slice of pie. The carton was surrounded by a dozen or more ketchup, mustard and jelly packets. It was here that Debbie froze. For an instant, her mind took her back to her childhood. It was a time when she was still inside her mother and everything was right and good and safe. She glanced down at her hands and they were trembling slightly.

Lord, if this is what I think it is and it is your will, I submit it all to you and to him, she thought joyfully.

"All that for a burger?" she teased and to help calm her nervousness.

"You'll see," he offered.

Inside the carton was a ring box. Inside the ring box was the most magnificent pear cut diamond engagement ring she had ever seen. Even though it was what she had just prayed about, the moment of truth still took her breathe away. At that same moment, Hitch felt comfortable in his assumption that Debbie knew sometime prior to opening the doggie bag what she might find. They have had many spirited discussions on love and the institution of marriage. And especially what God thought about love and marriage. Hitch also felt comfortable in his assumption that she knew nothing about his plans to ask her to be his lawfully wedded wife... on Easter no less. With that in mind, he felt it only fair to give her a moment or two to reflect on this life altering decision before popping the question. After all, she knew about his contemptible and cowardly track record at being a husband. But, if she were to accept his proposal, Hitch would dedicate himself to her wellbeing - till death do they part.

The two moments were up.

"Sùilean Soilleir, I do not consider myself worthy of you," he began humbly and truthfully. "But, will you marry me?"

"Yes, mo luaidh, with all my heart, I will," she replied softly.

These periods when the human parents were away from the cabin for hours at a time were mostly peaceful. Nothing too exciting ever happened indoors when compared to outdoors. Wallace would normally take this additional quiet time to get a little more shut-eye. As usual, what he became was simply a big, shifting obstacle course for one or more kittens. Fang would try to keep them away, but found it impossible to entertain more than two at a time. There was no reason to shame mom cat for allowing her kids to run amok. How could they when the poor thing had to deal with these four rambunctious rascals all night and whenever Wallace and Fang were outside enjoying their freedoms. In the end, however, the kittens would all tucker out soon enough and find somewhere along Wallace's warm fuzzy perimeter to fall back asleep... until feeding time.

Then, there were days like today.

The disturbance was coming from the attic. It started soon after Hitch and Debbie left for church before dawn. The spirited, unintelligible chatter, and loud, sporadic banging would stop whenever Wallace stood just outside the attic door and barked. He was there to inform whoever it was making the racket, that they were - not only disturbing the peace - but had no business messing around in their attic.

In no uncertain terms, he insisted they leave the premises immediately or suffer the worst possible consequences.

But, then again, there was no way a three-dimensional human being or animal could have made it through the house and up the stairs without Wallace and Fang knowing about it. That, according to Wallace, was all the evidence he needed to believe the cabin was haunted. He had tangled with ghosts before and reason was not their strong suit. Stern warnings and brute force were all they understood. Besides, they were on his turf now.

This was not the enchanted forest, so Fang was not so quick to jump to that conclusion. She did, however, find it unsettling that the intruders managed to slip past them undetected. That, according to Fang, was all the incentive she needed to get to the bottom of this noise in the attic. Opening doors that were not locked was child's play for Fang. It was what to do once the attic door was opened that concerned her. The plan she presented to Wallace was simple: give the intruders enough space for them to leave the cabin peacefully.

"No chase," she implored.

"No chase," he grumbled.

Fang depressed the lever handle with her good paw and allowed the attic door to swing open. Wallace and Fang were immediately hit with a blast of warm musty air. The unfinished room full of junk that stretched from one end of the cabin to the other was still and quiet. It was well past daybreak now and the natural light from the six dormer windows without curtains helped illuminate the path of destruction caused by the intruder's disregard for another person's personal property. To anyone's knowledge, there was nothing of tremendous value up here. Nothing in the attic was Hitch's beforehand. It was, more or less, the kind of stuff collected over the many years of running a private "Bed & Breakfast" and left behind by the previous owners.

The one open dormer window presented the clue as to how the invaders were able to gain access to the attic and, from all appearances, on how they were able to leave. The window was not damaged. Therefore, it was most likely not fully closed or left wide open by mistake – perhaps for ventilation. They were about to leave when a faint rustling noise could be heard behind them. Turning back around, Wallace and Fang watched in amazement as two boxes along the wall began to move on their own. Both boxes seemed to be heading towards the open window. About two feet short of the window, up popped the masked faces of two raccoons. It was Bonnie and Clyde.

There was never a chance for Wallace to catch up to them before they escaped out the window, but he gave it his best shot. If that weren't enough excitement for one day, all four kittens had worked their way up two flights of stairs, slipped past Fang while she was distracted and disappeared into the multiple layers of junk. Fortunately, she had the presence of mind to close the window before the search for inquisitive kittens began. Otherwise, they may have had to summon mom cat up here to get one or more of them off the roof. Still, it would take Wallace and Fang a good half an hour to hunt down the elusive little tykes, trap them, pick them up without puncturing their thin skin, carry them down two flights of stairs and - once all were accounted for – go back to shut the attic door.

It was not five minutes after all was said and done, when Wallace and Fang heard the Jeep pull up. So much for any additional shut-eye. The front door opened and, as Hitch and Debbie walked in, Wallace and Fang strolled out. There was the usual happy greeting and a few pleasantries shared in the passing, but this was not the time or place for chit-chat. The specifics on how each had spent Easter Day so far would be sorted out later - after the packing for the return home was complete.

Easter Day. What a glorious day knowing there is a good God and that he knows us by name (Jn 10:25-30). For Wallace and Fang, the glorious day would continue while lying side by side on the porch listening to the beautiful melodies of the songbirds, smelling the many fragrancies of the wind and watching two racoons wrestling playfully as they made their way across the far side of the yard... wait... what?

"Stop right there!" Wallace barked at the two attic vandals.

Wallace recognized Bonnie and Clyde immediately and was now in a runner's position with every fiber in his body on stand-by. If Fang's injured paw were 100%, he would be giving them a good run for their money right now. But she needed him now. Wallace knew there would be other opportunities for chasing these two reckless bandits. So, reluctantly, he sat back down. The two racoons took notice of Wallace's hesitation and began referring to him in many unflattering terms – even making funny faces at him.

"Wallace..." Fang began sweetly.

He knew what she was going to say before she said it...
and he would be fine with the decision.

"No chase," Wallace stated somberly.

"Yes chase," she replied calmly.

"Yes chase?" he repeated for verification.

"Go get 'em, my love," she barked... more or less.

Notes

(With Audio Recommendations)

Chapter 1 – Prophets and Profiteers

"Dissention of Darwinism" (statement); issued by conservative think tank, Discovery Institute, Seattle, Washington. Part of a series on Intelligent Design verses Darwin's theory of evolution; 2001.

"Compassion International" (Christian humanitarian aid organization); Founded in 1952 by Rev. Everett Swanson. It is headquartered in Colorado Springs, Colorado. This is a child-advocacy ministry and its purpose is the pairing of compassionate people with children living in extreme poverty - spiritual, economic, social, and physical poverty. Each child is linked to only one sponsor at a time. Phone (800) 336-7676. Call now.

Chapter 2 – Bright Eyes and Fang

"Cairo" (Belgian Malinois); member of U.S. Navy SEAL Team Six. Also see, "No Ordinary Dog" (Book); written by Will Chesney,

SEAL Team Operator and Cairo's handler. Published by St. Martin's Press; April 21, 2020.

Chapter 3 – The Passion

"Claxton Fruit Cake" (bakery); Claxton, Georgia. Italian pastry-maker, Savino Tos, immigrated to the US in the early-1900's and opened Claxton Bakery in 1910. Long time employee, Albert Parker, acquired the bakery in 1945. The high-quality fruit cake - with the unique horse and buggy label – became a hit after WWII and continues to be a hit - especially during the Christmas season.

"Easter Oratorio: Kommt, eilet und laufet "Come, hasten and run" BWV 249); Johann Sebastian Bach (1685–1750), composer. First performance on Easter Sunday, 1 April 1725.

Audio Recommendation (YouTube)

"Bach - Easter Oratorio, BWV 249 - Gardiner - Classical Vault 1" performed by Monteverdi Choir; English Baroque Soloists; John Eliot Gardiner, conductor; Live recording, London, 2013.

Chapter 4 – Enchanted Forest

N/A

Chapter 5 – That Wiccan Boy Can Sing

"Le Fay's Herr Schwarz Grant Stinnett" (bass guitar); German bass manufacturing company founded in 1987 by Reiner Dobbratz. His brother, Meik Dobbratz, would join Le Fay later. Address: Sandkamp 7, D-25368, Kiebitzreihe, Germany. Email: inquiry@lefay.de.

"Wicca" (Neo-Pagan religion); the origins of modern Wicca can be traced to a retired British civil servant, Gerald Brosseau Gardner (1884–1964) and commonly referred to as "Gardnerian Wicca." Followers often use the pentagram, or five-pointed star, as the main symbol of their religion. Other historical occultists include; Aleister Crowley, Doreen Valiente, Alexander Sanders, Victor and Cora Anderson.

"Hartke LX8500 Tone Stack EQ preamp and HyDrive HD410 cabinets" (bass amplifier and speakers); American company founded by Larry Hartke and Ron Lorman. They released their first products, an aluminum cone, free edge tweeter and a 2-way bookshelf system with an eight-inch aluminum woofer, under the Hartke name, in 1980. Manufacturing factory in Meriden, Connecticut. Corporate address: 278-B Duffy Ave. Hicksville, NY 11801.

"Sennheiser" (audio headphones); German company founded in 1945 by Prof. Dr. Fritz Sennheiser. Its first product was a voltmeter and manufactured under the company name, Laboratorium Wennebostel (shortened, "Labor W"). Labor W was renamed Sennheiser electronic in 1958. In 1987,

Sennheiser was awarded at the 59th Academy Awards for its MKH 816 shotgun microphone. In 2021, Sennheiser sold its consumer audio division to Swiss-based hearing-aid manufacturer, Sonova. Corporate address: Am Labor 1, 30900 Wedemark, Germany.

"Für Elise" (song); Ludwig van Beethoven (1770–1827), German composer. "For Elise" or "Bagatelle No. 25 in A minor" for solo piano. Bagatelle is a short piece of music. It is not known who "Elise" was for certain. Two possibilities are; Beethoven's friend, Therese Malfatti von Rohrenbach zu Dezza (1792–1851) and German soprano singer, Elisabeth Röckel (1793–1883). The song was one of Ludwig van Beethoven's most popular compositions, but was not published during his lifetime. It was discovered in 1867, or 40 years after his death.

Audio Recommendation (YouTube)

"Für Elise" Performed by Lang Lang" (2019). Lang Lang is a Chinese virtuoso pianist (b. 1982). He performs Beethoven's "Für Elise" on the Steinway "Black Diamond" Limited Edition piano.

"Alice's Adventures in Wonderland" (book); written by English author, Lewis Carroll (pen name) and illustrated by John Tenniel. Carroll's name given at birth was Charles Lutwidge Dodgson (1832–1898). The book was originally published in 1865 and received positive reviews. The book's sequel, "Through the Looking-Glass" was published in 1871.

[Author's Note: It is said that, at a very young age, Lewis Carroll, suffered through a fever that left him deaf in one ear. I know, firsthand, some of the challenges he faced in life]

Chapter 6 – Cabin In the Woods

"Ëgadiyóhšö and Awë:iyö" (ancient squirrel names); the actual words and phrases spoken by the Seneca Nation of American Indians. The dictionary was compiled by Wallace Chafe (among others) in an online book entitled, "English – Seneca Dictionary" (pdf). The Seneca traditionally lived between Seneca Lake and the Genesee River in western New York. They were the largest of the six native American tribes that comprised the Iroquois Confederacy - formed between 1350 to 1600. The other five tribes were the Cayuga, Mohawk, Oneida, Onondaga and Tuscarora. The Tuscarora tribe originated from North Carolina and joined the Confederacy in 1722.

"Romeo and Juliet" (play); written by William Shakespeare (1564–1616). The tragedy is believed to have been written between 1591 and 1595. It was first published in 1597. The play was among Shakespeare's most popular during his lifetime and depicted the romance between two Italian youths from feuding families.

"Jeep Gladiator Rubicon" (mid-size pickup truck); The Jeep Gladiator is manufactured in Toledo, Ohio by the Jeep division of Stellantis North America (formerly FCA US). It was introduced in 2018 and went on sale in the spring of 2019.

The four-door, five-passenger Gladiator features exterior and interior styling similar to the Jeep Wrangler (JL). Taylor Langhals was the lead exterior designer on the Gladiator.

Chapter 7 – In God's Hand

"Tesla" (electric vehicle); American automotive company now headquartered in Austin, Texas. Founded in 2003 (San Carlos, CA) by Elon Musk, Martin Eberhard, JB Straubel, Marc Tarpenning, and Ian Wright. In 2021, Tesla moved its corporate headquarters from California to Texas after Elon Musk had enough of California's anti-business regulatory and tax policies.

Chapter 8 – Palm Sunday – Part I

N/A

Chapter 9 – Palm Sunday – Part II

"Millennial and Gen Z" (age ranges); "Millennials" (or Generation Y), were born between 1981 and 1996 (15 years); "Generation Z" were born between 1997 and 2012 (15 years). Gen Alpha refers to the group of individuals born between 2013 and 2025.

> [NOTE: Members of Generation Alpha are often the children of Millennials and the younger siblings of Generation Z]

"The Last Supper" (painting); painting by the Italian High Renaissance artist Leonardo da Vinci (1452–1519). It measures 460 cm × 880 cm (15 ft × 29.1 ft) and is located at the monastery of Santa Maria delle Grazie in Milan, Italy. The painting depicts Jesus seated at the table with the Twelve Apostles the night before he was crucified. Specifically, it was the moment just after Jesus announces that one of his apostles will betray him (as described in the Gospel of John).

"Bösendorfer" (piano); Bösendorfer is an Austrian piano manufacturer. It was founded in 1828 by Ignaz Bösendorfer, an Austrian musician. It is one of the oldest piano manufacturers in the world. It is now a wholly owned subsidiary of Yamaha Corporation (2008). Bösendorfer is unusual in that it produces 97 and 92-key models in addition to instruments with standard 88-key keyboards.

"The Lord of the Rings" (movies); "The Lord of the Rings" is an epic novel written by English author and scholar J. R. R. Tolkien (1892–1973). The three-part movie series based on Tolkien's novel included; The Fellowship of the Ring (2001), The Two Towers (2002), The Return of the King (2003). All three films were directed by Peter Jackson. The production companies for all three were New Line Cinema, WingNut Films, Saul Zaentz Film. Aragorn was played by American actor, Viggo Peter Mortensen Jr. (b. 1958). Legolas was played by English actor, Orlando Jonathan Blanchard Copeland Bloom (b. 1977).

Chapter 10 – Say You Love Me

"Jonas Brothers" (American pop rock band); Formed in 2005 and consists of three brothers: Kevin Jonas, Joe Jonas, and Nick Jonas (youngest). The band have released six albums: It's About Time (2006), Jonas Brothers (2007), A Little Bit Longer (2008), Lines, Vines and Trying Times (2009), Happiness Begins (2019), and The Album (2023). Four of those albums reaching the No. 1 spot on Billboard's "Top Album Sales" chart: A Little Bit Longer, Lines, Vines and Trying Times, Happiness Begins and The Album. Priyanka Chopra Jonas is one of India's highest-paid actresses and winner of the Miss World 2000 pageant. Her numerous accolades include two National Film Awards and five Filmfare Awards. Nick and Priyanka were married in 2018.

Chapter 11 – It's Hard to Explain

"Bryce Harper" (Major League Baseball player); Right fielder for the National League (NL) Philadelphia Phillies. Harper (b. 1992) was drafted by the Washington Nationals (NL) in the 1st round (1st) in 2012. He signed on as a "Free Agent" with the Philadelphia Phillies on March 2, 2019. Career titles; 2012 NL Rookie of the Year, 2015 NL Hank Aaron Award (Best Hitter), 2015 NL Most Valuable Player (MVP), 2021 All-MLB (Best Player) Team 1, 2021 NL Hank Aaron Award (Best Hitter), 2021 NL MVP, 2022 NL NLCS (National League Championship Series) MVP.

"Your Feet's Too Big" (Jazz song); composed by Fred Fisher with lyrics by Ada Benson (1936). Recorded by Fats Waller in 1939. Thomas Wright "Fats" Waller (1904–1943) was a Jazz pianist virtuoso, prolific songwriter and entertainer. The lyrics "Your pedal extremities are colossal, to me you look just like a fossil," "You know, your pedal extremities really are obnoxious," and "One never knows, do one?" were ad-libbed by Waller. In 1926, he signed with the RCA Victor Label and recorded many more hits, such as "Jitterbug Waltz," "Honeysuckle Rose," and "The Joint is Jumpin."

Audio Recommendation (YouTube)

"Fats Waller - your feet's too big" (song); song was performed in the revue of Waller tunes, "Ain't Misbehavin'" (1978).

"Dr. R.C. Sproul" (American Reformed Theologian); Dr. Robert Charles Sproul (1939–2017) was an ordained pastor in the Presbyterian Church in America and founder of Ligonier Ministries (1971). Their mission is to proclaim, teach, and defend the holiness of God in all its fullness. Email service@ligonier.org for more information.

Chapter 12 – Music to My Ears

"Kyrie Eleison" (Christian song and prayer); Ancient Greek " Κύριε ἐλέησον" (Kūrie eléēson). The English translation is "Lord, have mercy." This Greek phrase is used three times in the New Testament: Matthew 15:22, "Have mercy on me, O

Lord, Son of David" (Ἐλέησόν με κύριε υἱὲ Δαβίδ); Matthew 17:15, "Lord, have mercy on my son" (Κύριε ἐλέησόν μου τὸν υἱόν); Matthew 20:30, "Lord, have mercy on us, Son of David" (Ἐλέησον ἡμᾶς κύριε υἱὸς Δαβίδ). This composition is used regularly in Christian liturgies.

Audio Recommendation (YouTube)

"Kyrie Eleison (song); soloist is Анастасия Гладилина (Anastasia Gladilina); Accompaniment by Хор Сретенского Монастыря (Sretensky Monastery Choir); Anastasia Gladilina is an enormously popular Russian singer. The Sretensky Monastery Choir was founded in 1397. The Russian monks standing behind her are the only music in this video. There are no musical instruments. Anastasia (Russian; meaning "Resurrection") was only fifteen years old when recorded in 2019.

"Our Hope Is Alive" (song); by Zach Sparkman (Lyricist) and Josh Sparkman (Composer/Arranger). Josh Sparkman (b. 1993) is the assistant pastor at Farmington Avenue Baptist Church in West Hartford, in addition to his roles as piano teacher and composer.

Audio Recommendation (YouTube)

"Our Hope Is Alive"- The Wilds Music - Official Lyric Video" (song); The Wilds is a non-profit organization focused on serving the local church with a wide variety of camping programs and Christian resources. Their mission is to present the Truth of God with the love of God so lives can be changed to the glory of God. Go to Wilds.org for more information.

"Lead Me to The Cross" (song); written by Brooke Fraser and first released by Hillsong United (2007). Brooke Fraser (b. 1983) is a New Zealand singer and songwriter best known for her hit single "Something in the Water"(2010). She released two studio albums with Columbia Records; "What to Do with Daylight" (2003) and "Albertine" (2006). "Flags," her third studio album with Sony Music Entertainment was released in 2010. "Brutal Romantic," through Vagrant Records, was released in 2014. Her first live album, "Seven" through Sparrow Records and Capitol Christian Music Group was released in 2022.

Audio Recommendation (YouTube)

"Francesca Battistelli - "Lead Me to The Cross" - Official Audio" (song); Francesca Battistelli (b. 1985) is an American Christian pop rock singer. This song was the fourth single off her debut album "My Paper Heart" which was released through Fervent Records (2008). "My Paper Heart" album was certified Gold by the RIAA

(Recording Industry Association of America) on July 13, 2012.

"Can It Be" (song); written by Adam Morgan (arr. Benjamin David Knoedler); published in 2020 by Majesty Music. Adam M. Morgan is an American politician (South Carolina House of Representatives from the 20th District), attorney (J.D. from University of South Carolina School of Law), filmmaker ("Operation Arctic: Viking Invasion") and president of Majesty Music (headquartered in Greenville, South Carolina).

Audio Recommendation (YouTube)

"Can It Be - Ben Farrell & The Hamilton Family" (song); title song for the Hamilton Family album "Can It Be." Album available at majestymusic.com

"Living Hope" (song); written by Phil Wickman and Brian Johnson (collab: Ed Cash and Jonathan Smith). Single released on March 30, 2018. Album "Living Hope" released on August 3, 2018, by Fair Trade Services. Philip David Wickham (b. 1984) is an American contemporary Christian musician, singer and songwriter. He has released nine albums: "Give You My World" (2003), "Phil Wickham" (2006), "Cannons" (2007), "Heaven & Earth" (2009), "Response" (2011), "The Ascension" (2013), "Children of God" (2016), "Living Hope" (2018), "Hymn Of Heaven" (2021), "I Believe' (2023 release date). Single "This is Amazing Grace" off the "Ascension" album became RIAA certified Platinum (2014). His latest Top 30 Christian singles include "Worthy of My Song - Worthy of It All" (2022) and "This Is Our God" (2023).

Audio Recommendations (YouTube)

"Phil Wickham - Living Hope - Official Music Video" (song); The music video released on March 29, 2018. The video features Wickham and his band performing the track in a dimly lit room.

"Nearer, Still Nearer" (song); written by Lelia N. Morris (1862–1929); song published in 1898. Lelia Naylor Morris was an American Methodist hymnwriter. She was born in Pennsville, Ohio. She began writing hymns and gospel songs in the 1890s. It has been said that she wrote more than 1,000 songs and tunes while doing her housework. She is buried in McConnelsville Cemetery, McConnelsville, OH.

Audio Recommendation (YouTube)

"Nearer, Still Nearer - Ben Burkholder - Cantate Domino Ensemble - 2022" (song); Ben Burkholder (Danville, PA), Composer. Seth Bergey, Conductor. Cantate Domino Ensemble was formed in 2019 to provide emerging Anabaptist composers with an avenue to present their music. The ensemble meets only once a year for a 3-day weekend to rehearse, perform, and record newly composed, a cappella music.

"Leonard Bernstein" (American conductor, composer and pianist); Born Louis Bernstein (1918-1990) in Lawrence, Massachusetts. It could be said that his fame began on November 14, 1943 with the New York Philharmonic. Without rehearsal, Bernstein stepped in for conductor Bruno Walter - who came down with the flu. The challenging program included works by Robert Schumann, Miklós Rózsa, Richard Wagner, and Richard Strauss. The New York Times would comment, "It's a good American success story. The warm, friendly triumph of it filled Carnegie Hall and spread far over the air waves."

"Oliver Twist; or, the Parish Boy's Progress" (book); novel written by English writer, Charles Dickens (1812–1870). The novel was first published in monthly instalments, from February 1837 to April 1839. Then published in a three-volume book set in 1838. Oliver Twist (innocent orphan) is the main character. Fagan (criminal mastermind) would recruit children to be his pickpockets.

Chapter 13 – Good Friday

"Origen" (also known as Origen of Alexandria or Origen Adamantius); Origen (c. 184 – c. 253) was a prominent Christian scholar and theologian. His greatest body of work is the "Hexapla." The Hexapla is a synopsis of six versions of the Old Testament: the Hebrew and a transliteration, the Septuagint (an authoritative Greek version of the Old Testament), the versions of Aquila, Symmachus, and Theodotion and, for the Psalms, two further translations (one being discovered by him in a jar in the Jordan Valley). Origen was imprisoned and tortured during the persecution of Christians under the emperor, Decius (c. 201 - 251).

"Augustine of Hippo" (also known as Saint Augustine); Augustine (354-430) was an influential theologian, philosopher, prolific writer. He was also the Bishop of Hippo Regius in Numidia, North Africa (Western Roman Empire). His greatest body of work comes from "Confessions" (c. 400) and "The City of God" (c. 413-426). In 1298, he was formally recognized as a "Doctor of the Church" by Pope Boniface VIII. Shortly before his death, Vandals (a Germanic tribe) besieged the city of Hippo in the spring of 430, destroying everything except for Augustine's cathedral and library - which they left untouched.

"Thomas Aquinas" (also known as Saint Thomas Aquinas); Thomas (1224-1274) was an Italian Dominican friar and priest, an influential philosopher and theologian. He has been described as being "the most influential thinker of the medieval period" and "the greatest of the medieval philosopher-theologians." His greatest body of works include the unfinished "Summa Theologica," or "Summa Theologiae" (1265-1274) and the "Summa contra gentiles" (1259-1265). He is also notable for his eucharistic hymns. In 1567, he was officially named "Doctor of the Church" by Pope Pius V.

"C. S. Lewis" (Irish-born scholar, novelist and Anglican lay theologian); Clive Staples Lewis (1898–1963). From 1925 to 1954 he was a fellow and tutor of Magdalen College, Oxford. From 1954 to 1963 he was Professor of Medieval and Renaissance English at the University of Cambridge. He is best known for writing a series of seven children's books called "The Chronicles of Narnia." He is also well known for his books on Christian apologetics, including "The Screwtape Letters" and "Mere Christianity." Lewis lived his life as an atheist through his 20s. With the support of his close friend, J.R.R. Tolkien, he would become a faithful Christian in 1931. Lewis described these changes in his autobiography "Surprised by Joy" (1955).

"Karl Marx" (German-born philosopher, economist and revolutionary socialist); Karl Marx (1818–1883), was the founder of "scientific communism." His most famous literary works are "The Communist Manifesto," published in 1848 (with Friedrich Engels) and the first volume of "Das Kapital," published in 1867 (the second and third volumes were published posthumously in 1885 and 1894, respectively). He was considered a "theoretical atheist." In the "Critique of the Hegelian philosophy of public law," he wrote, "Religious misery is at once the expression of real misery and a protest against it. Religion is the groan of the oppressed, the sentiment of a heartless world, and at the same time the spirit of a condition deprived of spirituality. It is the opium of the people."

"Friedrich Nietzsche" (German philosopher); Friedrich Wilhelm Nietzsche (1844–1900) became the youngest person to hold the Chair of Classical Philology at the University of Basel in 1869 (age of 24). He is probably most famous for writing "God is dead, and we have killed him" from his otherwise, dull, book "Thus Spoke Zarathustra." He also argued that the development of science and emergence of a secular world would eventually lead to the death of Christianity. In 1889, at age 44, he collapsed and afterward suffered a complete loss of his mental faculties. He lived his remaining years in the care of his mother until her death in 1897 and then with his sister **Elisabeth Förster-Nietzsche** until his death in 1900.

"Bertrand Russell" (Welsh-born mathematician, philosopher, and pacifist); Bertrand Arthur William Russell (1872–1970) was awarded the Nobel Prize in Literature in 1950 "in recognition of his varied and significant writings in which he champions humanitarian ideals and freedom of thought." He was also a member of Humanists UK's Standing Advisory Council, as well as President of Cardiff Humanists, until his death. In his book "Why I am Not a Christian," he states that "religions are both harmful and untrue." However, when asked in a radio debate, how he could explain the existence of the universe, his reply was, "I should say the universe is just there, and that's all."

"Theophrastus Redivivus" (book); Author is unknown. Exact date book was published is unknown (most likely around 1650). Only four copies of Theophrastus Redivivus remain, all in Latin. Theophrastus (c. 371–287 BC) was a lesser-known Greek philosopher and pupil of the well-known Greek philosopher, Aristotle (384–322 BC). The unknown author of this book refers to himself as being the "second Theophrastus" or "Theophrastus Redivivus" (Latin: meaning "The revived Theophrastus"). The philosophical position proclaimed throughout the book is "materialistic atheism."

Chapter 14 – Dueling Cantatas

N/A

Chapter 15 – You're Just Who I Needed

"Beethoven's String Trio No. 1 in Eb major, op. 3, mvt. 1" (song); Ludwig van Beethoven (1770–1827), German composer. All five of his "trios" for violin, viola, and cello were written in the 1790s and published in Vienna. The genre of "string trio" was one which occupied Beethoven for only a few years. He would stop writing string "trios" after starting his impressive cycle of sixteen string "quartets" in 1798.

Audio Recommendation (YouTube)

"Beethoven's String Trio Op. 3" - The United States Air Force Band" (song); the performance took place on December 15, 2020 marking the 250th anniversary of Ludwig van Beethoven's birth. Performed by USAF STRING TRIO; Master Sgt. Luke Wedge on violin, Technical Sgt. Mattew Maffett on viola, Master Sgt. Christine Lightner on cello.

"Bonnie and Clyde" (American criminals); Bonnie Elizabeth Parker (1910–1934) and Clyde Chestnut "Champion" Barrow (1909–1934) were best known for robbing banks during the Great Depression. They are believed to have murdered at least nine police officers and four civilians. Their poor choice of careers (and their lives) would end on May 23, 1934 by police in Bienville Parish, Louisiana.

Milton Keynes UK
Ingram Content Group UK Ltd.
UKHW050200130724
445574UK00014B/723